HUNTING AND GATHERING

Born in 1970, Anna Gavalda was a teacher whose collection of stories, *I Wish Someone Were Waiting for Me Somewhere*, shot her to fame in her native France. *Hunting and Gathering (Ensemble, c'est tout)* has sold over a million copies in France, is being filmed starring Audrey Tautou and is a best-seller in several countries. Gavalda's work, including another short novel, *Someone I Loved*, has been translated into thirty-six languages. The mother of two young children, she lives and writes just outside Paris.

ANNA GAVALDA

Hunting and Gathering

TRANSLATED BY
Alison Anderson

VINTAGE BOOKS
London

Published by Vintage 2007

2 4 6 8 10 9 7 5 3 1

Originally published in French as
Ensemble, c'est tout

First published in Great Britain in 2006 by
Chatto & Windus
Random House, 20 Vauxhall Bridge Road,
London SW1V 2SA

www.vintage-books.co.uk

Addresses for companies within The Random House Group Limited
can be found at: www.randomhouse.co.uk/offices.htm

The Random House Group Limited Reg. No. 954009

A CIP catalogue record for this book
is available from the British Library

ISBN 9780099494072

Printed and bound in Australia by
Griffin Press

For Muguette
(1919–2003)
Body unclaimed.

Part One

1

Paulette Lestafier wasn't as crazy as they said. Of course, she knew what day it was, since that was all she had left to do now. Count the days, wait for them, and forget. She knew perfectly well that today was Wednesday. And what's more, she was ready. She had her coat on, she'd found her basket, and gathered all her discount coupons together. She could even hear Yvonne's car in the distance . . . But what can you do, the cat had been outside the door, hungry, and it was while she was leaning over to put his bowl back on the floor that she fell and banged her head against the bottom step.

Paulette Lestafier often fell, but that was her secret. Mustn't tell anyone, ever.

'Not anyone, you hear?' she'd threaten, silently. 'Not even Yvonne, or the doctor, not to mention the boy . . .'

So she would get up again slowly, wait for things to go back to normal, rub herself with some Synthol and hide those damn bruises.

Paulette's bruises never turned blue. They were yellow, green or violet, and they stayed on her body for a long time. Far too long. For several months, sometimes. It was hard to hide them. People asked her why she always dressed as if it were the middle of winter, why she always wore stockings and never took off her cardigan.

The boy was the one who pestered her most: 'Hey Grandma? What's going on? Take off all that stuff, do you want to die of heat?'

No, Paulette Lestafier wasn't crazy at all. She knew those huge bruises that never went away would get her into trouble some day.

She knew how useless old women like her ended up. Old women who let weeds take root in their vegetable garden and who held on to furniture to keep from falling. Old women who couldn't thread needles or remember how to turn the volume up on the TV. And who would try every single button on the remote control and finally just unplug the thing, crying tears of rage.

Tiny, bitter tears, head in hand, in front of a defunct television.

So? Is that it? No more sound, ever, in this house? No more voices, ever? Simply because you can't remember the colour of the button? Even though he'd put coloured stickers on there, your grandson, stuck them on, just for you! One for the channels, one for the sound and one for the power button. Come on, Paulette, just stop your crying and look at those stickers!

Stop shouting at me like that, all of you . . . They've been gone for ages, those stickers, they came unstuck almost right away. I've been looking for that button for months and I can't hear a thing, all I have is the picture, with a tiny whisper of sound.

So stop your shouting, or you'll make me deaf into the bargain.

2

'Paulette, Paulette, are you there?'

Yvonne muttered crossly. She was cold and pulled her shawl tighter across her chest, then muttered some more. She didn't like the idea of being late at the supermarket.

That was one thing she couldn't stand.

She went back to her car with a sigh, switched off the ignition and picked up her hat.

Paulette must be down at the end of the garden. She was always out there at the end of her garden, sitting on a bench next to the empty rabbit hutches. She'd sit there for hours, from morning to night – upright, motionless, patient, her hands on her lap and her eyes vacant.

Paulette would talk to herself, calling to the dead, praying to the living.

She talked to the flowers, to her heads of lettuce, to the birds and to her own shadow. Paulette was losing her mind and she no longer knew which day was which. Today was Wednesday, and Wednesday was shopping day. Yvonne had been coming to get her every week for over ten years; now she raised the latch on the gate and groaned, 'If it isn't such a crying shame . . .'

A shame to be getting so old and alone, and they'd be late at Intermarket, and now there wouldn't be any shopping trolleys left near the check-out.

Wait a minute. The garden was empty.

Even crotchety Yvonne was beginning to worry. She went to the back of the house and put her hands on either side of her eyes to peer through the windowpane, trying to get to the bottom of this silence.

'Sweet Jesus!' she exclaimed, when she saw her friend's body sprawled on the kitchen tiles.

Yvonne was so overwhelmed that she made the sign of the cross any old way, mixing up the Son with the Holy Ghost, and she let fly a few small curses too, then she went to get a tool out of the shed. She broke the window with a hoe and with a colossal effort managed to drag herself up on to the windowsill.

It wasn't easy for her to cross the room, kneel down, then lift her friend's head from the pink puddle where it lay bathed in a mixture of blood and milk.

'Hey! Paulette! You're not dead, are you?'

The cat was licking the floor, purring, supremely indifferent to the unfolding drama, or to what was appropriate, or to the fact that there was broken glass all over the place.

3

Yvonne didn't really like the idea, but the paramedics had asked her to go along in the ambulance in order to deal with the administrative problems and formalities for admission to emergency.

'You know this lady?'

She was offended: 'I most certainly do! We were at infant school together!'

'Get in, then.'

'What about my car?'

'Your car won't run away. We'll bring you back later.'

'All right,' she sighed, resigned. 'I'll get my shopping done later.'

It was pretty uncomfortable in there. They'd pointed to a tiny stool next to the stretcher and she wedged herself in there the best she could. She clung to her handbag and nearly fell off the stool every time they went round a bend.

There was a young man in there with them. He was complaining because he couldn't find a vein in his patient's arm, and Yvonne didn't like the way he was carrying on: 'Stop yelling,' she muttered, 'stop it, what on earth are you trying to do, anyway?'

'Put her on a drip.'

'A what?'

The way the young man looked at her, she understood she'd better just be quiet and keep her little monologue to herself: 'Just look at that, just look at the way he's twisting her arm, would you just look at that . . . It's awful. Better not look. Blessed Virgin, pray for . . . Hey! You're hurting her!'

The paramedic was on his feet, adjusting a little screw on the tube. Yvonne counted the bubbles and went on praying as best she could. It was hard to concentrate, what with the siren.

She was holding her friend's hand in her lap, smoothing it as if it were the hem of a skirt, mechanically. She was too sad and frightened to show more tenderness than that . . .

Yvonne Carminot sighed, examined the wrinkles, the calluses, the dark spots here and there; her friend's nails were still in fairly good shape, but hard, dirty and split. She held her own hand next to Paulette's and compared them. Of course she was younger, and a little bit plumper, but above all she hadn't suffered as much in her time on earth. She hadn't worked as hard, she'd had a greater share of caresses. And when was the last time she'd had to toil in the garden . . .? Her husband still grew their potatoes, but for everything else it was better to shop at Intermarket. The vegetables were already clean, and you didn't have to pull the lettuce apart to look for slugs. And then she had so many people close to her: there was dear Gilbert and Nathalie and the little ones to fuss over. Whereas Paulette – what did she have left in life? Nothing. Not a single good thing. Her husband was dead, her daughter was a slut, and her grandson never came to see her. Nothing but worries, nothing but memories, a rosary of little sorrows.

Yvonne grew thoughtful: so was that it, was that all there was to life? Such a weightless, unrewarding thing? And yet Paulette had been a beautiful woman, and a kind one, too. She used to be so radiant. But now? Where had it all gone?

Just then the old woman's lips began to move. Yvonne instantly abandoned her pointless philosophizing: 'Paulette, it's Yvonne. Everything's fine, Paulette. I came to take you shopping and –'

'Am I dead? Is that it, am I dead?' she muttered.

'Of course not, Paulette! Of course not. The idea! You're not dead!'

'Oh,' she replied, closing her eyes. 'Oh –'

There was something terrible about that 'Oh.' A disappointed little syllable, disheartened, full of resignation.

Oh, so I'm not dead. I see. Too bad. Oh, forgive me.

Yvonne wasn't about to go along with that.

'Come on, my little Paulette, you've got to live! You've got to live, for goodness sake!'

The old woman shook her head. Almost imperceptibly, very

gently. A minute, stubborn, sad regret. A minute revolt.

Perhaps the first.

Then silence. Yvonne didn't know what to say. She blew her nose then took her friend's hand again, more delicately.

'They're going to put me in a home, aren't they?'

Yvonne started: 'Of course they're not going to put you in a home! Not at all! And why are you saying that? They're going to take care of you and that's all. In a few days you'll be back home again.'

'No. I know perfectly well I won't.'

'Well, I never! Now, that's a thing! And why should I, young man?'

The paramedic was gesturing to her to speak more quietly.

'And my cat?'

'I'll look after your cat. Don't worry.'

'And what about Franck?'

'We'll call Franck, we'll call him right away. I'll take care of it.'

'I can't find his number. I've lost it.'

'I'll find it.'

'But you won't disturb him, will you? He works hard, you know.'

'Yes, Paulette, I know. I'll leave him a message. You know what it's like nowadays. Kids all have mobile phones. You can't disturb them any more.'

'You tell him that I, that I –'

Paulette began to sob.

The vehicle started up the drive to the hospital, and Paulette Lestafier murmured through her tears: 'My garden. My house. Take me back to my house, please.'

Yvonne and the young stretcher-bearer were already on their feet.

4

'Date of your last period?'

She was already behind the screen, struggling into her jeans. She sighed. She knew he would ask her that question, she just knew it. And yet she'd had her strategy all planned; she'd tied her hair back with a really heavy silver barrette and stood on the fucking scale clenching her fists and trying to weigh herself down as much as possible. She'd even wiggled a bit to try to move the needle. But it hadn't worked, of course, and now she'd have to listen to a little sermon.

She knew it from the way he frowned a few minutes earlier when he pressed her abdomen. Her ribs and hipbones were too prominent, her breasts were downright ridiculous and her thighs were hollowed-out, and that was the last thing he wanted to see.

She fastened her belt buckle slowly. She had nothing to fear this time. This was a medical visit for work, not school. He'd give her some bla-bla for appearance's sake and then she'd be out of there.

'Well?'

She was sitting across from him, and she smiled.

That was her deadly weapon, the secret rabbit she could pull out of the hat. Smile at people when they're bugging you: no one's ever found a better way to change the subject. Unfortunately, the dork had gone to the same charm school. He put his elbows on the desk, crossed his hands, and then delivered his disarming smile. She had no alternative but to respond. She might have expected as much: he was cute, and she couldn't help closing her eyes when he placed his hands on her stomach.

'Well? No lies, okay? Otherwise I'd rather you didn't answer.'

10

'A long time.'

'That's obvious,' he grimaced, 'that's obvious. Forty-eight kilos and one metre seventy-three, at this rate you'll be able to fit between the glue and the poster before long.'

'What poster?' she asked naively.

'On a billboard.'

'Oh, I see! Sorry, I didn't know the expression.'

He was about to say something then changed his mind. He reached over for his prescription pad, sighed, then once again looked her straight in the eyes:

'Are you eating?'

'Of course I'm eating!'

A sudden wave of weariness came over her. She was sick of all this talk about her weight, downright fed up. For nearly twenty-seven years everyone had been bugging her about it. Couldn't they just change the record? She was here, for God's sake! She was alive, after all. Doing as much as anyone else. She was just as cheerful, sad, brave, vulnerable and exasperating as any other young woman. There was a person inside her! There was somebody there!

For pity's sake, couldn't they talk to her about something else for a change?

'You do agree, forty-eight kilos isn't a lot.'

'Yes,' she conceded, defeated, 'yes, I agree. It's been a long time since I weighed that little. I –'

'You?'

'No. Nothing.'

'Tell me.'

'I . . . I've had better times in my life, I think.'

He didn't react.

'Will you make out the certificate for me?'

'Yes, yes, you'll get your certificate,' he replied, shrugging, 'uh, what did you say the name of the company was?'

'Which company?'

'This one, where we are, I mean yours –'

'All-Kleen.'

'Sorry?'

'All-Kleen.'

'Capital A l-l-c-l-e-a-n.'

She corrected him: 'No, it's k-l-e-e-n. I know, it doesn't make sense. They should have called it All-clean c-l-e-a-n, but I think they wanted something different . . . Looks more professional, more, like, tuh-rendy . . .'

He didn't get it.

'And what do they do exactly?'

'Who?'

'This company.'

She leaned back, stretching her arms out in front of her and, deadly serious, in a flight attendant's voice, began to rehearse the mission statement of her new job:

'Ladies and Gentlemen, All-Kleen will satisfy your every need where cleaning is concerned. For individuals or businesses, in your home or office, with clients as diverse as property managers, professional offices, agencies, hospitals, housing developments, apartment buildings and workshops, All-Kleen will be there on the spot to offer you immediate satisfaction. All-Kleen tidies, cleans, sweeps, vacuums, waxes, scrubs, disinfects, shines, polishes, deodorizes and leaves you with a healthy environment. We adapt our schedule to fit your needs, and we are flexible and discreet. Our work is meticulous, our rates are competitive. All-Kleen – professionals at your service!'

She'd delivered this remarkable spiel in one breath. Her classy little doctor sat there speechless:

'Is that some kind of joke?'

'Course not. Anyway, you're about to meet the dream team, they're waiting just outside the door.'

'And what's your role in all that?'

'I just told you.'

'That's what you do, really?'

'Yup, I tidy, clean, sweep, vacuum, wax – the whole caboodle.'

'You're a cleaning la—'

'Uh-uh. I'm the cleaning operative, if you don't mind.'

He couldn't tell if she was serious.

'Why are you doing it?'

She opened her eyes wide.

'Well, what I mean is why are you doing *this job*? And not something else?'

'Why shouldn't I?'

'Well, wouldn't you rather be doing something a bit more –'

'Rewarding?'

12

'Yes.'

'No, I wouldn't.'

He sat like that a little while longer, his pencil in the air, his mouth open, then he looked at his watch to read the date, and questioned her without raising his head:

'Last name?'

'Fauque.'

'First name?'

'Camille.'

'Date of birth?'

'11 February 1977.'

'There you go, Ms Fauque, you're fit for work.'

'Great. How much do I owe you?'

'Nothing, that is, All-Kleen pays.'

'Aaah, All-Kleen!' she exclaimed, getting up with a theatrical gesture, 'here I come, one hundred per cent fit to clean your toilet, isn't that great?'

He walked her to the door.

He wasn't smiling any more, and had put his conscientious bigshot doctor mask back on.

As he was opening the door for her, he held out his other hand:

'A few kilos, won't you try? For my sake?'

She shook her head. That sort of thing was a waste of time with her. Blackmail and sympathy – she'd had her fair share.

'I'll see what I can do,' she said. 'I'll try.'

Samia went in after her.

Camille walked down the steps of the van feeling her jacket pockets for a cigarette. Fat Mamadou and Carine were sitting on a bench making comments about the people walking by, and complaining because they wanted to go home.

'Well?' laughed Mamadou, 'what the hell were you doin' in there? I got my train to catch! He put a spell on you or what?'

Camille sat on the ground and smiled. Not the same kind of smile, a transparent smile, this time. She couldn't mess with Mamadou, Mamadou was way too smart for her.

'Is he nice?' asked Carine, spitting out a bit of chewed fingernail.

'Fabulous.'

'I knew it!' said Mamadou triumphantly, 'I was sure! Didn't I tell you and Samia she was stark naked in there?'

'He'll make you stand on the scales.'

'Who, me?' cried Mamadou. 'Me? He thinks I'm gonna get on his scales?'

Mamadou weighed at least a hundred kilos. She pounded her thighs, 'Not on your life! If I get on those scales, I'll flatten them and him along with them! What else did he do?'

'Maybe he'll give you an injection,' suggested Carine.

'Injection for what?'

'No, no injections,' Camille reassured her, 'he'll just listen to your heart and lungs.'

'Oh, that's okay.'

'And he'll touch your stomach.'

'What?!' she frowned, 'what the hell, just let him try! If he touches my stomach, I'm gonna eat him alive. Little white doctors, they taste goo-od.'

She exaggerated her accent and rubbed the colourful cloth of her dress.

'Yeah, they make *real* good yum-yum. So my ancestors told me. Fried up with cassava and cockscombs. Mmmm-mm!'

'And what about that Bredart, what's he gonna do to her?'

Bredart – Josy was her first name – was a regular bitch, their resident shit-stirrer and punch bag and vicious to boot. She also happened to be their boss. 'Chief Worksite Manager' is what it said, clearly, on her badge. Bredart made life miserable, within the limited means at her disposal, but even that was tiring.

'Josy? Nothing. As soon as the doctor gets a whiff of her, he'll ask her to put her clothes back on, pronto.'

Carine wasn't wrong. Josy Bredart, in addition to all the qualities listed above, perspired profusely.

When it was Carine's turn, Mamadou pulled a wad of papers from her bag and placed them in Camille's lap. Camille had promised her she'd take a look, and now she was trying to make sense of the whole bloody thing:

'What's this?'

'It's the form from the social services.'

'No, all these names, here?'

'My family, what'd you think?'

'Which family?'

'Which family? Which family? My very own family, use your head, Camille!'

'All these names – this is your family?'

'Every single one of them,' she said proudly.

'How many kids do you have, anyway?'

'I got five, and my brother got four.'

'But why are all of them on here?'

'Where, here?'

'Yeah, on this paper.'

'It's easier this way because my brother and sister-in-law live at our place and we have the same letter box so –'

'Yeah but that won't do, they say that won't do. You can't have nine children –'

'And why not?' she retorted, 'my mother, she had twelve!'

'Hang on, don't get carried away Mamadou, I'm just telling you what it says here. They're asking you to explain the situation, and to come in with all the birth certificates.'

'What for?'

'Well I guess it's not legal, your thing. I don't think your brother and you are allowed to put all your kids on one form –'

'Yeah but my brother, he got nothing!'

'Is he working?'

'Course he's working. He does the motorways.'

'And your sister-in-law?'

Mamadou wrinkled her nose:

'She don't do nothing. Not a thing, I tell you. She won't budge, that mean old bitch, she never moves her big fat ass at all!'

Camille smiled to herself: what on earth would a big fat ass be in Mamadou's eyes . . . ?

'Do they both have papers?'

'Yes, of course they do.'

'Well, then let them file a separate declaration.'

'But my sister-in law, she don't want to go to the social services and my brother, he works all night long so daytime he's asleep, you see?'

'I see. But right now, how many kids are you getting benefit for?'

'For four.'

15

'For four?'

'Yeah, that's what I been trying to tell you from the beginning, but you're like all white folks, you're always right and you never listen.'

Camille exhaled, a little sigh of irritation.

'The problem I wanted to tell you about is that they forgot my Sissi.'

'So which number kid is Mysissi?'

'She's not a number, you idiot!' seethed Mamadou. 'She's my youngest. Little Sissi.'

'Oh, Sissi.'

'Yes.'

'So why isn't she on here?'

'Hey, Camille, you doing this on purpose or what? That's what I been asking you since a while back.'

Camille didn't really know what to say.

'The best would be to go and see the social services people with your brother or sister-in-law and all your papers and explain it to the lady there.'

'Why you say the "lady"? Which lady, anyway?'

'Any old lady!' said Camille, getting annoyed.

'Okay, all right, don't get so worked up. I was just asking you a simple question 'cause I thought you knew her.'

'Mamadou, I don't know anyone at the social services. I've never been there in my life, don't you see?'

Camille handed her papers back to her, along with a jumble of small ads, pictures of cars, and phone bills.

She heard Mamadou grumbling, 'She said "the lady" so I ask her which lady, that's normal 'cause there's men there too, so how can she know, if she's never been there, how can she know it's a lady? There's guys there too. Is she Mrs Know-it-all or what?'

'Hey, are you sulking?'

'No, I'm not sulking. Just you says you gonna help me and you don' help me. And that's it, that's all!'

'I'll go with you all then.'

'To the social services?'

'Yes.'

'You'll speak to the woman?'

'Yes.'

'And what if it's not her?'

Camille thought it might be time to sacrifice some of her usual cool, but just then Samia came back: 'Your turn, Mamadou . . .' To Camille she said, 'Here, the doctor's phone number.'

'What for?'

'What for? What for? How the hell should I know? To play doctors and nurses, bozo! He asked me to give it to you.'

The doctor had written his mobile number on a prescription slip and added: *I'm prescribing a good dinner, call me.*

Camille crumpled the piece of paper and tossed it in the gutter.

'You know,' added Mamadou, rising heavily to her feet and pointing at Camille with her index finger, 'if you fix things for me and my Sissi, I'll ask my brother to fix it so you find yourself a sweetheart . . .'

'I thought your brother did motorways.'

'Motorways, and spells and undoing spells, you name it.'

Camille rolled her eyes.

'What about me?' Samia burst in. 'Can he find me a guy?'

Mamadou walked past her, scratching the air in front of her face:

'Hey you, damn it, you give me back my bucket first and then we'll talk!'

'Shit, stop bugging me! I don't have your bucket, it's mine. Your bucket was red.'

'Get lost, damn you,' she hissed, walking away, 'daa-aamn.'

Mamadou hadn't even finished climbing the steps and already the van was rocking. Have fun in there, thought Camille, smiling, as she picked up her bag. Good luck . . .

'You coming?'

'I'll catch you up.'

'What're you doing? You taking the metro with us?'

'No. I'll walk home.'

'That's right, you live over there in the fancy neighbourhood . . .'

'Yeah, really.'

'So long, see you tomorrow.'

'Bye, girls.'

Camille was invited for dinner at Pierre and Mathilde's place. She left a message to cancel, relieved that she had got their answering machine.

The ever so light Camille Fauque went on her way, her feet on the

17

ground thanks only to the weight of her backpack or, harder to gauge, the weight of the stones and pebbles which rattled around inside her body. That's what she should have told the doctor about. If she had really wanted to . . . Or if she'd had the courage? Or the time, maybe? Time, surely, she reassured herself, not entirely convinced. Time was a notion she could no longer grasp. Too many weeks and months had gone by that she hadn't even been a part of, and her tirade, earlier, that absurd monologue where she was trying to convince herself that she was just as resilient as the next girl, was nothing but a pack of lies.

What was the word she had used then? 'Alive,' was that it? That's ridiculous; Camille Fauque wasn't alive.

Camille Fauque was a ghost who worked at night and piled up stones by day. A ghost who moved slowly, spoke little, and with a graceful shimmy made herself scarce.

Camille Fauque was the sort of young woman you always saw from behind, fragile and elusive.

But we shouldn't trust that little scene we just watched unfold, for example, however casual it might have seemed. However easy and natural. Camille had been lying. Merely trying to feed the right answers to the doctor; she made an effort, controlled herself, and replied, 'present' to avoid being noticed.

But she couldn't stop thinking about the doctor. She didn't care about his mobile number, but she wondered if she hadn't missed an opportunity, all the same. He seemed the patient type, more attentive than the others. Maybe she should have . . . at one point she had almost . . . She was tired, she should have put her elbows on the desk too, and told him the truth. Told him that if she wasn't eating at all, or almost nothing, it was because the stones were taking up all the room in her belly. That she woke up every day with the feeling she was chewing gravel, that even before she opened her eyes she was suffocating. And that the world around her had become mean-ingless, and every new day was like a weight that was impossible to lift. So she cried. Not that she was sad, but to make it pass. The flood of tears, in the end, helped her to digest the pile of stones and get her breath back.

Would he have listened? Would he have understood? Of course he would have. And that was precisely why she'd kept quiet.

She didn't want to end up like her mother. She refused to open that box. Once she started she didn't know where it would lead. Too far, much too far, too deep and too dark. All things being equal, she just didn't have the guts to look back.

Give them the answers they want, yes, but don't look back.

She went into Franprix downstairs from her place and forced herself to buy a few things to eat. As a gesture to the young doctor's kindness, and to Mamadou's laugh. Mamadou's expansive laughter, the dumb job at All-Kleen, that bitch Bredart, Carine's unbelievable stories, the squabbles, the cigarettes they shared, the physical fatigue, their crazy uncontrollable giggles and the foul moods they got into sometimes – all of that helped her to live. It really did, it helped her to live.

She wandered up and down the aisles a few times before she made up her mind, bought some bananas, four yogurts, and two bottles of water.

There was that bloke from her building. A tall, strange guy with trousers that were way too short, glasses held together with sticking plaster, and the behaviour of a Martian. The minute he picked something up he put it back down, took a few steps then changed his mind, picked it up again, shook his head and finally left the check-out line, when it was his turn at the till, to go and put the thing back where it belonged. Once she even saw him leave the store then go back in to buy the jar of mayonnaise that he'd rejected only seconds before. Funny, sad clown playing to the gallery, stuttering in front of the salesgirls, and wringing her heart.

Sometimes she saw him in the street or outside their front door, and it was always crisis mode with him, major hassles or emotional meltdown. Sure enough, there he was, fumbling and muttering as he stood before the digital lock.

'Is something wrong?' she asked.

'Ah! Oh! Um, excuse me.' He was twisting his hands together. 'Good evening Mademoiselle, forgive me, so sorry to bother – I am bothering you, aren't I?'

What a bummer, she never knew whether to laugh or to feel sorry for him. His pathological shyness, his incredibly convoluted way of speaking, the words he used and his perpetually spacey gestures: it all made her feel really ill at ease.

'No, no, don't worry about it. Did you forget the code?'

'Goodness, no. At least not as far as I know . . . well . . . I didn't look at it that way. My God, I –'

'Maybe they changed it?'

'You really think they might have?' he asked, as if she had just informed him that the end of the world was nigh.

'Well, let's find out. 342B7 –'

The door clicked.

'Oh, I get so confused, what a muddle. I – But that's what I did, too, I don't get it . . .'

'Don't worry about it,' she said, leaning against the door.

He made as if to hold the door for her, and as he was trying to put his arm above her, he missed and knocked her hard on the back of her head.

'Oh gosh! I didn't hurt you did I? I'm so clumsy, honestly, please excuse me, I –'

'Don't worry about it,' she said for the third time.

He didn't move.

'Uh,' she begged at last, 'could you shift your foot because you've trapped my ankle there and it really hurts.'

She was laughing. Nervously.

When they were in the hall, he rushed toward the glass door to let her through.

'Oh sorry, but I'm not going that way,' she said, pointing to the other side of the courtyard.

'You live in the courtyard?'

'Well, not really . . . under the roof more like.'

'Oh, that's great.' He was tugging on the strap of his bag which was caught on the brass door handle. 'That, that must be really nice.'

'Well, yeah,' she said, making a face and moving away quickly, 'that's one way of looking at it.'

'Have a nice evening, Mademoiselle!' he called. 'My regards to your parents!'

Her parents . . . what a weirdo, that guy. She remembered one night – since it was always the middle of the night when she got home, as a rule – she'd found him in the hall, in his pyjamas and hunting boots, with a box of dried cat food in his hand. He seemed really upset and asked her if she hadn't seen a cat. She said no and followed him for a few steps into the courtyard, looking for the cat in question. 'What does he look like?' she asked. 'I'm afraid I don't know.' 'You don't know what your cat looks like?' He stiffened: 'How should I know? I've never had a cat in my life!' She was dead tired so, shaking her head, she'd left him there. There was definitely something creepy about the guy.

'The fancy neighbourhood . . .' She remembered Carine's words as she walked up the first of the one hundred and seventy-two steps between herself and the slum she called home. Fancy neighbourhood, yeah right. She lived on the seventh floor of the service stairway of a smart building which looked out onto the Champ-de-Mars, so in that respect, yes, you could say she lived in a nice area because if she climbed onto her stool and leaned out perilously far to the right, it was true, she could just make out the top of the Eiffel Tower. But for all the rest, sweetheart, for all the rest, it's really not what you think.

She clung to the banister, coughing her lungs out, dragging her bottles of water behind her. She tried never to stop. Ever. Not on any floor. One night she had stopped and she couldn't get going again. She'd sat down on the fourth floor and fallen asleep with her head on her knees. When she woke up it was horrible. She was frozen stiff and it took her a few seconds before she understood where she was.

Before going out she had closed the shutters, afraid there was going to be a storm, and now she sighed, thinking what a furnace it would be up there. When it rained, she got wet; when it was fine, like today, she suffocated; and in winter, she shivered. Camille knew all the climatic conditions inside out, she'd been living there for over a year. She couldn't complain, finding this roost had been a blessing, and she could still remember Pierre Kessler's embarrassed expression the day he had pushed open the door of this dump in front of her and handed her the key.

It was tiny, dirty, cluttered, and a godsend.

When Pierre had found her on his doorstep a week earlier, Camille was famished, dazed and silent. She had spent the last few nights on the street.

At first, when he saw the wraith on his landing, he was apprehensive:

'Pierre?'

'Who's there?'

21

'Pierre . . .' moaned the voice.

'Who is it?'

He switched on the light and his apprehension grew.

'Camille? Is that you?'

'Pierre,' she sobbed, shoving a small suitcase in his direction, 'you have to keep this for me . . . It's all my stuff you see, and it'll get stolen, they'll steal it, all of it, everything. I don't want them to take my tools because I'd just die, do you understand? I would absolutely die.'

He thought she was delirious.

'Camille, what are you talking about? And where have you been? Come in!'

Mathilde appeared behind him, and Camille collapsed on the doormat.

They undressed her and put her to bed in the back room. Pierre Kessler pulled a chair up to the bed and looked at her, appalled.

'Is she asleep?'

'I think so.'

'What happened?'

'I have no idea.'

'But look at the state she's in!'

'Ssssh.'

Camille woke up in the middle of the night and ran a bath, very slowly, so as not to wake them. Pierre and Mathilde weren't asleep, but they decided it was better to leave her alone. They let her stay for a few days, gave her a second set of keys, and asked no questions. They were truly a blessing, that couple.

From his parents Pierre had inherited a maid's room, in the building where they used to live; now he offered it to Camille, pulling the little tartan suitcase, the one that had brought her to them, out from under the bed:

'Here you go,' he said.

Camille shook her head. 'I'd rather leave it –'

'Out of the question,' he said sharply, 'you take it with you. It has no business here.'

Mathilde went with her to a furniture outlet, helped her to choose a lamp, a mattress, some bed linen, a few pots and pans, an electric hotplate, and a minute fridge.

'Do you have any money?' she asked, before saying goodbye.

'Yes.'

'Will you be all right, sweetheart?'

'Yes,' said Camille again, fighting tears.

'You want to keep the keys to our place?'

'No, no, it's okay. I . . . what can I say . . . what is . . .'

She was crying.

'Don't say anything.'

'Thanks?'

'Yes,' said Mathilde, pulling her close, 'thanks, that's okay, that's fine.'

They came to see her a few days later.

They were breathless from climbing the steps, and collapsed onto the mattress.

Pierre laughed and said that this reminded him of his youth, and he launched into 'La Bo-hèèème'. They drank champagne from plastic cups, while Mathilde pulled all sorts of delicious treats out of a big bag. Emboldened by the champagne and a sense of well-being, they dared to ask Camille a few questions. She answered some of them, and they didn't press her.

Just as they were leaving, and Mathilde had already gone down a few steps, Pierre Kessler turned around and took Camille by the wrists:

'You've got to work, Camille . . . Now you have *got* to work.'

She lowered her eyes.

'I feel like I've been working a lot lately. A whole lot.'

He squeezed harder, almost hurting.

'That isn't work and you know it!'

She raised her head, held his gaze. 'Is that why you've been helping me? To tell me that?'

'No.'

Camille was trembling.

'No,' he repeated, letting go, 'no. Don't be silly. You know very well we've always thought of you as our own child.'

'Prodigal or prodigy?'

He smiled and added, 'Get to work. You've got no choice, anyway.'

She closed the door behind them, put away the dinner things and found a big catalogue from Sennelier's art supply store in the bottom of the bag. A Post-it informed her: *Your account is still open.* She didn't feel like leafing through the catalogue, so she drank the rest of the wine straight from the bottle.

But she'd listened to Pierre, all right. She was working.

Work nowadays was cleaning up other people's shit, and that suited her just fine.

They really were dying of heat in there. The day before, Super Josy had warned them: 'Don't complain, girls, these are the last nice days we'll get. Winter will be here soon and we'll be freezing our butts off. So no grousing, eh?'

For once she'd been right. It was the end of September and the days were getting shorter before their very eyes. Camille thought that maybe she'd do things differently this year, like go to bed earlier and get up in the afternoon so she could see the sun. Her thoughts took her by surprise, and her mind was elsewhere as she turned on the answering machine:

'It's your mum. Well . . .' laughed the voice, 'that is, if you still know who I'm talking about. You know – Mum? Isn't that the word that darling little children use when they're talking to their biological parent? Because you do have a mother, Camille, remember? Sorry about the unpleasant reminder, but this is the third message I've left since Tuesday. I just wanted to know if we're still having lunch to –'

Camille interrupted the message and put the yogurt she had just started back into the fridge. She sat down cross-legged, grabbed her tobacco and tried to roll a cigarette. Her hands wouldn't cooperate. She started again several times before she was able to roll the paper without tearing it. Concentrating on every gesture as if this were the most important thing in the world, biting her lips until they bled. It was so unfair. So unfair to be taking shit like this from a tiny piece of cigarette paper when she had actually managed to get through an almost normal day. She had talked, listened, laughed, even *socialized*. She had simpered for that doctor and made a promise to Mamadou. That might not seem like much, and yet . . . It had been a long time since she had promised anything. To anyone, ever. And now all it took was a few sentences from an answering machine to mess up her mind, drag her back down and leave her flat out, crushed beneath the weight of a scarcely believable mass of rubble.

5

'Mr Lestafier!'

'Yes, boss?'

'Telephone.'

'No, boss.'

'Whaddya mean, no?'

'I'm busy, boss! Ask them to call back later.'

The boss shook his head and went back into the sort of closet which served as an office behind the serving hatch.

'Lestafier!'

'Yes, boss!'

'It's your grandmother.'

Sniggers all around.

'Tell her I'll call her back,' he said; he was in the middle of boning a piece of meat.

'You're pissing me off, Lestafier! Come and take this fucking phone. I'm not your private switchboard operator.'

Franck wiped his hands on the cloth which hung from his apron, mopped his forehead with his sleeve and, making a slicing gesture across his neck, said to the boy at the next work station:

'If you so much as touch a thing . . .'

'Take it easy,' the boy replied, 'go and order your Christmas presents, Granny's waiting.'

'Asshole.'

He went into the office and picked up the receiver with a sigh:

'Grandma?'

'Hello, Franck. This isn't your grandmother, this is Yvonne Carminot speaking.'

'Madame Carminot?'

'Oh, it's been so hard to track you down. First I called the Grands Comptoirs and they told me you didn't work there any more, so I called –'

'What's up?' he interrupted.

'Oh dear God, it's Paulette.'

'Hold on a second. Don't move.'

He got up, closed the door, picked up the phone, sat down again, shook his head, went pale, searched the desk for something to write on, said a few more words then hung up. He pulled off his chef's hat, put his head in his hands, closed his eyes and sat like that for a few minutes. His boss was staring at him through the glass door. Finally Franck stuffed the piece of paper into his pocket and went out.

'You okay, mate?'

'I'm okay, boss.'

'Nothing serious?'

'Broke her hip.'

'Oh, that happens a lot with old people. My mother broke her hip ten years ago, you should see her now. A regular mountain goat.'

'Say, boss –'

'Let me guess. You're going to ask for the rest of the day off?'

'No, I'll do the lunch service and I'll do the evening set-up during my break, but I'd like to leave after that.'

'And who'll do the hot service tonight?'

'Guillaume. He can do it.'

'Does he know how?'

'Yes, boss.'

'How do I know he'll know what to do?'

''Cause I say so, boss.'

His boss made a face and shouted at a boy who was walking by, telling him to change his shirt. Then he turned back to Franck and added, 'Go ahead, but I warn you, Lestafier, if there's another balls-up during the evening service, if I have to make a single comment, even one, you hear – I'll hold you responsible, is that clear?'

'Clear, boss.'

He went back to his station and picked up his knife.

'Lestafier! Go back and wash your hands! We're not out in the sticks here!'

'Piss off,' Franck muttered, closing his eyes. 'Piss off, all of you.'

He went back to work in silence. After a few minutes his commis asked, 'You okay?'

'No.'

'I heard what you were telling old fatso . . . Broken hip, that it?'

'Yeah.'

'Is it serious?'

'Nah, don't think so, but the problem is that I'm on my own.'

'On your own for what?'

'For everything.'

Guillaume didn't get it, but preferred to leave Franck alone with his problems.

'So if you heard what I was telling the boss, that means you're clear about tonight?'

'Yes.'

'Can you handle it?'

'There's a trade-off . . .'

They went on working in silence, one leaning over his rabbits, the other over his *carré d'agneau*.

'My motorbike . . .'

'What about it?'

'I can lend it to you on Sunday.'

'The new one?'

'Yeah.'

'Wow,' said Guillaume, sighing, 'you do love your granny. It's a deal.'

Franck made a face.

'Thanks.'

'Huh?'

'What?'

'Where is your old lady?'

'Tours.'

'But then you're gonna need your bike on Sunday if you have to go and see her.'

'I'll work something out.'

The boss's voice interrupted them: 'Silence please, gentlemen! Silence!'

Guillaume sharpened his knife and used the cover of noise to murmur, 'Hey, it's okay. You can lend me the bike when she's better.'

'Thanks.'

'Don't thank me. I'll steal your station instead.'

Franck Lestafier nodded, smiling.

He didn't say another word. The service seemed to take longer than usual. He had trouble concentrating, barked when the chef passed the orders and tried not to burn himself. He almost screwed up a *côte de boeuf*, and couldn't stop cursing under his breath. He thought about what a fucking mess his life would be over the next few weeks. It had already been complicated enough thinking about his granny and going to see her when she was healthy, so now . . . What a hassle, big-time, fuck. This was the last thing he needed. He'd just bought himself a really expensive motorbike on credit as long as his arm, and he'd committed to a number of extra jobs just to make the monthly payments. How was he going to be able to fit her in on top of all the rest? Whatever. He didn't want to admit it to himself, but there was a silver lining. Fat Titi had just souped up the bike's engine and this way he'd be able to try it out on the motorway.

If everything went okay, he'd have a great ride and he'd be there in just over an hour.

Franck sat on alone in the kitchen with the dishwashing guys during the break. He went over his supplies, inventoried his merchandise, numbered the slabs of meat and left a long note for Guillaume. There was no time to stop by his house, so he took a shower in the locker room, found a cleaning product to wipe his visor and left the place with his head in a whirl.

Happy and worried at the same time.

6

It was just before six when Franck wedged the bike's kickstand onto the asphalt of the hospital car park.

The woman at reception told him visiting hours were over and he'd have to come back the next day after ten. He insisted; she was firm.

He put his helmet and gloves on the counter: 'Hold on a minute here, just one minute. I don't think you understand, okay?' He was trying hard not to get annoyed. 'I've come all the way from Paris and I have to go back there later, so if you could –'

A nurse came over.

'What's going on?'

This one was more imposing.

'Yes hello, I, um, sorry about the bother, but I have to see my grandmother who was brought in yesterday as an emergency and I –'

'Your name?'

'Lestafier.'

'Oh, yes.' She gestured something to her colleague. 'Come with me.'

The nurse explained the situation briefly, gave him a run-down on the operation, told him what the rehabilitation period would involve and asked for details about the patient's lifestyle. Suddenly bothered by the smells and the engine noise still thrumming in his ears, Franck had trouble following her.

'Here's your grandson!' the nurse announced gaily as she opened the door. 'You see? I told you he'd come! Okay, I'll leave you now,' and to Franck she added, 'Come and see me in my office, otherwise they won't let you out.'

He didn't have the presence of mind to thank her. What he saw there, in the bed, broke his heart.

He turned aside to try to pull himself together. Removed his jacket and sweater, and looked for somewhere to hang them up.

'It's hot in here, isn't it.'

His voice sounded strange.

'You okay?'

The old lady, who was bravely trying to smile at him, closed her eyes and began to cry.

They'd removed her dentures. Her cheeks seemed terribly hollow and her upper lip was sucked into her mouth.

'So! You been partying again, that it?'

It cost him a superhuman effort just to use that bantering tone.

'I talked with the nurse, you know, she said the operation was very successful. So now you've got a nice little piece of metal in you.'

'They're going to put me in a home.'

'Of course not! What are you talking about! You're going to stay here for a few days and then you'll go to a convalescent home. That's not a home, it's like a hospital only not as big. They'll pamper you and help you to walk and then, hey presto! Back into Paulette's garden.'

'How long for?'

'A couple of weeks . . . afterwards it'll depend on you. You'll have to make an effort.'

'You'll come and see me?'

'Of course I'll come. I've got a beautiful motorbike, you know.'

'You don't drive too fast, I hope.'

'Bah, it's a regular tortoise.'

'Liar . . .'

She was smiling through her tears.

'Stop it, Grandma, otherwise I'll start crying too.'

'No you won't. Not you, you never cry. Even when you were just a little kid, even the day you twisted your arm, I never saw you shed a single tear.'

'Cut it out, all the same.'

He didn't dare take her hand because of all the tubing.

'Franck?'

'I'm here, Grandma.'

'It hurts.'

'That's normal, it'll pass, you have to get some sleep now.'

'It really hurts.'

'I'll tell the nurse before I leave, I'll ask her to give you some-thing.'

'Are you leaving right away?'

'Of course not!'

'Talk to me a little. Tell me what you've been up to.'

'Wait, let me switch off the light, it's really hideous, the lighting in this place.'

Franck raised the blinds and the room, which faced west, was suddenly bathed in a gentle twilight. Then he moved the armchair to the other side so he could take her good hand between his own.

At first it was hard to find the words, he'd never been one for fancy talk or telling stories. He began with little things, the weather in Paris, the pollution, the colour of his Suzuki, a description of his menus and that sort of nonsense.

And then, with the help of the fading day and his grandmother's almost peaceful face, he found more precise memories, and the intimate things it was harder to say. He told her why he'd split up with his girlfriend, the name of the new girl he'd got his eye on, how he was getting on at work, his exhaustion. He did an imitation of his new flatmate and he heard his grandmother laughing gently.

'You're exaggerating . . .'

'I swear I'm not. You'll find out when you come to see us, you'll see.'

'Oh, but I don't want to go up to Paris.'

'So we'll come down here, and you'll make us a nice meal.'

'You think so?'

'Yes. You can make your potato cake.'

'Oh no, not that, that's just country food.'

Then he told her about the atmosphere in the restaurant, how the chef would fly off the handle, or the day a minister came into the kitchen to congratulate him, or the skill of young Takumi, or the price of truffles. He told her the latest about Momo and Madame Mandel. Finally he fell quiet to listen to her breathing and he realized she'd fallen asleep. He got up without making any noise.

Just as he was about to go out the door Paulette called him back:

'Franck?'

'Yeah?'

31

'I haven't told your mother, you know.'

'You were right.'

'I –'

'Ssh. Go to sleep now, the more you sleep the sooner you'll be on your feet.'

'Was I right?'

He nodded and put a finger to her lips.

'Yes. Go on, go to sleep now.'

He was dazzled by the harshness of the neon lights and it took him for ever to find his way out. The nurse he'd spoken to earlier stopped him on his way.

She pointed to a chair and opened Paulette's file. She began by asking a few practical and administrative questions, but Franck didn't react.

'Are you all right?'

'Tired.'

'Have you eaten?'

'No, I –'

'Hold on. I've got something right here.'

She pulled a tin of sardines and a packet of crackers from the drawer.

'Maybe this will do you?'

'And what about you?'

'No problem. Look, I've got loads of biscuits. Want something strong with that?'

'No thanks. I'll get a Coke from the machine.'

'Go ahead, I'll have a little glass of something to keep you company but . . . don't tell anyone, okay?'

He munched, answered all her questions, then picked up his gear.

'She says it hurts.'

'She'll feel better tomorrow. We've put some anti-inflammatory in her drip and she'll feel better when she wakes up.'

'Thanks.'

'It's my job.'

'I meant for the sardines.'

He drove fast, collapsed on his bed, hid his face in the pillow to keep from breaking down. Not now. He'd managed for so long, he could hang on just a bit longer.

7

'Coffee?'

'No, Coke please.'

Camille took little sips. She was sitting with her elbows on the table in a café opposite the restaurant where her mother had told her to meet. She now placed both hands flat on the table on either side of the glass and closed her eyes, breathing slowly. No matter how infrequent these lunches were, they always played havoc with her insides. She would leave again bent double, staggering, feeling like she had been scraped raw. As if her mother were trying, with a sadistic and probably unconscious diligence, to pick at scabs and open a thousand little scars one by one. In the mirror behind the bottles Camille could see her now, going through the door into the Jade Paradise. She smoked a cigarette, went to the toilet, paid for her drink and crossed the street. Hands in her pockets, and her pockets crossed over her stomach.

Camille saw her mother's hunched figure and sat down across from her, taking a deep breath:

'Morning, Mum.'

'Aren't you going to kiss me?'

'Good morning, Mum,' she said more slowly. 'How are things?'

'Why do you ask?'

Camille held on to the edge of the table to stop herself from getting up again right away.

'Because that's what people usually say when they meet.'

'I'm not "people".'

'What are you, then?'

33

'Oh, please, don't start, okay?'

Camille turned her head and looked at the ghastly decor of pseudo-Asian stucco and bas-reliefs. The tortoise-shell effect and 'mother-of-pearl' inlay were made of plastic, and the lacquer was yellow formica.

'It's nice here.'

'No, it's horrible. But I don't have the means to invite you to the Tour d'Argent, so there. Anyway, even if I did, I wouldn't take you there. The way you eat it would be money down the drain.'

Great atmosphere.

Camille's mother began to giggle sarcastically.

'Though you could go there without me because you do have money. It's an ill wind –'

'Stop right now,' threatened Camille, 'or I'll leave. If you need money, just tell me and I'll lend you some.'

'That's right, I hear you've got a job now, a good job, interesting to boot. Cleaning lady. Really hard to imagine for someone who's as messy as you are. You never fail to astonish me, you know that?'

'Stop, Mum, stop right there. We can't go on like this. We *cannot*, don't you see? At least I can't. Change the subject, please. Change. The. Subject.'

'You had a nice job and you went and ruined everything.'

'A nice job. Like hell . . . And I don't miss it at all, either. I wasn't happy there.'

'You didn't have to stay there all your life. And anyway, what is "happy" supposed to mean? That the new "in" word or something? Happy! Happy! If you think we're here on earth to frolic around and pick daisies, you're just plain naive, young lady.'

'No, no, you can relax, that's not what I think at all. I've been in good hands so I know we're here to have a hard time. You said so often enough.'

'Are you ready to order?' asked the waitress.

Camille could have kissed her.

Her mother spread her pills on the table and counted them with one finger.

'Aren't you sick of taking all that crap?'

'Don't talk about what you don't know. I'd be long dead if it weren't for these pills.'

'What makes you say that? And why don't you take off those

awful glasses? There's no sun in here.'

'I feel better with them. This way I see the world the way it is.'

Camille decided to smile, and patted her mother's hand. It was either that or go for her neck and strangle her.

Her mother smiled, moaned a bit, talked about her loneliness, her back, the stupidity of her colleagues and the woes of co-ownership. She ate with gusto and frowned when her daughter ordered a beer.

'You drink too much.'

'Yes, you're right! C'mon, cheers. For once you're not saying something stupid.'

'You never come to see me.'

'And now? What am I doing here, then?'

'Always the last word, right? Just like your father.'

Camille froze.

'Ah, you don't like it when I talk about him, do you,' she declared triumphantly.

'Mum, please . . . Don't go there.'

'I'll go wherever I like. Aren't you going to finish your plate?'

'No.'

Her mother shook her head disapprovingly.

'Look at you. You're a skeleton. If you think that's what the boys like –'

'Mum –'

'What, "Mum?" I worry about you, that's normal, you don't bring children into the world to watch them waste away in front of your eyes!'

'So why did you bring me into the world, then?'

The moment she said it Camille realized she'd gone too far and now her mother would put on her drama queen act. There would be nothing new, she'd seen it a thousand times and her mother had it down pat: emotional blackmail, crocodile tears, and suicide threats. At random or in order.

She wept, reproached her daughter for leaving her just like the girl's father had done fifteen years earlier, said she was an ungrateful child and wondered what earthly reason she had left for living.

'Give me a single reason to be here, one single reason.'

Camille rolled a cigarette.

'Did you hear me?'

'Yes.'

'Well?'

Camille was silent.

'Thank you my dear, thank you. Your answer couldn't be any clearer.'

She sniffed, put two luncheon vouchers on the table, and walked out.

Just don't get emotional; the sudden departure has always been the apotheosis, the curtain coming down in a way, on her mother's theatrics.

Usually the star would wait until after dessert, but it's true they'd been in a Chinese restaurant and her mother didn't especially like fried bananas, lychees and other sorts of sickly sweet nougats.

No. She mustn't get emotional.

It was never easy, but Camille had learned the tricks of her own little survival kit long ago. So she resorted to her usual tactic and tried to focus on what she knew for sure. There were a few really simple tenets, full of common sense. Hastily assembled little crutches she could reach for when she had to see her mother. Because there wasn't much point in these forced encounters – absurd and destructive as they were – if her mother didn't get something out of them. And Catherine Fauque did get something out of them, for sure: being able to use her daughter as a doormat was very gratifying. And even if she often stomped off with an outraged flourish in the middle of dinner, she always went away satisfied. Satisfied and replete. With all her abject good faith and pathetic vindictiveness intact, and an ample supply of grist to the mill for next time.

Camille had taken a while to figure this out and, moreover, she hadn't managed it on her own. She'd had help. Some of the people who knew her, above all in the early days, when she was still too young to judge her mother, had given her the keys to understanding her mother's attitude. But that was in the old days, and all those people who'd looked out for her then were no longer around.

And nowadays the kid was having a very hard time of it.

She really was.

8

The table had been cleared and the restaurant was emptying. But Camille didn't move. She kept smoking and ordering coffees so they wouldn't kick her out.

A toothless old Asian man in the back of the restaurant was jabbering and laughing to himself.

The young woman who had served them was standing behind the bar. She was drying glasses, and from time to time she scolded the old man in their language. He would frown, sit quietly for a minute, then start up again with his nonsensical monologue.

'Are you getting ready to close?' asked Camille.

'No,' the girl replied, putting a bowl down in front of the old man, 'we stop serving but we stay open. You want another coffee?'

'No, no thanks. Can I stay a little bit longer?'

'Yes, sure! You can stay. As long as you're here, it gives him something to think about.'

'You mean I'm the one who's making him laugh like that?'

'You or anyone.'

Camille stared at the old man, then smiled at him.

Gradually, the anxiety her mother had plunged her into began to fade. She listened to the sounds coming from the kitchen: running water, pots and pans, the radio, and incomprehensible refrains in a shrill key which had the young girl jiggling her feet, keeping time. Camille watched the old man as he lifted long noodles with his chopsticks, dribbling broth all down his chin, and she suddenly felt as though she was in the dining room of a real house.

There was nothing on the table in front of her other than her coffee cup and tobacco pouch. She moved them over to the next table and began to smooth the tablecloth.

Slowly, very slowly, she ran the flat of her hand over the cheap, stained paper that covered the table.

She went on doing this for several long minutes.

Her mind grew calmer and her heartbeat accelerated.

She was afraid.

She had to try. *You have to try.* Yes, but it's been such a long time since –

Ssh, she murmured to herself, ssh, I'm here. It will be fine, sweetheart. Look, it's now or never. Go on, don't be afraid.

She raised her hand a few inches from the table and waited for it to stop trembling. Good, you see? She reached for her backpack and rummaged inside: there it was.

She brought out the little wooden box and put it on the table. She opened it, took a small rectangular stone and rubbed it against her cheek; it was soft and warm. Then she unfolded a blue cloth and lifted out a stick of ink; there was a strong scent of sandalwood. Finally she unrolled a little mat of bamboo slats in which two brushes nestled.

The larger one was of goat hair, and the other, much finer, of hog bristle.

She stood up, took a pitcher of water from the counter and two phone books, and bowed slightly to the crazy old man.

She put the phone books on her seat so she'd be able to stretch her arms out without touching the table, poured a few drops of water on to the slate stone and began to grind the ink. The voice of her master echoed in her ear: *Turn the stone very slowly, little Camille. Oh, even slower than that! And longer. Maybe two hundred times because, you see, as you do that you're loosening your wrist and preparing your mind for great things. . . . Don't think about anything any more – stop looking at me, you naughty girl! Concentrate on your wrist, it will guide you for the first stroke and it is the first stroke alone which counts, that is what will give life and breath to your drawing.*

When the ink was ready, she disobeyed her master and began with little exercises on a corner of the paper tablecloth to recover the memories, all too distant. She made five spots to begin with, from deepest black to the most diluted, to remind herself of the ink's

38

colours, but then when she tried different strokes she realized she had forgotten almost all of them. A few remained: the loosened rope, the hair, the raindrop, the rolled thread and the ox's hairs. Then came the points. Her master had taught her over twenty of them, but she remembered only four: the circle, the rock, the rice and the shiver.

Enough. Now you're ready. She picked up the finer brush between her thumb and index finger, held her arm above the table-cloth and waited a few more seconds.

The old man, still rambling on in his corner, encouraged her by closing his eyes.

Camille Fauque emerged from a long sleep, with a sparrow, then two, then three, then an entire flock in flight, birds with a mocking look in their eye.

She hadn't drawn a thing in over a year.

*　*

As a child she had never been talkative, spoke even less than nowadays. Her mother had obliged her to take piano lessons and Camille hated it. Once, when the teacher was late, she picked up a thick magic marker and painstakingly drew a finger on each key. Her mother had wrung her neck and her father, to make the peace, showed up the following weekend with the address of a painter who gave lessons once a week.

When her father died, not long after, Camille stopped speaking. Even during her drawing lessons with Mr Doughton (she pro-nounced it Doggton) whom she liked so much; even with him she would not speak.

The old Englishman didn't take offence, and he continued to come up with ways to teach her technique, even in silence. He would give her an example and she would copy it, merely moving her head to say yes or no. Between the two of them, and only there, in that place, things were fine. Her mute silence even seemed to suit them. He didn't have to struggle for the words in French, and she concentrated more readily than her fellow pupils.

But one day, when all the other pupils had left, he broke their tacit agreement and spoke to her while she was amusing herself with the pastels:

'You know, Camille, who you make me think of?'

She shook her head.

'Well, you make me think of a Chinese painter called Zhu Da. Do you want me to tell you his story?'

Camille nodded but he had turned around to switch off his kettle.

'I can't hear you, Camille, don't you want me to tell you the story?'

Now he was staring at her.

'Answer me, young lady.'

She gave him a black look.

'I beg your pardon?'

'Yes,' she said finally.

He closed his eyes contentedly, poured a cup and came to sit next to her.

'When he was a child, Zhu Da was very happy . . .'

He took a swallow of tea.

'He was a prince of the Ming dynasty. His family was very rich and very powerful. His father and grandfather were painters and famous calligraphers, and little Zhu Da had inherited their gift. So just imagine, one day, when he wasn't even eight years old yet, he drew a flower, a simple lotus flower floating on a pond. His drawing was beautiful, so beautiful that his mother decided to hang it in their sitting room. She claimed that thanks to the drawing you could feel a fresh little breeze in the huge room and you could even smell the flower's perfume when you walked by the drawing. Can you imagine? Even the perfume! And his mother was surely not an easy person to please . . . With both a husband and a father who were artists, she must have seen a few things by then . . .'

He took another sip from his cup.

'So, Zhu Da grew up in this carefree world full of pleasure, and he was sure that he too would be a great artist one day. Alas, when he turned eighteen, the Manchus seized power from the Mings. The Manchus were a cruel and brutal people who did not care for painters and writers. They forbade them to work. That was the worst thing anyone could do, you can well imagine. Zhu Da's family knew no peace after that, and his father died of despair. From one day to the next the son, who had been a mischievous kid, who loved to laugh, sing, say silly things or recite long poems, did the most incredible thing . . . Oh! Now who's this, then?' asked Mr Doughton, turning to his cat, which had just settled on the windowsill, and deliberately starting a long conversation in baby talk with the creature.

'What did he do?' Camille murmured, finally.

Mr Doughton hid his smile in his bushy moustache and went on as if nothing had happened:

'He did the most incredible thing. Something you'd never imagine. He decided to stop speaking for ever. For ever, do you hear? Not a single word would leave his lips! He was disgusted by the attitude of the people around him, those who denied their traditions and their beliefs just so they would be viewed favourably by the Manchus; he didn't want to speak to any of them ever again. Devil take them all! Every last one! Slaves! Cowards! So, he wrote the word *Mute* on the door of his house, and if there were people who tried to talk to him all the same, he would unfold a fan in front of his face, on which he had also written *Mute*, and he'd wave it every which way to make them go away.'

Little Camille was captivated.

'The problem is that people can't live without expressing themselves. No one can. It's impossible. So Zhu Da, who, like everyone, like you and me for example, had a lot of things to say, Zhu Da had a brilliant idea. He went off into the mountains, far away from all those people who'd betrayed him, and he began to draw. And from then on, that is how he would express himself, how he'd communicate with the rest of the world: through his drawings. Would you like to see them?'

Mr Doughton went to fetch a big black and white book from his shelves, and put it down in front of her.

'Look, isn't this beautiful? So simple. Just one stroke, and there you are. A flower, a fish, a grasshopper. Look at this duck, how angry it looks; or these mountains in the mist. And you see how he's drawn the mist? As if it were nothing, just an emptiness. And these chicks, see them? So soft you want to stroke them. Look, his ink is like down, his ink is soft . . .'

Camille was smiling.

'Would you like me to teach you to draw like this?'

She nodded.

'You want me to teach you?'

'Yes.'

When everything was ready, when he had finished showing her

how to hold the brush, and explaining to her how important the first stroke was, she was puzzled. She didn't really understand what she was supposed to do, and she thought she had to complete the entire picture in one stroke, without lifting her hand. It was impossible.

She thought about it for a long time, then looked around, and stretched out her arm.

Camille drew a long wavy line, a bump, a point, another point, brought her brush back down in a long wiggly stroke, then came back to the initial wavy line. She decided to cheat when the teacher wasn't looking, and lifted the brush to add a big black spot and six little half-strokes. She'd rather disobey than draw a cat without whiskers.

Malcolm, her model, was still sleeping in the window and Camille, eager to be true to life, finished her drawing with a fine rectangle around the cat.

She then got up and went to stroke the cat, and when she turned around, she saw her teacher was looking at her strangely, almost angrily:

'Did you do this?'

So he had seen her picture, seen that she had lifted the brush off the paper several times. She made a face.

'Did you do this, Camille?'

'Yes.'

'Come over here please.'

Not very proud of herself, she went and sat beside him.

There were tears in Mr Doughton's eyes.

'This is magnificent, what you've done, you know. Magnificent. You can hear the cat purring. Oh, Camille.'

He reached for a big paint-splattered handkerchief and began noisily blowing his nose.

'Listen, lass, I'm just an old fellow and a bad artist to boot, but listen carefully now. I know that life's not easy for you, I imagine it's not always very cheery at home and I heard about your dad, but . . . No, don't cry . . . Here, take my handkerchief. But there's one thing I've got to tell you: people who stop talking go mad. Zhu Da, for example, I didn't tell you this before, but he went mad and he was very unhappy as well. Very very unhappy and very very mad. He only found peace again when he was an old man. You're not going to wait to be an old woman, now, are you? Tell me you're not.

You're very gifted, you know. You're the most gifted of all the students I've ever had, but that's not a reason, Camille; that's not a reason. The world today is not like in Zhu Da's time and you have to start speaking again. You've got to, do you understand? If you don't, they'll put you away with people who really are mad, and no one will ever see all your beautiful pictures.'

They were interrupted by her mother's arrival. Camille got up and said to her, in a hoarse, unsteady voice, 'Wait a minute, I haven't finished putting my things away.'

One day, not long ago, she received a poorly wrapped parcel with this letter:

> *Hello.*
>
> *My name is Eileen Wilson. That probably doesn't mean anything to you, but I was Cecil Doughton's friend, he used to be your drawing teacher. I'm very sad to inform you that Cecil passed away two months ago. I know you will appreciate me telling you (forgive my poor French) that we buried him in his native Dartmoor that he loved so dear, in a cemetery with a lovely view. I put his brushes and his paintings in the earth with him.*
>
> *Before dying he asked me to give you this. I think he would be happy knowing that you are using it and thinking of him.*
>
> *Eileen W.*

Camille could not hold back her tears when she unwrapped the box of Chinese painting tools – the same box she was using at this very moment . . .

*

Intrigued, the waitress came to clear away the empty coffee cup and she glanced over at the tablecloth. Camille had just drawn a cluster of bamboo stalks. The leaves and stems were the most difficult thing to get. *One leaf, lass, a simple leaf blowing in the wind, took the masters years of work, even an entire lifetime . . . Play with contrasts. You've got only one colour to work with and yet you can suggest everything . . . Concentrate harder. If you want me to carve you your seal some day, you've got to make your leaves much lighter than that . . .*

The paper was really poor quality, and it curled and absorbed the ink much too quickly.

'May I?' asked the waitress.

She held out a packet of clean tablecloths. Camille moved back and put her work on the floor. The old man was grumbling; the girl scolded him.

'What's he saying?'

'He's complaining because he can't see what you're doing.'

She added, 'He's my great-uncle. He's paralysed.'

'Tell him the next one will be for him.'

The girl went back to the bar and spoke to the old man. He calmed down and looked fiercely at Camille.

For a while Camille stared back at him, then using the entire surface of the tablecloth she drew a little laughing man who looked just like him, running through a paddy field. Camille had never been to Asia but for a background she improvised a mountain in the mist, some pine trees and rocks, and even Zhu Da's little hut on a promontory. She portrayed her old man with a Nike cap and a jacket, but she'd left him with bare legs and wearing only a traditional loincloth. She added a few splashes of water at his feet, and a group of children chasing after him.

Camille leaned back to inspect her work.

There were a few details she was dissatisfied with but, in the end, the old fellow looked happy, truly happy. So she opened the little pot of red cinnabar and set her seal on to the picture in the middle of the right-hand side. She stood up, cleared the old man's table, put a plate under the tablecloth to prop it up, then went back for the picture and arranged it in front of him.

No reaction.

Oops, she thought, maybe I've offended him.

When his great-niece came back from the kitchen, he let out a long, sorrowful moan.

'I'm sorry,' said Camille, 'I thought that –'

The girl made a gesture to interrupt her, went to fetch a pair of thick glasses from behind the counter and slid them on to the old man's nose below his cap. He nodded ceremoniously and began to laugh. A child's laughter, clear and happy. There were tears there too, then he laughed again, rocking back and forth with his arms crossed over his chest.

'He wants to drink some sake with you.'

'Great.'

44

The girl brought out a bottle, he shrieked something, she sighed and went back to the kitchen.

When she returned, she had a different bottle and the entire family in tow: an older woman, two middle-aged men, and a teenager. They were all laughter, shouting, bowing and bursts of enthusiasm. The men tapped him on the shoulder and the boy gave him a high five.

Then each of them returned to what they were doing, and the girl put two little glasses down in front of Camille and the old man. He nodded to her then emptied his glass before filling it again.

'I warn you, he's going to tell you his life story,' said the girl.

'No problem. Woah, this is strong.'

The girl walked away, laughing.

They were alone now. The ancestor was chattering away, and Camille listened earnestly, nodding with her nose whenever he pointed to the bottle.

It was no easy thing to stand up and get her things together. She bowed goodbye over and over to the old fellow, then stood giggling and helpless by the door, tugging on the door handle; till the girl had to come and help her to push it open.

'You should feel at home here, any time, okay?' she said. 'You can come and eat here whenever you want. If you don't come, he'll be mad. And sad, too.'

Camille was completely drunk when she showed up at work.

Samia said excitedly, 'Hey, did you find a guy or something?'

'Yes,' confessed Camille, sheepishly.

'No kidding?'

'Yes.'

'Nah, it's not true . . . What's he like? Is he cute?'

'Really cute.'

'Really, that's way cool. How old is he?'

'Ninety-two.'

'Hey, you're bullshitting me, idiot, how old is he?'

'All right, girls, whenever you're ready!'

There was Miss Josy, pointing at her watch.

Camille walked away, giggling, tripping over the hose of the vacuum cleaner.

9

More than three weeks had gone by. Franck was working every Sunday as a catering assistant in another restaurant on the Champs-Elysées, and every Monday he travelled to his grandmother's bedside.

Paulette was in a convalescent home a few miles north of the town, and from first light on she'd be waiting for him to come.

As for Franck, he had to set his alarm, head like a zombie down to the corner café, drink two or three coffees in a row, climb on to his motorcycle, then head off to catch up on his sleep in a hideous leatherette armchair by his grandmother's bed.

When they brought her dinner in on a tray, Paulette would put her finger to her lips and, with a jerk of her head, indicate the big baby curled up there, keeping her company. She watched over him jealously, and made sure that the jacket covered his chest properly.

She was happy. He was there. Really there. All hers.

Paulette didn't dare call the nurse to ask her to raise the bed; she took her fork gingerly between her fingers and ate in silence. She hid things in her night table – bits of bread, a portion of cheese, and some fruit, for Franck when he woke up. Then she quietly pushed the tray away and folded her hands across her stomach with a smile.

Lulled by her young man's breathing and the sudden rush of memories, Paulette closed her eyes and dozed. She'd lost him so many times already, so many times. She sometimes felt she'd spent her life hunting for him: in the garden, in the trees, at the neighbours', where he'd be hidden in the stables or slumped in front of the television, then at the café, of course; and now she hunted for

46

him on little scraps of paper where he would scribble phone numbers which were never the right ones.

She'd done her best, though, she really had. Fed him, kissed him, cuddled and reassured and scolded; punished and consoled but none of it had done a bit of good . . . No sooner did that kid know how to walk than he'd be scampering off somewhere, and once he had three hairs on his chin that was it. He was gone.

Sometimes when she was daydreaming she'd wince, and her lips would tremble. Too much sorrow, too much waste, and so many regrets. At times it had been so, so hard. But she mustn't think about all that, anyway, he was waking up, his hair tousled and his cheek marked by the seam on the armchair.

'What time is it, Grandma?'

'Nearly five.'

'Fuck, already?'

'Franck, why are you always saying that f-word?'

'What about, "goodness-gracious-me", already?'

'Are you hungry?'

'I'm okay, thirsty more like. I'll just go and stretch my legs.'

So there we are, thought Paulette, that's it.

'Are you leaving?'

'Course not, I'm not leaving, for fu— for goodness sake.'

'If you see a red-haired man with a white coat, can you ask him when I'm supposed to get out of here?'

'Yeah, yeah,' said Franck as he went out the door.

'A tall man with glasses and a –'

He was already in the corridor.

'Well?'

'I didn't see him.'

'Oh?'

'C'mon Grandma,' he said gently, 'you're not going to start that crying again, are you?'

'No, but I . . . I've been thinking about the cat, and my birds. And it's been raining all week long and I'm worried about my tools. I didn't put them away and they're going to rust, for sure.'

'I'll go by the house on my way home and take care of it.'

'Franck?'

'Yes?'

'Take me with you.'

'Oh, Grandma . . . Don't do this to me, every time. I can't take it.'

She took hold of herself.

'The tools . . .'

'What?'

'You need to oil them with neat's-foot oil.'

He looked at her and blew out his cheeks. 'Hey, if I have time, okay? Right, this is all very well, but you have your gym class now, you know. Where's your Zimmer?'

'I don't know.'

'Grandma.'

'Behind the door.'

'C'mon, old girl, get up, you want to see some birds? I'll show you some birds!'

'Bah, there's no birds here. Just vultures and raptors.'

Franck smiled. He loved it when his grandma was bitchy.

'You okay?'

'No.'

'Now what's the matter?'

'It hurts.'

'Where?'

'Everywhere.'

'Everywhere, that's impossible, can't be. Show me the exact spot.'

'Inside my head.'

'That's normal. Hey, we all hurt inside our heads. C'mon, introduce me to your girlfriends.'

'No, go the other way. I don't want to see that lot, I can't stand them.'

'And what about that old guy in the blazer, he's not bad, is he?'

'That's not a blazer, stupid, that's his pyjamas, plus he's as deaf as a post. And pretentious to boot.'

As long as she was putting one foot behind the other and bad-mouthing her fellow inmates, everything would be cool.

'Okay, I'm on my way.'

'Now?'

'Yes, now. If you want me to take care of your hoe . . . I've got to get up early tomorrow and I don't have anyone to bring me breakfast in bed.'

'Will you call me?'

He nodded.

'That's what you say and then you never do.'

'I don't have time, Grandma.'

'Just say hello and then hang up.'

'Okay. To be honest, I don't know if I can make it next week. My boss is taking us for a night on the town.'

'Where?'

'The Moulin Rouge.'

'Really?'

'Nah, I wish. We're going to the Limousin to see the guy who sells us his livestock.'

'What a funny idea.'

'That's my boss all over. He says it's important.'

'So you won't be coming?'

'I don't know.'

'Franck?'

'Yes?'

'The doctor . . .'

'I know, the red-headed guy, I'll try and get hold of him. And you do your exercises like you're supposed to, okay? I hear the physio isn't too pleased with you.'

When he saw her astonished expression he added, facetiously, 'So you see, I do telephone from time to time.'

He put away the tools, ate the last strawberries from the vegetable garden, and sat there for a moment. The cat wound its way between his legs, mewing hoarsely.

'Don't worry, puss, don't worry. She'll be back.'

The jangle of his mobile roused him from his lethargy. It was a girl. He did his rooster act; she giggled like a clucking chicken.

She invited him to a film.

All the way home he rode at over a hundred miles an hour, trying to think up a way to get laid without having to sit through the film. He wasn't crazy about the cinema. He always fell asleep before the end.

10

In mid-November, when the cold weather began its dirty work of undermining everyone's morale, Camille finally decided to head for the nearest DIY store, in order to improve her chances of survival. She spent her entire Saturday there, wandering up and down the aisles, touching the wooden panels, admiring the tools, the nails and screws, the door handles, the curtain rods, the tins of paint, the mouldings, the shower cabinets and sundry chrome mixer taps. She then went to the gardening section and made an inventory of everything she might dream of having: gloves, rubber boots, the combined hoe and fork, chicken coops, sowing buckets, organic fertilizer, and seed packets in their infinite variety. She spent as much time observing other customers as she did inspecting the wares: a pregnant woman among the pastel wallpapers; a young couple arguing about a hideous wall lamp; a sprightly man with an air of early retirement about him, in his Timberland shoes, and with spiral notebook in one hand and a carpenter's yardstick in the other.

The school of hard knocks had taught her to beware of any certainty or projects for the future, but there was one thing Camille knew for sure: some day, a long long way down the road, when she'd be quite old, even older than now, with white hair, a zillion wrinkles and brown spots all over her hands, she'd have her own house. A real house with a copper pot for making jam, and sweet biscuits in a tin hidden deep inside a dresser. A long farmhouse table, nice thick wood, and cretonne curtains. She smiled. She had no idea what cretonne was, or even if she'd like it, but she liked the way the words went together: cretonne curtains. She'd have a guest room and – who knows, maybe even some guests? A well-kept little garden, hens who'd provide her with tasty boiled eggs, cats to chase after the field mice and dogs to chase after the cats. A little plot of aromatic herbs, a fireplace, sagging armchairs and books all around. White tablecloths, napkin rings unearthed at flea markets, some sort of device so she could listen to the same operas her father used to listen to, and a coal-fired range where she could let a rich beef and carrot stew simmer all morning long.

A rich beef and carrot stew. What was she thinking.

A little house like the ones that children draw, with a door and two windows on either side. Old-fashioned, discreet, silent, overrun with Virginia creeper and climbing roses. A house with those little fire bugs on the porch, red and black insects scurrying everywhere in pairs. A warm porch where the heat of the day would linger and she could sit in the evening to watch for the return of the heron.

And an old greenhouse she could use as a studio. Well, that wasn't sure. So far, her hands had always betrayed her and maybe it was better not to rely on them.

Maybe she couldn't rely on her hands to give her a sense of peace after all.

But then what could she rely on? she wondered, suddenly anxious.

What?

She pulled herself together and called out to a sales assistant before she lost it completely. Little cottages deep in the woods, that was all well and good, but in the meantime she was freezing at the end of a damp corridor and this young man in his bright yellow polo-neck was bound to help her:

'You say the air is getting in?'

'Yes.'

'Is it a skylight?'

'No, a louvred window.'

'Those things still exist?'

'Unfortunately . . .'

'Here, this is what you need.'

He handed her a roll of sealing strip that could be nailed in place, especially designed for 'window weatherproofing' and made of long-lasting, washable, waterproof PVC-backed foam. Hallelujah, thought Camille.

'Do you have a staple gun?'

'Nope.'

'A hammer and nails?'

'Not that either.'

She followed him all round the store like a little dog while he filled her basket.

'What about heaters?'

'What do you have at the moment?'

'An electric radiator which blows a fuse during the night, and which stinks as well.'

He took his role very seriously and gave her a proper lecture on the subject.

In a learned tone of voice he sang the praises of various heaters, gave a running commentary on others, and compared the merits of fan, radiator, infrared, ceramic, oil and convection – until Camille felt dizzy.

'What should I get?'

'Well, that's really up to you.'

'But that's the thing, I just can't tell.'

'Get an oil heater, they're not too expensive and they heat well. The Calor Oléo is not bad.'

'Is it on casters?'

'Well . . .' he said hesitantly, checking the technical specifications, '*mechanical thermostat, cord storage, adjustable power, integrated humidifier, bla-bla-bla, casters!* Yes, ma'am!'

'Cool. That way I can put it near the bed.'

'Well . . . if you don't mind me saying so . . . you know, a guy does the job just as well. In bed, he gives off heat . . .'

'Yes, but there's no cord storage.'

'Fair enough.'

He was smiling.

On her way to the till to get the warranty, she spotted a fake fireplace with fake embers, fake logs, fake flames and fake fire dogs.

'Hey, what's that?'

'An electric fireplace, but I don't recommend it, it's a rip-off.'

'No, go on, show me!'

It was the Sherbone, an English model. Only the English could invent something so ugly and kitsch. Depending on the intensity of the heat (1,000 or 2,000 watts), the flames rose higher. Camille was in raptures: 'It's fantastic, it looks like a real one!'

'You seen the price?'

'No.'

'532 euros, it's insane. A useless gadget. Don't be fooled.'

'What the hell, it doesn't mean anything to me in euros, anyway.'

'It's not hard, just calculate roughly 3,500 francs for a gizmo that won't heat you half as well as the Calor at less than 600 francs.'

'I want it.'

Here was a young man full of good sense, but Camille just closed her eyes and handed over her credit card. She'd come this far, she might as well pay for the delivery as well. When she told them she was on the seventh floor without a lift, the woman looked at her askance and told her it would cost an extra ten euros.

'No problem,' replied Camille, squeezing her buttocks.

He was right. It was insane.

Yes, it was insane, but the place where she was living wasn't much better. Fifteen square metres under the roof, which left her about six to stand up in, with a mattress right on the floor, a tiny sink in one corner which looked more like a urinal and doubled as both kitchen and bathroom sink. A hanging rail for a wardrobe and two stacked cardboard boxes as shelves. A hotplate on top of a camping table; a mini-fridge that served as work surface, dining room and coffee table. Two stools, a halogen lamp, a little mirror and another cardboard box for a kitchen cupboard. What else? The tartan suitcase where she'd stored some of the materials she still had left, three art portfolios and . . . No, that was it. So much for the tour of the property.

Down at the end of the hall to the right the toilets were Turkish-style, and the shower was above the toilet. All you had to do to take a shower was to place the specially provided mouldy grating over the hole.

Camille didn't have any neighbours, or maybe just a ghost or two: from time to time she could hear murmuring behind door no. 12. On her door there was a padlock and, tacked to the doorframe in pretty violet lettering, the name of the former tenant: *Louise Leduc*.

A little servant girl from the nineteenth century.

No, Camille was not at all sorry she had bought her fireplace, even though it cost her nearly half her salary. Oh, what the hell – for all the use she made of her salary. On the bus she fell to daydreaming, wondering who she could invite over to inaugurate the heater.

A few days later, she found her victim: 'Guess what, I've got a fireplace!'

'I beg your pardon? Ah! Oh! It's you. Hello there. Beastly weather, isn't it?'

'You said it. Why did you just take your hat off?'

'Well I – I, um, I'm greeting you, aren't I?'

'Oh, come on, put it back on. You'll catch your death. I was looking for you actually. I wanted to invite you to dinner by the fire one evening.'

'Me?' he choked.

'Yes, you.'

'Oh, no, but I, uh, why? Really, it's –'

'It's what?' she said, suddenly tired. They stood there shivering outside their favourite grocer's.

'That is –'

'Can't you make it?'

'No, it's just – it's just such an honour!'

'Oh,' she laughed, 'such an honour. Not at all, you'll see, it will be a very simple occasion. You'll come, then?'

'Well, yes, yes, I'd be delighted to share your table –'

'It's not really a table, you know.'

'Oh, really?'

'It'll be more like a picnic. A bite to eat, informal.'

'Excellent, I do like picnics. I can even bring my blanket and my basket, if you like.'

'Your basket of what?'

'My picnic basket.'

'One of those things with dishes?'

'Yes, there are plates, and cutlery and a tablecloth, four napkins, a corksc—'

'Oh yes, that's a very good idea. I don't have any of those things. So shall we say this evening?'

'Well, this evening, I don't know –'

'You what?'

'Well, I haven't warned my flatmate.'

'I see. But then he can come too, that's no problem.'

'What, him? No, not him. To start with I don't know if . . . well, if he's quite the thing. I – Let's get this straight, I'm not talking about his behaviour, even if, well, I don't behave like that, you see, no, it's more that – Oh, and besides, he's not here this evening. Or any other evening for that matter.'

'Let's see if I've got this right,' said Camille, taking a deep breath, 'you can't come because you haven't warned your flatmate who's never there anyway, is that right?'

He looked down and fiddled with the buttons on his coat.

'Hey, you're not, like, obliged, you know. You don't have to say yes.'

'It's just that –'

'Just what?'

'No, nothing. I'll come.'

'Tonight or tomorrow? Because after that I'm back at work until the end of the week.'

'Okay,' he murmured, 'okay, tomorrow. You'll be there, right?'

She shook her head.

'What a song and dance! Of course I'll be there, since I'm the one inviting you!'

He gave her an awkward smile.

'See you tomorrow?'

'See you tomorrow, Mademoiselle.'

'Eight o'clock all right?'

'Eight o'clock sharp. I'll make a note of it.'

He bowed and turned on his heels.

'Hey!'

'I beg your pardon?'

'You have to take the service stairs. I'm on the seventh floor, door no. 16, you'll see, it's the third on the left.'

He gestured with his hat, to let her know he'd heard.

11

'Come in, come in! You look great!'

'Oh,' he blushed, 'it's just a boater. It belonged to my great-uncle and I thought, for a picnic . . .'

Camille couldn't believe her eyes. The boater was only the cherry on the cake. He'd tucked a silver-knobbed walking stick under his arm, he was wearing a light suit with a red bow tie; and now he was handing her an enormous wicker trunk.

'This is your basket?'

'Yes . . . but wait, there's something else.'

He disappeared down the corridor and came back with a bunch of roses.

'That's nice of you.'

'These aren't real flowers, you know.'

'Excuse me?'

'No, I believe they're from Uruguay. I would have preferred real roses from a garden, but in the middle of winter it's, it's –'

'It's not possible.'

'Yes, that's it. Not possible.'

'Well, please come in, make yourself at home.'

He was so tall that he had to sit down at once. He struggled to find his words but for once, the problem was not his stuttering but rather his utter bewilderment.

'It's, it's . . .'

'It's small.'

'No, it's, how to put it – it's sweet. Yes, it's terribly sweet and . . . er, picturesque, wouldn't you say?'

'Very picturesque,' repeated Camille, laughing.

He was silent for a moment.

'You really live here?'

'Well, yes.'

'Nowhere else?'

'Nowhere else.'

'All year round?'

'All year round.'

'It's rather small, isn't it?'

'My name is Camille Fauque.'

'Of course, delighted to meet you. Philibert Marquet de La Durbellière,' he announced, standing up and banging his head on the ceiling.

'All that?'

'I'm afraid so.'

'Don't you have a nickname?'

'Not that I know of.'

'So, see my fireplace?'

'I beg your pardon?'

'There, my fireplace.'

'Ah, there it is. Very nice,' he added, sitting back down and stretching his legs out in front of the plastic flames, 'very very nice. Like being in an English cottage, don't you think?'

Camille was happy. Her instinct had been right on. He might be a strange bird, but he was a perfect specimen.

'It's lovely, isn't it.'

'Magnificent! Does it draw well, at least?'

'Perfectly.'

'And what do you do for wood?'

'Oh you know, what with the storms we're having . . . All you have to do is bend down, these days.'

'Alas, I am only too aware of that. You should see the undergrowth at my parents' place, it's a real disaster. But what do you use here? This is oak, no?'

'Exactly!'

They smiled at each other.

'How does a glass of wine sound?'

'Perfect.'

Camille was awestruck by the contents of the picnic trunk. Not a thing was missing, the plates were porcelain, the cutlery was silver-plated and the glasses were crystal. It even contained a salt shaker, a pepper mill, an oil flask, coffee and tea cups, embroidered linen napkins, a vegetable dish, a sauce boat, a fruit bowl, a box for toothpicks, a sugar bowl, fish knives, and a special pot just for making hot chocolate. And the entire set was emblazoned with his family coat of arms.

'I've never seen anything so lovely.'

'You can see why I didn't come yesterday. If you only knew how long it's taken me to clean it and get everything shining.'

'You should have said!'

'You really think if I had said, "Not this evening, I've got to clean my trunk," you wouldn't have thought I was out of my mind?'

Camille was careful not to make any comment.

They spread the tablecloth on the floor and Philibert Whatsisname laid the place settings.

Like two children christening a new dolls' tea set, they sat cross-legged, delighted, excited, acting ever so properly and making a big effort not to break anything. Camille didn't know how to cook, so she had stopped in at Goubetzkoï's and bought an assortment of tarama, salmon, marinated fish and onion chutneys. They filled all the great-uncle's little bowls with painstaking care, and to reheat the blinis on the hotplate they fashioned an ingenious sort of grill pan from an old lid and some tin foil. They stashed the vodka in the roof gutter, and all they had to do was raise the blind and reach out for more. Opening and closing the window made the room chilly, to be sure, but the fireplace crackled and drew its fire from God.

Camille as usual drank more than she ate.

'Do you mind if I smoke?' she asked.

'Please . . . But I'd like to stretch my legs. They've gone to sleep.'

'Stretch out on my bed.'

'Oh, no, I, uh, couldn't do that.'

The least emotion and he was at a loss for words again, and mislaid his faculties.

'Oh go on, it's actually a sofa-bed.'

'Well in that case . . .'

'Maybe we should call each other *tu* instead of *vous*, Philibert?'

He went pale.

'Oh, no, for myself I couldn't possibly, but you, you –'

'Stop! Cut the lights up there! I didn't say a thing, not a thing! And, anyway, I think it's like, great to say *vous* to people, perfectly charming, it's –'

'Picturesque?'

'Exactly!'

Philibert didn't eat a lot either, but he was so slow and fastidious that Camille the perfect little hostess congratulated herself on planning a cold meal. She had also bought some *fromage blanc* for dessert, after standing paralysed gazing into the window of a patisserie, utterly disconcerted and incapable of choosing a cake. She brought out her little Italian coffee pot and drank her brew in a cup so delicate she was sure it would break if she closed her teeth on it.

Neither of them was naturally talkative. Nor were they used to sharing meals any more. So they didn't really know how to behave, and it was hard to leave their comfortable solitude behind. But because they were polite, they made the effort for appearance's sake. Acted jolly, raised their glasses, talked about the neighbourhood. The check-out girls at Franprix, for example: Philibert liked the blonde one, Camille preferred the one with aubergine-coloured hair; tourists, the illumination of the Eiffel Tower, the dog pooh. Totally unexpectedly, Camille's guest turned out to be a charming conversationalist: he knew how to keep the talk going, and came up with an endless variety of trivial and titillating topics. French history was his passion, and he confessed that he spent most of his time in Louis XI's jails, in François I's antechamber, at table with peasants from the Vendée in the Middle Ages or at the Conciergerie with Marie-Antoinette, a woman for whom he nursed a veritable devotion. Camille had only to launch into a theme or mention an era and Philibert would respond with a host of spicy details . . . Costumes, courtly intrigues, the amount of the salt tax or the genealogy of the Capetians.

It was very entertaining.

She felt as though she were surfing an Internet history site.

Click, and you got a summary.

'Are you a teacher or something?' she asked.

'No, I . . . that is . . . I work in a museum.'

'Are you a curator?'

'My, what a fancy word! No, I'm more on the . . . commercial side.'

'Oh,' she nodded gravely, 'that must be fascinating. Which museum?'

'Depends, I move around. And you?'

'Oh, me . . . nothing so interesting I'm afraid. I, like, work in offices.'

She looked put out and at the sight of her expression, he had the tact not to pursue the matter.

'I have a nice *fromage blanc* with apricot jam. Would you like some?'

'With pleasure. And you?'

'Oh, thanks, but with all these little Russian goodies, I feel stuffed.'

'You don't have to worry about getting fat.'

Fearful that he had said something hurtful, he quickly added, 'You're very, uh, graceful. Your face reminds me of Diane de Poitiers.'

'Was she pretty?'

'Oh, more than pretty!' He blushed. 'I, you – have you never been to the Château at Anet?'

'No.'

'You should go. It's a marvellous place. It was a gift from her lover, King Henri II.'

'Really?'

'Yes, it's very beautiful, a sort of hymn to love, wherever you go, their initials are intertwined – in stone, in marble, in iron, in wood, on her grave. It's very touching, too. I seem to recall that her cosmetic jars and hair brushes are still there, in her dressing room. I'll take you there some day.'

'When?'

'In the springtime, perhaps?'

'For a picnic?'

'That goes without saying.'

They sat in silence for a moment. Camille tried to ignore the holes in his shoes and Philibert did likewise with the damp stains all along the walls. They made do with gingerly sipping their vodka.

'Camille?'

'Yes?'

'Do you really live here all the time?'

'Yes.'

'Well . . . uh, to, I mean . . . to use the facilities . . .'

'On the landing.'

'Oh?'

'Do you need to go?'

'No, no, I was just asking.'

'Are you worried about me?'

'No, I mean, yes – it's just it's so Spartan here, that's all.'

'I appreciate your concern . . . But I'm okay. Really, I promise, and now I have this great fireplace!'

He did not seem quite as enthusiastic about the fireplace.

'How old are you? If that's not indiscreet of course.'

'Twenty-six. I'll be twenty-seven in February.'

'Like my little sister.'

'You have a sister?'

'Not just one, six!'

'Six sisters!'

'Yes, and one brother.'

'And you live on your own in Paris?'

'Yes, well, with my flatmate.'

'Do you get along okay?'

When he did not reply, she pressed him further, 'Not that well?'

'Yes, yes, it's okay. We never see each other, anyway.'

'Oh?'

'Let's just say it's not exactly the Château at Anet.'

She laughed.

'Does he work?'

'That's all he does. He works, sleeps, works, sleeps. And when he's not sleeping he brings girls back. He's a strange fellow, barking seems to be his primary mode of communication. I cannot understand what those girls see in him. Or, uh, I do have my own theory on the matter, but there you are . . .'

'What does he do?'

'He's a cook.'

'Oh? And does he at least make you some nice meals?'

'Never. I've never once seen him in the kitchen. Except in the morning to chastise my poor coffee pot.'

'Is he a friend of yours?'

'Gracious, no. I found him through an ad he'd left on the counter at the bakery across the street: *Young chef at the Vert Galant seeks room for midday siesta during his break.* In the beginning he only came for a few hours a day but now, there you go, he's there all the time.'

'Does it bother you?'

'Not at all. I even suggested it. Because you'll see, well you'll understand, that my place is a bit too big for me. And then, he knows how to do everything. I can't even change a light bulb, so it suits me fine. He can do anything and he's an incorrigible rogue, to boot . . . Since he's been there my electricity bill has melted away like snow in the sun.'

'You mean he fiddled with the meter?'

'I get the impression he fiddles with everything he lays his hands on. I don't know how good a cook he is, but as a handyman, he's first rate. And since everything is falling to bits in my place . . . No, well, I like him all the same. I've never had a real chance to talk to him at any length, but I think that he, well, I don't know . . . Sometimes I get the feeling I'm sharing a roof with a mutant.'

'Like in *Alien*?'

'I beg your pardon?'

'Nothing.'

Since Sigourney Weaver had never messed around with a king, Camille thought it best to drop the matter.

Together they put everything away. When he saw her tiny sink, Philibert begged her to let him wash the dishes. His museum was closed on Mondays, so he had all day to do them.

They made a great show of parting.

'You'll come to my place next time.'

'With pleasure.'

'But I'm afraid I don't have a fireplace.'

'Hey. Not everyone has the good fortune to have a cottage in the heart of Paris.'

'Camille?'

'Yes?'

'You'll take care of yourself, won't you?'

'I'll try. And you too, Philibert.'

'I . . . I . . .'

'What?'

'I have to tell you. The truth is, I don't really work in a museum, you know. I work outside. In shops, I mean. I – I . . . sell postcards.'

'And I don't really work in an office, either. More like outside, too. I clean for people.'

They exchanged a resigned smile, and said goodbye, rather sheepishly.

Rather sheepishly, and relieved, too.

Altogether a very successful Russian dinner.

12

'What's that noise?'

'Don't worry, it's the Grand Du-duke.'

'But what the hell is he doing? Sounds like he's flooding the kitchen.'

'So what, who cares. Come over here, you.'

'No, leave me alone.'

'C'mon, get over here. Why don't you take off your T-shirt?'

'I'm cold.'

'Go on, come over here.'

'He's weird, isn't he?'

'Completely out to lunch. You should have seen him when he went out earlier, with his walking stick and his clown's hat. I thought he was on his way to a fancy dress ball.'

'Where was he going?'

'See some girl, I think.'

'A girl!'

'Yeah, think so, I don't know. Who cares anyway, hey, turn around, shit.'

'Leave me alone.'

'Hey, Aurelie, you're starting to piss me off.'

'Aurelia, not Aurelie.'

'Aurelia, Aurelie, same difference. All right. And your socks, you going to keep them on all night, too?'

13

Camille put her clothes on top of her new stove, even though it was strictly forbidden, stayed in bed as long as possible, got dressed under her duvet and warmed the buttons of her jeans between her hands before pulling them on.

The PVC weatherproofing didn't seem to be working very well and she had had to move her mattress to get away from the horrible draught drilling a hole in her forehead. Now the bed was against the door and this made it a real hassle to get in and out. She was constantly having to tug it this way or that just to move three steps. Is this any way to live, she wondered; what a dump. And what the hell, she'd given in, she was pissing into her own sink now, holding on to the wall so there was no danger of the sink coming unstuck. As for her Turkish baths, the less said the better.

So she was dirty. Well, maybe not quite dirty, but not as clean as usual. Once or twice a week, when she was sure they were out, she went to the Kesslers'. She knew which days their cleaning woman was there, and the woman would hand her a big towel with a sigh. They weren't exactly taken in. Camille always left with a bit of food or an extra blanket. But one day Mathilde came home and managed to corner her while she was still drying her hair:

'Wouldn't you like to come back here to stay for a while? You could have your old room.'

'No, thank you, both of you, but it's okay, really. I'm fine.'

'Are you working?'

Camille closed her eyes.

'Yes, yes.'

'How are you doing? Do you need money? If you gave us something, Pierre could advance you some money, you know.'

'No, I don't have anything finished just yet.'

'And what about all the paintings at your mother's place?'

'I don't know . . . I have to go through them. I don't feel like it.'

'And your self-portraits?'

'They're not for sale.'

'So what are you working on exactly?'

'Stuff.'

'Have you been by the Quai Voltaire?'

'Not yet.'

'Camille?'

'Yes.'

'Can't you turn that bloody hairdryer off? So we can hear each other better?'

'I'm in a hurry.'

'So what are you doing these days?'

'Sorry?'

'How is life, I mean, what's going on with you at the moment?'

So that she'd never have to be subjected to this sort of questioning ever again, Camille rushed down the stairs of their building four steps at a time and barged into the first hairdresser's she could find.

14

'Shave me,' she said to the young man standing behind her in the mirror.

'Excuse me?'

'I'd like you to shave my head, please.'

'Like a billiard ball?'

'Yes.'

'No, I can't do that.'

'Yes, yes, you can. Just take your shaver and do it.'

'No, hey, this isn't the army here. I don't mind cutting it really short, but not like a billiard ball. That's not the sort of thing we do here – huh, Carlo?'

Carlo was reading the racing form behind the cash desk.

'What?'

'This young lady wants us to shave her head.'

The other man made a gesture as if to say, I don't give a fuck, I just lost ten euros in the seventh race, so don't go pissing me off.

'Half a centimetre.'

'Pardon?'

'I'll cut it to half a centimetre, otherwise you won't even dare show your face outside this place.'

'I have a hat.'

'I have my principles.'

Camille smiled, nodded her head in agreement and felt the buzzing of the blades against her neck. Strands of hair scattered on to the floor while she gazed at the stranger emerging in the mirror. She didn't recognize herself, couldn't remember what she'd looked like only a moment earlier. And she didn't care. From now on it wouldn't be such a hassle to go and have her shower on the landing, and that was the only thing that mattered.

She questioned her reflection in silence: Well? Wasn't that the whole idea? Learn to cope, even if it meant being ugly, even if it meant losing sight of her own self, so that she'd never owe anybody anything?

No, seriously, was that it?

She ran her palm over her bristly scalp and had a real urge to cry.

'You like it?'

'No.'

'I warned you –'

'I know.'

'It'll grow.'

'You think so?'

'I'm sure of it.'

'Another one of your principles.'

'Can I borrow a pen?'

'Carlo?'

'Mmm?'

'A pen for the young lady.'

'We don't take cheques for less than fifteen euros.'

'No, it's for something else.'

Camille pulled out her pad and drew what she saw in the mirror.

A bald girl with a hard gaze, holding a pen belonging to a bad-tempered punter, while a young man leaning on a broom handle looks down at her, bemused. She wrote down her age and got up to pay.

'That's me?'

'Yes.'

'Blimey, you draw really well.'

'I try.'

15

The ambulance man – not the same one as last time, Yvonne would have recognized him – was stirring his spoon round and round in his mug.

'Is it too hot?'

'Pardon?'

'The coffee. Is it too hot?'

'No, it's fine, thanks. We're not quite done but I have to file my report here.'

At the far end of the table sat a disconsolate Paulette. This time, she knew, her number was up.

16

'You had lice or something?' asked Mamadou.

Camille was pulling on her overall. She wasn't in the mood to talk. Too many of those stones, too cold, too fragile.

'You cross or something?'

Camille shook her head, wheeled her cart out of the garbage room and headed for the lifts.

'You going up to the fifth floor?'

'Uh-huh.'

'And why is it always you does the fifth floor? It's not right! Don't you let them push you around like that. You want I speak to the boss? I don't give a shit, I can make a stink, you know! Sure as hell! I don't give a shit.'

'No, thanks, Mamadou. Fifth floor, whatever, they're all the same to me.'

The other girls didn't like that floor because it was where the bosses had their private offices. The other floors, the *"ho-pen spay-siz"* as Bredart called them, in heavily accented English, were easier and, more to the point, quicker to clean. All you had to do was empty the wastepaper baskets, line the armchairs up against the walls and run the vacuum cleaner all over. You could go at it to your heart's content, and it didn't matter if you banged into the feet of the furniture because it was all cheap stuff anyway and nobody gave a shit.

But on the fifth floor, each office required a whole rather fastidious ritual: empty the wastepaper baskets, the ashtrays, gut the shredders, and clean the desks with the utmost respect for the warning not to touch a thing, not to move even the tiniest paper clip; and, on top of all that, there were the little adjacent meeting rooms and secretaries' offices: those bitches went and stuck Post-its all over the place as if they were giving orders to their own private cleaning woman, even though they couldn't possibly afford a real one at home. *And be sure to do this and be sure to do that and last time you moved the lamp and broke the thingamajig and whine and moan and bitch.* The kind of trivial remarks that really annoyed Carine or Samia, but didn't bother Camille. Whenever one of their notes was too ridiculously anal, she would write *Me no speak French* at the bottom of the Post-it and stick it right in the middle of the computer screen.

On the lower floors, the white-collar workers would put their stuff away, more or less, but here it was considered more chic to leave everything all spread out. Just so people would know you were overworked, that you really didn't want to have to leave your post, but that you'd be back any minute now to resume your position at the Great Helm of the world. Hey, why not, sighed Camille. Whatever . . . everyone has their dreams and illusions.

But there was one guy, all the way down at the end of the hall on the left, who was really beginning to piss her off. So what if he was some effing bigshot – that guy was a pig and things had gone on long enough. Not only was his office filthy, it also reeked of superiority.

Camille had lost count of the number of times she'd had to empty out plastic cups with their flotsam of cigarette butts, or how many crusts of stale sandwiches she'd had to pick up, and she'd never given it any further thought until this evening. But tonight she didn't feel like doing what she was doing. So she picked up Mr Piglet's trash – old nicotine patches wadded with hair, chewing gum stuck to the edge of the ashtray, used matches and crumpled balls of paper, and all the other gross leftovers of his presence, and she scooped it all into a little pile on his desk on his smart zebu-skin blotter, with a note: *Monsieur, you are a pig, and I ask you please henceforth to leave this place as clean as possible. P.S. Look down by your feet – there's a very useful thing known as a wastepaper basket.* To her tirade she added a nasty drawing featuring a little pig in a three-piece suit leaning down to see what sort of strange contraption was hiding under his desk. She then went to find her co-workers to help them finish the corridor.

'What are you laughing at?' asked Carine.

'Nothing.'

'You can be so weird.'

'What's next?'

'The stairs over in B.'

'Again? But we just did them.'

Carine shrugged her shoulders.

'Shall we go?'

'No, we have to wait for Super Josy for the report.'

'What report?'

'I dunno. Seems we're using too much of some product.'

'Wish they'd make up their minds, the other day we weren't using enough. I'm going to have a smoke out on the pavement, you coming?'

'It's too cold.'

Camille went out alone and leaned against a lamppost.

'. . . 2 December 2003 . . . 00.34 . . . −4°C': a string of luminous letters on an optician's storefront.

That's when she found the answer she should have given Mathilde Kessler earlier that day when she'd asked, with a hint of annoyance in her voice, how Camille's life was at the moment.

'. . . 2 December 2003 . . . 00.34 . . . −4°C.'

There, that's how life was at the moment.

17

'I know! I know all that! But why are you making such a big deal? It's nonsense, anyway!'

'Now listen, young Franck, in the first place, you are not going to take that tone with me and, secondly, you have no right to lecture me. I'm the one who's been looking after her for almost twelve years, going to see her several times a week, taking her to town and making sure she's okay. Over twelve years, you hear? And so far no one can say that you've been that much involved. Never a word of thanks, never a sign of gratitude, nothing. Even that other time when I went with her to the hospital and visited her every day at the beginning: would it ever have crossed your mind to call me or send me a flower, huh? Well, in a way it doesn't matter because I'm not doing it for you, but for her. Because she's a good woman, your grandmother. A good woman, you understand? I'm not blaming you, son, you're young and you live far away and you've got your own life, but sometimes it gets to be a bit too much for me, you know? A bit too much. I have a family, too, and I have my own worries and problems with my health so I'm going to come right out with it: it's time for you to start taking responsibility.'

'You want me to louse up her life and stick her in the pound just because she left a pot on the stove, is that it?'

'There you go! You're talking about her as if she were a dog!'

'No, I'm not talking about her. And you know damn well what I'm talking about. You know damn well that if I put her in an old people's morgue, she won't be able to stand the shock. Shit! You saw the song and dance she made last time round.'

'There's no need to be obscene, you know.'

'Sorry, Madame Carminot, I'm sorry. But I don't know where I am any more. I – I can't do it to her, you understand? For me it would be like killing her.'

'If she goes on living alone, she'll end up killing herself.'

'And? Wouldn't that be better?'

'That's the way you see things, but I don't go along with it. If the postman hadn't come just in time the other day, the whole house would have gone up in flames; and the problem is that the postman isn't always going to be there. And neither will I, Franck. Neither will I. It's just all too much now. Just too much responsibility. Every time I come over I wonder what I'm going to find, and on the days when I don't come, I can't sleep. When I call her and she doesn't answer, I get sick with worry and I always end up going over there to see where she's wandered off to. That fall she took really shook her up, she's not the same woman any more. She stays in her bathrobe all day, doesn't eat, doesn't speak, doesn't read her post. Only yesterday I found her out in the garden in her underwear. She was completely frozen, poor thing. It's no life for me, I'm always imagining the worst. We can't leave her like this. We can't. You have to do something.'

Franck was silent.

'Franck? Hello? Franck, are you there?'

'Yes.'

'You have to get used to the idea, young man.'

'No way. I'm willing to stick her in a hospice because I don't have a choice, but don't ask me to get used to the idea. That's impossible.'

'Pound, old people's morgue, hospice . . . Why can't you just call it a "retirement home?" '

'Because I know how it's going to end.'

'Don't say that, there are some very nice places. My husband's mother, for instance, she –'

'And what about you, Yvonne? Can't you take care of her for good? I'll pay you . . . I'll give you whatever you want.'

'No, thanks for offering, but I can't, I'm too old. I don't want the responsibility, I've already got my Gilbert to look after. And besides, Paulette needs medical care.'

'I thought she was your friend.'

'She is.'

'She's your friend, but you don't mind shoving her into her grave.'

'Franck, take that back, right now.'

'You're all the same. You, my mother, and everyone else, the whole lot of you. You say you care for other people, but then as soon as it comes to rolling up your sleeves, where are you?'

'Don't you dare put me in the same category as your mother! How could you! You're unbelievably ungrateful, young man, mean and ungrateful.'

She hung up.

It was only three in the afternoon but Franck knew he wouldn't be able to sleep.

He was exhausted.

He pounded the table, thumped the wall, lashed out at everything in reach.

Then he put on his jogging gear and collapsed on the first bench he came to.

It was only a little whimper to begin with, as if someone had just pinched him, but then his entire body gave way. He started trembling from head to foot, his chest split open and released a huge sob. The last thing he wanted, fuck, the last thing. But he couldn't help it. He wept like a big baby, like a useless moron, like some guy who was about to take the only person on the planet he'd ever loved and consign her to her grave. The only person, too, who'd ever loved him.

Franck was bent double, racked with sorrow and smeared with snot.

When he finally accepted that there was no way he could stop, he wrapped his sweater around his head and folded his arms.

He was hurting, he was cold, and he was ashamed.

He stood under the shower with his eyes closed and his face held up to it, until there was no more hot water. He cut himself shaving because he didn't have the guts to face himself in the mirror. He didn't want to think about it. Not now, not for the time being. The dike wasn't strong, and if he let go, thousands of images would swamp his brain. He'd never seen his grandma anywhere else, only there in her house – her mornings in the garden, her days in the kitchen, and in the evening, by his bedside . . .

*

When Franck was a kid he suffered from insomnia. He had night-mares and would scream and call out to his grandma, and he swore to her that when she closed the door his legs went down a deep hole and he had to cling to the bars of his bed to keep from going down there after them. All his teachers had suggested consulting a psychologist, but the neighbours shook their heads gravely and advised taking him to some other kind of quack to have his nerves put right. As for Paulette's husband, he wanted to stop her going upstairs. You're spoiling the boy! he said, You're the one who's driving him crazy! For Christ's sake, just love him a bit less! Just let him cry for a while, he'll stop pissing so much for a start, and you'll see, he'll go to sleep just the same.

And Paulette would say yes to everyone, nice as pie, but she didn't do what anyone said. She'd make Franck a glass of hot sugared milk with a bit of orange flower water and, sitting by him on her chair, she held his head while he drank. There, you see, I'm right here. She folded her arms, sighed, and dozed off when he did. Or sometimes even before he did. It was nothing serious; as long as she was there, everything would be all right. He could stretch out his legs.

'I warn you, there's no more hot water,' said Franck to Philibert.

'Oh, dear, how irritating for you . . . I don't know what to say, you –'

'Stop apologizing. Shit! I'm the one who emptied the tank, okay? I did it. So don't you apologize!'

'I'm sorry, I just thought –'

'You know what? You're starting to piss me off. If you want to go on being a doormat, that's your problem.'

Franck left the room and went to iron his work clothes. He absolutely had to buy some new jackets because he didn't have enough to see out the week. He didn't have time. There was never enough time, never the time to do a fucking thing.

He had only one day off a week, he was damned if he was going to spend it at some old folks' home in the back of beyond, watching his grandmother cry her eyes out.

Philibert was already settled in his armchair with his parchments and all his heraldry crap.

'Philibert?'

'I beg your pardon?'

'Listen, hey, I'm sorry about what happened earlier, I've got a lot of shit going on at the moment and I'm up to there with it, okay? Plus, I'm shattered.'

'It doesn't matter.'

'Yes, it does matter.'

'What matters, you see, is to say that you're sorry *for* doing something, not that you're sorry *about* something. It's linguistically too vague, and the other person cannot know whether you are apologizing or just expressing some generalized regret . . .'

Franck stared at him for a minute before shaking his head.

'You really are one weird guy, you know that?'

As he went out of the door, he added, 'Hey! Have a look in the fridge, I brought you something. I can't remember what it is, some duck, I think.'

Philibert said thank you to a draught of cold air.

Franck was already in the hallway, cursing, because he couldn't find his keys.

He took up his station in complete silence, did not flinch when the boss took the pan from his hands in order to show off, clenched his teeth when an undercooked *magret* was sent back, and rubbed at the hob so hard it was as if instead of simply cleaning it he were trying to scrape off fine iron filings.

As the kitchen emptied, Franck waited around for his mate Kermadec to finish sorting his tablecloths and counting his napkins. When Kermadec found him in a corner leafing through *Bikers' Journal*, he gestured with his chin, 'What you want, chef?'

Lestafier tilted his head back and wiggled his hand in front of his mouth.

'I'm coming. A few more odds and ends and I'm all yours.'

They had meant to do the rounds of the bars, but by the time they left the second one, Franck was already dead drunk.

That night he fell into a deep hole, but not the one from his childhood. A different one.

18

'Okay, well, I wanted to say I was sorry about, I mean sorry *for* . . . I wanted to ask you . . .' said Franck.

'Ask what, kiddo?' said Yvonne.

'Well, ask you to forgive me.'

'I've already forgiven you, forget it. I know you didn't mean what you said, but you should mind your manners all the same. You have to be good to the people who behave right towards you. You'll see, when you get older, you won't meet that many.'

'You know, I've been thinking about what you said yesterday, and even if it sticks in my throat to say it, I know you're right.'

'Of course I'm right. I know old people, I see plenty of them here, all day.'

'So, uh –'

'What?'

'The problem is I've got no time to take care of it, I mean to find her a place and all that.'

'So you want me to take care of it?'

'I'll pay you for your time, you know.'

'Don't you start being obscene with me again, young man, I'm willing to help you, but you're the one who's going to have to tell her. You have to explain the situation to her.'

'Will you come with me?'

'If it makes it easier for you, but you know, she knows perfectly well what I think about the whole thing. She's been getting herself in such a state ever since I first brought it up.'

'You have to find her a really classy place, okay? With a nice room and beautiful grounds all around.'

'It's very expensive, you know.'

'How expensive?'

'Over a million a month.'

'Uh, hang on, Yvonne, what are you talking here? We have euros now, okay?'

'Oh, euros. Well I'm talking the way I'm used to talking and for a good home, you have to pay upwards of a million old francs a month.'

There was a silence while Franck did some mental arithmetic.

'Franck?'

'That's – that's what I earn.'

'You have to go to the social services and ask them for housing assistance, see how much your granddad's pension comes to, then put together an ADHP application and send it off.'

'What's the ADHP?'

'Assistance for dependent and handicapped persons.'

'But . . . She's not exactly handicapped, is she?'

'No, but she'll have to act the part when they send the assessor over. Mustn't look too sprightly or they won't give you much.'

'Aw fuck, what a hassle . . . Sorry.'

'I'm blocking my ears.'

'I'll never have time to fill in all the forms. Maybe you could help out with this initial stuff for me?'

'Not to worry, I'll bring it up at the Club next Friday, it's sure to cause a stir.'

'Thank you so much, Madame Carminot.'

'Don't mention it. It's the least I can do, after all.'

'Right, well, I better get to work.'

'I hear you're cooking like a chef now?'

'Who told you that?'

'Madame Mandel.'

'Oh.'

'Oh, my word, if you could just hear her. She's still talking about it! You made "*lièvre à la royale*", some sort of hare, that evening?'

'I don't remember.'

'Well she does, believe me! Just one thing, Franck?'

'Yes?'

'I know this is none of my business, but . . . your mother?'

'What about my mother?'

'I don't know, but I was wondering if she shouldn't be contacted too. Maybe she could help pay.'

'Now you're being obscene and you know it, Yvonne, it's not as if you'd never met her, either.'

'You know, sometimes people change.'

'Not her.'

Yvonne was silent.

'No,' he repeated, 'not her. Okay, I'm out of here, I'm running late.'

'Bye, Franck.'

'Uh, Yvonne – '

'Yes?'

'Can you try to find somewhere a little bit cheaper?'

'I'll see, I'll let you know.'

'Thanks.'

It was so cold that day that Franck was glad to be at his galley slave's station in the warmth of the kitchen. The boss was in a good mood. They'd had to turn diners away for lack of tables, and he'd just learned that he'd be getting a good review in some glossy upmarket magazine.

'With this weather, kiddos, tonight we'll be able to bring out the foie gras and the vintage wines! We're done with salads and chiffonades and all that rubbish. Fi-nito! I want everything looking good and tasting great so that the customers leave here feeling ten degrees warmer! Let's roll! Light those burners, boys!'

19

Camille was having trouble going down the stairs. She felt stiff and achy all over, and had a terrible headache. As if someone had planted a knife in her eye and was gleefully and delicately turning the blade whenever she moved. When she got to the entrance she leaned against the wall to keep her balance. She was shivering and suffocating at the same time. For a moment she thought of going back to bed, but the idea of climbing seven flights of stairs seemed even more impossible than the idea of going to work. At least in the metro she could sit down.

As she stepped out of the entrance she bumped into a bear. Her neighbour, wrapped in a long cloak.

'Oh excuse me, Monsieur,' he said, 'I –'

He looked up.

'Camille, is that you?'

She had no strength to start up a conversation, and tried to dodge past him.

'Camille! Camille!'

She buried her face in her scarf and hurried away. The effort soon obliged her to lean against a parking meter to keep from falling over.

'Camille, are you all right? My God, just look at you, what have you done to your hair? You look terrible! Your hair, your beautiful hair . . .'

'I have to get going, Philibert, I'm late already.'

'But it's bitter cold out, my dear! Don't go bare-headed, you'll catch your death. Here, take my *shapka* at least.'

Camille made an effort to smile.

'Did this belong to your uncle too?'

'Goodness, no! To my ancestor, more like it, the one who accompanied Napoleon on his campaigns in Russia.'

He wedged the hat on to her head, down to her eyebrows.

She tried to joke. 'You mean this thing went through the battle of Austerlitz?'

'Exactly. And Berezina too, I'm afraid. But you're so pale, are you sure you're feeling all right?'

'I'm just a little tired.'

'Tell me, Camille, you're not too cold up there in the attic?'

'I don't know . . . Okay, I, I've got to get going . . . Thanks for the hat.'

The heat in the metro carriage made her drowsy and she fell asleep. When she woke up they were at the end of the line. She turned to face the other direction and pulled her furry bear hat down over her eyes so that she could cry from exhaustion. God, it was a smelly old thing.

When at last she got out at her stop the cold was so piercing that she had to sit down in a bus shelter. She collapsed sideways across the seats and asked a young man standing there to hail her a taxi.

Camille climbed up to her room on her knees and fell across the mattress. She had no strength to get undressed and, for a split second, she wondered if she might be about to die, right there and then. Who would know? Who would care? Who would weep for her? She was shivering with heat, and sweat enveloped her in an icy shroud.

20

At around two in the morning Philibert got up for a glass of water. The tiles of the kitchen floor were freezing and a vicious wind was rattling the windowpanes. For a moment he stared out at the deserted avenue and murmured childhood phrases: *Here comes winter, killing the poor folk.* The outdoor thermometer indicated minus six and he could not help but think of that little slip of a thing up in the attic. Was she asleep? And what on earth had she done to her hair, poor wretch?

He had to do something. He couldn't just leave her like that. Well sure, but his education, his fine manners, his discretion, had him trapped in a tangled web of endless self-interrogation.

Was it ever appropriate to disturb a young woman in the middle of the night? How would she take it? And after all, she might not be alone. And what if she were naked? Oh, no. He dared not even think about it. And now, like characters in Tintin, an angel and a demon were having a squabble over on the other pillow.

Well, maybe the characters weren't quite the same . . .

A frozen angel was saying, 'But listen, the poor child will be dying from the cold,' while the demon, his wings pinched, retorted, 'I know that, my friend, but it simply isn't done. You'll go and enquire after her in the morning. Now go to sleep, I beg you.'

Philibert observed their little quarrel without taking part, tossing and turning, ten, twenty times; he asked them to pipe down, then finally took away their pillow so he wouldn't have to listen any more.

*

At three fifty-four he was groping for his socks in the dark.

The ray of light from under her door gave him courage.

'Mademoiselle Camille?'

Then, slightly louder, 'Camille? Camille? It's Philibert.'

No answer. He tried one last time before turning back. He was already at the end of the corridor when a muffled sound called him back.

'Camille, are you there? I was worried about you and I, I –'

'. . . door . . . open,' she moaned.

The garret room was icy. Philibert had trouble getting through the door because of the mattress, and he stumbled against a pile of discarded clothes. He knelt down, lifted one blanket, then another, then a quilt, and finally came to her face. She was drenched in sweat.

He put his hand on her forehead:

'You've got a raging temperature! You can't stay like this, not here, not all alone. And what happened with your fireplace?'

'. . . no strength to move it . . .'

'Do you mind if I take you with me?'

'Where?'

'To my place.'

'I don't feel like moving . . .'

'I'll carry you in my arms.'

'Like Prince Charming?'

Philibert smiled. 'All right, I see, you're so feverish that now you're delirious.'

He pulled the mattress over to the middle of the room, removed her heavy shoes and lifted her up with an exemplary lack of grace.

'I guess I'm not as strong as a real prince. Uh, can you try to slide your arms around my neck, please?'

She dropped her head on to his shoulder and he was troubled by the acrid smell which rose from her neck.

The abduction was a disaster. At every turn Philibert bumped his sleeping beauty into something, and with every step he took he almost toppled over. Fortunately he had remembered to take the service key with him and only had to go down three flights. He went through the pantry and the kitchen, almost dropped her ten times along the corridor, then finally laid her down on his Aunt Edmée's bed.

'Listen, I ought to undress you a bit, I think. I . . . rather . . . you, well, it's all very embarrassing.'

She had closed her eyes.

Right.

Philibert Marquet de La Durbellière found himself in an extraordinarily tricky situation.

He thought of the daring deeds of his ancestors, but neither the Convention of 1793, nor the conquest of Cholet, nor the courage of Cathelineau or the bravery of La Rochejaquelin seemed to be of the slightest conceivable use at the moment.

The irate angel was now perched on Philibert's shoulder, with Baroness Staffe's etiquette guide under his arm . . . and he went at it with a vengeance: 'Well, my fine friend, you're pleased with yourself, aren't you? Ah! He's in a fine situation, is our valiant knight! Congratulations are in order, surely. And now? What are you going to do now?' Philibert was completely disoriented. Camille murmured, ' . . . thirsty . . .'

Her saviour rushed to the kitchen, but the killjoy devil was waiting there on the edge of the sink: 'Attaboy! Go on! And what about the dragon? Aren't you going to go off and slay the dragon?' 'Oh, shut your face!' replied Philibert. His sudden courage had bolstered him, and he went back to his patient's bedside with a lighter heart. In the end it wasn't all that complicated. Franck was right: sometimes a few rude words were more effective than a long speech. Feeling brighter, Philibert helped her to drink, then took his courage in both hands: he undressed her.

It was no easy task because Camille was wrapped in more layers than an onion. First he took off her coat, then her denim jacket. Then a sweater, another sweater, a turtleneck and finally he arrived at a sort of long-sleeved vest. Right, he said to himself, I can't leave this thing on her, you could practically wring it out. Well, never mind, I'll see her – well, her bra . . .

Horror of horrors! Jesus and Mary and all the saints! She isn't wearing one!

Philibert quickly pulled the sheet up over her chest. Right. Now for her bottoms. This was a little easier because he was able to manoeuvre by working under the covers. He pulled with all his strength on her trouser legs. God be praised, her knickers didn't come off with her trousers.

'Camille? Do you have the strength to take a shower?'

No answer.

He shook his head disapprovingly, went into the bathroom, filled a jug with hot water into which he splashed a little eau de Cologne, and armed himself with a flannel.

Courage, soldier!

He pulled back the sheet and began to freshen her up gently with the edge of the flannel to begin with, then more boldly.

Philibert scrubbed her head, neck, face, back, armpits, breasts since he had to (and could you even really call them breasts?), stomach and legs. For the rest, well, she'd have to manage. He wrung out the flannel and put it on her forehead.

He had to get her some aspirin now. He pulled so hard on the knob of the drawer in the kitchen that the entire contents spilled out on to the floor. Rats. Aspirin, aspirin.

Franck was standing in the doorway, one arm up under his T-shirt, scratching his stomach.

He yawned loudly and said, 'What the hell's going on? What is all this shit?'

'I'm looking for aspirin.'

'In the cupboard.'

'Thanks.'

'Got a headache?'

'No, it's for a friend.'

'Your girlfriend from the seventh floor?'

'Yes.'

Franck cackled, 'Hey, wait, you were with her just now? Up there?'

'Yes. Out of the way, please.'

'No way, I don't believe it. So you're not a virgin any more!'

His sarcasm followed Philibert down the hall:

'Hey! Is she giving you the crap about a headache already on the first night? Shit, you're not off to a great start, mate . . .'

Philibert closed the door behind him, turned around and muttered audibly, 'And you shut your face, too.'

He waited for the tablet to stop fizzing before disturbing her one last time. He thought he heard her whispering 'Daddy.' Unless it was 'Don't, don't' because she probably wasn't thirsty any more. He couldn't tell.

He dampened the flannel again, pulled back the sheet and paused for a moment.

Speechless, frightened, and proud of himself.

Yes, proud of himself.

21

Camille woke up to the sound of U2. At first she thought she was back at the Kesslers' and she nearly dozed off again. Then, confused, she thought, No, that's not possible. Neither Pierre, nor Mathilde, nor their maid would ever stick Bono on full blast like that. There was something funny going on. Slowly she opened her eyes, moaned from the throbbing in her skull and waited in the half-dark until things came into focus.

But where was she? What the . . .

Camille turned her head. Her entire body ached in protest. Her muscles and joints and what little flesh she had all refused to budge. Clenching her teeth, she managed to move up a few centimetres. She was shivering and drenched in sweat all over again.

The blood was pounding in her temples. With her eyes closed she waited a moment, motionless, for the pain to subside.

Gingerly she opened her eyes and saw that she was in a strange bed. The light hardly penetrated the gaps in the inner shutters or the enormous velvet curtains which hung lopsided on either side of the window, sliding off their rods. Facing the bed below a spotty mirror was a marble fireplace. The room was papered with a flowered design; she could not quite make out the colours. There were paintings everywhere, portraits of men and women dressed in black who seemed as astonished to find her there as she was herself. Then she turned toward the bedside table and saw a lovely engraved jug next to a Scooby-Doo glass which used to be a mustard jar. She was dying of thirst and the jug was full of water, but she didn't dare touch it: in what century had it been filled?

Where the hell was she, and who had brought her into this museum?

A sheet of paper lay folded in half next to a candlestick: 'I didn't dare to disturb you this morning. I've gone to work. I'll be back around seven. Your clothes are folded on the wing chair. There's some duck in the fridge and a bottle of mineral water at the foot of the bed. Philibert.'

Philibert? What on earth was she doing in this guy's bed?

Help.

Camille thought hard, trying to summon even a trace of some unlikely debauchery, but her memory would not take her beyond the boulevard Brune . . . She'd keeled over on her side in a bus shelter and begged some tall guy with a dark coat on to call a taxi . . . Was that Philibert? No, and yet . . . No, it wasn't him, she would have remembered.

Someone had just turned off the music. She could hear steps, grunts, a door slamming, a second door, then nothing. Silence.

Camille was desperate but she waited a little while longer, attentive to the slightest sound, already exhausted at the idea of having to move her poor carcass.

She pushed back the sheets and lifted the duvet which seemed as heavy as a dead donkey.

When her feet hit the floor, her toes curled up. A pair of oriental kid slippers was waiting at the edge of the carpet. She stood up and saw that she was dressed in a man's pyjama top, put her feet in the slippers and threw her denim jacket over her shoulders.

She turned the door handle gently and found herself in an immense corridor, very dark, at least fifteen metres long.

Now where was that toilet . . .

No, that was a closet, and that was a kid's room with two twin beds and a moth-eaten rocking horse. Here? How could she tell? This must be a study – there were so many books piled on a table in front of the window that the daylight could scarcely enter. A sabre and a white scarf hung on the wall along with a horsetail attached to the end of a brass ring. A real tail from a real horse. Kind of special, as relics go.

There! The toilet!

The seat was wooden, as was the handle of the flush. The bowl, given its age, must have witnessed generations of fannies in crinolines. Camille felt a bit reticent at first, but it all worked perfectly. The flush made a disconcerting amount of noise. As if Niagara Falls were crashing down all around her.

She was getting dizzy, but she continued her journey in search of a bottle of aspirin. In one of the rooms she discovered an incredible mess. Clothes were strewn everywhere among magazines, empty beer cans and scraps of paper: pay slips, complicated recipe cards, the instruction manual for a GSXR and various reminder notices from the tax office. Someone had put a horrible multicoloured duvet on the lovely Louis XVI bed, and a few spliffs lay at the ready on the fine marquetry of the bedside table. Well, it certainly smelled like the lair of some wild beast . . .

At the end of the hall she found the kitchen. It was a cold room, grey and sad, with a floor of pale old tiles picked out with black cabochons. The work surfaces were marble and nearly all the cupboards were empty. There was nothing, except perhaps the presence of an antique Frigidaire, to indicate that anyone actually lived here. Somehow she found a tube of effervescent aspirins, took a glass from next to the sink and sat down on a formica chair. The ceiling was dizzyingly high and she noticed how white the walls were. The paint must be very old, lead-based; the years had given it a smooth patina. It was neither off-white nor eggshell; this was the white of rice pudding or insipid cafeteria desserts. Mentally Camille mixed up a few tints and promised herself she'd come back one day with two or three tubes of paint to get a clearer picture.

On the way back down the hall she got lost and thought she'd never find her room again. As she collapsed on the bed it crossed her mind that she ought to call that old cow at All-Kleen, but then she fell asleep at once.

22

'Are you all right?'

'Is that you, Philibert?'

'Yes.'

'Am I in your bed?'

'My bed? No, but – but. No, please, listen. I would never –'

'Where am I?'

'In the apartments of my aunt Edmée, Auntie Mée to her friends. How are you feeling, my dear?'

'Exhausted. I feel like I've been under a steam roller.'

'I called a doctor.'

'Oh, no! You shouldn't have!'

'I shouldn't have?'

'Oh, well maybe, yes, I suppose you did the right thing . . . I'll need sick leave from work in any case.'

'I'm heating up some soup.'

'I'm not hungry.'

'You have to force yourself. You need to recoup and rally the troops to drive the enemy virus back beyond the border. Why are you smiling?'

'Because you're talking as if it were the Hundred Years' War.'

'Not quite as long, I trust! Oh, listen, that must be the doctor.'

'Philibert?'

'Yes?'

'I have nothing with me, no chequebook, no money, not a thing.'

'Don't worry. We'll work something out later on . . . Once the peace treaty is signed.'

23

'Well?' asked Philibert anxiously.

'She's asleep.'

'Oh?'

'Is she a member of your family?'

'A friend.'

'What sort of friend?'

'Well, she's a, uh, neighbour, a neighbour friend,' mumbled Philibert.

'Do you know her well?'

'No. Not very.'

'Does she live alone?'

'Yes.'

The doctor frowned.

'Is something bothering you?'

'You might put it that way. Do you have a table? Somewhere I can sit down?'

Philibert led him into the kitchen. The doctor pulled out his prescription pad.

'Do you know her name?'

'Fauque, I think.'

'You think or you're sure?'

'How old is she?'

'Twenty-six.'

'Sure?'

'Yes.'

'Does she work?'

'Yes, for a cleaning outfit.'

'Pardon?'

'She cleans offices.'

'Are we talking about the same person? The young woman who is resting in the big Polish-style bed at the end of the corridor?'

'Yes.'

'Do you know her schedule?'

'She works nights.'

'Nights?'

'Well, in the evening, when the offices are empty.'

'Is something wrong?' Philibert dared to ask.

'Well, yes. Your friend is completely exhausted, she has no strength left. Were you aware of that?'

'No. Well, yes. I thought she looked somewhat under the weather but I . . . Well, I don't know her all that well you see, I . . . I just went to check on her last night because she doesn't have any heating and –'

'Listen, I'll tell you frankly how things stand: given the state of her anaemia, her weight, and her blood pressure, I could have her hospitalized right now; only when I mentioned this to her she looked so panicked that . . . Well, I don't have a medical record for her, I don't know her past or her antecedents, and I don't want to rush to any conclusions, but once she feels better, she needs to undergo a series of tests, that much is clear.'

Philibert was wringing his hands.

'In the meantime, one thing is for sure: you have to build her up. You really have to get her to eat and sleep, otherwise . . . I'm prescribing ten days' sick leave for now. Here's a prescription for paracetamol and Vitamin C, but I can't emphasize it enough: none of this can possibly replace a good rare steak, a big bowl of pasta, vegetables and fresh fruit, do you understand?'

'Yes.'

'Does she have any family in Paris?'

'I don't know. What about her temperature?'

'That's a simple flu bug. There's nothing you can do for it, just wait for it to pass. Make sure she doesn't cover herself too much, keep her out of draughts and make her stay in bed for a few days.'

'Right.'

'Now you look like something's bothering you. Well, maybe I've made things out to be worse than they really are, but not a whole lot, to be honest. You will look after her, won't you?'

'Yes.'

'Tell me, is this your place?'

'Uh, yes.'

'How many square metres altogether?'

'A little over three hundred.'

'Well, I'll be!' he whistled. 'Maybe this is a personal question but do you mind if I ask what you do for a living?'

'Noah's Ark.'

'Pardon?'

'No, never mind. How much do I owe you?'

24

'Camille, are you asleep?'

'No.'

'Look, I have a surprise for you.'

He opened the door and rolled her fake fireplace into the room.

'I thought you might enjoy it.'

'Oh . . . That's kind of you, but I'm not going to stay here, you know. I have to go back upstairs tomorrow.'

'No.'

'What do you mean, no?'

'You'll go back up when the barometer does, in the meanwhile you'll stay here and get some rest, that's what the doctor said. And he's given you ten days off.'

'That much?'

'Yes indeed.'

'I have to send it in.'

'I beg your pardon?'

'The doctor's certificate.'

'I'll get you an envelope.'

'Wait a minute – no, I don't want to stay that long, I really don't.'

'You'd rather go to the hospital?'

'Don't make jokes about that.'

'I'm not joking, Camille.'

She began to cry.

'You won't let them, will you?'

'Do you remember the War of Vendée?'

'Well, not especially, no.'

'I'll lend you some books. In the meanwhile just remember you are staying with the Marquet de La Durbellière family, and we've no fear of the Bleus here.'

'The Bleus?'

'The French revolutionaries. The Republic. They want to put you in a public hospital, do they not?'

'Probably.'

'So if you stay here you'll have nothing to fear. I will pour boiling oil on the stretcher-bearers from the top of the stairwell!'

'You are completely out of your flipping mind.'

'Aren't we all, a bit? Why did you shave your head, for example?'

'Because I didn't feel like washing my hair out on the landing.'

'Do you remember what I told you about Diane de Poitiers?'

'Yes.'

'Well, I just came upon something in my library, hang on a second.'

He came back with a dog-eared paperback, sat on the edge of the bed, and cleared his throat:

The entire Court, with the exception of Madame d'Étampes, of course (I'll tell you why, later on), *agreed that Diane de Poitiers was simply ravishing. All the ladies copied the way she walked, her gestures, her hairstyles. She served, in fact, to establish the canon of beauty, one which all women, for over a hundred years, would seek in desperation to emulate:*

Three white things: skin, teeth and hands.

Three black: eyes, eyebrows and eyelids.

Three red: lips, cheeks, nails.

Three long: body, hair, hands.

Three short: teeth, ears, feet.

Three narrow: mouth, waist, toes.

Three wide: arms, thighs, calves.

Three small: nipples, nose, head.'

'Rather nicely put, don't you think?'

'And do you think I look like her?'

'Yes, well, according to certain criteria.'

He blushed red as a beetroot.

'Not – not all, of course, but you – you see, it's a question of allure, of grace, of, of –'

'Are you the one who took my clothes off?'

His glasses had fallen on to his knees and he began stu-stuttering as never before.

'I, I, yes, well, very ch-chastely, I p-p-promise you, I c-c-covered you f-f-first, I –'

She handed him his goggles.

'Hey, don't get so worked up! I just wanted to know, that's all. Uh, was he here too, the other guy?'

'Wh-who?'

'The cook.'

'No. Of course not. Obviously.'

'That's better. Oh, my head really aches.'

'I'm going down to the pharmacy. Do you need anything else?'

'No. Thanks.'

'Good. Ah, yes, have to tell you: we don't have a telephone here. But if you need to get in touch with anyone, Franck has a mobile phone in his room and –'

'That's okay, thanks. I have a mobile, too. I just have to get my charger from upstairs.'

'I'll go if you like.'

'No, no, it can wait.'

'So be it.'

'Philibert?'

'Yes?'

'Thank you.'

'Oh, go on.'

There he stood, with his trousers that were too short, his jacket that was too tight, and his arms that were too long.

'This is the first time in a long long time that anyone's looked after me like this,' said Camille.

'Go on.'

'Really, it's true. I mean . . . without expecting anything in return. Because you, like – you're not expecting anything, are you?'

He was outraged.

'No, but . . . what on earth are you thinking?!' he spluttered.

She had already closed her eyes again.

'I'm not thinking a thing, I'm just telling you: I have nothing to give.'

25

Camille had lost track of the days. Was it Saturday? Sunday? She hadn't slept like that for years.

Philibert had just looked in to offer her a bowl of soup.

'I'm getting up. I'm going to come and sit in the kitchen with you.'

'Are you sure?'

'Of course! I'm not, like, made out of icing sugar, you know.'

'Okay, but don't come in the kitchen, it's too cold in there. Wait for me in the little blue sitting room.'

'Sorry?'

'Oh, of course, that's right, it's not really blue any more since it's empty. The room that's by the entrance, you know the one?'

'Where there's a sofa?'

'Well, a sofa, that's saying a lot. Franck found it on the pavement one evening and he brought it up with one of his friends. It's very ugly but quite practical, I must admit.'

'Tell me, Philibert, what is this place exactly? Who does it belong to? And why are you living here as if you were squatting?'

'I beg your pardon?'

'As if you were camping?'

'Oh, it's a sordid story of an inheritance, I'm afraid. The kind you hear every day. Even in the best families, you know . . .'

He seemed truly distressed.

'This was my maternal grandmother's home, and she died last year. So while we are waiting for the inheritance to be sorted out, my father asked me to come and live here, to keep out the – what did you call them just now?'

'Squatters?'

'That's it, squatters. But not those drugged boys with safety pins in their nose, no, I mean people who are much better dressed and much less elegant: our own cousins.'

'Your cousins have designs on the place?'

'I think they've already even spent the money they hoped to get out of it, poor things! A family council was held at the lawyers', the outcome being that I have been designated porter, guard and night watchman. Of course, there was a bit of intimidating manoeuvring in the beginning . . . Moreover, a lot of furniture vanished into thin air as you may have noticed, and I've often opened the door to the bailiffs, but everything seems to be back to normal now. Henceforth it's up to the court to find a solution to this sorry affair.'

'How long will you be here for?'

'I don't know.'

'And don't your parents, like, mind you putting up strangers like that cook, or me?'

'They don't need to find out about you, I imagine. As for Franck, they were actually rather relieved. They know how clumsy I am. But, well, they haven't the faintest idea what he's like, fortunately. They think I met him through the church!'

He laughed.

'You lied to them?'

'Let's just say I was a tad . . . evasive?'

Camille had shrunk so much that she could tuck her shirt tails into her jeans without having to unbutton them first.

She looked like a ghost. But as if to prove the opposite, she stared into the big mirror in her room and made a face, then tied her silk scarf around her neck, put on her jacket and ventured off into the incredible Haussmannian labyrinth of the apartment.

Eventually she stumbled upon the horrid sagging sofa and walked around the room, looking out at the ice-covered trees on the Champ-de-Mars.

Just as she was slowly turning around, her mind still in a fog, her hands in her pockets, she gave a start and was unable to restrain an idiotic little cry of shock.

Right behind her, dressed entirely in black leather, with boots and a helmet, stood a tall man.

'Uh, hello,' she finally managed to blurt.

Saying nothing in reply, the black leather man turned on his heels.

In the hall he took off his helmet and went into the kitchen rubbing his hair:

'Hey, Philou, say man, who is that poofter you've got in the living room? One of your fellow boy scouts or something?'

'I beg your pardon?'

'The fairy who's behind my sofa.'

Philibert, who was already flustered enough as it was by the enormity of his culinary disaster, lost some of his aristocratic nonchalance:

'The fairy, as you call her, is called Camille,' he said flatly. 'She is my friend, and I'd ask you to behave like a gentleman because I have every intention of having her here to stay for some time.'

'Okay, okay. Take it easy. She's a girl, you say? Are we talking about the same character? The skinny guy with no hair?'

'She is indeed a young woman.'

'You sure?'

Philibert closed his eyes.

'You mean he's your girlfriend? She, that is? Say, what are you making for her there? Pickled aardvark vomit?'

'It's soup, actually.'

'That? Soup?'

'Exactly. Potato and leek soup from Liebig's.'

'Their stuff is crap. And you've burned it, too. It'll be disgusting. What did you add to it?' he asked, as he raised the lid, horrified.

'Uh . . . little cubes of cheese and pieces of brown bread.'

'Why'd you do that?'

'It's the doctor. He asked me to help her get back on her feet.'

'Well, if she manages to get back on her feet after a meal like this . . . congratulations! If you want my opinion, you'll make her fall down dead more like.'

He reached in the fridge for a beer and went off to shut himself into his room.

When Philibert went back to his protégée, she was still somewhat disconcerted: 'Is that him?'

'Yes,' he murmured, lowering the big tray on to a cardboard box.

'Doesn't he ever take his helmet off?'

'Yes, he does, but when he comes back on Monday evenings he's always in a foul mood. I generally try to stay out of his way on Mondays.'

'Is it because he has too much work?'

'No, that's just it, he doesn't work on Mondays. I don't know what he does. He leaves early in the morning and always comes back in a stinking mood. Family problems, I think. Here, help yourself while it's hot.'

'Uh, what is it?'

'Soup.'

'Oh?' said Camille, trying to stir Philibert's mystery chowder.

'Soup the way I make it. A sort of borscht if you prefer.'

'Aaah. Perfect,' she said, laughing.

Nervously, again.

Part Two

Part Two

1

'Have you got a minute? We need to have a talk here.'

Philibert always had hot chocolate at breakfast and his special pleasure was to turn off the flame just before the milk boiled over. More than a ritual or a mania, this was his daily little victory. His exploit, his invisible triumph. The milk would subside and the day could begin: Philibert was master of the situation.

But that morning he felt disconcerted, even aggressed by his flatmate's tone, and he turned the wrong knob. The milk gushed over and an unpleasant smell instantly filled the room.

'I beg your pardon?'

'I said, we have to talk.'

'Let's talk,' answered Philibert, calmly, running water into the pan to soak. 'I'm listening.'

'How long is she going to be here?'

'I beg your pardon?'

'Oh, c'mon, stop acting clever, okay? Your little chick? How long is she going to be here?'

'As long as she likes.'

'You've got the hots for her, is that it?'

'No.'

'Liar. I can tell, from your performance. Your fine manners, your airs of lord and master, all that.'

'Are you jealous?'

'Hell, no. That's all I need. How can I be jealous of a bag of bones? Hey, do I have Sally Army written all over my forehead or something?'

105

'You're not jealous of me, not jealous of her – so maybe you just feel it's become a bit too crowded here all of a sudden and you don't feel like moving your tooth mug a scant few inches to the right?'

'Well, what can I say? Your fancy phrases . . . Every time you open your mouth it's as if your words have to get written down somewhere, they sound so good.'

Philibert didn't reply.

'Hey, I know this is your place and all, that's not the problem. You can invite who you want, give a home to who you want, go ahead and open a soup kitchen if you feel like it but shit, I don't know, we were a good little team, the two of us, no?'

'Do you think so?'

'Yeah I think so. Okay – I know I have my moods and you have all your weird hangups, all your junk, your obsessive compulsive disorder, but on the whole things were going fine until today.'

'And why should they change?'

'Pfff . . . I can see you know nothing about women, Philibert. Careful, I'm not saying that to hurt you, okay? It's just true, that's all. The minute you let a girl in, all hell breaks loose, man. Everything gets complicated, everything becomes a pain in the arse and even the best buddies end up shouting at each other, you know. Now why are you laughing?'

'Because the way you express yourself . . . like a cowboy. I didn't know I was your . . . buddy.'

'Okay, forget it. I just think you could have talked to me about it beforehand, that's all.'

'I was going to talk to you.'

'When?'

'Here, right now, over my bowl of chocolate, if you'd just left me the time to make it properly.'

'I'm sorry about – no, I'm not supposed to say sorry *about*, right? I'm sorry *for* doing whatever it was I did, right?'

'Exactly so.'

'You on your way to work?'

'Yes.'

'Me too. C'mon. I'll buy you a hot chocolate downstairs.'

When they were in the courtyard, Franck fired his last round:

'On top of everything else, you don't even know who she is, where she comes from, or anything, that girl.'

106

'I'm going to show you where she comes from. Follow me.'

'Huh. You won't get me climbing up seven flights of stairs.'

'I will too. I am absolutely counting on you to do just that. Follow me.'

This was the first time in their entire acquaintance that Philibert was asking Franck to do something. Franck grumbled as much as he could and followed him up the service stairway.

'Shit, it's freezing in here!'

'This is nothing. Wait until we get up under the roof.'

Philibert opened the padlock and pushed the door.

Franck was silent for a moment, then said, 'This is where she sleeps?'

'Yes.'

'You sure?'

'Come here, I want to show you something else.'

He led Franck down the corridor, kicked another wobbly door and added, 'This is her bathroom. The toilet below, the shower above. You have to admit it's pretty ingenious.'

They went back down the stairs in silence.

Franck said nothing until after his third coffee: 'Okay, just one thing, then. You explain to her that it's really important for me to get my sleep in the afternoon and all that.'

'Yes, I'll tell her. We'll both tell her. But in my opinion it won't be a problem because she'll be sleeping, too.'

'Why?'

'She works at night.'

'What does she do?'

'Cleans houses.'

'What?'

'She's a cleaning lady.'

'Are you sure?'

'Why should she lie to me?'

'How do I know? Could be she's actually a call girl.'

'She would be more, er, curvaceous?'

'Yeah, you're right. Hey, you're not so dumb!' he added, giving Philibert a big slap on the back.

'Oh, w-watch it, you've made me drop my cr-croissant, i-idiot. Look, it's like an old je-je-jellyfish now.'

107

Franck didn't care, he was reading the headlines of the *Parisien* on the counter.

Outside the café they shook themselves as if to banish the cold.
    'Hey – '
    'What?'
    'Hasn't that chick got any family?'
    'You see,' began Philibert, tying his scarf, 'that is precisely the sort of question I've never allowed myself to ask you.'
    Franck looked up and smiled at him.

When he got to work he asked his commis to put some bouillon aside for him.
    'And hey.'
    'What?'
    'The good stuff, okay?'

2

Camille decided to stop taking the half-tablet of Lexomil every evening that the doctor had prescribed. On the one hand she couldn't stand the sort of half-comatose state she was floundering in, and on the other she didn't want to run the risk of getting accustomed to it. All through her childhood she had been witness to her mother's hysteria at the thought of trying to sleep without her pills, and those crises had had a lasting traumatic effect.

Camille had just awoken from yet another nap and had no idea of the time, but she decided to get up, give herself a good shake and, for a change, get dressed then go up to her place to see if she was ready to pick up the thread of her little life where she had left it.

On her way through the kitchen to take the back stairs she came upon a note stuck under a bottle filled with a yellowish liquid.

Reheat in a saucepan, make sure you dont boil it. Add the noodles when its bubbling and let it cook 4 minutes, stiring gentley.

It didn't look like Philibert's handwriting.

The lock had been broken and the little she owned on this planet – her last ties to the past, her tiny little realm – had been devastated.

Instinctively she rushed to the little tartan suitcase gaping open on the floor. No, that was okay, they hadn't taken anything and her art portfolios were still there.

Her mouth twisted to one side, her heart in her throat, she steeled herself to tidy up and see what was missing.

Nothing was missing, and for good reason: she didn't own a

thing. Well, there had been a clock-radio. That was it. What carnage for one little piece of junk she probably paid next to nothing for at a Chinese shop.

Camille picked up her clothes, piled them into a box, bent down to retrieve her suitcase and left the room without a backward glance. She waited until she was in the stairway and then she let it all out.

Outside the pantry she blew her nose, put her stuff down on the landing, and sat on a step to roll a cigarette. The first one in a long time . . . The automatic timer on the overhead light had switched off, but it didn't matter, quite the reverse.

Quite the reverse, she murmured, quite the reverse.

She thought about that nasty theory which held that as long as you were on your way down, there was no point in trying anything new and you had to wait until you touched bottom before you could give that salutary little kick which was the only thing that would help you back up to the surface.

Right.

She'd done that now, no?

She glanced at her box, ran a hand over her angular face and jumped back to leave room for some nasty insect that was scampering between two cracks.

Uh, say that again? She'd done that now, no?

When Camille went into the kitchen, it was Franck's turn to jump.

'Ah! You're up. I thought you were asleep.'

'Hello.'

'Franck Lestafier.'

'Camille.'

'Did you, did you see my note?'

'Yes, but I –'

'Are you moving your things? You need a hand?'

'No, I . . . well this is all I've got left, to be honest. I've been burgled.'

'So, shit.'

'Yup, like you say. That about sums it up. Well, I'm going back to bed, because I feel kind of dizzy and –'

'Want me to fix the consommé for you?'

'Pardon?'

110

'The consommé?'

'Consumer what?'

'The bouillon!'

'Oh, sorry. No. Thanks. I'm going to get some sleep.'

'Hey!' he shouted when she was already in the hall, 'the very reason you feel dizzy is because you're not eating enough!'

Camille sighed. Diplomacy, diplomacy . . . Given that she had a right clever one here, better not screw up in the first scene. So she went back into the kitchen and sat down at the end of the table.

'You're right.'

Franck began muttering to himself. Make up your mind . . . Of course I'm right . . . Fuck it anyway . . . Now I'll be in a rush.

He turned his back and set to work.

He poured the contents of the saucepan into a soup plate, then took a folded paper towel out of the fridge and proceeded to unfold it with care. Inside was some sort of green stuff that he cut into tiny slivers over the steaming soup.

'What's that?' she asked.

'Coriander.'

'And what do you call those little noodles?'

'Pearls from Japan.'

'Really? That's a pretty name.'

He grabbed his jacket and slammed the front door as he went out, shaking his head: *Really? That's a pretty name.*

What a dickhead, that girl.

3

Camille sighed and pulled the soup plate absent-mindedly towards herself, thinking about her burglar. Who'd done it? The ghost in the corridor? Some stray visitor? Did they get in from the roof? Was there a chance they'd come back? Should she mention it to Pierre?

The smell – the *fumet*, more like – of the bouillon stopped her from brooding. Mmm, it was wonderful; she almost felt like draping her napkin over her head to turn it into an inhalation. What on earth was in it? It was a very particular colour: warm, oily, golden brown, cadmium yellow. With the translucent pearls and the emerald slivers of chopped herb, it was a joy to behold. She stayed like that for a few seconds, respectfully, with her spoon poised, then she took a first sip, quite slowly because it was very hot.

Camille then found herself in the same state as Marcel Proust, minus the childhood: 'intent upon the extraordinary thing that was happening . . .' and she finished her plate religiously, closing her eyes between each spoonful.

Maybe it was just that she'd been dying of hunger without knowing it, or maybe it was because for three days she'd been forcing herself, with a grimace, to swallow down Philibert's cartons of soup, or maybe it was because she hadn't been smoking as much as usual, but in any event, one thing was certain: never in her life had she had such a pleasurable experience of solitary dining. She got up to see if there was anything left in the bottom of the pan: alas, no. She lifted the soup plate to her lips, not to miss a drop, then clicked her tongue, washed the dish and reached for the open packet of noodles. Lining up some of the pearls on top of Franck's note, she wrote 'Wow!' with them, then went back to bed, where she ran her palm over her nicely distended tummy.

Sweet Jesus, thank you.

4

The end of Camille's convalescence went by too quickly. She never saw Franck, but she knew when he was there: doors slamming, stereo, television, animated conversations on the phone, rowdy laughter and harsh swear words – and none of it was really natural, she could tell. He was the restless type, and he let his life reverberate to the four corners of the apartment, like a dog who'd piss everywhere to mark its territory. There were times Camille really wanted to go back to her room upstairs to be on her own again and not be beholden to anyone. But other times she didn't. Other times she would begin to shiver at the very idea of sleeping on the floor again, or of climbing up seven flights of stairs, clinging to the banister so she wouldn't fall.

So it was complicated.

She didn't know where she belonged any more, and besides, she liked Philibert. Why was she always berating herself, beating her breast, with clenched teeth? For the sake of her independence? What the hell kind of victory was that? She'd scarcely talked about anything else for years – and for what? How far had she come? To a dump where she spent her afternoons smoking one cigarette after the other, rehashing her destiny yet again? It was pathetic. She was pathetic. Here she was going to be twenty-seven years old and up to now she hadn't managed to produce a single thing she could call her own. No friends, no memories, not one reason to be the least bit kind to herself. What had happened? Why had she never managed to clasp her hands together and keep just two or three precious things between them? Why?

Camille grew thoughtful. She felt rested. And when that sweet gangly monkey would come and read to her, then quietly shut the door behind him – rolling his eyes to the ceiling since that other baboon was listening to his 'Zulu' music – Camille would smile at him and, for a moment, escape the force of the hurricane.

She had begun drawing again.

Just like that.

For no particular reason. For her own sake. For the pleasure of it.

She had picked out a new sketchbook, the last one, and broke it in by recording everything she saw around her: the fireplace, the designs on the curtains, the window catch, the goofy smiles of Shaggy and Scooby-Doo, the picture frames, the paintings themselves, the lady's cameo and the gentleman's severe-looking riding coat. A still life of her clothes with her belt buckle left on the floor; clouds, a vapour trail, the treetops beyond the ironwork of the balcony; and a self-portrait taken from her bed.

Because of the spots on the mirror and her short hair, she looked like a kid with chicken pox.

It felt as natural as breathing to be drawing again. Turning the pages without thinking, stopping only to pour a little India ink into a small dish and refill her pen. She had not felt this calm, this alive, so simply alive, for years.

But it was Philibert, the way he had about him, that she liked best of all. He would get so absorbed by his own stories, his face suddenly so expressive or passionate or crestfallen (oh, poor Marie-Antoinette!), that she asked for permission to sketch him.

Of course he stuttered a bit in the beginning, a pure formality, then just as quickly forgot about the sound of the pen scratching across the paper.

Sometimes it went:

'*But Madame d'Étampes did not fall in love in the same way as Madame de Châteaubriant, she could scarcely be satisfied with mere trifles. She dreamt above all of obtaining favours for herself and her family. Indeed, she had thirty brothers and sisters. Courageously, she set to work.*

'*She was clever, and she knew how to take advantage of every spare moment which the need to catch her breath between two spells of embracing afforded her, in order to wrench from the King – now sated and out of breath – the nominations or advances she desired.*

'Finally, all the Pisseleu family were endowed with important duties, generally of an ecclesiastic nature, for the King's mistress was "the religious sort".

'Antoine Seguin, her maternal uncle, became abbot of Fleury-sur-Loire, bishop of Orléans, cardinal, and finally, archbishop of Toulouse. Charles de Pisseleu, her second brother, had the abbey at Bourgueil and the Bishopric of Condom.'

He raised his head: 'Condom. You have to admit it's rather naughty.'

And Camille would hurry to capture that particular smile, the amused rapture of a young man who could leaf his way through the history of France the way others would flip through a magazine full of tits 'n' bums.

Or it might be something like:

'. . . as the prisons had become inadequate, Carrier, an all-powerful autocrat, surrounded by deserving collaborators, opened new jails and requisitioned ships in the harbour. Soon typhoid fever would ravage the thousands of people incarcerated in abominable conditions. The guillotine could not keep up, so the proconsul ordered that thousands of prisoners be shot, and to the firing squads he assigned a "burial corps". Then, as the number of prisoners in the city continued to grow, he invented the drownings.

'For his part, General Westermann wrote: "Citizens of the Republic, the Vendée no longer exists. Beneath our sword of freedom, with its women and children, it has died. I have buried it in the swamps and forests of Savenay. Upon your orders, I have crushed the children beneath the hooves of my horses and massacred the women who – these women at least – will no longer give birth to brigands. I do not have a single prisoner with which to reproach myself."'

And all it took was a shadow sketched across his tense face.

'Are you drawing or are you listening?'

'I'm listening while I draw.'

'That Westermann. That same monster who served his fine new motherland with so much fervour, well, just imagine, he was captured with Danton a few months later and lost his head alongside him.'

'Why?'

'Accused of cowardice. He was a "wet".'

*

At other times Philibert would ask Camille's permission to sit in the wing chair and the two of them would read in silence.

'Philibert?'

'Mmm?'

'The postcards?'

'Yes?'

'Are you going to do that for long?'

'I beg your pardon?'

'Why don't you make this your profession? Why don't you try to become a historian or a professor? It would give you the right to delve into all those books during your working hours and you'd get paid as well!'

He put the tome down on the worn corduroy that covered his bony knees and removed his glasses to rub his eyes.

'I've tried. I have a degree in history and I took the entrance exam to the École des Chartes three times, but each time I failed.'

'You weren't good enough?'

'Oh, I was!' He blushed. 'Well, at least, I think so, I humbly believe that, but I – I've never been able to take exams, I get too nervous, each time my eyesight gets worse, I can't sleep, I lose my hair and I even lose my teeth! And all my faculties. I read the questions, I know the answers, but I cannot write a single line. I sit there petrified, staring at the blank paper.'

'But you got your baccalaureate? And your degree?'

'Yes, but I paid the price. And never the first time round. And it really wasn't difficult. I got my degree without ever having set foot inside the Sorbonne, unless it was to go and listen to lectures by the great professors I admired, and who had nothing to do with my own curriculum.'

'How old are you?'

'Thirty-six.'

'But with your degree you could have been teaching, couldn't you?'

'Can you see me in a classroom with thirty kids?'

'Sure.'

'No. The very idea of addressing an audience, no matter how small, makes me break into a cold sweat. I . . . I have problems – I have problems . . . relating to people.'

'But at school? When you were little?'

'I didn't go to school until I was twelve. And, what's more, it was a boarding school. It was a horrible year. The worst in my life. As if they'd thrown me in at the deep end and I didn't know how to swim.'

'So what happened?'

'Nothing. I still don't know how to swim.'

'Literally or figuratively?'

'Both, General, sir.'

'You never learned how to swim?'

'No. What for?'

'Well, so you could go swimming!'

'Culturally, we come rather from a generation of infantry and artillery, you know.'

'What on earth are you on about? I'm not talking about going off to fight a war! I'm just talking about going to the seaside. And why didn't you go to school earlier to start with?'

'My mother was teaching us.'

'Like Saint Louis's mother?'

'Exactly.'

'What was her name again?'

'Blanche de Castille.'

'That's right. And why was that? Did you live too far away?'

'There was a local elementary school in the next village, but I only lasted a few days there.'

'How come?'

'Because it was a state school.'

'Oh, that old thing about the republicans, is that it?'

'That's it.'

'Hey, that was over two hundred years ago! Things have evolved a bit since then.'

'Changed, I don't deny. Evolved . . . I'm not sure.'

Camille looked at him in silence.

'Does that shock you?' said Philibert.

'No, no, I respect your . . .'

'My values?'

'Yes, I suppose, if that's the right word, but how do you make a living, then?'

'I sell postcards!'

'But that's wild. Unbelievable, what a story.'

'You know, compared to my parents, I have . . . evolved, as you say, I've acquired a certain distance, all the same.'

'What are they like?'

'Well . . .'

'Stuffed? Embalmed? Immersed in a jar of formaldehyde with the fleur de lys?'

'There is a bit of that, indeed,' he conceded, amused.

'Please tell me that they don't go around in one of those sedan chair things, do they?'

'Well, only because they can't find anyone to carry it for them any more!'

'What do they do?'

'I beg your pardon?'

'For a living.'

'They own land.'

'That's all?'

'It involves a lot of work, you know.'

'But, uh . . . Are you, like, very rich?'

'No, not at all. On the contrary.'

'This is wild. And how did you manage at boarding school?'

'I managed. Thanks to Liddell and Scott.'

'Who were they?'

'They're not people. Liddell and Scott is a heavy Greek dictionary that I carried around in my schoolbag and that I used as a catapult. I'd hold my bag by the strap, swing it to get momentum and . . . tally-ho! Cleave the enemy in two.'

'And then?'

'Then what?'

'Well, now?'

'Well, my dear, now things are very simple, you have before your eyes a magnificent example of *homo degeneraris*, that is, a creature totally incapable of life in society, out of synch, out to lunch, a perfect anachronism.'

Philibert was laughing.

'So how will you manage?'

'I don't know.'

'Are you seeing a shrink?'

'No, but I met this young woman where I work, a sort of amusing, tiring nutcase who's been badgering me to go with her to her drama class one evening. And she's been through every imaginable shrink in the book and she claims that the theatre is much more effective.'

'Really?'

'That's what she says.'

'But other than that, do you ever go out? Don't you have friends? No like-minded people? Some contact with . . . the twenty-first century?'

'No, not a great deal. And you?'

5

Life returned to normal. Camille braved the cold when night fell to take the metro in the opposite direction from the labouring masses, and she observed all the strained faces.

Mothers who fell asleep with their mouths open against the steamy windows, on their way to pick up their kids in the poorer suburban neighbourhoods; women covered in cheap costume jewellery briskly turning the pages of their *TV Week* with pointed, moistened index fingers; men in soft leather loafers and patterned socks highlighting improbable reports as they sighed noisily; young executives with greasy skin who passed the time playing Tetris on their not yet paid for mobile phones.

And then all the others, those who did nothing more than cling instinctively to the strap to keep their balance. Those who saw nothing, no one. They didn't see the Christmas ads – golden days, golden gifts, salmon for next to nothing and foie gras at wholesale prices – nor their neighbour's paper, nor the pain in the arse with his outstretched hand and his whiny plea rehashed a thousand times over, nor even that young woman sitting just across from them, sketching their mournful gazes and the folds of their grey overcoats.

Camille exchanged a few pleasantries with the building security officer, got changed as she held on to her trolley, pulled on a pair of shapeless overalls and a turquoise nylon blouse stamped *Professionals at your service,* and warmed up, busying herself like a condemned man until it was time for the next blast of cold air, her umpteenth cigarette, and the last metro.

When Super Josy saw Camille, she rammed her fists deep into her pockets and her face creased into an almost tender grimace:

'Well, I'll be damned, here's a ghost. And I'm out ten euros,' she grumbled.

'Pardon?'

'A bet I had with the other girls. I didn't think you'd come back.'

'Why?'

'Dunno, just a gut feeling. But hey, no problem, I'll pay up. Okay, gang, this is all very well, we need to get a move on. With this bad weather they're trashing everything. To the point you wonder if their mothers ever showed these folks how to use a doormat. Just look at that, have you seen the corridor?'

Mamadou, dragging her feet, said to Camille: 'You been sleeping like a big baby all week long, right?'

'How do you know?'

'Because of your hair. It been growing too quick.'

'Are you okay, Mamadou? You don't look so hot.'

'I'm okay, I'm okay.'

'You've got problems?'

'Oh, problems . . . Got sick kids, the husband gambles away his pay cheque, sister-in-law she gets on my nerves, a neighbour been shitting in the lift and the phone line been cut, but otherwise I'm okay.'

'Why'd he do that?'

'Who?'

'The neighbour?'

'Why, I don't know, but I told him, and next time, he's gonna eat his shit. And I mean what I say. What you laughing at, huh?'

'What's wrong with your kids?'

'One of 'em's coughing and the other one has gastroenteritis. Okay, c'mon, let's stop talking 'bout all that because it makes me too sad and when I'm sad I'm no damn use to anybody.'

'And your brother? Can't he make them better with all that black magic he does?'

'And what about the racetrack? Don't you think he could pick a few winners from time to time? Oh no, don't talk to me 'bout that good-for-nothing scum, okay?'

The piglet on the fifth floor must have taken Camille's drawing to heart: his office was more or less tidy. Camille drew an angel as seen from behind, a pair of wings emerging from his suit and a nice halo.

At the apartment they were beginning to get their bearings. The awkwardness of the first days, the hesitant dance and all their embarrassed gestures were slowly changing into a discreet, everyday choreography.

Camille got up in the late morning, but made certain she was always back in her room by three when Franck came home. He left again at around six thirty, sometimes passing Philibert in the stairway. Camille would share a pot of tea or have a light dinner with Philibert before going to work herself; she was never back before one in the morning.

Franck was never asleep at that time: he'd be listening to music or watching television. The scent of pot wafted from underneath his door. Camille wondered how he managed to keep up such a frenetic pace, and very quickly she had her answer: he didn't.

So from time to time he'd blow a fuse. He would throw a fit when he opened the refrigerator and found food that had not been put away in the right place, or was poorly wrapped, and he'd take out the offending items and put them on the table, knocking over the teapot and calling Philibert and Camille every rude name in the book:

'Fuck! How many times do I have to tell you? The butter goes into a butter dish because otherwise it absorbs all the other smells! And the cheese! Clingfilm wasn't invented for dogs, shit! And what the hell is this? Lettuce? Why did you leave it in a plastic bag? Plastic ruins everything! I've already told you, Philibert. Where are all those containers I brought home the other day? And what about this lemon? What's it doing in the egg compartment? You cut open a lemon, you wrap it up or put it upside down on a plate, *capisce*?'

Then off he went with his can of beer and our two criminals waited for the backdraught from the door before picking up the thread of their conversation:

'Did she really say, "*If there is no more bread, then let them eat cake*"?'

'Of course not, come on. She would never have uttered such rubbish. She was a very intelligent woman, you know.'

Of course they could have put their cups down with a sigh and answered back, told Franck that for someone who never ate there anyway and who only used the fridge to store his six-packs he was over-reacting . . . But it really wasn't worth the trouble.

Since he was the yelling type, well, let him yell.

Let him yell.

Besides, that's what he expected. The slightest excuse to be at their throats. Camille's, especially. He held her in his sights and wore an outraged expression whenever their paths crossed. No matter that she spent the vast majority of her time in her own room, they were bound to run into each other, and she felt the full force of the murderous vibes which, depending on her mood, made her feel awkward or coaxed out a half-smile.

'Hey, what's with you? What you laughing at? Something wrong with my face?'

'No, no. Nothing, it's nothing.'

And she would hurry to change the subject.

In the communal rooms, Camille was on her best behaviour. She tried to leave the place as clean as you would hope to find it on entering; when Franck wasn't there she locked herself in the bathroom and hid all her toilet articles; she wiped the sponge over the kitchen table two times rather than once, emptied her ashtray into a plastic bag that she tied carefully before putting it in the garbage; tried to be as discreet as possible, hugged the walls, dodged the bad vibes and ended up thinking maybe she'd leave earlier than planned.

She'd freeze up there – never mind, she wouldn't keep bumping into that stupid dickhead; so much the better.

Philibert was sorry:

'But Camille, Camille, you are mu-much too intelligent to allow yourself to be in-intimidated by that oversized beanpole, don't you see? You are a-above all that, aren't you?'

'No, that's just it. I'm on exactly the same level. As a result, it really gets to me.'

'Whatever do you mean? You two are not on the same planet, not at all! Have you, have you ever seen his ha-handwriting? Have you ever heard the way he laughs when he listens to that inane TV presenter's vulgar commentary? Have you ever seen him reading anything besides the motorcycle blue book? Hang on a minute, he has the mental age of a two-year-old! Not his fault, poor guy. I imagine he started up in a kitchen somewhere when he was still a boy and he's never been anywhere else. Go on, take a step back. Be more tolerant, "stay cool", as you say.'

Camille didn't answer.

'You know what my mother would say whenever I dared to evoke – in barely a whisper – even a quarter of half the horrible things my little roommates would in-inflict on me?'

'No?'

'"Learn, my son, that a toad's drool cannot touch the white dove." That's what she would say.'

'And did it make you feel better?'

'Not at all! Quite the reverse!'

'So, you see . . .'

'Yes, but with you, it's not the same. You're not twelve years old any more. And besides, it's not a question of drinking the piss of some sn-snotty-nosed little kid.'

'They made you do that?'

'I'm afraid so.'

'Well, in that case, I can see that some bla-bla about a white dove, uh –'

'You might say that I never quite swallowed the white d-dove stuff. Incidentally, I can still feel it, right here,' he laughed bitterly, pointing to his Adam's apple.

'Yeah. Hmm.'

'And then the truth of it is really bloody simple and you know it as well as I do: Franck is je-jealous. Jealous as a tiger. Put yourself in his place. He had the apartment all to himself, wandered in and out as he pleased, more often than not wearing just his underwear or in the wake of some terrified little goose. He could shout and swear and burp to his heart's content, and our relationship was limited to a few exchanges of a practical nature on the state of the plumbing or the supplies of toilet paper.

'I almost never left my room and I used earplugs when I needed to concentrate. He was the king here. So much so that he must have felt like this was his place, so to speak. And then you came along and *boom*. Not only did he have to start zipping up his flies, but now he has to witness our shared affinities, as well, he can hear us laughing sometimes and he listens to bits of our conversation and probably doesn't understand much of what we're talking about. It must be rather hard for him, don't you think?'

'I didn't think I was, like, taking up so much room.'

'No, you – you're very discreet, on the contrary, but you want me to – to tell you? I think he's a bit intimidated by you.'

'Well, that beats everything! Me? Intimidate someone? You must be joking. Hey, he's just dripping with scorn, I've never seen anything like it in my life!'

'Shh. He hasn't got much culture, that's a fact, but he's far from being an ignoramus either, that guy there, and you don't exactly box at the same weight as his girlfriends, you know. Have you run into any of them since you've be-been here?'

'No . . .'

'Well, wait till you see them. It's truly amazing. Whatever happens, I implore you, dear Camille, stay above the madding crowd. For my sake.'

'But I won't be staying here very long, I mean, you know that.'

'Neither will I. Neither will Franck, but in the meantime, let's try to be good neighbours. The world is already a sufficiently dreadful place without us falling out, is it not? And you m-make me stutter when you say st-stupid things.'

Camille got up to switch off the kettle.

'You don't seem convinced,' said Philibert.

'Yes, yes, I'm going to make an effort. But you know I'm not very good when it comes to power struggles. I usually, like, throw in the towel before I try to defend myself.'

'Why?'

'Because.'

'Because it doesn't take as much effort?'

'Yes.'

'That's not a good strategy, be-believe me. In the long run, you'll end up losing.'

'I already have ended up losing.'

'Speaking of strategies, I'm going to attend a fascinating conference on the military art of Napoleon Bonaparte next week, would you care to join me?'

'No, but you go, hey, I'm all ears: tell me about Napoleon.'

'Ah! A vast topic! Would you like a slice of le-lemon?'

'Whoa, take it easy! No more lemons for me! No more of anything, anyway.'

He rolled his eyes at her:

'A-above the madding crowd, remember that.'

6

Time Regained, as the name of choice for a place where everyone was going to snuff it, was really appropriate.

Franck was in a foul mood. His grandmother hadn't said a word to him ever since she'd started living there, and the minute he hit the outskirts of Paris he'd have to start digging really deep into his skull to come up with some stuff to tell her. On his first visit he'd run out of things to say, and they'd sat there glaring at each other for the entire afternoon. In the end, he stood watch by the window and made comments about everything he could see going on in the car park below: old folks being loaded into vehicles, others being unloaded, couples arguing, children running around between the cars, that one there who had just been smacked, a young woman crying, a Porsche Boxster, a Ducati, the spanking new 5 Series, and the incessant coming and going of the ambulances. A truly memorable day.

Yvonne Carminot had taken charge of the moving, and Franck had shown up in all innocence on that first Monday, without any idea what to expect.

There was the place itself, to start with. Given the state of their finances, he'd had to fall back on a hastily constructed public retirement home located in the outskirts of town between a Buffalo Grill and an industrial waste dump. Urban development zones one after the other, a conglomeration of concrete shit. A very big conglomeration of concrete shit in the middle of nowhere. He'd got lost, and had ridden around for over an hour in a labyrinth of all sorts of gigantic warehouses, looking for a non-existent street name, stopping at every roundabout to try and decipher some fucking incomprehensible map, and when finally he put his bike on its stand and took off his helmet, he was almost blown off his feet by a gust of wind. 'Hey, what the fuck is going on? Since when do they put old people in wind tunnels? They say that the wind eats into their brains . . . Oh shit, tell me this isn't true, she's not around here somewhere, please, tell me I made a mistake . . .'

The heat in that place would send you to your grave, and as Franck drew nearer to his grandmother's room, he felt his throat getting tighter and tighter and tighter until he needed several minutes before he could utter a single word.

All these wrinkly old people – ugly, sad, depressing, moaning and groaning, with the sounds of slippers slapping and dentures rattling and sucking, with their huge bellies and skeletal arms. That one over there with a tube up his nose, and another one whimpering all alone in his corner, or this old creature completely folded over in her wheelchair as if she were recovering from an attack of lockjaw. You could even see her stockings and her nappy.

And the heat, Jesus! Why didn't they ever open the windows? To make them kick the bucket all the sooner?

The next time Franck came, he kept his helmet on all the way to room 87 so he wouldn't have to see anything, but a nurse nabbed him and told him to take it off because he was frightening the inmates.

His grandma wouldn't speak to him, but she nevertheless looked him right in the eye, defiantly, rebelliously, to fill him with shame: 'Well? Are you pleased with yourself, son? Answer me. Are you proud of what you've done?' That is what she said over and over, in silence, while Franck pulled aside the net curtain to check on his motorbike.

He was too irritated to fall asleep. He pulled the armchair up next to her bed, hunted for words, phrases, anecdotes, and trivial nonsense until finally, tired of struggling, he switched on the television. He didn't watch it, but kept his eyes on the wall clock behind it and began the countdown: in two hours I'm out of here, in one hour I'm out of here, in twenty minutes . . .

That week, exceptionally, he came on Sunday because Potelain didn't need him. He walked through the hall quick as he could, just shrugging his shoulders at the garish new decorations and at all those poor old folks wearing pointed hats.

'What's going on, is it carnival time?' he asked the woman in a white coat next to him in the lift.

'They're rehearsing a little performance for Christmas. You're Madame Lestafier's grandson, right?'

'Yes.'

'She's not very cooperative, your grandmother.'

'Oh?'

'No. That's putting it mildly. A real stubborn one.'

'I thought she was just like that with me. I thought with you she'd be, well, easier.'

'Oh, she's charming with us. A treasure. As sweet as can be. But it's with the other residents that there's a problem. She doesn't want to see them and she'd rather not eat than go down to the dining room.'

'So what does that mean? She's not eating?'

'Well, eventually we gave in. She stays in her room.'

Paulette wasn't expecting Franck until the next day, she was surprised to see him, and didn't have time to put on her indignant old lady act. For once she wasn't sitting up in bed, grumpy and stiff as a post; she was over by the window, sewing.

'Grandma?'

Oh rats, she would have liked to put on her pinched expression, but she couldn't stop herself from smiling.

'You looking at the scenery?'

She almost felt like telling him the truth: 'Are you making fun of me? What scenery? No. I've been watching and waiting for you, son. That's what I do all day and every day. Even when I know you're not coming, here I am. I'm always here. You know, now I recognize the sound of your motorbike from a distance, and I wait and watch for you to take off your helmet before I jump into bed and put my grumpy face on.'

But Paulette got a grip and merely grumbled as usual.

Franck slid down on to the floor at her feet and leaned against the radiator.

'You okay?' he asked.

'Mmm.'

129

'What are you up to?'

She was silent.

'You angry or something?'

Still she said nothing. They glowered at each other for a good quarter of an hour, then Franck rubbed his head, closed his eyes, sighed, slid over a few inches so he was facing her straight on, and started off in a monotonous voice:

'Listen to me, Grandma, listen carefully:

'You used to live on your own, in a house you loved, and I loved it too. In the morning you'd get up at dawn, make your coffee with chicory and drink it while you looked at the colour of the clouds to try and predict the weather. Then it was time to feed everyone, right? Your cat, the neighbours' cats, the robins, all the sparrows and blue tits in creation. Then out with the secateurs to tidy up the flowers, even before you made yourself look nice. Then you'd get dressed, wait for the postman on his rounds, or the butcher. Fat Michel, that crook who always cut you three hundred grams of steak when all you wanted was a hundred, even though he knew damn well you didn't have any more teeth . . . But you never said a thing. You were too afraid that when he came the following Tuesday he'd forget to blow his horn for you. You'd just boil up the rest of the beef to add some taste to the soup. Around eleven, it was time to take your shopping bag and go on down to old Grivaud's café to buy your paper and your two-pound loaf of bread. Even though you hadn't been eating bread for the longest time, you bought it all the same . . . because you're a creature of habit. And for the birds. Sometimes you'd run into an old girlfriend who'd had a look at the obituaries before you had and you'd talk about your dead folks and sigh. Then you'd give her my news. Even if you didn't have any news. As far as they were concerned, I was already as famous as Bocuse, right? For nearly twenty years you'd been living alone, but you went on using a clean tablecloth and setting a nice table, with a wine glass and flowers in a vase. If I remember right, in the springtime it was anemones, daisies in the summer and in winter you'd buy a bouquet at the market, and at every meal you'd mutter that it was an ugly bouquet and you'd paid way too much for it. In the afternoon you took a little nap on the sofa, and that big tomcat of yours just might condescend to sit on your lap for a while. Then you'd finish what you'd started in the garden or the vegetable plot that morning. Oh, the vegetable garden . . . Not a lot to do in there any more, but it still gave you a few things to eat, and whenever Yvonne bought her carrots at the supermarket you could feel that glow of satisfaction; supermarket carrots were the height of dishonour.

'Evenings were starting to drag though, weren't they. You hoped I might call, but I didn't call, so you switched on the television and waited for all that crap to knock you senseless. Until the commercials woke you up with a jolt. You went around the house holding your shawl tight against your chest and you closed the shutters. That sound – shutters creaking in the half-light – you can still hear it today and I know this because it's the same for me. Paris is so tiring that you can't hear a thing any more, but those sounds – the wooden shutters and the shed door – all I have to do is listen carefully and I can still hear them.

'So maybe I didn't call you, but I was still thinking about you, you know. And whenever I came out to see you, I didn't need Saint Yvonne to take me to one side and clutch my arm while she filed her report to understand that it was all going downhill. I didn't dare say anything to you, but I could tell that the garden wasn't so neat any more and that the vegetable plot was beginning to look shabby. I could see you didn't take such good care of your appearance any more either, that your hair was a really weird colour and your skirt was on back to front. And the stove was dirty, and the incredibly ugly sweaters you went on knitting for me were full of holes, and your socks didn't match and you bumped into things every time you turned around. Yes, don't look at me like that, Grandma. I could see those enormous bruises you tried to hide under your cardigans.

'I could have got on your case about all this ages ago. Could have dragged you to the doctor's and shouted at you to stop wearing yourself out with that old spade that you could hardly lift any more; I could have asked Yvonne to spy on you and watch your every move and send me the results of your tests. But I didn't. I figured it was better to leave you in peace and the day when it all fell apart, yeah, well, at least you'd have no regrets, and neither would I. At least you'll have had a good life. A happy one. No sweat. Right up to the end.

'Now that day's come. Here we are, now, and you have to face it, Grandma: instead of making a face when you see me you should be thinking how lucky you are to have lived over eighty years in such a great house and –'

She was crying.

'– and on top of it all, you haven't been fair with me. Is it my fault I'm far away and there's only me? Is it my fault you're a widow? Is it my fault you didn't have any other kids, only my crazy mother, to look after you now? Is it my fault I don't have any brothers or sisters who could share these visiting days?

'Nope, it's not my fault. My only mistake was to choose such a lousy profession. All I do is work like a dog, and you know? The worst of it is that even if I wanted, there's nothing else I know how to do. Do you even realize that I work every day except Mondays? And Mondays I come and see you. Hey, don't act so surprised. I told you that I was working extra on Sundays to pay for my motorbike, so you see, I don't have a single morning when I can just stay in bed. I start every morning at eight thirty and in the evening I'm never out of there before midnight. That's why I have to sleep in the afternoon or I'll never make it.

'So. You see? That's it, that's my life: nothing. I do nothing. I see nothing. I know nothing and the worst is I understand nothing. In all this crap there was one good thing, and only one, and that was the place I'd found with that weird guy I told you about. The aristocrat, remember? Okay, well even that's up shit creek now. He brought home some girl who's there now, who lives with us and she pisses me off to a point you can't even imagine. And she's not even his girlfriend! I don't know if that guy will ever even get laid some day – sorry – if he'll ever go all the way. Nope, she's just some poor girl he took under his wing and now the atmosphere is hea-vy in that apartment and I'm going to have to find something else. Well okay, maybe it's no big deal and I've moved so many times already that one address more or less, same difference, I can always get myself sorted out out. But for you, I can't sort anything out, don't you see? For once I have a boss who's cool. Maybe I'm always telling you about how he shouts a lot and all that, but still, he's really fair. You know where you are with him, and he's a good guy. I really feel like I'm making progress with him, you see? So I can't just ditch him like that, in any case not before the end of July. Because I told him about the situation with you, you know, I told him I wanted to come back here to work so I'd be closer to you and I know he'll help me, but at the level I've reached now, I don't want to take just any old job. If I come back here, I've got to be either second chef in a cool new gastro place, or chef in a regular place. I don't want to be the bottlewasher any more, I've done my time. So you have to be patient and stop looking at me like that because otherwise, frankly: I won't come and see you any more.

'I'll say it again, I've got one day off a week, and if that day off is going to get me depressed, then that's the end of the line for me. And now the holidays are coming and I'm going to be working harder than ever, so you have to help me, too, for Christ's sake.

'Wait, one last thing. There's a woman here told me that you didn't want to mix with the others, and in a way I understand because they don't really look like a bundle of joy, but you could at least just do the minimum. You never know, there might be another Paulette around here somewhere, hidden in her room and as lost as you are. Maybe she'd like to talk about her garden and her fantastic grandson, but how is she supposed to find you if you just sit there sulking like some schoolgirl?'

Paulette looked at her grandson and did not know what to say.

'Okay, that's it. I've got that off my chest and now I can't even get up because my arse – sorry – my bum is sore. So? What are you sewing?'

'Is that you, Franck? Is it really you? That's the first time in my life I've heard you talk for so long. You're not sick or anything?'

'Nope, I'm not sick, I'm just tired. I'm fed up, understand?'

She stared at him for a long time then shook her head as if, at last, she were coming out of a daze. She picked up her sewing:

'Oh, this is nothing. It belongs to Nadège, this nice young woman who works here in the morning. I'm mending her sweater. And could you thread the needle for me, I don't know where I've put my glasses.'

'Don't you want to get back in bed and I'll sit in the armchair?'

No sooner had he slumped into the chair than he fell asleep.

The sleep of the righteous.

'What's this?'

'Dinner.'

'Why don't you go down?'

'They always feed us in our rooms at night.'

'But what time is it?'

'Five thirty.'

'Are they out of their flipping minds? They feed you at five thirty?'

'Yes, that's how it is on Sundays. So they can leave early.'

'Jeez. What is this stuff? It stinks, don't you think?'

'I don't know what it is and I'd rather not know.'

'What's that? Fish?'

'No, looks more like scalloped potatoes, don't you think?'

'No way, it smells like fish. And what's that brown thing?'

'Stewed fruit.'

'What?'

'Yes, I think so.'

'You sure?'

'Oh, I don't know any more.'

They had reached this point in their investigation when the young woman came back in: 'All set? Was it okay? You all done?'

'Wait a minute,' said Franck, 'you just brought this thing in two minutes ago. Give her some time to eat in peace!'

The woman turned and closed the door briskly.

'It's like this every day, but it's worse on Sundays. They're all in a hurry to leave. You can't blame them, can you.'

The old lady looked down.

'Oh, poor Grandma. God what a bloody mess this all is. A bloody mess.'

Paulette folded her napkin.

'Franck?'

'Yeah?'

'Forgive me.'

'Nah, it's me. Nothing's going the way I want. But it's no big deal, it's been going on so long I'm beginning to get used to it.'

'May I take your tray now?' The young woman was back.

'Yes yes, go ahead.'

'Please congratulate the chef, miss,' added Franck, 'it's delicious.'

'Well, then. I'd better get going.'

'Could you wait until I get into my nightgown?'

'Go ahead.'

'Help me get back up.'

He heard the sound of water running in the bathroom and, when she was slipping in under the sheets, he turned away modestly.

'Switch off the light, son.'

She turned on the bedside lamp.

'Come and sit here, just two minutes.'

'Two minutes, okay? I don't live next door you know.'

'Two minutes.'

She placed her hand on his knee and asked him the last question he might have expected: 'Tell me, that young woman you were talking about earlier, the one who lives with you, what's she like?'

'She's skinny, stupid, pretentious, and as weird as my flatmate.'

'Goodness.'

'She . . .'

'She what?'

'She's like some intellectual. Nah, not like, she is an intellectual. With Philibert they're always with their noses in books and like all those intellectuals they can sit there talking for hours about stuff no one gives a shit about, but what's even weirder is that she works as a cleaning lady.'

'Really?'

'At night.'

'At night?'

'Yeah. Like I said, really weird. And you should see how skinny she is. Makes you shudder.'

'Doesn't she eat?'

'How would I know? And what do I care?'

'What's her name?'

'Camille.'

'What is she like?'

'I just told you.'

'Her face?'

'Hey, why are you asking me all this?'

'To keep you here longer. No – because I'm interested.'

'Well, she has very short hair, almost shaved off, sort of brown. She has blue eyes, I think. I don't know – well, light, in any case. She . . . oh, what the hell do I care, I told you.'

'What about her nose?'

'Normal. I think she has freckles, too. She – why are you smiling?'

'No reason, I'm listening . . .'

'No way, I'm out of here, you're starting to get on my nerves.'

7

'I hate December. All these holidays, it's so depressing.'

'I know, Mum. That's the fourth time you've said that since I got here.'

'It doesn't make you depressed?'

'So what else is new? Have you been to the cinema?'

'Why on earth would I go to the cinema?'

'You going down to Lyon for Christmas?'

'I have to. You know what your uncle's like. He couldn't care less about my life, but if I miss his turkey, it'll be all hell to pay. You coming with me this year?'

'No.'

'Why not?'

'I'm working.'

'Sweeping up the needles from the Christmas trees, I suppose,' she said sarcastically.

'Exactly.'

'Are you making fun of me?'

'No.'

'Still, I can see how you might. It's the height of misery after all, isn't it, to have to sit there with all those jerks around the Christmas pudding?'

'Don't exaggerate. They're still nice people.'

She made a dismissive sound and said, 'Nice people – that's depressing, too, but hey . . .'

'My treat,' said Camille, intercepting the bill. 'I have to get going now.'

'Hey, you cut your hair, didn't you,' said her mother when they were outside the metro station.

'I wondered when you were going to notice.'

'It is really awful. Why did you do it?'

Camille ran down the stairs as fast as she could.

Air, quickly, air.

8

Camille knew the girl was there even before she saw her. From the smell.

A sort of sweet and cloying perfume, nauseating. She dashed for her room and caught a glimpse of them in the living room. Franck was sprawled on the floor, laughing stupidly as he watched the girl sway her hips. The music was on full blast.

'Evening,' blurted Camille as she went by.

Closing her door, she heard him mutter, 'Ignore her. Who gives a shit, okay? Go on, keep moving – yeah . . .'

It wasn't music, it was noise. Enough to drive you crazy. Walls, picture frames, even the floor, everything vibrating. Camille waited a few more minutes then went to interrupt: 'Hey, you'd better turn it down. We'll get in trouble with the neighbours.'

The girl stopped moving and began to giggle.

'Hey Franck, is that her? Is that her, huh? Are you the Conchita?'

Camille stared at her for a long time. Philibert was right: it was truly amazing.

A distillation of silliness and vulgarity. Platform shoes, jeans with frills and flounces, black bra, fishnet sweater with holes, home-styled highlights and rubbery lips: picture perfect.

'Yes, it's me,' said Camille. Then looking at Franck, 'Turn it down, please.'

'Christ, you know how to piss me off. Just go away. Go on, back to beddy-byes in your basket.'

'Isn't Philibert around?'

'Nah, he's off with Napoleon. Go on, back to your basket, I said.'

The girl was laughing louder than ever.

'Where's the loo, hey, where's the loo?'

'Turn it down or I'll call the cops.'

'Yeah sure, you do that, call the cops and stop pissing us off. Go on! Get the hell out of here, I said!'

Unlucky. Camille had just spent a few hours with her mother.

But Franck had no way of knowing that.

So, unlucky.

Camille turned on her heel, went into Franck's room, trampled over his stuff, opened the window, unplugged the stereo and tossed it out, from the fourth floor.

She went back into the living room and stated calmly, 'That's fine. No need to call the cops after all.'

Then, as she turned to go, 'Hey, close your mouth, codface, you might swallow a fly.'

She locked herself in. He pounded on the door, shouted, brayed, threatened her with the worst sort of revenge. All that time she looked at herself in the mirror with a smile on her face, and saw a very interesting self-portrait there. Pity she was in no state to draw anything: her palms were too damp.

She waited until she heard the front door slam before she ventured back out into the kitchen to eat a bite, and then she went to bed.

He took his revenge in the middle of the night.

At four in the morning Camille was awoken by a long drawn-out clamouring coming from the room next door. He grunted, she moaned. He grunted, she moaned.

Camille sat up and waited for a moment in the dark, wondering if it might not be best just to throw her stuff together there and then, and head for home.

No, she murmured, no, that's just what he wants. What a racket, I swear to God, what a racket. They must be doing it on purpose, it's impossible otherwise. He must have asked her to overdo it, there's no way. Hey, did she come with a special wah-wah pedal or something, stupid cow?

Franck had won.

She'd made her decision.

She couldn't get back to sleep.

She rose very early that morning and silently got to work. She took the sheets off the bed, folded them, and found a big bag to take them to the laundry in. She got her things together and piled them into the same little box she had come with. She felt horrible. It wasn't so much the idea of going back up there which bothered her, but of leaving this room. The scent of dust, the light, the soft rustling of the silk curtains, the cracking noises, the lampshades, the misty mirror. The strange impression of living outside time. Far from the world. Philibert's ancestors had eventually accepted her and she'd had a grand time drawing them in different guises and situations. The old Marquis above all had turned out to be much funnier than expected. Younger, jollier. She unplugged her fireplace and regretted the lack of any cord storage. She didn't dare roll it along the corridor so she left it by the door.

Then she took her sketchbook, made herself some tea and went to sit in the bathroom. She had promised herself she'd take it with her. It was the loveliest room in the house.

She moved all of Franck's things out of the way – his Mennen X deodorant for 'us guys', his scruffy old toothbrush, his Bic razors, his gel for sensitive skin – that beat everything – and his clothes which stank of stale fat. She tossed everything into the bathtub.

The first time she'd come in here she couldn't help but exclaim with delight, and Philibert had told her that the entire bathroom was a Porcher model, from 1894. It had been one of his great-grandmother's whims: she was one of the most elegant Parisiennes of the Belle Époque. A bit too elegant in fact, if you were to judge by his grandfather's eyebrows whenever he talked about her and told stories of her escapades. Better than Offenbach.

When the bathroom was first installed, all the neighbours gathered to complain because they thought it was going to go through the floor; then they came to admire and ooh and ah. It was the finest in the whole building, perhaps in the entire street.

It was intact, a bit chipped here and there, but intact.

Camille sat on the laundry basket and drew the shape of the tiles, the friezes, the arabesques, the huge porcelain bathtub with its four lion's-claw feet, the worn chrome, the enormous showerhead which had been inoperable since World War I, the soap dishes scalloped like holy water fonts, and the towel racks coming loose from the wall. The empty perfume flasks: *Shocking* by Schiaparelli, *Transparent* by Houbigant, *Le Chic* by Molyneux, the boxes of *La Diaphane* talcum powder, the blue irises which lined the bidet; and the sinks, so well-wrought, so elaborate, so loaded with flowers and birds that she'd always felt reluctant about putting her hideous wash bag down on the yellowed shelf. The original toilet bowl was no more, but the cistern was still fixed to the wall. Camille completed her inventory with a sketch of the swallows that had been flitting to and fro up there for over a century.

Her sketchbook was nearly full. Only two or three more pages.

She didn't have the heart to leaf through it, and she saw this as a sign. End of sketchbook, end of holiday.

She rinsed out her mug and left, closing the door behind her very quietly. While the sheets were spinning she went to Darty's near the Madeleine and bought a new stereo for Franck. She didn't want to owe him anything. She hadn't had time to see the make of his stereo, so she let herself be guided by the salesman.

She liked that, being guided.

When she came back, the apartment was empty. Or silent. She didn't try to find out which. She left the Sony box outside his door, piled the sheets on to her former bed, bade farewell to the ancestors' gallery, closed the shutters, and rolled her fireplace as far as the pantry. She couldn't find the key. Never mind; she put her box on top of the fireplace along with her kettle, and left for work.

As evening fell and the cold air did its dreary work, she could feel a dryness in her mouth, a pit in her stomach: the stones were back. She tried to use her imagination to keep from crying, and eventually persuaded herself that she was like her mother: holidays just irritated her.

She worked alone and in silence.

Camille didn't feel like carrying on with this journey. Might as well face the facts: she wasn't going to make it.

She would go back up there, into Louise Leduc's room, and check out.

At last.

*

142

A little note on Monsieur Erstwhile Piglet's desk roused her from her sordid thoughts:

Who are you? enquired a cramped, black handwriting.

She put down her spray bottle and her dusters, took a seat in the enormous leather armchair and looked for two sheets of white paper.

On the first she drew a sort of Yosemite Sam, hairy and toothless, leaning on a mop and smiling maliciously. A litre of red wine stuck out from the pocket of her blouse: *All-Kleen, professionals etc.*, confirming, *Well, this is me.*

On the second sheet she drew a 1950s pinup. Hand on hip, mouth like a hen's arse, one leg at an angle, and breasts squeezed into a pretty lace apron. She was holding a feather-duster, retorting, *What do you mean? This is me.*

She used a highlighter to give herself pink cheeks.

Because of the time wasted on this nonsense, Camille missed the last train and had to walk home. Puh, maybe it was just as well. Another sign in the end. She'd almost touched bottom, but not just yet, was that it?

One more effort.

Another few hours in the cold and that would be it.

When she pushed open the front door she remembered that she hadn't returned her keys and that she had to get her stuff out into the service stairway.

And write a little note to her host, perhaps?

Camille headed for the kitchen and was annoyed to see that there was a light on. Surely it would be Lord Marquet de La Durbellière, sad-faced knight, with his plum in his mouth and his arsenal of phoney pretexts to make her stay. For a split second she thought of turning back. She didn't have the strength to listen to his waffling. But okay, just in case she didn't die tonight, she did need her heater.

9

He was at the other end of the table, fiddling with the opener on his beer can.

Camille closed her hand around the door handle and felt her nails go right into her palm.

'I was waiting for you,' he said.

'Oh?'

'Yeah.'

She was silent.

'Don't you want to sit down?'

'No.'

They remained like that, in silence, for a long while.

'Have you seen the keys to the back stairs?' she asked, finally.

'In my pocket.'

'Give them to me.'

'No.'

'Why?'

'Because I don't want you to leave. I'm the one who's gonna leave. If you're not here, Philibert will be angry with me until the end of his days. Earlier today when he saw your box he already went berserk, and he hasn't been out of his room since. So I'm going to leave. Not for your sake, for his. I can't do that to him. He'd get the way he was before and I don't want that. He doesn't deserve it. He helped me when I was in deep shit so I don't want to hurt him. I don't want to see him suffer, or squirm like some worm whenever anyone asks him a question, no way, never again. He was already better before you got here but since you've been here he's almost normal and I know he's not taking as many pills either. You don't need to leave. I've got a mate who can put me up until after the holidays.'

Silence.

'Can I have one of your beers?'

'Go ahead.'

Camille poured a glass and sat down across from him.

'Can I light a cigarette?'

'Go ahead, I said. Pretend I'm not here.'

'No, I can't do that. It's impossible. When you're in the room, there's so much electricity in the air, so much aggressive energy that I can't be natural, so . . .'

'So, what?'

'So I'm like you, would you believe, I'm tired. Not for the same reasons, I suppose. I don't work as hard, but the result's the same. Different, but the same. It's my head that's tired, know what I mean? And plus, I want to leave. I realize I'm really not cut out to live with other people and I –'

'You?'

'No, nothing. I'm tired, I said. And you're incapable of talking to people in a normal way. You're always shouting, you're always so . . . in your face . . . I guess it's because of your work, the atmosphere in the kitchen which rubs off on you . . . What do I know . . . And to be honest, I don't really care. But there's one thing for sure: I'm going to give you back your privacy.'

'No, I'm the one who's leaving you guys, I have no choice, like I said. You matter more to Philou, you've become more important than me.

'That's life,' he added, laughing.

And, for the first time, they looked each other in the eye.

'I fed him better than you will, that's for sure! But I really don't give a fuck about Marie-Antoinette's white hair. I really don't, not a camel's fart about any of that and that was my undoing. Oh, hey, thanks for the stereo.'

Camille rose to her feet. 'It's more or less the same one, no?'

'Probably.'

'Great,' she concluded dully. 'Okay, the keys?'

'Which keys?'

'Come on.'

'Your stuff is back in your room and I made your bed for you.'

'An apple-pie bed?'

'Shit, you really are a bitch, know that?'

She was going to leave the room when he tipped his chin toward her sketchbook:

'Are you the one who does those?'

'Where'd you find it?'

'Hey, take it easy, it was here, on the table. I just looked at it while I was waiting for you.'

She was about to pick it up when he added, 'If I say something nice to you, will you promise not to bite my head off?'

'You can always try.'

He took the sketchbook, flipped through a few pages, put it back down and waited a moment longer, until finally she turned around, and then he said:

'This is brilliant, you know. Really beautiful, really well drawn. It's . . . Well, this is just me saying it, I don't know that much about it, nothing at all even – but I've been waiting for you for almost two hours, in this kitchen where you freeze your balls off, and I didn't notice the time go by. I wasn't bored for one second. I looked at all these faces, here, old Philou and all these other people. You really captured them, you really make them look beautiful . . . And the flat, too. I've been living here for over a year and I thought it was empty – well, I didn't notice a thing. But you – well, they're really good, okay?'

Camille was quiet.

'Hey, now why are you crying?'

'Just nerves, I suppose.'

'That's a whole other ballgame. D'you want another beer?'

'No thanks, I'm going to bed.'

While Camille was in the bathroom she heard Franck banging loudly on Philibert's door, shouting, 'C'mon man! It's okay! She didn't disappear! You can go and take a leak now!'

She thought she could see the Marquis smiling at her from between his sideburns as she turned out her lamp, and she fell asleep at once.

10

The weather was gentler. There was a gaiety, a lightness, something in the air. People were rushing around hunting for presents, and Josy B. had dyed her hair yet again. A mahogany tint, really gorgeous, which set off the frames of her glasses. And Mamadou had bought a magnificent hairpiece. One evening, between two floors, Mamadou gave them a hairdressing lesson while the four of them clinked glasses, knocking back the bottle of sparkling wine they'd bought with the money from Josy's winning lottery ticket.

'But how long do you have to stay at the hairdresser's to get the hair plucked from your forehead like that?'

'Oh, not long, two maybe three hours. Some hairstyles take a lot longer, though. For my Sissi it took over four hours.'

'Over four hours? And what does she do all that time? Does she behave?'

'Of course not, she doesn't behave! She does like we do, she laughs, she eats, she listens to us tell our stories. We tell a lot of stories . . . Lots more than you guys do.'

'And what about you, Carine? What do you do for Christmas?'

'I put on two kilos. And you Camille, what d'you do for Christmas?'

'I lose two kilos. Just joking.'

'You going to be with your family?'

'Yes,' she lied.

'Okay, this is all very well, but,' said Super Josy, tapping on the face of her . . . etc. etc.

*

147

On the desk she read, *What is your name?*

Maybe it was just a coincidence, but the photo of his wife and kids had vanished. Hmm, how predictable, this guy. She threw out the sheet of paper and did some hoovering.

The atmosphere was lighter in the apartment, too. Franck no longer slept there and was in and out like an arrow when he came for his nap in the afternoon. He hadn't even taken the new stereo out of the box.

Philibert never made the slightest reference to what had happened in his absence the evening he was at the Invalides. He was the sort who couldn't stand the slightest change. His equilibrium hung on a thread and Camille was just beginning to realize the magnitude of what he had done, coming to get her that night . . . How he must have had to force himself. She also thought about what Franck had said about Philibert's medication.

Philibert informed Camille that he was going on holiday and would be absent until mid-January.

'Are you going to your château?'

'Yes.'

'Are you glad to be going?'

'Well, I suppose I'll be glad to see my sisters.'

'What are their names?'

'Anne, Marie, Catherine, Isabelle, Aliénor and Blanche.'

'And your brother?'

'Louis.'

'Only names of kings and queens.'

'Indeed.'

'And what happened to your name?'

'Oh, my name . . . I'm the ugly duckling.'

'Don't say that, Philibert. You know, I don't understand much about your aristocracy business and I've never had much time for your names beginning with "de". To tell you the truth, I even think it's a tiny bit ridiculous when you get down to it, a bit . . . old-fashioned, but one thing is for sure: you, Philibert, are a prince. A real prince.'

'Oh,' he blushed, 'a modest gentleman, a little provincial country squire at best . . .'

'A fine little gentleman, that's for sure. Hey, don't you think we could cut the formality and start saying "*tu*" to each other next year?'

'Ah! My little suffragette is back! Always another Revolution! I'd find it really hard to call you "*tu*".'

'Well, I wouldn't. I would like to be able to speak to you the way I'd speak to a friend and say, Philibert, thanks for all you – *tu* – have done for me, because you may not know it, but in a way you've saved my life . . .'

He didn't answer. He was looking down at the floor, once again.

11

She got up early to see him off at the station. He was such a bundle of nerves she had to take his train ticket out of his hand to get it stamped for him. They went for a cup of hot chocolate but he didn't touch it. As the departure time drew near, she saw his face grow tense. His tics had come back, and it was once again the poor bugger from the supermarket who was sitting opposite her. A tall young man who was needy and gauche and who had to keep his hands in his pockets to keep from scratching his own face when he adjusted his glasses.

She put a hand on his arm:

'You okay?'

'Oh, yes, fine, you've got an eye on the time, right? Right?'

'Ssh,' she scolded gently. 'Hey, everything's going to be fine. Everything is fine.'

He tried to agree.

'Is it that stressful to be going to see your family?'

'N-no,' he said, while nodding yes with his head.

'Think about your little sisters.'

He smiled.

'Which one is your favourite?'

'The – the youngest.'

'Blanche?'

'Yes.'

'Is she pretty?'

'She's – she's more than pretty. She – she's really gentle with me.'

Farewell kisses were out of the question, but Philibert grabbed her by the shoulder when they were on the platform:

'You – you'll take good care of yourself, won't you?'

'Yes.'

'Are you going to be with your f-family?'

'No.'

'No?' He made a face.

'I don't have any little sisters to make the rest easier to bear . . .'

'I see.'

From the window, he lectured her:

'Above all, d-don't let our little Escoffier in-intimidate you, all right?'

'No, no,' she reassured him.

He added something which she did not hear because of the loudspeakers. To be on the safe side she nodded yes yes, and the train pulled away.

She decided to walk back, but took a wrong turn without realizing it. Instead of heading left down the boulevard Montparnasse as far as the École Militaire, she went straight and ended up on the rue de Rennes. It was because of the boutiques, the Christmas garlands, the atmosphere.

She was like an insect, drawn to the light and the warm blood of the crowds.

Camille wanted to be one of them, to be like them – busy, excited, in a hurry. She wanted to go into shops and buy silly things so she could spoil the people she loved. She began to walk more slowly: who, in fact, did she love? Come on, come on, she scolded, lifting the collar of her jacket, don't start, please, there was Mathilde and Pierre and Philibert and her comrades of the mop. Surely here in this jewellery shop she could find some pretty things for Mamadou, who was so careful about her looks. And for the first time in a very long time, Camille did the same thing everyone else was doing at the same time everyone else was doing it: she was walking along, trying to work out how much her bonus would be. For the first time in a very long time she stopped thinking about tomorrow. And that wasn't just a manner of speaking. It really was about tomorrow, the very next day.

For the first time in a long time the very next day seemed . . . conceivable. Yes, that was exactly it: conceivable. She had a place where she liked to live. A strange, idiosyncratic place, like the people living there. She closed her fist around the keys in her pocket and looked back on the last few weeks. She had met an extra-terrestrial. An odd but generous individual, who stood a thousand leagues above the horde and yet did not act the least bit conceited. Then there was that other strange bird. Well, with him it was a bit more complicated. She didn't see what you could get out of him other than stories about bikers and sauté pans, but at least he'd been moved by her sketchbook, well, moved was a bit strong perhaps, let's just say affected. He was a bit more complicated but probably simpler, too: the operating instructions seemed to be fairly basic . . .

Yes, she had come quite a way, she thought, shuffling along behind the strolling shoppers.

This time last year she had been in such a pitiful state that she couldn't say her own name to the fellow from the emergency rescue who'd picked her up, and the year before that she'd been working so hard she didn't even realize it was Christmas; her 'benefactor' had been careful not to remind her for fear she might not keep up the pace. So what: she could say it now, no? She could say those few words which would have singed her lips not so very long ago: she was fine, she felt fine, and life was beautiful. There, she'd said it. C'mon, stop blushing, you fool. Don't look back. No one heard you muttering your inane gibberish, rest assured.

She was hungry. She went into a bakery and bought a few *chouquettes*. Perfect little choux pastry things, light and sweet. She stood licking her fingertips for a long time before she dared go back into a shop to look for some small presents for everyone. Perfume for Mathilde, jewellery for the girls, a pair of gloves for Philibert and some cigars for Pierre. Could she decently be less conventional? No. These were the easiest Christmas presents on earth and they were perfect presents.

Camille finished her shopping near the Place Saint-Sulpice and walked into a bookshop. Here too, first time in a long time. For so long she didn't dare go into places like this. It was hard to explain, but it hurt too much, it – No, she couldn't bring herself to say it. Such a weight of sadness, such cowardice, the risks she had no longer wanted to take. Going into bookshops, cinemas, exhibitions, or even just glancing in the windows of art galleries: that had meant pointing to her own mediocrity, her spinelessness, it had meant reminding herself that one day she had thrown in the towel, in despair, and that she couldn't remember what it was like, before . . .

To go into any of those places which existed by the grace of the sensibility of a few individuals was to be reminded of how futile her own life was.

She preferred the aisles of the local Franprix.

Who might understand? Not a soul.

It was a private struggle. The most invisible of all. The most persistent, too. And how many nights of office cleaning, toilet scrubbing, and solitude would she have to inflict upon herself to get through it?

She avoided the art section, she knew it only too well, she'd spent a lot of time here back when she was trying to complete her studies at the École des Beaux-Arts, then, later, for less noble purposes. Anyway, she had no intention of going there now. It was too soon. Or too late, precisely. It was like the business of the salutary little kick. Wasn't she at a time in her life when she should no longer count on the help of the great Masters?

Ever since Camille had been old enough to hold a pencil, people had been telling her that she was gifted. Very gifted. Too gifted. Very promising, much too clever, or too spoiled. Often they were sincere, at other times their words were more ambivalent, their compliments didn't take her anywhere, and today, now that she was good for nothing except frenetically filling up sketchbooks like a leech, she told herself she'd gladly exchange her two barrelfuls of dexterity for a teaspoon of artlessness. Or for a magic slate, why not. Bingo! and nothing left upstairs. No more technique, no more references, no more know-how, nothing. Begin all over again, from scratch.

A pen, you see, you hold it between your thumb and your index finger. No, wait, you hold however you want. After that, it's not hard, you don't even think about it. Your hands don't exist any more. The important thing happens elsewhere. No, this won't do, it's still too pretty. You're not being asked to come up with something pretty, you know. No one gives a damn about pretty. There are children's drawings and glossy magazines for that. So put on your mittens, little genius, little empty shell, yes, go on, put them on I tell you, and maybe at last you'll see, you'll draw an almost perfect failed circle.

So there she was wandering among the books. She felt lost. There were so many and she'd lost track of what was current for so long that all the covers with their bright red publicity belly bands made her dizzy. She looked at the jackets, read the blurbs, checked to see how old the authors were and made a face whenever she saw that they were born after her. Not a very smart way to choose a book . . . She went over to the paperbacks. The cheap paper and small type were less intimidating. The jacket of this one, a picture of a kid with a helmet and an old typewriter was weird, but she liked the way it began:

If I could tell you only one thing about my life it would be this: when I was seven years old the mailman ran over my head. As formative events go, nothing else comes close; my careening, zigzag existence, my wounded brain and faith in God, my collisions with joy and affliction, all of it has come, in one way or another, out of that moment on a summer morning when the left rear tire of a United States postal jeep ground my tiny head into the hot gravel of the San Carlos Apache Indian Reservation.

Not bad, that. Added to which, the book was square and fat and dense. There was dialogue, and bits of letters copied out and fun subtitles. She went on leafing through it and roughly a third of the way into the book came upon this passage:

'Gloria,' Barry said in his phony, doctorly way. 'This is your son Edgar. He's waited a long time to see you.'

My mother looked everywhere in the room but at me. 'Got any more?' she said to Barry in a light, airy voice that made my insides clench and hold.

Barry sighed, yanked open the fridge and pulled out a can of beer. 'This is the last one. We'll have to get more later.' He set it on the table in front of my mother and gave her chair a gentle shake. 'Gloria, it's your boy. Here he is.'

And gave her chair a gentle shake . . . perhaps that's what's meant by technique?

When she stumbled on this passage, near the end, she closed the book. Now she knew.

There's nothing to it, really. I go out with my notepad and people spill their guts to me. I show up on their doorsteps and they offer their life stories, their small triumphs, their secret angers and regrets. I usually put away my notepad, which is just for show anyway, and listen patiently until

*they've said all they have to say. After that is the easy part. I go home, sit
down in front of my Hermes Jubilee, and do what I've been doing every day
for the past twenty years: I type up all the gritty details.*

A head run over in childhood, a mother who was out to lunch,
and a little notebook deep in his pocket . . .

What an imagination.

A little further along Camille came upon Sempé's latest collection.
She undid her scarf and jammed it, together with her coat, between
her legs so it would be easier to give full rein to her admiration. She
turned the pages slowly and – the same thing happened every time
– her cheeks flushed pink. There was nothing she loved so much as
this world of great dreamers, the precision of his artwork, the
expressions on his characters' faces, the glass porches of suburban
bungalows, the old ladies' umbrellas and the infinite poetry of
everyday situations. How did he do it? Where did he find it all?
There they were: the candles, incense burners and large baroque
altar of Camille's favourite little bigot. This time, the lady was sitting
at the back of the church, holding a mobile phone and turning
slightly to one side as she said, *'Hello, Marthe? It's Suzanne. I'm at
Sainte-Eulalie-de-la-Rédemption, you want me to put in an order for you?'*

Delicious.

A gentleman in the bookshop turned around to stare when he
heard Camille laughing out loud, a few pages further along. It was
nothing special, though, just a fat lady talking to a pastry chef who
was hard at work. He was wearing a pleated chef's toque and a
vaguely world-weary expression, and he had an exquisite little pot
belly. The lady was saying, *'After all this time, I've remade my life, but
you know, Robert, I've never forgotten you.'* And she was wearing a hat
in the shape of a cake, a sort of chocolate confection with cream
identical to the one the pastry chef had just finished . . .

It didn't take much, just two or three strokes of ink; and yet you
could see that the character was fluttering her eyelashes with a
certain nostalgic languor, with the cruel nonchalance of women who
know they are still desirable . . . Little Ava Gardners of the Parisian
suburb, little femmes fatales with the latest Clairol rinse . . .

Six tiny pen strokes to convey all that: How did Sempé do it?

Camille put the treasure back in its place, musing that the world
could be divided into two kinds of people: those who understood

Sempé's drawings, and those who didn't. However naive and Manichean it might appear, her theory seemed to her to be spot-on. She knew a woman, for example, who, whenever she leafed through a *Paris-Match* and came upon one of Sempé's vignettes, could not help complaining, 'I really don't see what's so funny. One day someone will have to tell me where I'm supposed to laugh.' As luck would have it, that person was her own mother. How unlucky could you get?

As she made her way toward the tills, Camille lifted her eyes and encountered Vuillard's gaze. Nor was this just a manner of speaking: he was looking right at her. Tenderly.

Self-portrait with cane and boater. She knew the painting but had never seen such a large reproduction of it. The cover of an enormous catalogue. So there must be an exhibition on at the moment? But where?

'At the Grand Palais,' confirmed one of the salesmen.

'Ah?'

It was a strange coincidence. She had been thinking incessantly about him over the last few weeks. Her room with its heavy drapes, the shawl over the chaise longue, the embroidered cushions, the overlapping carpets and the warm light of the lamps: more than once the thought had occurred to her that it was like being inside one of Vuillard's paintings. Like being in the bowels of something, a cocoon, timeless, reassuring, stifling, even a bit oppressive.

She leafed through the display copy and was seized by another bout of acute admirationitis. It was so, so beautiful. This woman, as seen from behind, opening a door. Her pink corsage, her long black sheath dress and the perfect curve of her hips. How did he manage to capture that movement? An elegant woman, as seen from behind: the slight sway of her hips.

With nothing but a little bit of black paint.

How was such a miracle possible?

The purer the elements, the purer the work. In painting, there are two methods of expression, form and colour; and the purer the colours the purer the beauty of the work.

Excerpts from the artist's journal were interspersed throughout the text.

His sleeping sister; the nape of Misia Sert's neck; nannies in the square; the motifs on the little girls' dresses; the portrait of Mallarmé with his leaden expression; the studies for the portrait of Yvonne Printemps with her sweet little carnivorous face; the scribbled pages of his diary; the smile of his girlfriend, Lucie Belin. To capture a smile is almost totally impossible, and yet Vuillard succeeded. For almost a century, although we have just interrupted her in her reading, this young woman has been looking up at us with a slightly weary movement of her neck, yet her smile is tender, as if to say, 'Ah, it's you?'

And there was a little canvas she'd never seen before – not even a canvas in fact, but a sketch. *The Goose.* An amazing thing. Four men, two of them in evening dress with top hats, trying to catch a goose who couldn't care less. The masses of colour, the brutal contrasts, the incoherence of perspective. How he must have enjoyed himself that day!

One hour and a stiff neck later, Camille finally raised her head and looked at the price: ouch, fifty-nine euros. No. It wasn't reasonable. Next month, maybe. She already had something else in mind: the music she had heard on the radio the other morning while sweeping the kitchen floor.

Ancestral gestures, a palaeolithic broom and a damaged tiled floor: she'd been grumbling between two of the black cabochons when a soprano's voice stopped her in her tracks, making every single hair on her forearms stand on end, one by one. Holding her breath, Camille went closer to listen to the announcer as the piece drew to its close: *Nisi Dominus* by Vivaldi, *Vespri Solenni per la Festa dell'Assunzione di Maria Vergine.*

Okay, enough daydreaming, enough drooling, enough money spent, time to go to work.

The cleaning took longer that night because one of their clients had just had their Christmas party, organized by the workers' council. Josy shook her head in disgust when she saw all the mess they'd made, while Mamadou scavenged dozens of mandarin oranges and mini Danish pastries for her kids. They all missed the last metro but it didn't matter: All-Kleen would pay for their taxis. Oh, the luxury! Giggling, they each chose a driver, and wished each other a merry Christmas in advance, because only Camille and Samia had signed up to work on the twenty-fourth.

12

The next day, Camille had lunch at the Kesslers'. No way to get out of it. It was just the three of them, and the conversation was animated. No awkward questions, no vague answers, no embarrassed silences. A real Christmas truce. No, wait, there was one instance, when Mathilde expressed concern about survival conditions in the maid's room, where Camille had to lie a bit. She did not want to talk about moving out. Not yet. A certain wariness. The obnoxious little punk hadn't left yet and one psychodrama could hide another.

Weighing her present, Camille said, 'I know what this is.'

'No.'

'I do!'

'Go on then, tell us, what is it?'

The package was wrapped in brown paper. Camille untied the gift ribbon, put the unopened package down flat in front of her, and took out her propelling pencil.

Pierre was beaming. If only this pig-headed young lady could get back to work . . .

When she had finished, she held up her drawing: the boater, the red beard, eyes like two dark buttons, the dark jacket, the doorframe and the tendrilled knob of his cane: it was exactly as if she had just copied the cover.

Pierre didn't get it right away.

'How did you do this?'

'I must have spent over an hour yesterday just staring at the cover.'

'Do you already have a copy?'

'No.'

He breathed a sigh of relief, then asked, 'Have you started working again?'

'A little bit.'

'Like this?' he asked, pointing to the portrait of Edouard Vuillard, 'still the little performing dog?'

'No, no . . . I've been filling sketchbooks . . . not much really, just little bits and pieces.'

'Are you enjoying it, at least?'

'Yes.'

He quivered. 'Ah, excellent. Can you show me something?'

'No.'

'And how is your mother?' interrupted Mathilde with her usual diplomacy. 'Still poised on the edge of the abyss?'

'Down at the bottom, more like.'

'So everything's fine, then?'

'Just fine,' said Camille with a smile.

The rest of the evening was spent holding forth about art. Pierre commented on Vuillard's work, seeking affinities, establishing parallels, and losing himself in endless digressions. Several times he got up to rummage in his library for proof of his insight and, after a while, Camille had to sit all the way at the far end of the sofa to make room for Maurice (Denis), Pierre (Bonnard), Félix (Vallotton) and Henri (de Toulouse-Lautrec).

In his capacity as an art dealer, Pierre was irritating, but as an enlightened amateur he was a delightful conversationalist. Of course he said his share of stupidities – and who didn't, where art was concerned? – but he said them well. Mathilde began to yawn and Camille finished the bottle of champagne. *Piano ma sano.*

When his face had almost disappeared behind the plumes of smoke from his cigar, Pierre offered to drive her back. She declined. She'd eaten too much and really needed the long walk.

The apartment was empty and seemed way too big. Camille shut herself in her room and spent the remaining half of the night with her nose buried deep in her Christmas present.

She slept a few hours in the morning and met up with her co-worker earlier than usual; it was Christmas Eve and the offices emptied out at five o'clock. They worked quickly, in silence.

Samia left first and Camille stayed for a moment to joke with the security guard:

'So did they make you put on that beard and bonnet?'

'Not likely. It was a personal and autonomous initiative to cheer things up!'

'And did it work?'

'Puh . . . yeah, really. No one gives a fuck. The only effect it had was on my dog. He didn't recognize me and he growled, silly bugger. I swear, I've had some really dumb dogs, but this one is the dog's bollocks.'

'What's his name?'

'Matrix.'

'Is it a female?'

'No, why?'

'Oh, nothing. Okay then, take care. Merry Christmas, Matrix,' she said to the big Dobermann lying at the guard's feet.

'Don't hope for an answer, like I said, he doesn't understand a thing.'

'Nah.' Camille laughed. 'I wasn't expecting anything.'

The guy was a regular Laurel and Hardy rolled into one.

It was almost ten at night. Elegant shoppers hurried this way and that, their arms filled with packages. The women's feet in their patent leather pumps were tired and aching; children zigzagged among the traffic cones and gentlemen checked details in their diaries as they stood by entry phones in doorways.

Camille watched all this activity with amusement. She was in no hurry, so she queued outside a chic delicatessen to buy herself a nice dinner. Or a nice bottle, rather. She didn't know what to choose. Finally, she pointed to a piece of goat's cheese and two walnut rolls. Well, it was mainly to go with her Pauillac.

She uncorked the bottle and placed it not too far from a radiator to bring it to room temperature. Then it was her turn: she ran a bath and stayed there for over an hour, her nose level with the steaming water. She got into her pyjamas, slipped on some thick socks and chose her favourite sweater. A priceless cashmere . . . vestige of a bygone era. She unpacked Franck's stereo, set it up in the living room, prepared a tray, switched off all the lights and curled up under her duvet on the old sofa.

She glanced quickly through the little booklet: *Nisi Dominus* was on the second CD. Right, the Vespers for Ascension – it wasn't exactly the right mass, plus she'd be listening to the psalms out of order all over the place . . .

Oh, so what difference did it make?

What earthly difference?

She pressed the remote button and closed her eyes: paradise.

Alone, in this huge apartment, with a glass of ambrosia in her hand, Camille was listening to the voices of angels.

Even the crystal pendants on the chandelier were quivering with well-being.

Cum dederit dilactis suis somnum.
Ecce, haereditas Domin filii: merces fructus ventris.

That was track number 5, and she must have listened to track number 5 at least fourteen times.

And still, even the fourteenth time she heard it, her ribcage shattered into a thousand pieces.

One day, when the two of them had been alone in the car and she had just asked him why he always listened to the same music, her father replied: 'The human voice is the most beautiful instrument of all, the most moving . . . And even the greatest virtuoso in the world will never be able to give you even a fraction of the emotion that a beautiful voice can give you. That is our share in the divine. It's something you begin to understand as you get older, I think. At least, as far as I'm concerned, it's taken me some time to realize . . . but, hey, would you rather hear something else? Do you want *The Little Fishes' Mummy?*'

She had already drunk half the bottle and had just started on the second CD when the light was switched on.

It was brutal, she put her hands over her eyes and the music suddenly seemed completely inappropriate, the voices incongruous, almost nasal. In two seconds the whole world returned to purgatory.

'Oh, you're here.'

She didn't respond.

'You didn't go home.'

'Up there?'

'No, your folks' place.'

'Well, no, as you can see.'

'Did you work today?'

'Yes.'

'Oh okay, sorry, huh, sorry. I didn't think there was anyone here.'

'No harm done.'

'Whassat you're listening to? Castafiore?'

'No, it's a mass.'

'Oh yeah? You religious?'

She really should introduce him to the security guard. They'd get on like a house on fire, those two. Even better than those little old guys in the Muppets.

'No, not 'specially. Do you mind switching the light off again, thanks.'

He did as she asked and left the room but it wasn't the same. The spell had been broken. She'd sobered up and even the sofa no longer felt like a cloud. She tried to concentrate, however, picked up the booklet and hunted for the spot she'd reached on the CD:

Deus in adiutorium meum intende.

God, come to my aid.

Yes, that was exactly right.

Apparently that stupid bozo was looking for something in the kitchen, shouting and taking revenge on every single cupboard door: 'Hey, have you seen the two yellow Tupperwares?'

Oh, Christ.

'The big ones?'

'Yeah.'

'No. Haven't touched 'em.'

'Christ almighty . . . You can never find a thing round here. What the fuck do you do with the dishes, eat them or something?'

Camille pressed pause and sighed: 'Can I ask you a very personal question? Why are you looking for a yellow Tupperware at two in the morning on Christmas Eve?'

'Because. I need it.'

Right, that was it, the mood was shot. She stood up and switched off the music.

'Is that my stereo?'

'Yes, I hope you don't mind –'

'Shit, it's really cool. You really went to town for me there, hey!'

'Yup, I really went to town for you there, hey!'

He stared at her, wide-eyed.

'Why are you repeating what I say?'

'No reason. Merry Christmas, Franck. Hey, let me help you find your beloved container. Look, there, on top of the microwave.'

Camille sat back down on the sofa while he rummaged through the refrigerator. Then he walked across the room without saying a word, and went to take a shower. She hid behind her glass: she'd probably used up all the hot water . . .

'Christ, who used up all the hot water, for fuck's sake?'

He came back half an hour later in his jeans, bare-chested.

Very casually, he lingered a moment longer before pulling on his sweater. Camille smiled: she could see him coming a mile off – no, make that half-way to the moon and back.

'Do you mind?' he asked, pointing to the carpet.

'Make yourself at home.'

'I don't believe it. You're eating?'

'Cheese and grapes.'

'And before that?'

'Nothing.'

He shook his head.

'It's really good cheese, you know. And these are very good grapes. And the wine is very good, too. Would you like some, by the way?'

'No. No, thanks.'

Phew, she thought. It would really have got on her tits to share the Mouton-Rothschild with him.

'Okay?'

'Sorry?'

'I'm asking if everything's okay,' he repeated.

'Uh, yes. And you?'

'Tired.'

'Are you working tomorrow?'

'Nah.'

'That's nice, that way you'll get some rest.'

'Nah.'

What a brilliant conversation, right?

He went over to the coffee table, picked up a CD box, and pulled out his weed.

'Shall I roll you one?'

'No, thanks.'

'You really are a goody two-shoes.'

'I prefer this,' she said, holding her glass in his direction.

'You're wrong.'

'Why, is alcohol worse than drugs?'

'Yeah. And you can believe what I say, because I've seen my share of winos in my life, you know. Besides, this isn't a drug. It's like a sweet, Quality Street for grown-ups.'

'If you say so.'

'Don't you want to try?'

'No, I know what I'm like. And I'm sure I'd like it.'

'And so what if you do?'

'So . . . It's just that I have a problem with voltage. I don't know how to explain it . . . I often get the feeling I've got a button missing, you know, some knob for adjusting the volume. I always go too far to one extreme or the other. I can never find the right balance and whatever I take a fancy to – well, it always ends badly.'

She was surprised at herself. Why was she confiding in him like this? Slightly tipsy, maybe?

'When I drink, I drink too much, when I smoke, I fuck myself up, when I love, I go out of my mind and when I work, it's into the ground. Dead. I don't know how to do things normally, quietly, I –'

'And when you hate?'

'Well, that I don't know.'

'I thought you hated me.'

'Not yet,' she smiled, 'not yet. You'll know when I do. You'll see the difference.'

'Okay. So, is your mass over?'

'Yes.'

'What shall we listen to now?'

'Uh, I'm not sure we like the same sort of stuff, to be honest . . .'

'We're bound to have one thing in common at least. Hang on. Let me think. I'm sure I'll find a singer that you like too.'

'Go on, then, find one.'

He was concentrating on rolling his joint. When he'd finished he went to his room then came back and crouched down by the stereo.

'So what is it?'

'A babe magnet.'

'Richard Cocciante?'

'No way.'

'Julio Iglesias? Tom Jones? Phil Collins?'

'No.'

'Andrea Boccelli?'

'Ssh.'

'Oh! I know! Roch Voisine!'

I guess I'll have to say . . . This album is dedicated to you . . .

'Nooo.'

'Yeeees.'

'Marvin Gaye?'

'Hey!' he said, spreading his arms. 'A babe magnet. Like I said.'

'I adore him.'

'I know.'

'Are we that predictable?'

'No, you're not at all predictable, unfortunately, but Marvin does it every time. I have yet to meet the girl who can resist him.'

'There haven't been any?'

'Not one, not one. Well, maybe a few, but I can't remember. They didn't count. Or else we didn't have a chance to get that far.'

'You've known a lot of girls?'

'What do you mean by "know"?'

'Hey! Why're you taking it off?'

'Because that's the wrong song, it's not the one I meant to put on.'

'No, wait, leave it! It's my favourite! You wanted "Sexual Healing", is that it? Pfff, you *guys* are the predictable ones . . . Do you know the story behind this album, at least?'

'Which album?'

'*Here My Dear.*'

'No, I don't listen to this one much.'

'You want me to tell you?'

'Hang on. Let me get settled. Pass me a cushion.'

He lit his joint and stretched out, Roman style, his head resting on his palm.

'I'm listening.'

'Well. I'm not like Philibert, okay, I'll just give you the rough outline. So, *Here My Dear*.'

'You mean me?' he said.

'Just listen. Marvin's first great love was a girl called Anna Gordy. They say that the first love is always the last, I don't know if that's true, but for him in any case it's obvious he would never have become who he was if their paths hadn't crossed. She was the sister of this bigshot at Motown, the founder I think: Berry Gordy. She was in with all the right people and he was just oozing with talent, raring to go, hardly twenty years old and she was almost twice that age when they met. Right: love at first sight, passion, romance, money and the whole caboodle, so off they went . . . She was the one who gave him his start, who put him on track, helped him, guided him, encouraged him and so on. A sort of Pygmalion, I suppose.'

'A what?'

'A guru, a coach, the rocket fuel . . . They had a lot of trouble having a kid so they finally adopted one; fast forward, it's 1977 and by now they were in deep trouble as a couple. He had gone sky high, he was a star, a kind of god. And their divorce, like all divorces, was a big mess. I mean, like, what could you expect, there was so much at stake. Anyway, it was getting vicious so to calm things down and sort out the business side, Marvin's lawyers suggested that all the royalties from the next album should end up in his ex's purse. The judge agreed and our idol rubbed his hands: he'd decided he'd write just any old rubbish so that would be one hassle out of the way . . . Except that it turned out he couldn't. You can't dash off a love story just like that. Well, okay, maybe some people manage but not him. The more he thought about it, the more he realized it was too good an opportunity . . . or too pathetic. So he shut himself away and wrote this marvellous song that tells their whole story: how they met, their passion, hatred, anger . . . you hear that? Anger, when it all goes wrong? Then how you calm down and a new love starts . . . It's a really beautiful gift, don't you think? He poured his guts out, gave everything he could for an album that wouldn't make him a cent no matter what.'

'Did she like it?'

'His ex?'

'Yes.'

'No, she hated it. She was mad with rage and for a long time she couldn't forgive him for washing their dirty laundry in public. Listen, there it is, "This is Anna's song", do you hear? Isn't it beautiful? You have to admit it doesn't sound anything like revenge. It's still about love.'

'Yeah.'

'Makes you think.'

'And you believe that?'

'What?'

'That the first love is always the last?'

'I don't know. I hope not.'

They listened to the end of the disc in silence.

'Hey, it's almost four in the morning, shit. I'll be in great shape again tomorrow.'

He got to his feet.

'You going to see your family?' she asked.

'What's left of it, yeah.'

'Not much left?'

'About this much,' he replied, holding his thumb and forefinger close together and squinting. 'And you?'

'This much,' she answered, passing her hand above her head.

'Okay, then, welcome to the club. Right. G'night.'

'Are you sleeping here?'

'Does it bother you?'

'Nah, nah, just wondered.'

He turned around: 'Are you sleeping with me?'

'Pardon?'

'Nah, nah, just wondered.'

He chuckled.

13

When Camille got up, at around eleven, Franck had already left. She made a big pot of tea and got back into bed.

If I could tell you only one thing about my life it would be this: when I was seven years old the mailman ran over my head.

At the end of the afternoon she tore herself away from the story to go and buy some tobacco. This would be tricky on a holiday, but never mind, it was mainly a pretext so the story could settle and she'd have the pleasure of meeting up with her new friend again a bit later on.

The major avenues of the 7th arrondissement were deserted. Camille walked a long time until she found a café that was open and while she was there she called her uncle. Some of the sting was removed from her mother's jeremiads (I ate too much and so on) by the distant cheer of family effusiveness.

There were already a lot of Christmas trees out on the pavement.

She stopped for a moment to watch the acrobats on rollerblades at the Trocadero, and she was sorry she had not brought her sketchbook with her. It wasn't so much their laborious leaping and jumping that interested her, but the ingeniousness of their props: wobbly springboards, little fluorescent cones, lines of bottles, upside-down pallets and a thousand other devices for them to break their necks on while their pants fell down.

She thought about Philibert . . . What was he doing at that very moment?

Before long the sun disappeared and the cold grabbed her by the neck. She ordered a club sandwich in one of the huge, plush brasseries which lined the square, and on the paper tablecloth she sketched the blasé expressions of the cute local boys as, with their arms around ravishing young women all buffed up like Barbie dolls, they compared the cheques their grandmothers had given them.

She read another quarter inch of *Edgar Mint*, then crossed back over the Seine, shivering.

She was dying of loneliness.

I'm dying of loneliness, Camille muttered to herself, I'm dying of loneliness.

Should she go to the cinema? Hmm . . . and afterwards, who would she talk about the film with? What use are emotions you keep all to yourself? Camille slumped against the front door to open it and felt a sharp disappointment when she found the apartment empty.

She did some housekeeping for a change, then picked up her book. I never knew a sorrow that an hour of reading could not assuage, said one of those great men. Let's check it out.

When she heard the jingle of keys in the lock she adopted the pose of a person who really doesn't care, tucking her legs up underneath her, wriggling on the sofa.

He was with a girl. A different one. Not quite as flashy.

They hurried along the corridor and shut themselves in his room.

Camille put on some music to drown out their romping.

Mmm.

Mind-numbingly infuriating would hardly describe it. Absolutely mind-numbing . . .

Finally, she picked up her book and migrated to the kitchen, at the far end of the apartment.

A little while later, she overheard their conversation at the door.

'What, you're not coming?' said the girl, sounding surprised.

'Nah, I'm knackered, don't feel like going out.'

'Hey wait a minute, you've got a bloody nerve. I dumped my whole family to be with you. You promised we'd go and eat out somewhere.'

'I'm knackered, I said.'

'Go for a drink, at least?'

'You thirsty? Want a beer?'

'Not here.'

'Yeah, but everything's closed today. And I have to work tomorrow.'

'I don't believe this. I may as well just piss off, right?'

'Aw, come on,' he said, more gently, 'you're not going to make a scene, are you? Come and see me tomorrow night at the restaurant.'

'When?'

'Around midnight.'

'Around midnight. As if. Hey, that's it.'

'You angry or something?'

'Ciao.'

Franck didn't expect to find Camille in the kitchen all wrapped up in her duvet.

'You here?'

She raised her eyes, without replying.

'Why are you looking at me like that?'

'Sorry?'

'Like I'm some piece of shit or something?'

'Not at all!'

'Oh yes, I can tell!' He was getting annoyed. 'Do you have a problem? Something get up your nose, maybe?'

'Hey, it's okay, leave me alone! I didn't say a thing. I couldn't care less about your life. Do what the hell you want. I'm not your mother!'

'Hey. That's more like it.'

'What's for dinner?' he asked, inspecting the interior of the fridge. 'Not a thing, of course. There's never anything in here. What do you and Philibert eat, anyway? Your books? The flies whose arses end up in your gabby mouths?'

Camille sighed and reached for the corners of her heavy shawl.

'You leaving? Did you eat?'

'Yes.'

'Oh yeah, I forgot, you've put on weight, looks like.'

'Listen,' she shouted, turning back, 'I don't pass judgment on your life, so hands off mine, okay? Anyway, aren't you supposed to go and live at a friend's after the holidays? Yes, you are, aren't you? So, that means we only have one week to go. We should be able to manage that, don't you think? So listen, the easiest thing would be that you just don't say another word to me.'

A bit later, he knocked on the door of her room.

'Yes?'

He tossed a package on to her bed.

'What's this?'

He had already gone back out.

It was a soft square. The paper was hideous, all wrinkled, as if it had already been used several times, and it smelled funny. A closed-in smell. Like a cafeteria tray.

Gingerly, Camille opened the package and at first glance thought it was one of those straggly things for mopping the floor. A dubious gift from the handsome hunk next door. But it wasn't, it was a scarf, very long and loose and rather badly knitted: a hole, a thread, two stitches, a hole, a thread, and so on . . . Some new kind of stitch? The colours were . . . different, to say the least.

There was a little note with it.

The handwriting of a turn-of-the-century schoolteacher, pale blue, wobbly, full of loops; apologetic.

Mademoiselle,
Franck wasn't able to tell me the colour of your eyes, so I put a bit of
everything. I wish you a Merry Christmas.
    Paulette Lestafier.

Camille bit her lip. Together with the Kesslers' book – which didn't really count either because the subtext went something like, Well, there are people who manage to put a body of work together – this was her only present.

God it was ugly. My God, it was lovely.

She stood on her bed and wrapped it seductively around her neck, as if it were a boa, to entertain a Marquis . . .

Poo poo pi doo, waah.

Who was Paulette? His mum?

She finished her book in the middle of the night.

Right. That was Christmas over with.

14

Same old boring, snoring drone. Sleep, metro, stupid job. Franck wouldn't speak to her and she avoided him as much as possible. He was almost never there at night.

Camille decided to get out more. She went to see Botticelli at the Luxembourg, and Zao Wou-Ki at the Jeu de Paume, but she rolled her eyes heavenward when she saw the queue outside the Vuillard. Besides, there was Gauguin just opposite! What a dilemma: Vuillard was great, but Gauguin . . . A titan! She stood there like Buridan's ass, torn between Pont-Aven in Brittany, Polynesian islands, or the Place Vintimille. It was horrible.

She ended up sketching the people standing in the queue, the roof of the Grand Palais, and the stairway to the Petit Palais. A Japanese woman came up and begged her to go and buy a Vuitton bag for her. She held out four five-hundred euro notes, jiggling in place as if it were a matter of life or death. Camille held out her arms.

'Look,' she said in English, 'look at me, I am too dirty.' She pointed to her clumpy shoes, her baggy jeans, her heavy truck driver's sweater, her idiotic scarf, and the military cap that Philibert had lent her. 'They won't let me into the shop.' The girl made a face, put away her banknotes and went up to someone else thirty feet down the line.

On an impulse, Camille made a detour down the Avenue Montaigne. Just to see.

The security guards were really impressive. She hated this area, where money had the least amusing things to offer: bad taste, power, and arrogance. She hurried past the window of the Malo cashmere shop: too many memories. And on home, by the riverbank.

At work, nothing to report. Once Camille had finished her shift it was the cold weather which was hardest to bear.

She went home alone, ate alone, slept alone and listened to Vivaldi, hugging her knees.

Carine had a plan for New Year's Eve. Camille didn't feel at all like going, but she'd already contributed her thirty euros so that they'd leave her alone, but also to back herself into a corner.

'You have got to go out,' she lectured herself.

'But I hate that sort of thing.'

'Why do you hate it?'

'I don't know.'

'Are you afraid of something?'

'Yes.'

'Of what?'

'I'm afraid of someone shaking up my insides. And besides . . . I can get the same feeling of going out when I get lost inside myself. I wander around . . . There's plenty of room in there actually.'

'Are you nuts? It's tiny! Come on, your insides are beginning to smell.'

That was the type of conversation between herself and her poor conscience that could nibble away at her brain for hours on end . . .

When she got home that evening, Camille found Franck out on the landing:

'Did you forget your keys?'

He didn't answer.

'Have you been here long?'

He made an irritated gesture in front of his mouth to remind her that he couldn't speak. She shrugged her shoulders. She was too old to be playing at that sort of idiotic game.

Franck went to bed without taking a shower, without smoking, without bugging her. He was done in.

*

173

He came out of his room at about ten thirty the next morning, he hadn't heard his alarm, and didn't even have the energy to complain. Camille was in the kitchen, he sat down across from her, poured himself a litre of coffee and waited a moment before he started to drink it.

'You okay?' she asked.

'Tired.'

'Don't you ever take any holiday?'

'Yes. Beginning of January. So I can move house.'

She looked out the window.

'Will you be here at around three?'

'To open the door for you?'

'Yes.'

'Yes, I'll be here.'

'Don't you ever go out?'

'Sure, from time to time, but I won't go out then because otherwise you can't get in.'

He shook his head like a zombie.

'Okay, I'm out of here, otherwise the boss'll scalp me.'

He got up to rinse out his mug.

'What's your mother's address?'

He stood stock still by the sink.

'Why do you ask?'

'To thank her.'

'To thank her –' He had a frog in his throat, couldn't speak, 'Thank her for what?'

'Well, for the scarf.'

'Aah. That's not my mother, she didn't make it, it was my grandma.' He seemed relieved. 'No one but her can knit like that.'

Camille smiled.

'Hey, you don't have to wear it, you know.'

'No, I like it.'

'I nearly fell off my chair when she showed it to me.'

He was laughing.

'And wait, you haven't seen a thing – wait'll you see Philibert's.'

'What's it like?'

'Orange and green.'

'I'm sure he'll wear it. He'll just be sorry he can't kiss her hand to thank her for it.'

174

'Yeah, that's what I thought when I was leaving her place. It's lucky for her it's you guys. You two must be the only people on the planet I know who could wear those horrors and not look completely ridiculous.'

She looked at him for a moment then said, 'Hey, do you realize you just said something nice?'

'You mean it's nice if I treat you like a clown?'

'Oh, sorry, I thought you meant that Philibert and I have a certain natural class.'

He paused, then said, 'Nah, I was talking about your . . . sense of freedom, I guess. How lucky you are to live the way you do and simply not give a damn.'

His mobile phone rang. Worse luck, just when he was trying to say something sort of philosophical.

'Hey boss, yeah, I'm on my way. Yes it's fine, I'm ready . . . Well hey, Jean-Luc can do them . . . Hey wait, boss, I'm in the middle of trying to get off with some girl who's way more intelligent than I am, so, yeah, it is taking longer than usual . . . What? No I haven't called him yet . . . Anyway, I told you he wouldn't be able to . . . Yes I know they're all swamped, I know . . . Okay, I'll take care of it . . . I'll call him right away . . . What was that? . . . Forget about it, with the girl? Yeah, I'm sure you're right, boss.'

'That was my boss,' he announced, flashing her a goofy smile.

'Oh, really?' She acted surprised.

He dried his mug and went out, catching the door just in time to stop it from slamming.

Okay, the girl could be a bitch but she was anything but stupid, and that was good.

With any other chick, he would have hung up and that was that. Whereas in this case he'd told her, That was my boss, to make her laugh, and she was so smart that she'd done the you-could-have-knocked-me-down-with-a-feather routine to return the joke. When you talked with her it was like playing ping-pong: she could keep the pace and send you a smash ball into the corner just when you least expected it, and as a result you got the feeling you weren't so clueless after all.

He went down the stairs holding on to the banister and he could hear the creaking of the cogs and gears inside his head. With Philibert it was the same, that's why he liked talking to him.

Because he knew he wasn't as thick as he might seem, but his problem was words, that was all . . . He never had the right words so he tended to get annoyed just to make himself understood. It was true, and it really pissed him off in the end, shit.

That was one of the reasons he didn't feel like leaving. What the fuck was he supposed to do over at Kermadec's place? Booze, smoke, watch DVDs and leaf through car maintenance magazines in the bog?

Great.

Back to square twenty years old.

He had trouble concentrating during his shift.

The only girl in the universe who could wear a scarf knitted by his grandma and still look pretty: and she'd never be his.

Life sucked.

He stopped off to see the pastry chef before leaving, got told off because he still hadn't called his former commis, and went home to bed.

He slept only one hour because he had to go to the laundrette. He picked up all his clothes and stuffed them into the duvet cover.

15

Whatever.

There she was again. Sitting next to machine number seven with her bag of wet laundry between her legs. Reading.

He sat down opposite her and she didn't even notice. That was something which always fascinated him. How she and Philibert could concentrate like that. It reminded him of a commercial he'd seen of a guy slowly savouring his Boursin cheese while the whole world collapsed around him. Lots of things reminded him of commercials these days. Probably because he'd watched so much TV when he was little.

He played a little game: imagine you've just come into this rotten Lavomatic on avenue de La Bourdonnais on December 29th at five in the afternoon and you see this figure for the first time in your life, what would you think?

He slumped into the plastic seat, put his hands deep in his jacket pockets and squinted.

First of all, you'd think it was a guy. Like the first time. Maybe not a drag queen but a really effeminate guy all the same. So you'd stop staring. Although . . . You'd still have your doubts. Because of his hands, his neck, the way he was rubbing his thumbnail along his lower lip. Yes, you'd hesitate. So maybe he would turn out to be a girl, after all? A girl dressed in a sack, as if she were trying to hide her body? You'd try to look elsewhere but you wouldn't be able to help yourself, and you'd look back again. Because there was something going on. There was some sort of special air around this person. Or a special light?

Yes. That was it.

If you just came in this crummy Lavomatic on avenue de La Bourdonnais on December 29th at five o'clock in the afternoon and you saw this figure in the dreary neon lights, this is exactly what you would say to yourself: Holy shit. An angel.

Camille raised her eyes just then, saw him, did not react right away, as if she had not recognized him, then finally smiled. A very faint smile, a slight brilliance, a little sign of recognition among regulars.

'Got your wings in there?' he asked, pointing to her bag.

'Sorry?'

'Nah, nothing.'

One of the dryers stopped turning and she sighed as she glanced at the clock. An old tramp went up to the machine and pulled out a jacket and a ragged sleeping bag.

Now this was interesting. A theory he had, about to be tested against the facts: no normally constituted girl would put her things in to dry after a tramp had used the dryer, and he knew what he was talking about, he'd clocked up nearly fifteen years of automatic laundries in his life.

He watched her closely.

Not the slightest movement of recoil or hesitation, not the slightest grimace. She got up, quickly shoved her clothes into the dryer, and asked him if he had any change.

Then she sat back down and picked up her book.

He was a bit disappointed.

Perfect people could be really boring.

Before plunging back into her book she called to him, 'Hey –'

'Yes.'

'If I give a washer-dryer to Philibert for Christmas, d'you think you could plumb it in before you leave?'

Franck couldn't say a thing.

'Why are you smiling? Did I say something stupid?'

'No, no.'

He waved his hand: 'You wouldn't understand.'

'Hey,' she said, tapping her middle and index fingers against her mouth, 'you've been smoking too much lately, don't you think?'

'In fact, you're a normal girl.'

'Why are you saying that? Of course I'm a normal girl.'

Silence.

'Are you disappointed?'

'No.'

'What're you reading?'

'A travel journal.'

'Is it good?'

'Great.'

'What's it about?'

'Oh, I don't know if you'd be interested.'

'No, to be honest, I'm not interested at all,' he scoffed, 'but I like it when you tell a story. You know, I listened to Marvin's record again yesterday.'

'You did?'

'Yeah.'

'And?'

'Well, the problem is I don't understand a thing. That's the reason I'm going to go and work in London, to learn English.'

'When are you leaving?'

'I was supposed to have a place after the summer, but it's all fucked-up at the moment. Because of my grandmother. Because of Paulette.'

'What's wrong with her?'

He sighed. 'I don't really feel like talking about it. Tell me about your travel journal instead.'

He drew his chair closer.

'Do you know Albrecht Dürer?'

'The writer?'

'No, the painter.'

'Never heard of him.'

'No, I'm sure you've seen some of his drawings. There are some very famous ones. A hare. Grass growing wild. Dandelions.'

He stared at her blankly.

'He's my personal god. Well, I have a few, but he's my number one god. D'you have any gods of your own?'

'Uh . . .'

'In your work? I don't know, like Escoffier, or Carême, Curnonsky?'

'Uh . . .'

'Bocuse, Robuchon, Ducasse?'

'Oh, you mean role models? Well, I have some but they're not well-known, or at least not as well-known. Not as flashy. You know Chapel?'

'No.'

'Pacaud?'

'No.'

'Senderens?'

'You mean the guy from Lucas Carton's?'

'Yes. That's wild you know all this stuff. How d'you do it?'

'Hold on, I know him by name, but I've never been there.'

'He's a really good chef. I even have one of his books in my room. I'll show you. Him and Pacaud, for me, they're the masters. And maybe they're not as well-known as the others, but that's because they're in the kitchen. Well, I mean, that's what I'm telling you, what do I know. That's just how I imagine them. Maybe I'm completely wrong.'

'But when you're with other chefs, you talk don't you? Tell each other your experiences?'

'Not a lot. We're not very chatty, y'know. We're too tired to spend our time gassing. We show each other stuff, tricks we've picked up, we exchange ideas, bits of recipes we find here and there, but it doesn't usually go any further.'

'That's a pity.'

'If we knew how to express ourselves, put words together in nice sentences and all that, we wouldn't be doing that kind of job, for sure. At least I would quit right away.'

'Why?'

'Because . . . it's not leading anywhere. It's slavery. Have you seen my life? Call that a life? Well, uh, anyway I don't like talking about myself. So what about that book, then?'

'Yes, my book. Well, it's the journal Dürer kept when he travelled through the Netherlands between 1520 and 1521. A sort of road journal or logbook. Above all it's a kind of proof that I'm wrong to think of him as a god. The proof that he was a normal kind of guy too. He counted his pennies, he got cross when he realized he'd just been ripped off by the customs officers, he was always disappointing his wife, couldn't help losing when he gambled, he was naive and gluttonous, macho and full of himself too. But hey, that's not all that important, really, it just makes him seem more human. And, uh – should I go on?'

'Yes.'

'Initially, if he wanted to go on this trip it was for a really serious reason, for his own survival and his family's and that of the people who worked for him in his studio. Up to that that point he'd been under the protection of Emperor Maximilian I. A total megalo-maniac who'd just given him the most insane commission: to represent him, the Emperor, at the head of a procession and immortalize him for ever. The work was finally printed a few years later and it measured over fifty-four metres in length. Can you imagine?

'For Dürer, it was manna from heaven. Years of work guaranteed. Then, as luck would have it, Maximilian died not long after that and as a result Dürer's annual income was no longer a sure thing. Major drama. So, off he goes on the road with his wife and servant in tow to suck up to Charles V, the future emperor, and Marguerite of Austria, the daughter of his former benefactor, because he absolutely had to have the official income continued.

'Those were the circumstances. So he was sort of stressed out at the beginning but that didn't stop him being the perfect tourist. Amazed by everything he saw – faces, customs, clothing – as he visited his peers, and other craftsmen, admiring their work, and he visited all the churches, and he bought a ton of trinkets straight off the boat from the New World: a parrot, a baboon, a tortoise shell, branches of coral, cinnamon, a stag's hoof, and so on. He was like a kid with it all. He even went out of his way to see a whale that had washed up on the shore of the North Sea and was decomposing. And of course he was drawing. Like a crazy man. He was fifty, he was at the height of his art and everything he touched – a parrot, a lion, a walrus, a chandelier or the portrait of the innkeeper – it was, it was . . .'

'Was what?'

'Well here, look.'

'No, wait, I don't know a thing about art.'

'You don't need to know anything! Look at this old man, isn't he great? And this handsome young man, see how proud he is? How sure of himself he looks? He looks a bit like you, actually. Same haughtiness, same dilated nostrils . . .'

'Oh, yeah? You think he's handsome?'

'Though he looks like the sort who deserves a good slap in the face.'

'That's his hat makes you think that.'

'Yeah, you're right,' she smiled, 'it must be the hat. And what about the skull, there, isn't it incredible? You get the feeling he's thumbing his nose at us, provoking us, "Hey, you too you guys, this is what's waiting for you." '

'Show me.'

'There. But what I like best are his portraits, and what kills me is how casually he just dashes them off. In this case, during his trip, they were mostly like hard currency, something to barter, nothing more: your know-how for mine, your portrait for some dinner, a rosary, a trinket for my wife or a rabbit-skin coat. Me, I'd love to have lived in those days. I think barter is a brilliant type of economy.'

'So what happened in the end? Did he manage to get his money?'

'Yes, but the price he paid . . . Fat Marguerite looked down her nose at him, even went so far as to refuse the portrait of her father that Dürer had made just for her, fat cow. So what did he do, swap it for a sheet! What's more, he came home sick, some nasty bug he picked up when he went to see the whale, actually. Marsh fever or something. Look, there's a free machine now.'

Franck got up with a sigh.

'Turn around, I don't want you to see my underwear.'

'Oh, I don't need to see it to imagine it. Philibert must be more the type to wear striped briefs but you, I'm sure you wear those tight little boxer shorts from Hom with stuff written on the waistband.'

'Hey, you're so smart. Go on, look the other way, anyway.'

He acted busy, went for the half-container of powder and leaned his elbows on the machine:

'Well, maybe you're not so smart after all. I mean otherwise you wouldn't be doing house cleaning, you'd be like your Dürer guy, there, you'd be working.'

Silence.

'You're right. I'm only smart in the men's underwear department.'

'Well, that's already something, isn't it? Might be a window of opportunity there for you. Hey, are you free on the thirty-first?'

'You got a party for me?'

'No. Some work.'

16

'Why not?

'Because I'm useless!'

'Wait, no one's going to ask you to cook! Just give a hand with the prep.'

'What's that?'

'Everything you prepare in advance to save time when the gun is fired.'

'So what would I have to do?'

'Peel chestnuts, clean chanterelles, skin and deseed the grapes, wash the lettuce . . . Basically a lot of really boring stuff.'

'I'm not even sure I could.'

'I'll show you everything, I'll explain really well.'

'You won't have time.'

'No . . . that's why I'd brief you beforehand. I'll bring some stuff back to the apartment tomorrow and I'll train you during my break.'

Camille stared at him in silence.

'Aw, c'mon, it'd do you good to see some people. You live with all these dead people, talking with guys who aren't even there to answer you. You're all alone all the time, no wonder you're not firing on all your cylinders.'

'I'm not firing on all my cylinders?'

'No.'

'Listen. I'm asking you as a favour. I promised my boss I'd find him someone to give a hand, and I can't find anyone. I'm in deep shit, now.'

Still her stubborn silence.

'C'mon . . . one last effort. After that I'll clear out and you'll never see me again in your life.'

'I had a party planned.'

'What time do you have to be there?'

'I don't know, around ten.'

'No problem. You'll be there, I'll pay your taxi.'

'Okay . . .'

'Thanks. Turn around again, my laundry's dry.'

'I have to leave anyway. I'm already late.

'Okay, see you tomorrow.'

'You sleeping here tonight?' asked Camille.

'No.'

'You disappointed?' said Franck.

'You can be so hea-vy . . .'

'Hey, I'm doing you a favour, okay? Because who knows, you might not be right about the boxer shorts!'

'Hang on a minute, if you knew how much I really don't give a stuff about your boxer shorts!'

'Too bad for you, then.'

17

'Shall we get started?'

'I'm listening. What's that?'

'What?'

'That case.'

'This? It's my knife case. My brushes, if you like. If I lost this, I'd be no good to anyone,' he sighed. 'You see what my life depends on? An old box that doesn't close properly.'

'How long have you had it?'

'Phew . . . Since I was a kid . . . It was my grandma who bought it for me when I started on my vocational training certificate.'

'Can I have a look?'

'Go ahead.'

'So tell me . . .'

'What about?'

'What each one is for. I like to learn.'

'So . . . The big one is the kitchen knife, or the chef's knife, you can use it for everything; the square one is for bones, joints, or to flatten the meat; and the little one is the all-purpose knife, the kind you find in every kitchen, why don't you take it just now, you're going to need it. The long one is a dicer for chopping and slicing vegetables, the little one there is a de-nerver for trimming and removing the fat from the meat, and its twin there, the one with the rigid blade, is for boning; the very thin one is for filleting fish and the last one is for slicing ham.'

'And this thing is to sharpen them.'

'That's a yes.'

'And this?'

'That's nothing, it's for decoration, but I haven't used it in a very long time.'

'What's it for?'

'For doing wonders. I'll show you some other day. Okay, you all set?'

'Yes.'

'Watch carefully, okay? Chestnuts, I better warn you right away, are a real hassle. These ones have already been soaked in boiling water so they'll be easier to peel. Well, that's if all goes well. Whatever happens, you mustn't spoil them. These little veins have to stay intact and visible. After the shell there's this cottony thing here, and you have to pull it off as delicately as possible.'

'But it takes for ever!'

'Hey. That's why we need you.'

Franck was patient. He went on to explain how to clean the chanterelle mushrooms with a damp cloth, and how to rub away the earth without spoiling them.

She was having fun. She was good with her hands. She was furious that she couldn't keep up with him, but it was fun. The grapes rolled through her fingers and she quickly got the knack of removing the seed with the tip of the knife blade.

'Okay, we'll go over the rest tomorrow. Lettuce and all that, you should be okay.'

'Your boss is going to see right away that I'm useless.'

'Well, obviously. But he doesn't have a lot of choice. What size are you?'

'I don't know.'

'I'll find you a pair of trousers and a jacket. And your shoe size?'

'Forty.'

'Got any trainers?'

'Yes.'

'They're not ideal but they ought to be okay for this one time.'

She rolled a cigarette while he was tidying up the kitchen.

'Where's your party?'

'Bobigny. At one of my co-workers'.'

'You're not worried about starting tomorrow morning at nine?'

186

'No.'

'I warn you, there's only one short break. One hour max. No lunch service but there will be over sixty place settings in the evening. Special menu for everyone. Should really be something. Two hundred and twenty euros per person I think. I'll try to let you go as early as possible, but I reckon you'll be there until eight o'clock at least.'

'And you?'

'Pfff . . . I'd rather not even think about it. New Year's Eve dinners are always the pits. But hey, it's well paid. And by the way, I'll ask for good pay for you, too.'

'Oh, that's not a problem.'

'Yes, yes, that is a problem. You'll see, tomorrow evening.'

18

'Time to go now. We'll have a coffee when we get there.'
  'But these trousers are way too big for me!'
  'Doesn't matter.'
  They crossed the Champ-de-Mars at a run.

Camille was surprised by the atmosphere of agitation and concentration which already reigned in the kitchen.
  It was suddenly so hot.
  'Here you go, boss. A brand new commis.'
  The boss grumbled something and waved them away with the back of his hand. Franck introduced her to a tall guy who didn't seem to be awake yet: 'This here's Sebastien. He's the *garde-manger* man. He'll also be your *chef de partie* and your big boss, okay?'
  'Nice to meet you.'
  'Mmm.'
  'You won't be dealing with him, but with his commis.'
  Turning to Sebastien, Franck asked, 'What's his name again?'
  'Marc.'
  'Is he here?'
  'In the cold store.'
  'Okay, I'm handing her over to you.'
  'What does she know how to do?'
  'Nothing. But you'll see, she does it well.'
  And he went to get changed in the locker room.
  'Did he show you how to do chestnuts?'
  'Yes.'

'Okay, there they are.' He pointed to a huge pile.

'Can I sit down?'

'No.'

'Why not?'

'No asking questions in a kitchen, you say, "Yes, sir," or "Yes, boss." '

'Yes, boss.'

Yes, asshole. Why on earth had she agreed to do this job? She'd go much faster if she could sit down.

Fortunately, a coffee pot was already on the boil. She put her mug down on a shelf and got to work.

A quarter of an hour later – her hands were already aching – Camille heard someone ask her: 'Everything okay?'

She looked up and was dumbfounded.

She didn't recognize him. Spotless trousers, an impeccably ironed jacket with a double row of round buttons and his name embroidered in blue letters; a little pointed bandana, immaculate apron and dishtowel, and his toque resting nice and tight on his head. She'd never seen him dressed any other way than as a consummate slob; she found him very handsome indeed.

'What is it?'

'Nothing. You're very handsome like that.'

And just look at him, bloody idiot, stupid fart, braggart, little provincial matador with his loud mouth, his big motorcycle and his thousands of bimbos notched on the butt of his battering ram: yes, that's him, the very same man – and he cannot stop himself from blushing.

'It's the uniform that does it, I expect,' she added with a smile, to let him off the hook.

'Yeah, that – that must be it.'

He moved away, bumped into a co-worker, and spattered him with insults.

No one spoke. All you could hear was the clack-clack of the knives, the glup-glup of the mixing bowls, the blam-blom of the swinging doors, and the phone ringing every five minutes in the boss's office.

Camille was fascinated, torn between concentrating on her work so she would not get told off, and looking up so she wouldn't miss a thing. She could see Franck in the distance, from behind. He seemed taller and much calmer than usual. It was as if she did not know him.

In a low voice she asked her fellow peeler:

'What does Franck do?'

'Who?'

'Lestafier.'

'He's the *saucier* and he's in charge of the meat.'

'Is it hard?'

The pimply boy rolled his eyes: 'Totally. The hardest thing of all. After the chef and the second, he's number three in the team.'

'Is he good?'

'Yeah. He's a jerk but he's good. I'd even say he's really good. And you'll see, the chef is always turning to him, not to the second. The second he has to keep an eye on, but Lestafier, he leaves him alone, even watches how he does it.'

'But –'

'Shh.'

When the boss clapped his hands to announce time for the break, she raised her head and made a face. Her neck ached, her back, her wrists, hands, legs, and feet all ached, and she hurt in other muscles she didn't even know she had.

'You want to eat with us?' Franck asked her.

'Do I have to?'

'No.'

'Then, I'd prefer to go out and walk around a bit.'

'Whatever. Are you okay?'

'Yes. It's hot in here, isn't it. You're working hard.'

'Are you kidding? This is nothing! There aren't even any customers!'

'Well . . .'

'You'll be back in an hour, okay?'

'Okay.'

'Don't go out right away, cool off a bit otherwise you'll catch your death.'

'All right.'

'You want me to come with you?'

'No, no. I feel like being alone.'

190

'You'd better eat something, okay?'

'Yes, Dad.'

Franck shrugged his shoulders: 'Tsk.'

Camille ordered a disgusting panini in a snack bar for tourists and sat down on a bench at the foot of the Eiffel Tower.

She missed Philibert.

She dialled the number of the château on her mobile phone.

'Hello, Aliénor de La Durbellière here,' said a child's voice. 'To whom do I have the honour of speaking?'

Camille was thrown.

'Uh, to – May I speak to Philibert, please?'

'We're having luncheon. Might I take a message?'

'He isn't there?'

'Yes, but we're having luncheon. I just told you –'

'Oh! Okay, right, no, nothing, just give him a kiss for me and tell him I wish him a Happy New Year.'

'Would you remind me of your name?'

'Camille.'

'Camille, just Camille?'

'Yes.'

'Very well then. Goodbye Madame Justcamille.'

Goodbye little squirt show-off.

What the hell was that all about? What sort of song and dance went on in that château?

Poor Philibert.

'In five separate batches of water?'

'Yes.'

'Well that'll be one clean lettuce!'

'That's the way we do it.'

Camille spent a ridiculous amount of time sorting and cleaning the salad leaves. Each leaf had to be turned over, calibrated and inspected with a magnifying glass. She had never seen salad leaves like this before, of every shape and size and colour.

'What's that?'

'Purslane.'

'And this?'

'Baby spinach.'

'And that?'

'Rocket.'

'And this?'

'Ice plant. Fig marigold to you.'

'What a lovely name.'

'Where are you from, anyway?' asked her neighbour.

She didn't pursue the matter.

Then she cleaned the herbs and dried them one by one in absorbent paper. Her job was to put them into small stainless steel containers and cover them carefully with clingfilm before distributing them into various cold boxes. She crushed walnuts and hazelnuts, peeled figs, rubbed an inordinate amount of chanterelles and rolled little mounds of butter between two ridged spatulas. She had to be careful not to make a mistake as she deposited one ball of unsalted butter and one of salted on to each saucer. At one point she was no longer sure and had to taste it with the tip of her knife. Yuck, she couldn't stand butter, so she was twice as careful from that point on. The waiters went on serving espresso coffees to whoever wanted them, and you could feel the pressure rising another notch with every passing minute.

Some of them didn't say a word, others swore in their beards and the boss acted like a speaking clock:

'Five twenty-eight, gentlemen . . . Six-oh-three, gentlemen . . . Six seventeen, gentlemen . . .' As if his heart's desire was to totally stress them out.

Camille had nothing left to do so she leaned against her work bench, raising first one foot then the other to relieve her legs. The guy next to her was practising making arabesques of sauce around a slice of foie gras on rectangular plates. With an airy gesture he would shake a little spoon and sigh as he inspected his zigzags. It never came out the way he wanted. And yet it looked lovely.

'What are you trying to do?'

'I don't know. Something a bit original.'

'Can I try?'

'Be my guest.'

'I'm afraid I'll spoil it.'

'No, no, go ahead, it's an old slice, it's just for practice.'

The first four attempts were hopeless, but by the fifth, she'd got the knack.

'Hey, that's really good, can you do it again?'

'No,' she laughed, 'I really doubt I could do it again. But . . . don't you have a pastry syringe? or something like that?'

'Uh . . .'

'Little pouch with a piping socket?'

'We do. Have a look in the drawer.'

'Can you fill one for me?'

'To do what?'

'Just an idea, you'll see.'

She leaned over, stuck out her tongue, and drew three little geese. Her co-worker called the boss over to show it to him.

'What the hell bullshit is this? C'mon . . . we're not working for Disney, you guys.'

He walked away, shaking his head.

Camille shrugged her shoulders sheepishly and went back to her salads.

'That is not cuisine. It's a gimmick,' grumbled the boss from the opposite end of the kitchen, 'and you know the worst of it? You know what kills me? It's that those idiots, they just love stuff like that. Nowadays that's what they want: a gimmick! Oh, well, it is a holiday after all. Okay, Mademoiselle, would you do me the honour of squirting your little farmyard on to sixty plates? And make it snappy.'

'Answer, "Yes, boss,"' whispered Marc.

'Yes, boss!'

'I'll never make it,' moaned Camille.

'Just do one at a time.'

'On the left or on the right?'

'On the left, it makes more sense.'

'It looks a bit sick, no?'

'Nah, it's funny. Anyway, you have no choice now.'

'I should have kept my mouth shut.'

'Rule number one. At least you'll have learned that. Here, this is the right sauce.'

'Why is it red?'

'Made from beetroot. Go on, I'll pass you the plates.'

They swapped places. She drew, he sliced the slab of foie gras, put it on the plate, sprinkled it with *fleur de sel* and coarsely crushed pepper, then handed the plate to a third guy, who added the salad as if he were working with gold leaf.

'What are they all doing?' asked Camille.

'They're going to eat. We'll go later. We have to open the ball, we'll go down when it's their turn to take over. Will you help me with the oysters?'

'Do we have to shuck them?!'

'No, no, just make them look nice. Actually, was it you peeled the green apples?'

'Yes. They're over there. Oh shit, looks more like a turkey, this one.'

'Sorry. I'll stop talking.'

Franck walked by, scowling. He thought they were a bit too casual. Or rather too cheerful.

He wasn't best pleased with the whole goose business.

'Are we having fun yet?' he asked, ironic.

'Doing what we can . . .'

'Just tell me, you don't have to heat it up, at least?'

'What did he mean by that?'

'Oh, it's a thing between us. The chefs who do the heating up feel like they've been entrusted with a supreme mission, whereas the likes of us, even if we make an enormous effort, they'll always look down on us. We don't touch the heat. You know him well, Lestafier?'

'No.'

'Oh yeah, that makes sense.'

'What?'

'Nah, nothing.'

While the others had gone off to eat, two black guys sluiced down the floor, then scraped it with a long rubber blade to make it dry faster. The boss was conversing with a very elegant man in his office.

'A customer already?'

'No, he's the maître d'.'

'Wow, he's classy.'

'They're all good looking, the ones who work on the floor. At the start of the work day, we're the ones who are clean and they go around vacuuming in their T-shirts and as the day goes by it tends to go the opposite way: we start to stink and get grubby and they walk by fresh as daisies, with their impeccable hairdos and suits.'

Franck came to see her as she was doing her last row of plates.

'You can get going if you want.'

'Well, no, I don't feel like leaving now. It'd feel like I'm missing the show . . .'

'Have you got some work for her?'

'Have I! As much as she wants. She can take over the salamander.'

'What's that?' asked Camille.

'That thing over there, a sort of grill that goes up and down. You want to do the toast?'

'No problem. Uh, actually, would I have time for a cigarette?'

'Sure, go on down.'

Franck went with her.

'You okay?'

'Great. He's a really nice kid, Sebastien.'

'Yeah.'

She was silent.

'Why the long face?'

'Because . . . I wanted to speak to Philibert earlier on to wish him Happy New Year and I got the brush-off from this snotty-nosed little girl.'

'Hey, I'll call him for you.'

'No. They'll be having dinner now.'

'Let me take care of it.'

'Hello? Excuse me for disturbing you, Franck de Lestafier speaking, Philibert's fellow lodger . . . Yes . . . The very one . . . Very nice to talk to you, Madame . . . Could I have a word with him, if you don't mind, it's about the boiler . . . Yes . . . Exactly . . . Au revoir, Madame.'

He winked at Camille, and she smiled as she exhaled her smoke.

'Philou? That you, angel? Happy New Year, sweetheart! I won't kiss you, but I'll pass you your little princess. What? Hey, who gives a fuck about the boiler! Listen, Happy New Year, the best of everything, and lots of kisses to your sisters. Well . . . only the ones who have big tits, okay?'

Camille took the phone, squinting. No, there was nothing wrong with the boiler. Yes, a big hug to you too. No, Franck hadn't locked her away in a closet. Yes, so did she, she thought about him often. No, she hadn't gone for her blood test yet. Yes, you too, Philibert,

Happy new Year to you.

'He sounded good, didn't he?' added Franck.

'He only stuttered eight times.'

'That's what I mean.'

When they went back to their stations, the wind changed. Those who hadn't yet put on their toque set it carefully on their head, and the chef leaned his belly against the serving hatch and folded his arms over it. You could have heard a pin drop.

'Gentlemen, to work.'

It was as if the temperature in the room was rising one degree per second. Everyone was suddenly busy, careful not to disturb his neighbour. Faces were tense. Stifled swear words ricocheted here and there. Some remained calm; others, like the Japanese fellow, seemed ready to implode.

Waiters stood single file by the serving hatch while the boss leaned over every single plate to inspect it, maniacally. The boy next to him used a tiny sponge to wipe any finger marks or splashes of sauce from the edge of the plate, and when the boss nodded, a waiter, clenching his teeth, would lift up the big silver tray.

Camille was doing the appetizers with Marc. She would put things down on a plate, some sort of chip or wedge of bark of a faintly reddish tint. She didn't dare ask any more questions. Then she added a few blades of chive.

'Get a move on, we don't have time for finishing touches this evening.'

She found a piece of string to hold up her trousers, and swore because her paper toque was for ever slipping down over her eyes. Her neighbour took a small stapler out of his knife box:

'Here you go.'

'Thanks.'

Then she listened to one of the waiters who was explaining how to cut the slices of brioche sandwich loaf into triangles, removing the crust.

'How toasted do you want them?'

'Well, golden, okay?'

'Go ahead, make a sample for me. Show me exactly the colour you want.'

'The colour, the colour . . . You can't tell by the colour, it's a

196

question of instinct . . .'

'Well, I'm a colour sort of person, so please make me a sample, otherwise I'll get stressed out.'

She took her assignment very seriously, and was never caught off guard. The waiters came for the toast, sliding each slice into the folds of a napkin. She would have liked a little compliment: 'Oh, Camille, your toast is superb!' but, oh well . . .

She caught a glimpse of Franck, from behind as usual, busy at his stove, like a drummer at his drums: bang a lid here, bang a lid there, a spoonful here, a spoonful there. The tall skinny guy, the number two or so she had gathered, was constantly asking him questions to which Franck rarely replied, and only then by means of an onomatopoeia. All his pans were copper and he had to use a cloth to pick them up. From time to time he must burn himself, for she often saw him lift his hand and shake it and then raise it to his mouth.

The boss was getting irritated. It wasn't going fast enough. It was going too fast. It wasn't hot enough. It was too cooked. 'Concentrate, gentlemen, concentrate!' he said, over and over.

The more the activity at her own station seemed to taper off, the busier it got on the other side. It was really something to watch. She saw how they were sweating and rubbing their brow on their shoulder the way cats do to wipe their head. Especially the fellow who was in charge of the rotisserie: he was bright scarlet and sucked on a bottle of water between each round trip he made with his poultry. (Funny things with wings, some much smaller than a chicken and others twice as big.)

'We're dying in here . . . how hot is it now, do you reckon?'

'No idea. Over there by the stove must be at least forty, fifty maybe? Those are the hardest jobs, physically. Here, take that over to the dishwasher. Mind you don't disturb anyone.'

Camille stared wide-eyed at the mountain of pans, baking trays, stewpots, stainless steel bowls, sieves and frying pans which stood piled in enormous dishwashing basins. Not a single white person on the horizon either, and the little guy she turned to merely took the implements from her hands, nodding his head. He obviously didn't speak a word of French. Camille stopped for a moment to gaze at him: every time she found herself face to face with someone who'd been uprooted from the ends of the earth, the little lights of her bargain basement Mother Teresa self began to flash frenetically:

where was he from? India? Pakistan? and what sort of life had he led to end up here? today? what boats? what trafficking? what hopes? at what cost? what had he had to give up, what were his fears? and the future? where did he live? with how many people? and where were his children?

When she understood that her presence was making him nervous, she went away again, shaking her head.

'Where's he from, the dishwashing guy?'

'Madagascar.'

Wrong again.

'Does he speak French?'

'Of course! He's been here for twenty years!'

Go and take a break, Miss Know-it-all.

She was tired. There was always some new thing to peel, chop, clean or put away. What a shit job . . . How did they manage to put up with it? What was the point of people stuffing their guts like this? They were going to burst! Two hundred and twenty euros, how much was that? Almost 1,500 francs. Jeez. Think what else they could do with that money. If they were clever they could afford a little trip. To Italy, for example. Sit down at a pavement café, drift off to the conversation of those pretty girls raising their little cups of thick, black, too-sweet coffee to their lips and, surely, telling each other the same rubbish as all girls the world over.

All the sketches, all the squares and faces and indolent cats and marvels you could have for that price. Books, records, even clothes: they could last a whole lifetime, whereas this . . . In a few hours, everything would be over, put away, digested, and evacuated.

She was wrong to reason like that, and she knew it. She was quite lucid. She had begun to lose interest in food as a child, because meal-times were synonymous with suffering. Moments that weighed heavily on a little girl who was an only child, and a sensitive one at that. A little girl alone with a mother who smoked like a chimney and tossed on to the table a meal prepared without a shred of tenderness. 'Eat up! It's good for you!' proclaimed her mother, as she lit another cigarette. Or alone with both her parents, Camille would look down in her lap as much as she could so as not to be caught in their net: 'Hey, Camille, you miss your daddy when he's not here, don't you? Isn't that right?'

Afterwards, it was too late. She'd lost any pleasure in food. Besides, there came a time when her mother didn't even prepare anything any more. Camille had developed her bird's appetite the way others became covered in acne. Everybody had bugged her about it, but she'd always been able to get around it. They had never managed to catch her out because she was one common-sense kid . . . She wanted nothing to do with their pathetic lives, but when she was hungry, she ate. Of course she ate, otherwise she wouldn't even be here any more. But without them. In her room. Yogurt, fruit, muesli, while she was doing other things. Reading, dreaming, drawing horses or copying out songs by Jean-Jacques Goldman.

Fly me away . . .

Yes, she knew her own weaknesses, and she would be a fool to judge those who were fortunate enough to enjoy sitting around a dinner table. But still . . . 220 euros for one meal, not even counting the wine, that was really lame, no?

At midnight, the boss wished them a Happy New Year and came to serve them all a glass of champagne:

'Happy New Year, Mademoiselle, and thank you for your ducks. Charles told me the customers were delighted. I knew they would be, unfortunately. Happy New Year, Monsieur Lestafier. Get rid of some of your bad temper in 2004 and I'll give you a rise . . .'

'How much, boss?'

'Ah! Don't get carried away! It is my infinite respect for you which will rise!'

'Happy New Year, Camille. Shall we . . . do you . . . shouldn't we kiss?'

'Sure, sure, of course, a kiss!'

'What about me?' said Sebastien.

'And me,' added Marc. 'Hey, Lestafier! Get back to your instrument, there's something boiling over!'

'Oh yeah, Ducon? Well, uh, she's done now, no? Maybe she can sit down?'

'Good idea. Come into my office, lass,' added the boss.

'No, no, I want to stay here until the end. Give me something to do.'

'Well, now we're just waiting for the pastry chef. You can help him decorate.'

She assembled wafers as thin as cigarette paper, crisped, crimped, creased in a thousand different ways; she played with flakes of chocolate, orange peel, candied fruit, arabesques of coulis and marrons glacés. The pastry boy watched her, clapping his hands together. 'You're an artist! This is one artist!' he said, over and over. The chef viewed such extravagance differently: 'Well, okay because it's this evening, but making things look pretty isn't the point. We don't cook to make things look pretty, for Christ's sake.'

Camille smiled as she topped the crème anglaise with a red coulis.

Alas, no, it wasn't enough just to make things pretty. Something she knew only too well.

At around two o'clock there was a sudden lull in the storm. The chef reached for his bottle of bubbly and some of the chefs had removed their toque. They were all exhausted but were making one last effort to clean their stations and get out of there as quickly as possible. Miles of clingfilm were unrolled to wrap everything, and the cold stores were a scene of pushing and shoving. There was a whole lot of commentary on the service and analysis of their performance: what they'd screwed up and why, whose fault it was, how the produce had been. Like athletes still steaming, they couldn't relax, and used the last of their strength to scrub down their stations the best they could. Camille thought it must be a way for them to work out their stress, and do themselves in, once and for all . . .

She helped out right to the end. Hunched over, cleaning the inside of a cold store.

Then she leaned against the wall and watched the flurry of young men around the coffee machine. Look at that one wheeling an enormous cart laden with sweet confections, chocolates, marsh-mallows, jams, mini-flutes, almond sponge fingers and so on . . . Hmm . . . and she felt like smoking a cigarette.

'You'll be late for the party.'

She turned around and saw an old man.

Franck was trying to look upbeat, but he was exhausted, drenched, slumping over, gaunt; his eyes were red and his features drawn.

'You look ten years older . . .'

'Could well be. I'm dead on my feet. I didn't sleep well and anyway I hate doing this sort of banquet. The same dish over and over. You want me to drop you off at Bobigny? I have a second helmet. I just have to finish my orders and we can go.'

'No. I don't feel like it any more, now. They'll all be high by the time I get there. The fun thing is getting drunk all at the same time, otherwise it's sort of depressing.'

'Okay, well, I'm going home, too, I can hardly stand up.'

Sebastien interrupted: 'We're just waiting for Marco and Kermadec, you wanna meet up afterwards?'

'No, I'm knackered, I'm going home.'

'What about you, Camille?'

'She's knackered too –'

'Not at all,' she interrupted, 'well, yes, but I still feel like partying!'

'You sure?' asked Franck.

'Well yeah, we have to ring in the new year don't we . . . so that it will be better than the last one, no?'

'I thought you hated parties.'

'I do, but this is my first good resolution, would you believe: "In 2003, I didn't believe in them, but in 2004 I'll go wild!"'

'Where are you going?' asked Franck with a sigh.

'Ketty's.'

'Oh no, not there, you know damn well –'

'Okay, what about La Vigie, then?'

'Not there either.'

'What a pain you are, Lestafier. Just because you claim to have laid all the waitresses within kilometres of here, there's nowhere left for us to go! Which one was it at Ketty's? The fat one with the lisp?'

'She didn't lisp!' Franck protested.

'No, when she was drunk she talked normally but when she was sober, she did lisp, actually . . . anyway, she doesn't work there any more.'

'You sure?'

'Yeah.'

'And the redhead?'

'The redhead doesn't either. Hey, what d'you care, anyway, you're with her, aren't you?'

'He is *not* with me!' protested Camille.

'Well, uh, you guys work it out between you, the rest of us are going to meet up when the others have finished.'

'Do you want to go?' asked Camille.

'Yes. But I'd like to take a shower first.'

'Okay. I'll wait for you. I'm not going back to the flat, otherwise I'll collapse.'

'Hey.'

'What?'

'Earlier on, you didn't kiss me.'

'Here you go,' she said, giving him a little peck on the forehead.

'That it? I thought in 2004 you were going to go wild.'

'Have you ever kept a single one of your resolutions?'

'No.'

'Me neither.'

19

Maybe because she was not as tired as they were, or because she held her alcohol better, it was not long before Camille had to order something besides beer to keep up with them. She felt like she had gone ten years back in time, to an era when she could still take certain things for granted . . . Art, life, the future, her talent, her lover, her place, her own little napkin ring here on earth and all that crap.

Well, it wasn't so unpleasant . . .

'Hey, Franck, you not drinking tonight or what?'

'I'm dead tired.'

'C'mon, not you. Aren't you on holiday, too?'

'Yes.'

'Well?'

'I'm getting old.'

'C'mon, have a drink. You'll sleep tomorrow.'

He held out his glass without much conviction: no, he wouldn't sleep tomorrow. Tomorrow he'd go to the Time Regained, the RSPCA for old folks, to eat crap chocolates with two or three abandoned grannies who'd play with their dentures while his own granny would look out the window and sigh.

Nowadays he had a pain in his gut from the moment he took the exit from the motorway.

He decided not to think about it, and emptied his glass in one gulp.

He stole sideways glances at Camille. Her freckles would surface and disappear depending on the time of day; it was a very strange phenomenon.

She'd told him he was handsome and now she was chatting up that big tall lump . . . whatever . . . all the same, he thought, with a sigh of disgust.

Franck Lestafier was feeling down.

He even felt a bit like crying.

And so what? What's wrong with you, man?

Where should I start? A shit job, a shit life, a grandma out west and a move coming up. Sleeping again on a rotten sofa bed, losing an hour at every break. No more seeing Philibert. No more teasing him to get him to learn to take a stance, answer back, get mad, or get his way, for Christ's sake. No more calling him my big candyfloss bunny. No more coming up with ways to set aside a nice doggy bag for him. No more impressing the girls with his king of France bed and his princess bathroom. No more hearing Philou and Camille talk about the war in 1914 as though they'd lived through it themselves, or about Louis XI as if they'd just had a pint with him. No more waiting for Camille to come in, or lifting his nose as he opened the door to sniff the air for cigarette smoke, a sign that she was already there. No more jumping on her sketchbook the minute her back was turned to see the day's drawings. No more going to sleep with the floodlit Eiffel Tower as his nightlight. And then he'd have to stay in France, sweat off a kilo with every service and put them back on again in beers afterwards. And go on obeying. Always. All the time. That's all he ever did: obey. And now he was stuck until . . . Go on, say it, until when, say it! Well, yeah, that was it. Until she snuffs it. As if he could only ever get his life together at the cost of greater suffering . . .

Fuck, I've had enough, all right? Can't you get off on someone besides me, now? Don't you believe me when I say I've had enough, okay?

My boots are full of shit, boys, so go and look somewhere else for me. As far as I'm concerned, that's it. I've done my bit.

She kicked him under the table.

'Hey, you okay?'

'Happy New Year.'

'Something wrong?'

'I'm going to bed. Ciao.'

20

Camille didn't stay long. They weren't exactly Foucault's crowd, either, those guys. They spent their time harping on about the really shit job they were doing, and there was good reason for it. And then Sebastien began to hit on her. If he'd wanted a chance to sleep with her, he should have been nicer to her that morning, stupid dickhead. That's how you could tell who were the good fucks: the boys who were nice to you even before they thought of getting you horizontal.

She found him curled up on the sofa.

'You asleep?'

'No.'

'Are you okay?'

'In 2004, I'll take to the floor,' he moaned.

She smiled: 'Well done . . .'

'Whaddya mean, I've been trying for ages to come up with a decent rhyme. I thought of, in the year 2004, I'll be greener than before, but you'd have thought I was going to throw up on you.'

'What a wonderful poet you're turning into.'

He fell silent. He was too tired to fool around.

'Put on some of that nice music we were listening to the other day.'

'No. If you're already sad, it won't help things.'

'If you put on your Castafiore, will you stay a little bit longer?'

'Length of one cigarette.'

'I'm up for it.'

And Camille, for the one hundred and twenty-eighth time that week, put on Vivaldi's *Nisi Dominus*.

'What's it about?'

'Hang on, I'll tell you. The Lord gratifies his friends in their sleep.'

'Great.'

'It's beautiful, isn't it?'

'I dunno,' he yawned. 'I don't know anything about it.'

'That's funny, that's what you said the other day about Dürer. But it's not something you can learn! It's just beautiful, that's all.'

'No, all the same. Whether you agree or not, it's still something you learn.'

She said nothing.

'Do you believe in God?'

'No. Well, yes. When I hear this kind of music, or go into a beautiful church or see a painting that moves me, an Annunciation for example, my heart fills up so much that I get the impression I believe in God, but that's wrong: it's Vivaldi I believe in. Vivaldi, or Bach, or Handel or Fra Angelico . . . They're the gods. The other one, the guy with the white beard, he's just a pretext. For me that's his only quality anyway: he was strong enough to inspire all the rest of them, all those masterpieces.'

'I really like it when you talk to me. Makes me feel more intelligent.'

'Go on.'

'No, really.'

'You've had too much to drink.'

'No. Not enough, actually.'

'Listen, this bit, isn't this beautiful, too? It's more cheerful. That's what I like about masses: the joyful moments, like the Glorias and all that, come and fish you back out just after those moments that make you sink. Like in life.'

A long silence.

'Are you asleep?'

'No, I'm watching the end of your cigarette.'

'You know, I –'

'You what?'

'I think you should stay. I think that everything you said about Philibert's potential reaction if I were to leave holds true for you too. I think he'd be really unhappy if you left, and by the same token you're just as accountable for his fragile equilibrium.'

'Uh, that last sentence, can you give it to me again in French?'

'Stay.'

'No. I – I'm too different from you two. You shouldn't mix up rags and napkins, as my grandma would say.'

'Okay, we're different, that's true, but how different? Maybe I'm wrong, but it seems we make up a good team of lame ducks the three of us, no?'

'You said it.'

'And besides, what does that mean, different? Okay, so there's me and I don't even know how to boil an egg, but I spent the entire day in your kitchen, and you who hardly listen to anything but techno, here you are falling asleep to Vivaldi. That's bullshit, your business about rags and napkins. The thing that prevents people from living together is their stupidity, not their difference. On the contrary, without you I'd never have been able to recognize a purslane leaf.'

'Fat lot of use that'll be.'

'That's bullshit too. Why "fat lot of use"? Why does there always have to be a notion of profitability? I don't give a fuck if it's useful or not, what I like is knowing it exists.'

'You see how different we are. Whether it's you or Philou, neither one of you is in the real world, you have no clue about life, how you have to struggle to survive and all that. I'd never met any intellectuals before you two, but you're just like I imagined.'

'And what did you imagine?'

He waved his hands:

'It went something like, "Tweet, tweet, oh the little birdies and the pretty little butterflies! Tweet, tweet, aren't they sweet! Care for another chapter, my dear? But of course, my dear, two, even, that will save me having to come back down to earth again. Oh, no! Don't do that, it's too terribly awfully stinky down there!"'

She stood up and turned off the music.

'You're right, we aren't going to make it. It's better if you leave. But let me say a thing or two before I wish you a pleasant trip: first of all, regarding intellectuals . . . It's easy take the piss out of them. Yeah, it's really easy. A lot of times they're, like, not very muscular and in addition, they're not really into fighting. It doesn't turn them on, the sound of marching boots, or medals, or big limos, so no, it's not hard to take the piss. All you have to do is rip the book from their hands, or the guitar or pencil or camera, and right away they turn into useless, clumsy oafs. As a matter of fact, that's usually the very first thing that a dictator does: break their glasses, burn their books or forbid their concerts, it doesn't cost him much and it can help him avoid all sorts of bother further down the line. But you see, if being an intellectual means you like to learn, that you're curious and attentive and can admire things and be moved by them and try to understand how it all hangs together, and try to go to bed a bit less stupid than the day before, well then, yes: I totally buy it, not only am I an intellectual but I'm proud to be one, really proud, even. And since I'm an intellectual, like you say, I can't help but read the motorcycle magazines that you leave lying around the bathroom and I know that the new BMW R 1200 GS has a little electronic gizmo that will keep you going even if you fill your tank with lousy petrol . . . So!'

'What the hell you on about now?'

'And since I'm an intellectual I went to borrow your *Joe Bar Team* comic books the other day and I sat there giggling all afternoon. Second thing: you really are the last person who has the right to lecture someone like me, man. You think your kitchen is the real world? Of course it isn't. Anything but. You never go out, you're always with the same people. What have you seen of the world? Not a thing. For over fifteen years you've been a prisoner of your rigid timetables, your caricature of a pecking order and your daily grind. Maybe that's the very reason you chose that job, after all? So you'd never have to leave your mother's womb and so you'd be sure you'd always be safe and warm with a ton of food around you. Who knows. You may work more and work harder than we do, that's a fact, but even if we're intellectuals, we still have to put up with the world. Tweet, tweet, we do have to go out every morning. Philibert goes to his little shop and I go to my dirty offices; and talk about working – well, we work. And your survival thing, right? Life is a jungle, a struggle for life and all that bullshit, we already know that by heart. We could even give you a few lessons if you wanted.

'On that note, good evening, good night and Happy New Year.'

'Sorry?'

'Nothing. I said you weren't in a very cheerful mood.'

'No, I'm cantankerous.'

'What's that mean?'

'Look it up.'

'Camille?'

'What.'

'Say something nice to me.'

'Why?'

'To start the year off nicely.'

'No. I'm not a jukebox.'

'Come on . . .'

She turned around: 'Leave your rags and napkins in the same drawer, life is more fun when there's a bit of mess.'

'And don't you want me to say something nice to you to start the year off nice?'

'No. Yes. Go on then.'

'You know what? Your toast was truly magnificent.'

Part Three

1

It was shortly after eleven the next morning when he went into her room. She had her back turned to him. She was still wearing her kimono, sitting by the window.

'What are you doing? Are you drawing?'

'Yes.'

'What are you drawing?'

'The first day of the year.'

'Show me?'

She raised her head and bit the inside of her cheek to keep from laughing.

He was wearing an unbelievably old-fashioned suit, style of Hugo Boss 1980s vintage, a bit too big on him and too shiny, with epaulettes like Goldorak, and a mustard yellow viscose shirt with a multicoloured tie. His socks matched his shirt, and his shoes, ammoniated pigskin, were killing his feet.

'Well, what?' he grumbled.

'No, nothing, you're . . . You look really chic.'

'Ha ha, very funny. I'm taking my grandmother out to a restaurant for lunch.'

'Well I must say . . .' she started, restraining her laughter, 'she'll be very proud to go out with a handsome fellow like you . . .'

'Very funny. You have no idea, it's driving me nuts. Anyway, I just have to get it over and done with.'

'Is that Paulette? The scarf lady?'

'Yes. That's why I'm here now. Didn't you tell me you had something for her?'

'Yes. Absolutely.'

Camille got up, moved the armchair and went to rummage in her little suitcase.

'Sit down.'

'What for?'

'For a present.'

'You're going to draw me?'

'Yes.'

'I don't want you to.'

'Why not?'

'. . .'

'Well, don't you know why?' she repeated.

'I don't like people looking at me.'

'I'll go fast.'

'No.'

'Suit yourself. I just thought that she would be pleased to have a little portrait of you. Same old story of barter, no? But I won't insist. I never insist. Not my style.'

'Okay then, but make it quick.'

'This is no good.'

'Now what?'

'That suit of yours . . . The tie and everything, it's no good. It's not you.'

'You want me to strip?' he snorted.

'Oh, yes, that'd be great! A nice nude,' she answered, without batting an eyelid.

'You joking or what?'

He was panicked.

'Of course I'm joking. You're much too old. And I'll bet you're way too hairy.'

'I am not! No way! I've got just the right amount.'

Camille laughed.

'Go on. Take off the jacket at least, and loosen your tie.'

'Pfff . . . took me for ever to do the knot.'

'Look at me. No, not like that. You look like you've got a broomstick up your arse, relax! I'm not going to eat you, silly, I'm just going to take a bite of your pictorial essence.'

'Oh, yes,' he begged, 'bite me, Camille, bite me . . .'

'Perfect. Hold that silly smile. That's exactly what I wanted.'

'You almost done?'

'Almost.'

'I'm bored. Talk to me. Tell me a story to pass the time.'

'Who do you want me to talk about this time?'

'You.'

'. . .'

'What are you going to do today?'

'Tidy up. Some ironing, too. And then I'll go for a walk. There's a beautiful light. I'll end up in a café or a tea room. Eat some scones with blueberry jam . . . Yum. And with a bit of luck, there'll be a dog. I'm collecting dogs in tea rooms these days. I have a special Moleskine sketchbook just for them, really nice. Before that I had one for pigeons. I'm an expert where pigeons are concerned. The ones in Montmartre, or the ones at Trafalgar Square in London, or in Venice on the Piazza San Marco, I've sketched them all.'

'Tell me –'

'Yes?'

'Why are you always all alone?'

'I don't know.'

'You don't like men?'

'Here we go. Any girl who doesn't respond to your irresistible charm has to be a lesbian, right?'

'No, no, I just wondered, that's all. You dress grunge, you shave your head, all that . . .'

Silence.

'Yes, yes, I do like boys. Girls too, by the way, but I prefer guys.'

'You've slept with girls?'

'Oh, yes, loads of times!'

'You having me on?'

'Yes. Okay, I'm done. You can get dressed.'

'Show me.'

'You won't recognize yourself. People never recognize themselves.'

'Why'd you make that big spot, there?'

'It's a shadow.'

'Oh?'

'It's called a wash.'

'And what's that, there?'

'It's your sideburns.'

'Oh?'

'You're disappointed, huh. Here, take this one, too. It's a sketch I made the other day when you were at your PlayStation.'

A big smile: 'Okay, there, yes! That's me.'

'I like the other one better but, oh well. Just put them inside one of your comic book albums to carry them.'

'Give me a sheet of paper.'

'Why?'

'Because. I can do your portrait too, if you want.'

He stared at her for a moment, leaned over his knees, sticking his tongue out, then handed her his scribblings.

'So?' she asked, curious.

He'd drawn a spiral. A snail's shell with a little black dot in the centre.

She didn't react.

'The little dot, that's you.'

'I, uh, I figured as much.'

Her lips were trembling.

He grabbed the paper back from her: 'Hey! Camille, hey, it was a joke! Just bullshit, nothing at all!'

'Yeah, yeah,' she confirmed, putting her fingers to her forehead. 'It's nothing at all, I'm well aware of that. Go on, get going, you're going to be late.'

He pulled on his leathers in the hallway and, ramming his helmet on to his head, shut the door.

The little dot, that's you.

What a jerk.

2

For once he wasn't dragging a backpack full of food with him, so he could lie flat out on his tank and let the speed do its fantastic job of scraping away all the crap: his legs hugging the bike, his arms outstretched, his chest warm and his helmet ready to crack, while he twisted his wrist to the maximum, to leave all the hassles behind and not think about another thing.

He was going fast. Much too fast. On purpose, just to see.

For as long as he could remember, Franck had always had an engine between his legs and a sort of itching in the palm of his hand and, for as long as he could remember he had never viewed death as something to be taken very seriously. Just one more thing to get on his nerves . . . And anyway . . . Since he wouldn't be around to suffer the effects of his own death, what did it really matter?

From the day he'd been able to rub two cents together Franck had gone into debt to buy bikes that were far too powerful for his little brain, and as soon as he had a few mates who knew how to fiddle things, he'd paid even more to gain a few millimetres on the speedo. He remained calm at traffic lights, never left any rubber on the asphalt, never compared size with other bikes, and saw no point in taking idiotic risks. It was just that whenever he had the opportunity, Franck would escape, go away on his own to blast off full throttle, and give his guardian angel a chance to work overtime.

He loved speed. He really did. More than anything on earth. More than girls, even. Speed had given him the only happy moments of his life: calm, free, a sense of peace. When he was fourteen, lying on his hayrick like a toad on a box of matches (it was an expression of the time), he was the king of the little back roads of Touraine; at twenty, he'd bought his first second-hand large-cylinder engine after sweating blood and tears all summer in a stinking dive near Saumur; and now it had become his sole pastime between two shifts: dreaming about a bike, then buying it, polishing it, wearing it out, dreaming of the next one, hanging around at the showroom, selling the previous bike, buying the next one, polishing it, and on, and on.

Without his bike, Franck would probably have been content simply phoning the old lady more often, just praying to the heavens she wouldn't start telling him her life story every time . . .

The problem was that the trick didn't seem to work so well any more. Even at 200 kilometres an hour, that sense of lightness eluded him.

Even at 210, even at 220, his brain was still spinning. No matter how he managed to weave his way, manoeuvre, slalom, and squeeze through, certain realities continued to cling to his jacket and gnaw away at his brain between two service stations.

And today, a first of January dry and brilliant like a newly minted coin, without his pannier, without his backpack and with nothing on the agenda other than a good feast with two adorable little grandmothers, Franck had finally sat up straight and no longer needed to stick out his leg in thanks to those cautious drivers who swerved abruptly to get out of his way.

He had given up the fight and it was enough just to get from A to B, listening to the same old scratched record: Why this life? How long for? And how could he get away from it? Why this life? How long for? And how could he get away from it? Why this life? How long? How long –

He was dead tired, and actually in a good mood. He had invited Yvonne to thank her and, he had to admit, so that she could make conversation for him. Thanks to her he'd be able to slip into automatic pilot. A little smile to the right, a little smile to the left, a few swear words to keep them happy and it would be time for coffee . . . awesome.

Yvonne would go and pick up Paulette from her cage and they would all meet up at the Hôtel des Voyageurs, a nice little restaurant full of tablemats and dried flowers, where he'd done his apprentice-ship – and where they were not about to forget him, either. That was back in 1990. Might as well be a thousand million light years ago.

What did he have back then? A Fazer Yamaha, wasn't it?

He zigzagged between the white lines and raised his visor to feel the sharp rays of the sun. He wasn't going to move house. Not right away. He could stay on there, in that outsize apartment where life had returned one morning with a girl from outer space. In a nightgown. She didn't talk a lot but ever since she had come, there'd been something more than silence. Philibert had finally started coming out of his room and they'd been having hot chocolate together in the morning. Franck didn't slam doors any more, so as not to wake her, and he fell asleep more easily when he could hear her moving around in the next room.

In the beginning he couldn't stand her, but now it was fine. He had tamed her . . .

Hey, did you hear what you just said?

What?

Go on, stop playing dumb. Tell the truth, Lestafier, look me in the eyes, do you really think you've tamed that girl?

Well, uh, no.

Right, that's more like it. I know you're not the brightest kid around but still . . . you had me worried there.

Hey, enough already, if I can't even joke around any more . . .

3

Under a bus shelter Franck zipped out of his leathers, and adjusted the knot of his tie as he went through the door.

The *patronne* spread her arms: 'Don't you look nice! I can see you buy your clothes in Paris now! René sends his love. He'll stop by after the service.'

Yvonne got up and his grandma gave him a tender smile.

'Well, girls? I can see you've spent the day at the beauty salon!'

They giggled over their kirs, and moved aside to let him see the view out on to the Loire river.

His grandma had got out her best suit with the paste brooch and the fur collar. The retirement home's hairdresser had done a fine job and her hair was the same salmon pink colour as the tablecloth.

'Hey, he's given you some great highlights, that hairdresser.'

'That's just what I was saying,' Yvonne interrupted, 'that colour suits her. Don't you think, Paulette?'

Paulette nodded, lapping it up, gently dabbing the corners of her mouth with the damask napkin. And devouring her grandson with her eyes, as she simpered behind the menu.

It was just as he had expected: yes, no, oh really?, you don't say!, well damn, pardon, shit, oops, and Jiminy Cricket were the only words he said, as Yvonne played the part perfectly.

Paulette didn't say much.

She was looking at the river.

The chef came to shoot the breeze for a while, and served them a vintage Armagnac which the old ladies initially refused, then sipped down as if it were a fine little communion wine. He told Franck stories about other chefs and asked whether he might ever come back to work there.

'Those bloody Parisians,' he said, 'they don't have a clue how to eat. The women are all on diets and the men only care about the bill. I'll bet you anything you never get any real lovers. At lunchtime there's no one but businessmen, who couldn't give a toss about what they're eating, and in the evening it's just couples celebrating their twentieth wedding anniversary and sulking at each other 'cause the car's badly parked and they're worried it'll get towed away . . . am I right?'

'Oh, you know, I don't really care one way or the other. I just do my job.'

'Well that's exactly what I mean! Up there you're just cooking for your paycheque! Why don't you come back down here, we can go fishing with my buddies.'

'Are you thinking of selling, René?'

'Bah. Who'd buy this place?'

While Yvonne went to get her car, Franck helped his grandmother find the sleeve of her raincoat:

'Here, she gave me something for you.'

Silence.

'Well, don't you like it?'

'Yes, yes.'

She started crying again: 'You're so handsome in this one.'

She pointed to the sketch he didn't like.

'You know, she wears it every day, that scarf you made.'

'Liar.'

'I swear!'

'Then you're right, she's not normal, that kid,' she added, wiping her smile with her handkerchief.

'Grandma, don't cry, we'll figure something out.'

'Yes. Feet first.'

Franck didn't know what to say.

'You know, sometimes I think I'm ready, and other times, I just, I –'

'Oh, my little grandma.'

And for the first time in his life, he put his arms around her and hugged her.

They said goodbye in the car park and he was relieved not to have to take her back to her miserable hole himself.

When he raised the kickstand, the bike felt heavier than usual.

He had a date with his girlfriend, he had cash, a roof, a job, he had even just found his Chico and Harpo, but he was dying of loneliness.

What a mess, he muttered into his helmet, what a fucking mess. He didn't repeat it a third time because what would be the point and anyway, it would only steam up his visor.

What a mess.

4

'You forgot your k—'

Camille didn't finish her sentence because she'd got the wrong person. It wasn't Franck, it was the girl from the other day. The one he'd thrown out on Christmas Day after screwing her.

'Franck's not at home?'

'No, he went to see his grandmother.'

'What time is it?'

'Uh, around seven, I think.'

'Do you mind if I wait for him here?'

'Course not. Come on in.'

'I'm not disturbing you?'

'Not at all! I'm just vegging out in front of the television.'

'You watch television?'

'I do, why?'

'I warn you, I'm watching the lamest thing there is. Nothing but girls dressed like whores and presenters in tight suits reading off teleprompters with their legs spread, trying to look virile . . . I think it's some sort of karaoke with celebrities but I don't recognize anyone.'

'Go on, you must know him, he's the guy from *Popstars*.'

'What's *Popstars*?'

'Yeah, I see, I was right, that's what Franck said, you never watch television.'

'Not a lot, no. But this sort of thing I love. It's like wallowing in some big warm pigsty. Mmm. They're all gorgeous, there's a lot of kissing and the girls are great at mopping up the mascara when they cry. You'll see, it's really moving.'

'Can I sit down?'

'Here.' Camille moved over and offered her the other end of her duvet. 'You want something to drink?'

'What are you on?'

'Aligoté Burgundy.'

'Hang on, I'll get a glass.'

'So what's going on?'

'I don't get it.'

'Pour me some, I'll tell you.'

They talked during the commercials. Her name was Myriam, she was from Chartres, she worked at a hairdresser's salon on the rue Saint-Dominique and she sublet a studio in the 15th arrondissement. They were worried about Franck, so they left him a message, then turned the sound back up when the show resumed. By the end of the third break they were friends.

'How long have you known him?'

'I don't know, must be about a month.'

'Is it serious?'

'No.'

'Why not?'

''Cause he never talks about anything but you! No, I'm kidding. He just told me you draw really well. Say, wouldn't you like me to fix you up while I'm here?'

'Sorry?'

'Your hair?'

'Now?'

'Well, yeah, because afterwards I'll be too drunk and I might cut your ear at the same time.'

'But you don't have anything with you, you don't even have any scissors.'

'Don't you have razor blades in the bathroom?'

'Uh, yes. I think Philibert still uses one of those palaeolithic cut-throat things . . .'

'What exactly are you going to do?'

'Make it softer.'

'Do you mind if we stand in front of a mirror?'

'You scared? You want to keep an eye on me?'

'No, just watch.'

While Myriam thinned her hair, Camille sketched them.

'Will you give it to me?'

'No. Anything you want, but not this one. I keep all my self-portraits, even condensed versions like this one.'

'Why?'

'I don't know. It's just, like, I feel like if I keep drawing myself long enough, some day I'll finally recognize myself.'

'When you see yourself in a mirror you don't recognize yourself?'

'I always think I look ugly.'

'And in your drawings?'

'In the drawings, not always, no.'

'Isn't that better?'

'You did sideburns, like Franck's.'

'It suits you.'

'You know Jean Seberg?'

'No, who's that?'

'An actress. She used to have her hair exactly like this, only she was blonde.'

'Oh if that's all that's missing, I can make you blonde next time.'

'She was really cute. She lived with one of my favourite writers. And then they found her dead in her car one day. How could such a pretty girl find the courage to destroy her own life? It's unfair, don't you think?'

'You should have drawn her beforehand, so she could have seen herself.'

'I was only two at the time.'

'That's another thing Franck told me.'

'About Seberg's suicide?'

'No, that you tell lots of stories.'

'It's because I like people. Uh – how much do I owe you?'

'Don't.'

'I'll give you a present then instead.'

Camille came back and held out a book.

'*King Solomon*, by Romain Gary. Is it good?'

'Better than good. Don't you want to try and call Franck again? I'm starting to get worried. Maybe he's had an accident.'

'Shh. There's no need to worry. He's just forgotten me. I'm beginning to get used to it.'

'Why do you go on seeing him, then?'

'So that I won't be alone.'

They'd started on the second bottle by the time he stood there removing his helmet.

'Well, what the fuck are you guys doing?'

'We're watching a porn movie,' they said, laughing. 'We found it in your room. It was hard to choose, wasn't it Mimi? What's this one called anyway?'

'*Take your tongue out so I can fart.*'

'Yeah, that's the one, it's great.'

'What the fuck are you talking about? I don't have any porn films!'

'No? That's weird . . . Maybe someone left it in your bedroom?' Camille gave him an ironic look.

'Or maybe you made a mistake,' added Myriam, 'you thought you were getting *Amélie* and you ended up with *Take your tongue –*'

'What the fuck –' He looked at the screen for a few seconds while they burst out laughing. 'You're completely trashed is what you are!'

'Yes . . .' they confessed.

'Hey,' called Camille as he was leaving the living room, muttering.

'Now what?'

'Aren't you going to show your fiancée how handsome you are today?'

'No. Don't piss me off.'

'Oh, please,' begged Myriam, 'show me, angel.'

'Striptease!' blurted Camille.

'Get it off!' said Myriam.

'Striptease! Striptease! Striptease!' they chimed.

Franck shook his head and rolled his eyes. He was trying to adopt an outraged expression, but couldn't do it. He was dead tired. All he'd wanted was to collapse on his bed and sleep for a week.

'Striptease! Striptease! Striptease!'

'Okay. You asked for it. Switch off the box and get ready with your little bank notes, girls.'

He put on 'Sexual Healing' – at last – and started with his biker's gloves.

And when the refrain came along –

get up, get up, get up, let's make love tonight
wake up, wake up, wake up, cause you do-o it right

– he tore open the last three buttons of his yellow shirt and swung it over his head, swivelling his hips in superb Travolta style.

The girls were tapping their feet and clutching their ribs.

All he had left was his trousers. He turned around and slowly slid them down, giving a little thrust of his hips towards one girl then the other, and when the top of his briefs appeared, a wide elastic band where you could read DIM DIM DIM, he turned towards Camille and winked at her. Just then the song came to an end and he quickly pulled up his trousers.

'Okay, this has been fun, but I'm going to bed.'

'Oh . . .'

'What a let-down.'

'I'm hungry,' said Camille.

'Me too.'

'Franck, we're hungry.'

'Well, the kitchen is that way, straight ahead then turn left.'

He came back a few minutes later in Philibert's tartan bathrobe.

'Hey? You not eating?'

'No, never mind. We're going to languish until we die. A Chippendale who gets dressed, a chef who doesn't cook – we're really out of luck tonight.'

'Okay,' he sighed, 'what do you want? Savoury or sweet?'

'Mmm, this is good.'

'Is justa some pasta, no?' he replied, modestly, in a mock-Italian voice.

'But what did you put in there?'

'Oh, just odds and ends.'

'It's delicious,' Camille reiterated. 'And for dessert?'

'*Bananes flambées*. You'll forgive me, ladies, but I'm making do with what's to hand. Anyway, you'll see. I warn you, the rum's not Old Nick from Monoprix!'

'Mmm,' they said again, licking their plates. 'What's next?'

'What's next is beddy-byes, and for whoever's interested, my room is thataway, at the far end on the right.'

Instead, they made some herbal tea and smoked a last cigarette while Franck dozed off on the sofa.

'Oh, is he bad or what, our Don Juan with his *healing*, his sexual baaalm,' squealed Camille.

'Yeah, you're right, he is baaad.'

He smiled in his half-comatose state, and put a finger to his lips, to ask them to be quiet.

When Camille went into the bathroom, Franck and Myriam were already there. They were too tired to play at 'after you, my dear' so Camille reached for her toothbrush while Myriam put hers away and wished her a good night.

Franck was leaning over the sink spitting out toothpaste and when he stood up, their eyes met.

'Did she do that for you?'

'Yes.'

'It looks good.'

They smiled at each other's reflections and it was a half-second that lasted longer than a usual half-second.

'Can I wear your grey wifebeater?' called Myriam from his room.

He was energetically scrubbing his teeth and turned again to the girl in the mirror, dribbling toothpaste all down his chin: 'Shreally dumbutIpweefertoshleeptogewahwizhzhoo.'

'Sorry?' she said, frowning.

He spat out, then said, 'I said, it's really dumb but I heard there's sleet tomorrow.'

'Yes,' she smiled, 'that is really dumb. It really is.'

Camille turned back to him: 'Listen, Franck, I have something important to tell you . . . Yesterday I confessed that I never keep any of my resolutions, but now there's one that I'd like us both to make, and try to respect.'

'You want us to stop drinking?'

'No.'

'Smoking?'

'No.'

'Well, what is it, then?'

'I'd like you to stop playing this little game with me.'

'What game?'

'You know what I mean . . . Your sexual planning routine, all your heavy little hints. I, uh, I don't want to lose you, I don't want us to fall out. I want us to get along, here, now . . . so that it will be a place . . . Well, you know what I mean, a place where all three of us can feel good. Calm, no complicated involvement. I . . . You . . . We . . . we're not going anywhere, the two of us, I hope you realize that, right? That is, I mean, we . . . Of course we could sleep together, but then what? The two of us, I mean it's a recipe for disaster and, well, it would be a pity to spoil everything, don't you think.'

He'd been thrown for a loop and it took him a few seconds before he caught on.

'Hey, what are you talking about? I never said I wanted to sleep with you! And even if I wanted, there's no way! You're way too skinny! What makes you think a guy would even want to touch you? Go and play with yourself, sister, while you're at it! You're out of your fucking mind!'

'You see I was right to warn you? You see how clear-headed I am? It could never work between us. I try to explain things to you as tactfully as possible and you have nothing else to offer in exchange but your little shit-faced aggro, your stupidity, bad faith and meanness. Thank goodness you'll never touch me! Thank goodness! As if I could ever want your filthy meaty paws and your chewed-up nails on my skin! Keep them for your waitresses!'

She gripped the door handle: 'Okay, I blew it. I should have kept my fucking mouth shut. What a fucking idiot. And I'm not usually like this. Not at all. I'm usually the kind to arch my back and leave on tiptoe as soon as I smell trouble.'

He was sitting on the edge of the bathtub.

'Yes, that's the way I usually behave . . . But just now, like a fool, I forced myself to speak to you because –'

He raised his head.

'Because what?'

'Because . . . I told you, I think it's important for this flat to remain a good, quiet place to be. I'm going to be twenty-seven and for the first time in my life I'm living somewhere where I feel good, where I'm happy to come home in the evening, and even if I haven't been here very long, okay, and even with all the mean things you've just thrown in my face, I'm still here, trampling on my pride so that I won't risk losing it . . . Uh, do you understand what I'm trying to say or is it just a load of bullshit as far as you're concerned?'

Franck didn't reply.

'Okay then, I'm fucking off, I mean, I'm going off to sleep.'

He couldn't help smiling.

'I'm sorry, Camille. I just seem to balls it all up when I'm around you.'

'Yes, you do.'

'Why is that?'

'Good question. Okay then: bury the hatchet?'

'Go ahead. I'm already digging.'

'Great. So, what about that kiss, then?'

'No. Sleep with you, maybe, but kiss you on the cheek, no way. To start with, it would be much too hard.'

'You're a fool.'

He took a moment to get up; he hunched over, looked at his toes for a long time, his hands, his nails, switched off the light, and then he took Myriam, distractedly, pushing her head down on the pillow so the other girl wouldn't hear.

5

Even though the conversation had cost her a great deal; even though she had got undressed that night barely touching her own body and with greater mistrust than ever, helpless and discouraged by all those bones sticking out in the most strategically feminine places – knees, hips, shoulders; and even though she had taken a while to fall asleep while counting all her defects, Camille was not sorry they had had that conversation. The next morning, from the way he moved, and joked around, and behaved attentively without making a big deal of it, and selfishly without even realizing it, she understood that her message had already got through.

Myriam's presence in her life made things easier, and even if Franck still treated her in an offhand way, he slept out more often and came home more relaxed.

Sometimes Camille missed their cheerful little banter. What a twit I am, she thought, it was fun . . . But such moments of weakness never lasted for long. She had coughed up often enough in her life to know the exact price of serenity: exorbitant. And anyway, where did things really stand between them? Where did sincerity leave off and the game begin? She was peacefully ruminating on the subject, sitting alone in front of a half-defrosted gratin, when she noticed a weird thing on the windowsill.

It was the portrait he'd made of her the day before.

A fresh lettuce heart had been placed at the opening to the snail shell.

She sat back down and stabbed the tines of her fork into her cold courgette with an idiotic smile.

6

They went together to buy a high-performance washing machine, and split the bill. Franck was delighted when the salesman retorted, 'But Madame is absolutely right,' and he proceeded to call her darling all through the demonstration.

'The advantage of these combo appliances,' declaimed the vendor, 'two-in-one, so to speak, is that you economize on space. We know only too well how it is for young couples trying to set up house these days.'

'Shall we tell him that we're a threesome in an apartment of four hundred square metres?' murmured Camille, touching his arm.

'Darling, please,' Franck replied, annoyed, 'let me hear what the man has to say, all right?'

She insisted he plumb it in before Philibert got back, 'Otherwise he'll be too stressed out,' and she spent an entire afternoon cleaning a small room next to the kitchen which must have been called the 'laundry room' once upon a time . . .

She discovered piles and piles of sheets, embroidered dishcloths, tablecloths, aprons and napkins in honeycomb weave. Old pieces of hardened soap and products that were all dried out and shrivelled inside ravishing boxes: salt crystals, linseed oil, whiting, alcohol for pipe-cleaning, Saint-Wandrille wax, Rémy starch, all soft to the touch like puzzle pieces made of velvet . . . An impressive collection of brushes of every size and bristle, a feather duster as lovely as a parasol, a boxwood grip for shaping gloves, and a sort of braided wicker racket for beating carpets.

Painstakingly she lined up all the treasures and committed them to a large sketchbook.

She'd decided to draw everything, so as to have something to offer Philibert the day he had to move out.

Every time she started tidying up somewhere, she inevitably ended up sitting cross-legged, immersed in huge hat boxes filled with letters and photos, and she spent hours on end with handsome moustachioed men in uniform, great ladies who had just stepped out of a painting by Renoir, and little boys dressed like little girls, right hand on a rocking horse at the age of five, on a hoop at the age of seven, and on a Bible at the age of twelve, shoulders turned slightly to show off the fine armband from their first communion, now that they were touched by grace.

Yes, she loved that place, and it was not unusual for her to glance at her watch and start suddenly: already time to gallop along the corridors of the metro, arrive at work and be told off by Super Josy pointing smugly at her watch. Bah.

'Where you off to?'
    'Work, I'm already way late.'
    'Put on your coat, it's freezing.'
    'Yes, Dad. By the way –'
    'What?'
    'Philou's due back tomorrow.'
    'Oh?'
    'I'm taking the evening off. Will you be here?'
    'Dunno.'
    'Right.'
    'Put a scarf on at –'
    The door had already slammed.

Make up your mind, he humphed, when I try to hit on her, it's all wrong, when I tell her to dress warmly, she makes fun of me. She's killing me, that girl . . .

New year, same chores. Same incredibly heavy waxing machines, same vacuum cleaners for ever jammed, same numbered buckets ('no more drama, girls!'), same bitterly hard-won products, same blocked sinks, same adorable Mamadou, same tired co-workers, same hyper Jojo. Nothing had changed.

Although she was in better shape, Camille had less enthusiasm. She'd left her stones at the door, had begun to work again, with a watchful eye on the daylight hours, and she no longer saw any reason to live life backwards. Morning was the time she was most productive, and how could she work in the morning when she never got to bed before two or three, exhausted by a job that was as physical as it was debilitating?

Her hands tingled, her brain was ticking over: Philibert was coming back, Franck was bearable, and the appeal of the apartment remained undeniable. She had an idea brewing in her head. A sort of fresco – no, not a fresco, the word was too pompous; but an evocation, yes, that's it, an evocation. A chronicle, an imaginary biography of the place where she lived. There was so much material, there were so many memories. Not just objects. Not just photos but a mood. An atmosphere. Murmurings, a few lingering heartbeats. These volumes, oil canvases, arrogant mouldings, porcelain light switches, exposed wires, metallic bedpans, little poultice jars, custom-made shoe trees, and all these faded, yellowed labels.

The end of a world.

Philibert had warned them: one day, perhaps even the very next day, they would have to leave, would have to snatch up their clothes, their books, their discs and souvenirs and the two yellow Tupperware containers, and leave everything else behind.

And after that? Who knew what would happen? At best things would be shared out; at worst, second-hand shops, the Salvation Army, a pavement skip. To be sure, the wall clock and the top hats would find a home, but the pipe-cleaning solvent and the drape of a curtain and the horse's tail with its little holy inscription – *In memoriam Venus, 1887–1912, proud bay with a speckled nose* – and the rest of the quinine in its blue bottle on the bathroom shelf – who would care about those things?

Convalescence? Drowsiness? Gentle dementia? Camille didn't know, either, when or how the idea came to her, but there it was, she'd fashioned this little pint-sized conviction – and it might even be the old Marquis who'd whispered it to her – that all of this, all this elegance and this dying world, this little museum of bourgeois art and tradition, had been waiting for her alone, for her gaze and her gentleness and her wonder-struck pen, to find the necessary resolve to disappear, at last.

Her crazy idea came and went, vanished during the day, often banished by a host of mocking faces: You poor child, what on earth are you on about? And who are you? And who could possibly be interested in any of this, tell me that?

But at night . . . oh, at night! When she came back from her horrible office towers, where she'd spent most of her time squatting down next to a bucket and wiping the drip from her nose with her nylon sleeve, bending over ten times, a hundred times, to throw away plastic cups and papers of no interest and following miles of pale, sinister underground passageways where insipid graffiti could not hide things like: *What about him? What does he feel when he's inside you?*; when she put her keys down on the chest by the front door and walked through this huge apartment on tiptoe, she could not help but hear them call out: 'Camille, Camille,' squeaked the floor; 'Don't let us go,' begged the antiques; "Zounds! Why the Tupperware and not us!' protested the old general from his death-bed photograph. 'Yes, exactly,' echoed a choir of copper buttons and the moth-eaten grosgrain, 'Why?'

So she sat in the dark and slowly rolled herself a cigarette to give them a chance to calm down. First of all, I don't give a damn about your Tupperware, second, I'm here, just wake me up before noon, bunch of smarty-pants . . .

And she thought about Prince Salina, going home alone on foot after the ball. The prince who had just witnessed, helpless, the decline of his world and who, when he saw vegetable peels and the bloodied carcass of an ox by the roadside, prayed to the heavens not to delay.

The guy on the fifth floor had left a box of Mon Chéri chocolates for her. He's crazy, laughed Camille, who offered them to her favourite boss, then let Yosemite Sam thank him for her: 'Well, thanks but hey, you don't have any filled with liqueur by any chance?'

I'm *sooo* funny, she sighed, putting down her sketch, so very funny.

And it was in that state of mind – dreamy, mocking, one foot in *The Leopard* and the other in filth – that she pushed open the door of the storage room behind the lifts where they left their bottles of bleach and all their crap.

Camille was the last to leave and was beginning to get undressed in the semi-darkness when she realized she was not alone.

Her heart stopped beating and she felt something hot run down her thighs: she had just pissed on herself.

'Is someone there?' she said, groping along the wall to find the light switch.

He was sitting on the floor, panicked, a crazed expression, his eyes hollowed by drugs or deprivation: she knew such faces by heart. He didn't move, he had stopped breathing and was holding his dog's muzzle between his hands.

They stayed like that for a few seconds, staring at each other in silence, long enough to understand that neither one of them was likely to die at the hands of the other, and when he moved his right hand to place a finger on his lips, Camille plunged him once again in darkness.

Her heart was beating again. All over the place. She grabbed her coat and stepped out, backwards.

'The code?' he moaned.

'P-pardon?'

'The entry code for the building?'

She couldn't remember it, mumbled something, and groping along the wall found her way to the exit, then was out in the street, quivering and covered in sweat.

The security guard called out: 'Cold out tonight, isn't it?'

Camille didn't reply.

'You okay? You look like you've seen a ghost.'

'Tired.'

She was frozen, pulled her coat tight over her soaking overall, and headed off in the wrong direction. When she finally realized where she was, she walked along the kerb to hail a taxi.

It was a luxurious estate car with a read-out indicating inside and outside temperatures (+21°, −3°). She spread her thighs, leaned her forehead against the window and spent the rest of the trip looking out at the little piles of humanity curled up over the air vents and in the alcoves of the entryways.

They were the stubborn, pig-headed ones who refused aluminium blankets because they didn't want to be seen in headlights, and they still preferred warm asphalt to the cold tiles of the homeless shelter in Nanterre.

Camille made a face.

Bad memories welling up in her throat.

And that wild ghost? He looked so young . . . And the dog? That was bloody stupid. He couldn't go anywhere with that dog. She should have talked to him, warned him against that big Matrix dog, and asked him if he was hungry. No, it was his dope he wanted. And the mongrel? When had he last had a ration of Pal? She sighed. What a bloody idiot she was. Worrying about some mongrel when half of the people on the planet were dreaming about a spot on top of an air vent, you stupid bitch. Go on, get to bed, you old cow, I'm ashamed of you. What is the point of it all, any of it? You switch off the light because you don't want to see him any more and then you worry away in the back of a huge limo chewing on your lace handkerchief . . .

Go to bed, okay?

The apartment was empty, Camille went looking for some alcohol, anything, drank enough of it to find her way to her pillow, then got back up in the night to throw up.

7

Hands in her pockets and nose in the air, she was hopping up and down beneath the arrivals and departures sign when a familiar voice gave her the information she was looking for:

'Arrival of the train from Nantes on platform 9 at 20.35. This train is delayed by 15 minutes. So what's new.'

'Hey! What are you doing here?'

'Well,' said Franck, 'I came to play gooseberry. Hey, you're all dolled up. What's this all about? Am I dreaming or is that lipstick?'

She hid her smile behind the holes in her scarf.

'You're an idiot.'

'No, I'm jealous. You never put on lipstick for me.'

'It's not lipstick, it's something for chapped lips.'

'Liar. Show me –'

'No. Are you still on holiday?'

'I start again tomorrow evening.'

'Oh? Is your grandma doing okay?'

'Yes.'

'Did you give her my present?'

'Yes.'

'And?'

'And she said that if you drew such a nice picture of me, it meant you must be madly in love with me.'

'What on earth –'

'Shall we go and get a drink?'

'No. I've been inside all day. I'm going to sit here and look at people.'

'Can I join you?'

They huddled on a bench between a newspaper stand and a ticket-stamping machine, and watched the merry-go-round of frantic travellers.

'Go on, run, man! Run! There you go – no, too laaate.'

'One euro? No, a cigarette if you want.'

'Can you explain to me why it's always the girls with the worst figures who wear those low-slung trousers? I just don't get it.'

'A euro? Hey, you already tried us a while ago, Grandpa!'

'Look at that little old lady with her Breton headdress, you got your sketchbook with you? No? That's too bad . . . And what about that guy, look how happy he is to see his wife.'

'Something not right there,' said Camille. 'She must be his mistress.'

'Why do you say that?'

'A man who comes rushing into town with his overnight kit and throws himself on a woman in a fur coat, kissing her on the neck . . . Woah, believe me, that's not on.'

'Pfff . . . Maybe it's his wife?'

'No way! His wife is in Quimper and she's putting the kids to bed as we speak! Hey, there's a real couple,' she laughed, pointing to a visibly middle-class man and woman who were quarrelling in front of a TGV barrier.

He shook his head: 'You know nothing.'

'You're just too sentimental.'

Then a little old couple walked by them at a snail's pace, bent, tender, cautious, holding each other by the arm. Franck elbowed her: 'Ah!'

'There, I concede.'

'I love stations.'

'So do I,' said Camille.

'If you want to get to know a country, you don't need to act the cretin in some tourist bus, all you have to do is visit the stations and the markets, and you get the whole picture.'

'I totally agree with you. Where have you been anyway?'

'Nowhere.'

'You've never been outside of France?'

'I spent two months in Sweden. Cook at the embassy. But it was winter and I didn't see a thing. You can't get a drink there. No bars, nothing.'

'And the stations? And the markets?'

'I never saw daylight.'

'Was it nice? Why're you laughing?'

'No reason.'

'Tell me.'

'No.'

'Why?'

'Because.'

'Uh-oh, some business with a woman, right?'

'No.'

'Liar, I can tell by your . . . your nose, it's getting longer.'

'Okay, shall we get going?' he asked, pointing to the platforms.

'Tell me first.'

'But it's nothing. Fucking stupid.'

'You slept with the ambassador's wife, is that it?'

'No.'

'With his daughter?'

'Yes! There! Bull's-eye! You happy now?'

'Very happy,' she conceded, simpering, 'was she cute?'

'A real dog.'

'Nooo.'

'Yes. Even a Swede who'd tanked up in Denmark on a Saturday night and got drunk as a skunk wouldn't have touched her with a bargepole.'

'Why you, then? Charity? For the good of your health?'

'Cruelty.'

'Tell me.'

'No. Unless you tell me that you were wrong and that the blonde there earlier was actually his wife.'

'I was wrong. The whore in her beaver skin coat really was his wife. They've been married sixteen years, they have four kids, they adore each other and at this very moment she is hurling herself at his flies in the car park lift with one eye on her watch 'cause she put a *blanquette* in the oven to reheat before she left and she'd like to make him come before the leeks get burnt.'

'Yuck. You don't put leeks in a *blanquette*.'

'No, really?'

'You're confusing it with a pot-au-feu.'

'So what about your Swedish girl?'

'She wasn't Swedish, she was French, okay? In fact it was her sister who was hitting on me. A spoiled little princess. A little bit of fluff got up like a Spice Girl, she was hot. I'll bet she was bored, too. So to pass the time, she'd stop by and sit her little arse down on our ovens. She was flirting with everyone, she'd dip her finger in my saucepans and lick it slowly while she looked up at me. Hey, you know me, I'm not a complicated guy, so one day I grabbed hold of her on the mezzanine and doesn't she start squealing, stupid bitch. That she'd go and tell her father and all that. Well, I'm not complicated but one thing I hate is cockteasers. So I had her big sister, just to teach her something about life.'

'But that's really mean, for the ugly one.'

'Everything is mean for the ugly ones, don't you know that?'

'And then?'

'After that, I left.'

'Why?'

He didn't answer.

'Diplomatic incident?'

'Yeah, you might call it that. C'mon, let's get going now.'

'I like it too, when you tell stories.'

'Yeah, what a story.'

'You have a lot like that?'

'No. As a rule I'm happier hitting on the cute ones.'

'We should go a little further down,' she fretted, 'if Philibert takes the stairs over there and goes up to the taxis, we'll miss him.'

'Don't worry, I know my Philou. He always walks dead straight ahead until he bumps into a pole, then he says sorry and lifts his head to look around and find the exit.'

'You sure?'

'Of course. Hey, this is far enough. You in love, or what?'

'Nah, but you know how it is. You climb out of the train with all your shit, you're a little groggy, a little discouraged. You're not expecting anyone to be there then boom! Someone's there after all, at the end of the platform, waiting for you. Haven't you ever dreamt that would happen to you?'

'I don't dream.'

'I don't dream,' she repeated in a cheeky, mock-gangster tone, 'I don't dream and I don't like cockteasers. May that be a warning, babe.'

He looked devastated.

'Hey, look,' she added, 'I think that's him, over there.'

Philibert was at the far end of the platform and Franck was right: he was the only one not in jeans or trainers, the only one with no soft bag or luggage on wheels. He held himself ramrod straight, walking slowly, carrying in one hand a big leather suitcase fastened with a military belt, and in the other a book that was still open.

Camille smiled: 'No, I'm not in love with him, but you see, he's the big brother I've always dreamt of having.'

'You an only child?'

'I . . . I'm not really sure any more,' she murmured, hurrying to her beloved half-blind zombie.

Of course he was confused, of course he stuttered, of course he dropped his suitcase on to Camille's foot, of course he apologized profusely and lost his glasses in the process. Of course.

'Oh, please, Camille, the way you do go on, like a little puppy, oh dear oh dear oh dear –'

'Hey, you don't have to tell me, I can't control her any more,' grumbled Franck.

'Here, take his suitcase,' she ordered, while she clung to Philibert's neck, 'you know, we have a surprise for you!'

'A surprise, oh my God, no . . . I don't really like surprises, you shouldn't have . . .'

'Hey, turtledoves! Would you mind not walking so fast? Your personal valet here is kind of tired. Shit, what you got in here? Suit of armour or what?'

'Oh, just a few books, nothing else.'

'Shit, Philou, you've already got a ton of books, couldn't you have left these ones at your château?'

'He's in fine fettle, our friend!' he whispered to Camille, 'and how are you?'

'Who? You mean both of us,' she said coyly, in response to his use of 'vous'.

'Uh, yes, you,' he insisted, still calling her 'vous'.

'Pardon?'

'You,' he stammered, using '*tu*' this time.

'Me?' she said again with a smile, 'I'm fine. I'm glad you're back.'

'Me too. Everything okay? No trenches in the apartment, no barbed wire? No sandbags?'

'No problems. He has a girlfriend at the moment.'

'Ah, I see. And did you have a nice celebration?'

'What celebration? Tonight's the celebration! And we're going to go out to eat somewhere. My treat!'

'Where?' grumbled Franck.

'La Coupole!'

'Oh, no . . . That's not a restaurant, it's a food factory.'

Camille frowned and said, 'Yes. La Coupole. I adore that place. You don't go there to eat, you go for the décor, for the atmosphere, for the people, and to be together.'

'What the hell does that mean, "you don't go there to eat"! That does it!'

'Well, if you don't want to come along, too bad, but I'm inviting Philibert. You can both think of this as my first crazy whim of the year!'

'We won't get in . . .'

'Of course we will. Or we'll wait at the bar.'

'And what about Monsieur le Marquis's vast library here? Am I the one who has to schlep it all the way there?'

'We can just leave it at the left luggage office and pick it up on the way back.'

'Well, maybe . . . Shit, Philou! Say something!'

'Franck?'

'Yes?'

'I have six sisters . . .'

'So?'

'So let me tell you, it's the simplest thing in the world: give in. What woman wants, God wants.'

'Who said that?'

'It's folk wisdom.'

'There we go! Starting all over again! You wear me out, the pair of you, with your quotations.'

Franck calmed down when Camille hooked her other arm through his, and on the boulevard Montparnasse, pedestrians moved aside to let them pass.

Seen from behind, they looked very sweet together.

On the left, the beanpole with his cloak straight out of Napoleon's retreat from Moscow; on the right, the well-built little guy with his *Lucky Strike* bomber jacket; and in the middle, a young girl – chirping, laughing, skipping and secretly dreaming of being lifted off the ground and hearing them say, 'On the count of three! One, two, three, yaaaaay!'

She held them as close as possible. All her equilibrium depended on it today. No further forward, nor back, but there, just there. Between these two kindly elbows.

The beanpole was inclining his head slightly, and the little well-built guy had his fists shoved down into his worn pockets.

Unbeknown to each other, both were thinking exactly the same thing: here we are, the three of us, now, famished, together, so let the good ship set sail, come what may.

For the first ten minutes, Franck was unbearable, criticizing every-thing in turn: the menu, the prices, the service, the noise, the tourists, the Parisians, the Americans, the smokers, the non-smokers, the paintings, the lobsters, his neighbour, his knife, and the revolting statue which would make him lose his appetite, for sure.

Camille and Philibert were having a good laugh.

After a glass of champagne, two glasses of chablis, and six oysters, he finally shut up.

Philibert, who was not used to drinking, kept laughing idiotically and for no particular reason. Every time he put his glass down he would wipe his mouth and imitate his village priest, launching into mystical, heartrending sermons which he concluded with 'Ah-men, aaah how happy I am to be here with you.' At the others' insistence he told them all the news from his damp little kingdom – his family, the floods, New Year's Eve with his fundamentalist cousins, and he described, in passing, a host of extravagant and unbelievable traditions and customs, with a deadpan humour they found enchanting.

Franck, above all, stared wide-eyed and every ten seconds let out a 'No?' 'No!' or 'No . . .'

'You say they've been engaged for two years and they've never . . . Go on. I don't believe it.'

'You should be on the stage,' urged Camille. 'You'd do a brilliant

244

routine. You know so many words and the way you say things is so clever. So deadpan. You could talk about the crazy charm of the old French aristocracy or something like that.'

'You think so?'

'I know so! Don't you agree, Franck? But . . . didn't you tell me about a girl at the museum who wanted to take you to her classes?'

'Yes, yes that's right, but I st-stutter too much.'

'No, when you're telling a story, you speak normally.'

'You – you think so?'

'Yes! C'mon! This'll be your New Year's resolution!' said Franck, raising his glass. 'On stage, Your Highness! And don't complain, okay, because that's one resolution that's not hard to keep.'

Camille prepared their crabs, breaking claws, pincers and shell, and made wonderful little open sandwiches for them. Since childhood she had adored seafood platters because there was always a lot to do and not much to eat. With a mountain of crushed ice between herself and her companions, she could play the part for an entire meal with no one interfering or pestering her. And this evening too, although she was already waving to the waiter for another bottle of wine, she had scarcely made a dent in her portion. She rinsed off her fingers, reached for a slice of rye bread with crab and leaned back against the booth with her eyes closed.

Click-clack.

Nobody move.

A moment in time.

Happiness.

Franck was telling carburettor stories to Philibert, who listened patiently, demonstrating once again his perfect upbringing and the kindness of his soul:

'To be sure, 89 euros is a considerable amount of money,' he opined gravely, 'and what does your friend think, fat, fat –'

'Fat Titi?'

'Yes!'

'Oh well, you know, Titi doesn't care. He's up to here with cylinder head gaskets.'

'Perfectly obvious,' he replied, sincerely sorry for Franck, 'Fat Titi is Fat Titi.'

He wasn't poking fun. Not the slightest trace of irony. Fat Titi was Fat Titi and that was that.

Camille asked who wanted to share *crêpes flambées* with her. Philibert preferred a sorbet and Franck was cautious:

'Hold on a minute. What sort of girl are you, anyway? The kind who says let's share and then you stuff yourself and bat your eyelashes? Or the kind who says let's share and then squabbles over the cherry? Or do you say let's share and then really share?'

'Order the crêpes, and you'll find out.'

'Yum, this is delicious.'

'Nah, they've been reheated, they're too thick and there's too much butter. I'll make you some one day and then you'll see the difference.'

'Anytime you're ready . . .'

'When you're a good girl.'

Philibert felt that the wind had veered, but he wasn't sure in which direction.

He was not the only one.

And that's what was so amusing.

Since Camille insisted, and what woman wants, etc., they began to talk about finances for the apartment: who would pay what, when and how? Who'd do the shopping? How much Christmas money for the concierge? Whose names on the letterbox? Should they have a phone line installed, and should they be intimidated by the incensed official letters about the television licence fee? And the housekeeping? Each of them would do their own room, that went without saying, but why was it always Camille or Philibert who were stuck with the kitchen and the bathroom? Speaking of the bathroom, said Camille, we need a wastebin; I'll take care of it. You, Franck, make an effort to recycle your beer cans and open the window of your bedroom from time to time, otherwise we'll all be infested . . . Same for the toilet. Please put down the seat and when there's no more toilet paper, say so. And can't we afford a decent vacuum cleaner, after all? That Bissel carpet sweeper dates from the First World War, it's done its time . . . Uh, and what else?

'So, Philou, my friend,' said Franck, 'now you understand what I meant when I said don't let a girl move in? See what I mean? See what a mess it makes? And just wait, this is only the beginning.'

Philibert Marquet de La Durbellière was smiling. No, he didn't see. He had just spent fifteen humiliating days at the receiving end of the exasperated stare of his pater familias, who could no longer hide his dissatisfaction. What sort of first-born son is it who isn't the least bit interested in farm tenancy, or forestry, or girls, or finance, let alone his social rank? A useless inept nitwit who sells postcards for the State and stutters when his little sister asks him to pass the salt. The only heir to the title, and not even capable of acting with a sense of his position when he speaks to the gamekeeper. No, he didn't deserve this, and every morning was cause for new despair when once again he found his son on all fours in Blanche's room, playing dolls with her.

'Have you nothing better to do, my son?'

'No, Father, but I – I – tell me, if you n-need me, I—'

But the door slammed before Philibert even finished his sentence.

'Let's pretend that you make the dinner and I'll go shopping, and after that we'll pretend that you make waffles, and after that we'll go to the park to walk the babies.'

'All right, my pumpkin, all right. We'll pretend whatever you want.'

Blanche, or Camille, for him it was the same: sweet little things who liked him and sometimes gave him a peck on the cheek. And for that Philibert was prepared to put up with his father's scorn, and buy fifty vacuum cleaners if that's what it took.

No problem.

As he had great respect for manuscripts, oaths, parchments, maps, and treaties of all sorts, Philibert was the one who cleared the coffee cups away and took a sheet of paper from his briefcase on which he wrote ceremoniously: 'Charter of the avenue Émile-Deschanel for the use of its occupants and other visit—'

He interrupted himself.

'And who was Émile Deschanel, children?'

'A president of the Republic?'

'No, the president was Paul. Émile Deschanel was a man of letters, a professor at the Sorbonne who was sacked because of his work *Catholicism and Socialism.* Or the other way round, I don't recall. Moreover, my grandmother was rather put out at having the name of that ruffian on her visiting cards. Well. Where was I?'

He went over everything that had just been concluded, point by point, including the toilet paper and the bin bags, and passed the new protocol around so that each of them could add his or her own clauses.

'This makes a regular Jacobin of me,' he sighed.

Franck and Camille reluctantly put down their glasses and wrote a lot of silly things.

Unruffled, Philibert brought out his stick of sealing wax and pressed his signet ring into the warm wax at the bottom of the paper before the stunned gaze of the other two, then folded the document in three and slipped it casually into his jacket pocket.

'Uh, do you always wander around with all your Louis XIV paraphernalia on you?' Franck asked, shaking his head.

'My wax, my seal, my salts, my golden écus, my coat of arms and my poison. To be sure, dear chap.'

Franck, who had recognized one of the waiters, went on a tour of the kitchen.

'I stand by what I said: a food factory. But a well-made factory.'

Camille picked up the tab, Yes, yes, I insist, you lot can do the hoovering; they retrieved the suitcase, stepping over a few more tramps here and there, and then Lucky Strike straddled his motorbike and the other two hailed a taxi.

8

She watched for him in vain the next day, the day after that, and the days which followed. No news. The security guard, with whom she now regularly had a chat (Matrix's right testicle hadn't descended, what a drama) didn't seem to know anything about him. And yet Camille knew he was around somewhere. Whenever she left a net bag full of bread, cheese, little salads, bananas and Fido dog food behind the bottles of detergent, it would systematically disappear. Never the tiniest dog hair or crumb, never the faintest odour. For a junkie he was remarkably well-organized, to such a degree that she even wondered about the recipient of her kindness. It might well be the other bozo who was feeding his unitesticular mutt for free. She explored discreetly, only to find that Matrix ate nothing but Vitamin B12-enriched dog biscuits with a soup spoon of castor oil for his fur. Canned food was crap. Why would you give your dog something you'd never want yourself?

Good point, why?

'But dog biscuits, that's the same thing, you'd never eat them yourself,' said Camille.

'Of course I would!'

'Yeah, really.'

'I swear!'

The worst of it was that she believed him. One-ball-only and One-brain-cell-only sitting there together nibbling on doggy chicken croquettes in front of a porn film in their over-heated hut in the middle of the night, that wasn't just a remote possibility. It even seemed quite appropriate.

Several days went by like this. Sometimes he didn't show. The baguette went hard and the cigarettes were still there. Sometimes he came by and took nothing but the dog food. Too much dope or not enough to enjoy a feast . . . Sometimes she wasn't able to bring anything. But she wasn't going to worry about it any more. Just a quick glance around the back of the storage room to see if she should empty out her bag or not.

Camille had other things on her mind.

At the apartment everything was fine, going smoothly, charter or no charter, Myriam or no Myriam, obsessive compulsive disorder or no obsessive compulsive disorder: everyone went merrily on their way without irritating their neighbour. They greeted one another in the morning and got gently stoned in the evening. Grass, hash, booze, incunabula, Marie-Antoinette or Heineken, it was each to his or her own trip, and Marvin for us all.

During the day, Camille made her sketches, and when he was there Philibert would read to her or give her a running commentary on his family albums:

'This is my great-grandfather. The young man next to him is his brother, Uncle Élie, and in front of them are their fox terriers . . . They used to organize dog races and it was the village priest – you can see him sitting there by the finish line – who designated the winner.'

'Hey, they had fun in their day, didn't they.'

'And a good job too. Two years later they left for the front in the Ardennes and six months after that they were dead, both of them.'

No, it was at work that everything was falling apart. First of all, the guy on the fifth floor had come up to her one night and asked her where she'd put his feather duster. Ha ha, he was so pleased with his joke that he followed her all the way down the hall shouting over and over, 'I'm sure it was you! I'm sure it was you!' Get lost, fat slob, you're in my way now.

No, it was my co-worker, she eventually barked, pointing to Super Josy who was busy counting her varicose veins.

Game over.

Secondly, she just couldn't stomach Ms Bredart any more.

She was as thick as two planks, had a tiny bit of power and abused it immoderately (site head at All-Kleen wasn't exactly head of the Pentagon, after all); she sweated, spat out her saliva, was always pinching the caps off ballpoint pens so she could pick at bits of meat stuck in her molars; and she would take Camille aside on every floor and whisper a racist joke, since Camille was the only other white person on the team.

Camille often had to cling to her floor mop simply in order not to scream in Josy's face, and the other day she'd finally begged her to keep her trashy thoughts to herself because she was beginning to grate on everyone's nerves.

'And who d'you think you are,' countered Josy, 'what makes you think you can talk to me like that? What the hell you doing here, anyway? What you doing with us? Spying or what? Matter of fact I was wondering that myself the other day. That maybe it was the bosses sent you to spy on us or summat like that. I seen on your payslip where the hell you live at and look how you talk and all, you're not one of us, are you. You stink bourgeois you do, you stink of money. You're one nosy bitch.'

The other girls didn't react. Camille gave a push to her trolley and started to walk away.

Then she turned round:

'Whatever Josy here has to say I don't give a damn because I despise her, but you lot, you are really useless. I opened my big mouth for your sake, so that she'd stop humiliating you, and I don't expect you to thank me, I really don't give a fuck about that either, but the least you could do is come and do the toilets with me. Because I may be bourgeois but it's me who always gets stuck with the toilets, in case you hadn't noticed.'

Mamadou made a funny noise with her mouth and dribbled a huge gob of spit at Josy's feet, a truly monstrous thing. Then she picked up her bucket, swung it in front of her and hit Camille in the buttocks:

'How can a girl with such a tiny ass have such a huge mouth? With you around, wonders will never cease.'

The others grumbled and groused and began to drift away. Camille didn't care about Samia; it was harder with Carine. Camille really liked her. Carine whose real name was Rachida, who didn't like her name, who was licking arse for that fascist pig. Well, that was one chick who'd go far.

From that day on, a new order reigned. But the work was still just as brainless and the atmosphere was sickening. Already quite a package.

Camille may have lost out on her industrial relations, but she was in the process of winning a friend. Mamadou had begun to wait for her outside the metro, and they teamed up. Mamadou talked while Camille did the work for two. It was not that Mamadou was trying to get out of doing her share, it was simply, sincerely, the fact that she was much too fat to be efficient. What took her a quarter of an hour, Camille could do in two minutes and, on top of it, she was aching all over. And she wasn't pretending. Her poor carcass could hardly take it any more: her monstrous thighs, her enormous breasts, her even bigger heart. If something inside her baulked at the idea of work, it made sense.

'You've got to lose weight, Mamadou.'

'Yes, indeedy. And you? When you going to come and try my homemade chicken?' she'd retort, every time.

Camille made a deal with her: I'll do the work, but you talk to me.

Who would have thought that such an innocent proposal would lead so far. Mamadou's childhood in Senegal, the sea, the dust, the little goats, the birds, the poverty, her eleven brothers and sisters, the old white priest who would remove his glass eye to make them laugh, her arrival in France in 1972 with her brother Léopold, the garbage cans, her failed marriage, her husband who was kind despite it all, her kids, her sister-in-law who spent her afternoons in the department stores while Mamadou did all the work, the kid who pooed again but in the stairway this time, all the parties they had, all the hassles, her cousin Germaine who hanged herself last year leaving behind two adorable twin girls, Sunday afternoons in the phone booth, her colourful African clothing, her recipes and a million other images that Camille never tired of. No need to read *Courrier International*, *Senghor* or the Seine–Saint-Denis edition of the *Parisien*: all you had to do was scrub a little harder and open your ears wide. And if Josy happened by, which was rare, Mamadou would bend over, give a little wipe to the floor and wait for the smell to disperse before raising her head again.

Story upon story, secret upon secret, Camille dared to ask more personal questions. Her co-worker told her some horrible things, or which seemed horrible to Camille at least, with a disarming nonchalance.

'But how do you manage all that? How do you hold up? How do you cope? A schedule like that is sheer hell.'

'Ta ta ta . . . don't talk about things you don't know about. Hell's a lot worse than what you know. Hell is when you can't see the folks you love. All the rest don't count. Say, don't you want me to get you some clean rags?'

'I'm sure you could find some work closer to home. Your kids shouldn't be staying alone at night, you never know what could happen.'

'My sister-in-law is there.'

'But you said you can't count on her.'

'Sometimes I can.'

'All-Kleen is a big company, I'm sure you could find a site nearer to home . . . You want me to help? Want me to ask for you? Write to the head of personnel?' said Camille, standing up.

'No, better leave well enough alone. Josy is who she is, but she turns a blind eye on a lot of things, you know. I'm such a fat gossip I'm even lucky to have this job, anyway. You remember that medical we had last autumn? That stupid little doctor? He wanted to give me a hard time because he said my heart was buried in too much fat or some bullshit or other, and it was Josy who fixed things for me, so you see, better not mess with things as they are.'

'Hang on . . . are we even talking about the same person? That old cow who's always treating you like you were the bottom of the shitheap?'

'Yes we are talking about the same person!' said Mamadou with a laugh. 'She's the only Josy I know, and thank God for that!'

'But you just finished spitting at her.'

'What do you mean I been spitting at her?' she said angrily, 'I wouldn't do that, hey.'

Camille emptied the shredder in silence. Whichever way you looked at it, life could deliver some odd colour combinations.

'Well, whatever, it's nice of you to offer. You're a good kid, you are. You have to come round the house one evening so's my brother can fix it so's you'll have a nice life with true love and lots of kids.'

'Aaargh.'

'What, "aaargh?" You don't want kids?'

'No.'

'Don't say that, Camille. You'll bring bad luck.'

253

'It already came.'

Mamadou gave her a nasty look: 'You should be ashamed talking like that. You have a job, a roof, two arms, two legs, a country, an admirer –'

'Excuse me?'

'Ah! Ah!' she said triumphantly, 'you think I didn't see you with Nourdeen downstairs? You always petting his big dog . . . you think my eyes are buried in fat too?'

Camille blushed.

To please her.

Nourdeen was hyper that evening and even plumper than usual in his law enforcement boiler suit, exciting his dog and acting as if he was Dirty Harry.

'Well, what's going on?' Mamadou asked him, 'why your dog growling like that?'

'I don't know what it is, but there's something funny going on. Don't hang around, girls. Don't stay here.'

Oh, he was in pig heaven just then, all he needed was a pair of Ray-Bans and a Kalashnikov.

'Don't stay here, I said!'

'Hey, calm down,' Mamadou replied, 'don't get youself so work-ed up.'

'Let me do my job, fat lady! I don't come and tell you how to hold your broom, do I?'

Hmm. What's bred in the bone . . .

Camille pretended to take the metro with Mamadou, then went back up the steps using the other exit. She walked around the block twice, and finally found them in the deep entryway of a shoe shop. He was sitting with his back against the shop window and his dog was asleep on his legs.

'You doing okay?' she asked casually.

He raised his eyes and it took him a moment to recognize her.

'Is that you?'

'Yes.'

'The food and stuff, too?'

'Yes.'

'Hey, thanks.'

Camille was silent.

'Does that loony have a gun?'

'I have no idea.'

'Okay, then. See you.'

'I can show you a place to sleep if you want.'

'A squat?'

'Sort of.'

'Who's there?'

'No one.'

'Is it far?'

'Near the Eiffel Tower.'

'No.'

'Suit yourself.'

She had hardly gone three steps down the street when a cop car, siren wailing, pulled up in front of hyper-excited Nourdeen. The boy caught up with Camille just as she was reaching the boulevard:

'What do you want in exchange?'

'Nothing.'

No more metro. They walked to the stop for the night bus.

'You go ahead and leave me your dog, they won't let you get on with him. What's his name?'

'Barbès. That's where I found him, the Barbès-Rochechouart metro station.'

'Right, like Paddington Bear.'

She took the dog in her arms and gave the driver a big smile; he didn't give a damn.

They met up at the back of the bus.

'What kind of dog is this?'

'Do we really have to talk, too?'

'No.'

'I put a new padlock on but it's symbolic. Here's the key. Just don't lose it, I only have one.'

She pushed open the door and added calmly, 'There's still some food in those boxes. Rice, tomato sauce and biscuits, I think. There are some blankets over there, and here's the electric radiator. Don't put it on full or it blows the fuse. There's a Turkish toilet on the landing. In theory, you'll be the only one using it. I say in theory because I've sometimes heard noise across the way but I've never seen anyone. And . . . what else? Oh, yes! I used to live with a junkie so I know exactly what will happen. I know that some day, maybe even tomorrow, you'll disappear and take everything with you. I know you'll try to pawn it all so you can pay for a good time. The radiator, the hotplates, the mattress, the sugar, the towels, everything. Okay. I know that. The only thing I ask is please be discreet. This isn't really my place either, so . . . So please don't get me in shit. If you're still here tomorrow, I'll go and see the concierge so there won't be any hassles. That's it.'

'Who drew that?' he asked, pointing to the trompe-l'œil. A huge window open on to the Seine with a seagull perched on the balcony.

'I did.'

'You used to live here?'

'Yes.'

Barbès sniffed around suspiciously then lay down in a ball on the mattress.

'I'll get going,' said Camille.

'Hey?'

'Yes?'

'Why you doing this?'

'Because the exact same thing happened to me. I was outside, and someone brought me here.'

'I won't stay long.'

'I don't care. Don't say anything. You never tell the truth, anyway.'

'I'm seeing people at the rehab, at Marmottan.'

'Yeah, sure. Right. Sweet dreams.'

9

Three days later Madame Perreira lifted aside the sublimely sheer net curtains at her door and called to Camille in the hall:

'Mademoiselle, hello?'

Shit, that didn't take long. What a hassle. And they'd even given him fifty euros.

'Hello.'

'Yes, hello. Say . . .'

She was making a face. 'Is he your frienda, that mucky pig?'

'Pardon?'

'The biker.'

'Uh . . . yes,' replied Camille, relieved. 'Is there a problem?'

'Not one, more like five! He's beginning to get on my nerves, that boy! No kidding! I'm getting reala fonda him. Come here and have a looka.'

Camille followed her into the courtyard.

'Wella?'

'I uh, I don't see anything.'

'The oil spots.'

Indeed, with a good magnifying glass you could clearly see five tiny little black spots on the cobblestones.

'Mechanics are all fine and good but it's a dirty job, so you tell him for me that newspapers aren't just for dogs, all right?'

Once she'd dealt with that problem, the concierge grew more affable. A little commentary on the weather: 'It's fine. It gets ridda all the vermin.' On the shiny brass door handles: 'Well for sure, to get them thata way, you gotta make an effort.' On the pushchair wheels full of dog shit. On the lady on the fifth floor who had just lost her husband, poor woman. And by then she'd calmed down completely.

'Madame Perreira . . .'

'That's me.'

'I don't know if you've noticed, but . . . I've got a friend staying up on the seventh floor.'

'Oh, I don't getta involved in your business, you know! People in, people out . . . I don't say I understand everything is-a going on, but anyway . . .'

'I mean the one who has a dog.'

'Vincent?'

'Uh . . .'

'Yes, Vincent! The guy witha AIDS, witha his little griffon?'

Camille was dumbfounded.

'He came to see me yesterdaya, because my Pikou wasa barking like crazy behind the doora, so we introduced them. That way it's easier. You know what they're like. They sniff the behinds once and for all and then is all squared awaya. Well, why you looking at me like that?'

'Why do you say he has AIDS?'

'Sweet Jesus, because he tolda me so himself! We drank a glass of port. You likea one, by the way?'

'No, no, I, well, thanks.'

'Ah yes, it's sad, but like I tell him, they can treat it now . . . they founda good medicine for it.'

Camille was so bemused that she forgot to take the lift. What the hell was that all about? Why weren't the rags with the rags and the napkins with the napkins?

Where the hell were they headed?

Life had been less complicated when she had nothing more to do than let her stones pile up.

No, come on, don't say that, stupid.

No, you're right. I won't say that.

'What's up?'

'Look at my sweater,' grumbled Franck with disgust. 'It's the fucking washing machine! Shit, this was one I really liked and all, but look! Just look! It's minute now.'

'Hang on, I'll cut off the sleeves and you can give it to the concierge for her rat.'

'That's right, go ahead and laugh. A brand new Ralph Lauren.'

'Well, all the more reason! She'll be delighted! On top of which she adores you.'

'Oh really?'

'She just said so again, "Ah, doesn't your friend cut a fine figure on his motorbike!"'

'No way.'

'I swear.'

'Okay then, why not. I'll take it down to her when I leave.'

Camille bit the inside of her cheek and custom tailored a chic little tube for Pikou.

'You know she'll give you a kiss on the cheek, lucky you.'

'No way, don't scare me!'

'And Philou?'

'You mean Cyrano? He's at his theatre class.'

'Really?'

'You should have seen him as he was heading out. Disguised again like I-don't-know-what . . . With a big cape and all.'

They laughed.

'I adore him.'

'Me too.'

She went to make some tea.

'Want some?'

'No thanks,' he replied, 'I have to get going. Hey –'

'What?'

'Don't you feel like getting out for a change?'

'Pardon?'

'When was the last time you got out of Paris?'

'Ages.'

'On Sunday we're slaughtering a pig, you want to come? I'm sure you'd find it interesting . . . I mean, for your drawing, huh?'

'Whereabouts?'

'At a friend's place, in the Cher region.'

'I don't know . . .'

'Yes you do! Ah, come on, you have to see this at least once in your life. Some day it will all be a thing of the past, you know.'

'I'll think about it.'

'You do that, think about it. That's your speciality, thinking about things. Where's my sweater?'

'Here,' said Camille, pointing to a magnificent pale green yappy-little-dog holder.

'Fuck. And it was a Ralph Lauren. I can't believe it, I swear to God.'

'Go on . . . you'll have two new friends for life.'

'Shit, he better not piss on my motorbike, bloody pop-eyed little runt!'

'Don't worry, it'll be fine,' she giggled, holding the door for him. And, adopting her best Portuguese accent, 'Yessa, yessa, I sweara, you frienda he cuts a fina figura on hisa motorbika.'

Camille ran to switch off the kettle, took her sketchbook and went to sit by the mirror. She began to laugh, finally. To laugh like crazy. Like a kid. She could just picture the scene: Mr Smart-Alec, always so smug, knocking casually on the window of the concierge's kiosk with his little offering of doggie felt and his balls on a silver tray. It was so good to laugh! So, so good. She hadn't done her hair, so she drew her spikes, her dimples, her silly mood and wrote: *Camille, January, 2004*, then took a shower and decided that yes, she would go somewhere for a change, with Franck.

That was the least she owed him . . .

A message on her mobile. Her mother. Oh, no, not today. To delete, press the star key.

Right, okay. Here we go. Star.

She spent the rest of the day listening to music, with her treasures and her box of watercolours. Smoking, nibbling, licking her sable-fur brushes, laughing to herself and grimacing when it was time to put on her overall.

You've done a great job clearing the terrain so far, she thought, trotting along to the metro, but there's still work to be done, you know that. You don't want to stop just yet, do you?

I'm doing what I can, I'm doing what I can.

Go on, we have faith in you.

No, no, don't have faith in me, it stresses me out.

Tsk, go on, hurry up. You're already very late.

10

Philibert was unhappy. He followed Franck around the apartment: 'It's not a good idea. You're leaving too late. In an hour it will be dark. It's going to freeze over. It's not a good idea. Leave to-tomorrow morning.'

'Tomorrow morning we're killing the pig.'

'But, but what sort of an idea is that! Ca-Camille,' he pleaded, wringing his hands, 'st-stay here with me, I'll take you to the Pa-Palace of Teas . . .'

'That's enough,' grumbled Franck, stuffing his toothbrush into a pair of socks, 'it's not exactly the end of the earth. It'll take us one hour.'

'Oh, d-don't say that. You're going to d-drive like a lunatic.'

'No, I won't.'

'But you will, I kn-know you.'

'Philou, cut it out! I won't drop her, I promise. You coming, Mademoiselle?'

'Oh, I – I –' fumbled Philibert.

'You what?' barked Franck.

'I have no-no one else but you two on earth.'

Silence.

'Oh, my God . . . I don't believe it. Bringing out the violins now.'

Camille stood on tiptoe to kiss Philibert: 'Me too, you're all I have on earth. Don't worry.'

Franck sighed.

'How the hell did I get mixed up with such a bunch of crackpots! Any more melodrama and we'll be drowning in soap bubbles!

We're not going off to war, fuck it! We'll be gone forty-eight hours!'

'I'll bring you back a nice steak,' said Camille, heading into the lift.

The doors closed on them.

'Hey.'

'What?'

'There's no steaks in a pig.'

'No?'

'Hell no.'

'Well, what is there?'

He rolled his eyes to the ceiling.

11

They had not even reached the Porte d'Orléans when Franck pulled over to the hard shoulder and motioned to Camille to get off the bike.

'Listen, there's something not quite right here.'

'What?'

'When I lean into the curves, you have to lean with me.'

'Are you sure?'

'Of course I'm sure! You'll run us off the road with your nonsense.'

'But I thought by leaning the other way I was keeping us balanced.'

'Fuck, Camille, I don't know how to give you a physics lesson but it has something to do with the centre of gravity, you see? If we lean together, the tyres grip better.'

'You sure?'

'Absolutely. Lean with me. Trust me.'

'Franck?'

'What is it? Are you scared? You can still get back on the metro, you know.'

'I'm cold.'

'Already?'

'Yes.'

'Okay. Let go of the handles and press yourself up against me. Get as close as possible and put your hands under my jacket.'

'Okay.'

'Hey?'

'What?'

'Don't take advantage, okay?' he added, mockingly, pulling her visor back down with a snap.

A hundred yards further along she was already icy cold again, by the time they turned off the motorway she was deep-frozen, and in the farmyard she could not feel her arms.

He helped her climb off and supported her as far as the door.

'Ah, there you are, well, what have we here?'

'A young lady who might as well be a fish-finger.'

'Come on in, please, come in. Jeannine! Here's our Franck with his girlfriend.'

'Oh poor wee thing,' lamented Jeannine, 'what on earth have you done to her? If that isn't a shame . . . She's completely blue, poor child. Out of the way, you lot. Jean-Pierre! Put a chair by the fire!'

Franck knelt down in front of Camille.

'Hey, you need to take your coat off now.'

No reaction.

'Here, I'll give you a hand. Let's start with your feet.'

He pulled off her shoes and three pairs of socks.

'There . . . that's better. Okay, now the rest.'

She was so rigid that it was only with enormous difficulty that he managed to get her arms out of her sleeves. There, there. Let me do it, little ice cube.

'Good lord! Get her something hot!' someone shouted.

Camille was the new centre of attention.

Or, how to defrost a Parisian girl without breaking her.

'I have some hot kidneys,' shouted Jeannine.

A flutter of panic from Camille where she sat by the fireplace. Franck rescued the situation: 'No, no, let me take care of it. You must have some bouillon kicking around,' he asked, looking under saucepan lids.

'That's from yesterday's chicken.'

'Perfect. I'll take care of it. Give her something to drink in the meantime.'

With each sip she took from the bowl, the colour began to return to her cheeks.

'Feeling better?'

She nodded.

'What did you say?'

'I said that's the second time you've fixed me the best bouillon in the world.'

'I'll make some more for you, don't worry. Can you come and join us at the table now?'

'Can I stay a bit longer by the fire?'

'Of course!' shouted the others. 'Leave her alone, Franck. We'll smoke her, like a side of ham!'

Franck reluctantly got up.

'Can you move your fingers?'

'Uh, yes.'

'You have to be able to draw, right? I'm happy to get some food for you but you've got to draw. You mustn't ever stop drawing, right?'

'Now?'

'Nah, not now, ever.'

She closed her eyes.

'Okay.'

'Right, I'm going. Give me your glass, I'll get you some more.'

And Camille gradually melted. By the time she went to join the others, her cheeks were on fire.

She listened to their conversation without understanding a word, admiring their features, smiling to the angels.

'Come on. One last swig and off to bed! Because tomorrow it's up early, guys. There's Gaston who'll be here at seven.'

Everyone stood up.

'Who's this Gaston?'

'Gaston is the guy who slaughters the pigs,' murmured Franck. 'Wait'll you see him, he's something else.'

'So this is it,' added Jeannine, 'here's the bathroom and over there on the table I laid out some clean towels. That okay?'

'Great,' answered Franck, 'great. Thanks.'

'No need for that, kiddo, we're just really happy to see you, you know that. And how's Paulette?'

He looked down.

'Okay, okay, we won't talk about it,' she said, squeezing his arm, 'it'll all work out, right?'

'You wouldn't recognize her, Jeannine.'

'Let's not talk about it, I said. You're on holiday now.'

When she had closed the door, Camille grew worried: 'Hey! There's only one bed!'

'Of course there's only one bed! You're in the country now, not at the Hotel Ibis!'

'Did you tell them we were together?' she groused.

'Of course not! I just said I was coming with a girlfriend, that's all!'

'Well, there you are.'

'Well, there you are, what?'

'A girlfriend, that generally means a girl you're having sex with. What the hell was I thinking?'

'Fuck, you really are a ball-breaker when you want to be, d'you know that?'

He sat on the edge of the bed while she got out her things.

'This is the first time,' he said.

'Pardon?'

'This is the first time I've ever brought anyone here.'

'That makes sense. Slaughtering pigs is not the most glamorous way to charm – '

'It has nothing to do with the pig. It has nothing to do with you, either. It's . . .'

'It's what?'

Franck lay across the bed and addressed the ceiling: 'Jeannine and Jean-Pierre had a son . . . Frédéric . . . A great guy, my best mate. The only one I've ever had, to be honest. We went to hotel school together and if he hadn't been there, I wouldn't have been there either. Anyway . . . He died ten years ago. Car accident. Not even his fault. Some fuckwit who jumped the lights. So you see . . . it's not like I'm Fred or anything, but we were similar. I come here every year. The pig's a pretext. They look at me and what do they see? Memories, words, and the face of their kid, he wasn't even twenty. Jeannine is always touching me, feeling me – why do you think she does that? 'Cause I'm the proof that he's still there. I'm sure she gave us her best sheets and that she's holding on to the banister, right now . . .'

'Was this his room?

'No. His is locked.'

'Why did you bring me here?'

266

'I told you, so you could draw and –'

'And what?'

'I dunno, I felt like it . . .'

He shrugged.

'And about the bed, it's not a problem. We can put the mattress on the floor and I'll sleep on the base. That okay, princess?'

'That's okay.'

'Have you seen *Shrek*? The cartoon?'

'No, why?'

'Because you remind me of Princess Fiona. Not quite as curvy, of course.'

'Of course.'

'C'mon . . . give me a hand? This mattress weighs a ton.'

'You're right,' she groaned. 'What the hell is in here?'

'Generations of peasants who died of fatigue.'

'Charming.'

'Aren't you getting changed?'

'I did . . . these are my pyjamas.'

'You're going to sleep in your sweater and socks?'

'Yes.'

'Shall I switch off the light?'

'Well, yeah.'

'You asleep?' she asked after a few minutes.

'No.'

'What are you thinking about?'

'Nothing.'

'Your youth?'

'Maybe. So, nothing. That's what I said.'

'Your youth was nothing?'

'Not a whole lot, at any rate.'

'Why?'

'Shit. If we head down that road, we'll still be there in the morning.'

'Franck?'

'Yes?'

'What's wrong with your grandmother?'

'She's old. She's alone. Her whole life she slept in a big comfy bed like this one with a woollen mattress and a crucifix above her head and now she's pining away in a sort of shit-awful metal box.'

'Is she in hospital?'

'Nah, an old folks' home.'

'Camille?'

'Yes?'

'Are your eyes open?'

'Yes.'

'Can you tell how dark the night is here? How beautiful the moon is? How the stars are shining? Can you hear the house? The pipes, the wood, the wardrobes, the clock, the fire downstairs, the birds and animals and the wind . . . Can you hear all that?'

'Yes.'

'Well, my grandma can't hear it any more. Her room looks over a car park that's lit all the time, and she just listens for the rattle of the food trolleys, conversations of the nursing aides, her neighbours moaning and their televisions blaring all night long. And it . . . it's killing her.'

'What about your parents? Can't they take care of her?'

'Oh, Camille.'

'What?'

'Don't let's go there. Go to sleep, now.'

'I'm not sleepy.'

'Franck.'

'Now what.'

'Where are your parents?'

'No idea.'

'What d'you mean, no idea?'

'I don't have any.'

Camille didn't know what to say.

'My father,' he continued, 'I never knew; a stranger who shot his load in the back of a car. And my mother, well . . .'

'What?'

'Well, my mother didn't really like the fact that some bastard whose name she couldn't even remember had shot his load like that so, uh . . .'

'What?'

'Nothing.'

'Nothing, what?'

'Well, she wanted nothing to do with him.'

'With who, the guy?'

'No, her little boy.'

'Your grandmother brought you up?'

'My grandmother and grandfather.'

'And did your grandfather die?'

'Yes.'

'You never saw her again?'

'Camille, I swear, you'd better stop. Otherwise you're going to have to take me in your arms afterwards.'

'No, go on. I'm willing to take that risk.'

'Liar.'

'You never saw her again?'

Silence.

'I'm sorry. I'll stop.'

She heard him turning over:

'I . . . until I was ten, I had no news from her. Well, no, actually I always got a present for my birthday and for Christmas, but later I learned that that was all a farce. Just another trick to get me all mixed up. A nice trick, but a trick all the same. She never wrote, but I know my grandma sent her my school photo every year. And then one year, go figure, I must have been cuter than usual – maybe the teacher had actually combed my hair that day – or the photographer pulled out a plastic Mickey Mouse to make me smile? Anyway, the little kid in the photo must've filled her with regret and she announced she was going to come and take me away with her. There was one hell of a mess . . . There was me screaming because I wanted to stay, my grandma trying to console me and saying over and over again that this was great, at last I'd have a real family, and she couldn't help bawling even louder than me, squeezing me up against her huge breasts . . . My granddad didn't say a thing. I'm not kidding, what a mess. You're smart enough to understand this sort of thing, right? But believe me, it was tough.

'After choking us off a few times, she finally turned up. I got in her car. She showed me her husband, her other kid, and my new bed.

'At first I really liked the idea, sleeping in a bunk bed, that kind of thing, and then that night I started crying. I told her I wanted to go

269

home. She answered that this was home now and I had to be quiet otherwise I'd wake up the little kid. That night and every night after that I wet my bed. It pissed her off. She said, I'm sure you're doing it on purpose, you can just stay wet, too bad. It's your grandmother, she spoiled you. And then I went crazy.

'I'd always lived in the fields, I went fishing every day after school, in winter my granddad would take me hunting, or to the café, or to pick mushrooms. I was always outdoors, always in boots, always throwing my bike into the bushes so I could hang out with the poachers and learn their trade, and then suddenly there I was in some rotten high-rise low-rent housing estate in some shit-faced suburb, stuck between four walls, a television and another kid who was raking in all the affection . . . so, I lost it. I – No. Never mind. Three months later she stuck me on the train and told me again and again that I'd spoiled it all.

'*You spoiled it all, you spoiled it all* . . . When I got into my granddad's Simca that was still going round and round in my little head. And the worst of it, you know, is that –'

'Is what?'

'Is that she shattered me into a million pieces, that bitch. Afterwards it was never the same. I wasn't a kid any more, I didn't want their cuddles and all that shit. Because the worst thing – it wasn't so much that she came to get me, the worst was all the bad stuff she said about my grandmother before she threw me out again. She really fucked with my head with all her lies. Said it was her mother who'd forced her to abandon me and then she threw her out. That she had done everything she could to take me with her but they'd pulled out the shotgun . . .'

'Was she bullshitting you?'

'Of course. But I didn't know that, not then. I didn't understand a thing any more and maybe on some level I wanted to believe her? Maybe it suited me to think we'd been separated by force and that if my granddad hadn't got out his blunderbuss, I would have had the same life as everyone and no one would have called me the son of a whore behind the church. "Your ma's a ho" is what they said, and "you're just a bastard". Words I didn't even understand. For me a hoe was a garden tool. What a loser.'

'And then?'

'After that I turned into a stupid fucker. I did whatever I could to get even. To make them pay for having deprived me of such a sweet mother.'

He was laughing.

'And I managed just fine. I smoked my granddad's Gauloises, stole money from the shopping kitty, caused all kinds of trouble at school, got expelled and spent most of my time on a moped or in the backroom of some café planning my next trick or feeling up some girl. Really nasty stuff. You've no idea. I was the chief. The best. King of the shit-stirrers.'

'And then?'

'And then, nighty night. To be continued in the next episode.'

'Well? Don't you want to take me in your arms now?'

'I'm not so sure. It's not like you got raped or anything.'

He leaned over her: 'So much the better. Because I don't want your arms. Not like that. Not any more. I played that little game long enough, but that's all over. It's no fun any more. It never works. Shit, how many blankets have you got there?'

'Uh . . . three, plus the duvet.'

'That's not normal. And it's not normal that you're always cold, and that you take two hours to recover from a ride on a motorbike. You have to put on weight, Camille.'

She didn't reply.

'You too, you – I don't really get the impression that you have a great album with pictures of your family laughing around you, do you?'

'No.'

'Will you tell me some day?'

'Maybe.'

'You know I . . . I won't bug you with this any more.'

'With what?'

'I was talking to you about Fred earlier on, saying he was my only friend, right, but I was wrong. I do have one other . . . Pascal Lechampy, the best pastry chef on earth. Remember his name, you'll see . . . This guy is a god. From a shortbread to a *saint-honoré*, via cakes, chocolate, *mille-feuilles*, nougat, cream puffs, whatever – everything he touches is transformed into something unforgettable. Delicious, beautiful, refined, amazing, and perfectly executed . . . I've met a few good workers in my life, but he's in a class by himself.

271

Perfection. And a really sweet guy to boot. Cream of the cream, a saint, a real softie. Well, turns out, this guy was enormous. Humongously enormous. Up to a point it wasn't a problem. He wasn't the only one. The problem was that he really stank. You couldn't stand next to him for one second without feeling like puking. Okay, I'll spare you the details, the way people made fun or made comments, the bars of soap they'd leave in his locker, all that sort of stuff . . . One day we were sharing a hotel room because I'd gone along with him to a contest to be his assistant. He gave his demonstration, and of course he won, but as for me, you can't imagine the state I was in by the end of the day. I couldn't even breathe any more and I'd decided to spend the night in a bar rather than stay another minute in his wake. What surprised me, though, was that he'd taken a shower in the morning, that much I knew, because I was there. Finally we got back to the hotel, I hit the booze so it would anaesthetize me, like, and in the end I started talking to him about it . . . You still there?'

'Yes, yes, I'm listening.'

'So I say, Shit Pascal, you stink. You stink of death, mate. What's going on for Christ's sake? Don't you wash or what? And then this big teddy bear, this monster of a guy, this pure genius with his big laugh and his mountain of fat starts crying, crying, crying. Like a fountain. Horrible, big baby-like sobs and everything, inconsolable, the idiot. Fuck, I felt bad. After a while he suddenly took all his clothes off, just like that, without warning. So I turned around, I was getting ready to go into the bathroom and he grabbed my arm and said, "Look at me, Lestaf, look at this shit." Fuck, I almost passed out.'

'Why?'

'His body to start with. It was downright gross. But more than anything – it was what he wanted to show me, it was . . . God, just thinking about it, I still feel like puking. He had this sort of rash, but like a crust, I don't know what it was, in the folds of his flesh. And that's what was stinking, this sort of oozing, bloody scabies. Fuck, I swear, I drank all night long to get over it. On top of that he told me it really hurt him when he washed but he would scrub like a crazy man to get rid of the smell and he'd sprinkle perfume all over himself and clench his teeth so he wouldn't cry. What a night; God it was horrible, when I think about it . . .'

'And then?'

'In the morning I dragged him to the hospital, to casualty. It was in Lyon, I remember . . . And even the doctor went all wobbly when he saw him. He cleaned his sores, gave him a ton of medicine, a long prescription with ointments and tablets all over the place. He bawled him out and told him he'd have to lose weight and in the end he said, "Why'd you wait so long?" No reply. And when we were on the platform at the station I pestered him again, too: "The doctor was right, man, fuck it, why did you wait so long?" "Because I was too ashamed," he answered, and he looked down. And there and then I swore that would be the last time.'

'Last time what?'

'That I'd give fat people a hard time. That I would look down on them, that . . . Well, you know what I mean, I was judging people by their appearance. So . . . to get back to you. Don't get jealous, the same thing applies for thin people. And never mind what I might be thinking, even if I'm sure that you'd be warmer and more appetizing if you were a few pounds heavier, I won't bug you with it any more. My drunkard's word of honour.'

'Franck?'

'Hey! We said we'd go to sleep now!'

'Will you help me?'

'What? To be warmer and more appetizing?'

'Yes.'

'No way. So that you'd get kidnapped by the first bearded wonder who comes along?' He clicked his tongue. 'I prefer you scrawny and with us. And I'm sure Philou would agree.'

Silence.

'Maybe a little bit then. As soon as I see your breasts starting to sprout too much, I'll stop.'

'Okay.'

'So what does this make me now, some kind of health guru? Shit, you're making me jump through all your hoops. How should we do this? For starters, no more doing your own shopping any more because you buy nothing but crap. Cereal bars and biscuits and cream desserts and all that, finito. I don't know what time you get up in the morning but from Tuesday on you have to remember that I'm the one who's feeding you, okay? Every day at three when I come home, I'll bring you a meal. Don't worry, I know girls, I won't give you duck confit or tripe. I'll make a good scrummy little dish just for you. Fish, grilled meat, tasty veggies, just stuff you'll really like. I'll make small amounts but you've got to eat it all or else I'll stop. And in the evening I'm not there so I won't bug you, but no snacking or nibbling, strictly forbidden, verboten! I'll go on making a big pot of soup at the beginning of the week for Philou the way I always have, and that's it. The idea is to get you hooked on my grub. So that every morning you'll get up wondering what's on the menu. I, uh, don't promise it'll be utterly amazing every single time, but it'll be good, you'll see. And when you start to fill out, I'll . . .'

'You'll what?'

'I'll eat you.'

'Like the witch in Hansel and Gretel?'

'You bet. And no use giving me a bone when I go to feel your arm because I'm not blind! And now I don't want to hear another word out of you. It's almost two in the morning and we have a long day tomorrow.'

'Do you know, you put on an act, but you're a nice person, you are.'

'Shut up.'

12

'Hey! Wake up, Michelin tyre lady!'

Franck put the tray at the foot of the mattress.

'Oh! Breakfast in bed . . .'

'Don't get excited. It's not me, it's Jeannine. C'mon, hurry up, we're late. And eat at least one slice of bread and jam, get some ballast, otherwise you'll regret it . . .'

No sooner had Camille stepped outside, her lips still smeared with café au lait, than someone handed her a glass of white wine.

'There you go, young lady! This'll give you courage!'

They were all there, the guests from the previous evening and everyone from the hamlet, fifteen people or so. And they were all exactly as you might imagine, stereotypical country folk with their mail-order clothes. The older women wearing smocks and the younger ones overalls. Tapping their feet, clutching their glasses, calling out to each other, laughing then suddenly falling quiet: Gaston had just arrived with his huge knife.

Franck took up the commentary:

'He's the pig-slayer.'

'I might have guessed.'

'Seen his hands?'

'Impressive.'

'Two pigs are getting it today. They're not fooled, they weren't fed this morning, so they know their number's up. They feel it. Look, there's the first one now. Got your sketchbook?'

'Yes, yes.'

Camille could not help but be startled. She had not imagined a pig could be so big.

They dragged the beast into the farmyard, Gaston whacked it with a club, they laid it on a bench and quickly tied it up, leaving its head dangling. Up to that point, it seemed all right because the beast was a bit out of it, but when the pig-slayer stuck his blade into the carotid, it was horrible. Instead of killing it, it was as if they'd woken it up. All the men rushing round it, blood spurting, the old grandma sticking a pan underneath, rolling her sleeve up to stir the blood. No spoon, nothing, her bare hand. Gulp. But still that wasn't too bad; what was unbearable was listening to him squeal. How he went on, and on. The more he bled, the more he squealed and the more he squealed, the less it sounded like a beast crying. It was almost human. A death rattle, a plea. Camille gripped her sketchbook, and the other people there, those who knew the whole ritual by heart, were not doing much better. Hey, another shot of Dutch courage.

'Absolutely, thanks.'

'You okay?'

'Yes.'

'Not drawing?'

'No.'

Camille, who wasn't born yesterday, tried to reason with herself and avoided making stupid remarks. For her the worst was still to come. For her, the worst was not the death itself. No, that was part of life, after all, but what seemed cruellest to her was when they brought out the second pig. Whether you believed in anthropomorphism or were simply squeamish, say what you liked, she didn't care, she really found it difficult to contain her emotion. Because that second pig had heard it all and he knew what had happened to his friend, and he didn't wait to be stuck before he started braying like a donkey. Well, 'like a donkey' is a stupid expression, like a pig that's having its throat cut.

'Shit, they could at least have blocked his ears!'

'With parsley?' asked Franck, laughing.

So then, yes, she had to draw, so she wouldn't see it any more. And she concentrated on Gaston's hands so she wouldn't hear.

It was no good. She was trembling.

When the squealing stopped, she put her sketchbook in her pocket and drew nearer. There, it was finished, she was curious, and with her glass she gestured toward the bottle.

They scorched the pigs with a blowtorch; there was a smell of grilled pork. Then they rubbed them with an astonishing brush: a wooden board on to which a whole series of upside-down beer caps had been nailed.

Camille sketched.

The butcher had begun his labour of chopping, and she went behind the block so that she would not miss any of his gestures. Franck was delighted.

'What's that?' she asked him.

'What?'

'That sort of transparent gluey ball?'

'The bladder. Actually it's not usually so full . . . it's making things difficult for him.'

'It's not making things difficult at all! There, here you go,' exclaimed the butcher, moving his blade.

Camille squatted down to look at the pig's bladder. She was fascinated.

Kids loaded down with trays went back and forth between the still smoking pig and the kitchen.

'Stop drinking.'

'Yes, Dr Health Guru.'

'I'm pleased. You did well.'

'Were you scared I wouldn't?'

'I was curious. Well, this is all very well, but I have work to do.'

'Where are you off to?'

'To get my gear. Go and sit somewhere warm, why don't you.'

She found them all in the kitchen, a whole row of perky housewives armed with wooden chopping boards and knives.

'Come over here!' shouted Jeannine. 'Here, Lucienne, make room for her by the stove. Ladies, may I introduce Franck's girlfriend, you know, the one I was telling you about a while ago. The one we resurrected, last night. Come and sit by us.'

The smell of coffee mingled with the frying of innards, and there was laughter, and chattering. A regular henhouse.

Franck arrived. Here he is! The chef! They giggled even more. When Jeannine saw him in his white chef's jacket, she became flustered.

Walking behind her toward the oven, he squeezed her shoulder. She blew her nose in her dishtowel and went back to laughing with the others.

At this precise moment in the story, Camille wondered whether she wasn't falling in love with him. Shit. This was not something she had planned on, not at all. No way, she thought, reaching for a chopping board. No way, it was only because he'd told her his Dickensian saga. She wasn't about to fall into that trap.

'Can you give me some work?' she asked.

They explained to her how to cut the meat into tiny pieces.

'What's it for?'

Answers came from all sides: 'Sausage! Salami! Andouilles. Pâté. Rillettes.'

'And what are you doing with that toothbrush?' – as she leaned over toward her neighbour.

'I'm washing the entrails.'

Yuck.

'And Franck?'

'Franck is going to be cooking for us. Blood pudding, poaching the andouilles and the delicacies.'

'What are the delicacies?'

'Head, tail, ears, trotters.'

Double-yuck.

Uh. His nutritionist thing: he did say it wouldn't start before Tuesday, right?

When he came back up from the cellar with his potatoes and onions and saw her peering over at her neighbours to find out how to hold the knife, he walked over and took it from her hands:

'Don't you get involved with this. Stick with what you're good at. If you cut your finger you'll be in deep shit. Stick with what you're good at, don't you see? Where's your sketchbook?'

Then, turning to the gossiping women: 'Hey, you don't mind if she draws you, do you?'

'Course not.'

'I do, my perm is all a mess.'

'C'mon Lucienne, you're not a beauty queen. In fact, we all know damn well you've got a wig!'

And that was the atmosphere: Club Med at the farm . . .

Camille washed her hands and sketched until evening. Indoors, outdoors. Blood, watercolours. Dogs, cats. Kids, old people. Fire, bottles. Smocks, cardigans. Under the table, fur-lined slippers. On the table, calloused hands. Franck from the back and her own face in the blurry convex surface of a stainless steel stewing pot.

To each of the women she offered a portrait – little shivers of delight – then she asked the children to show her the farm so she could get some fresh air. And sober up a bit too.

Kids in Batman sweatshirts and rubber boots were running in every direction, laughing as they captured hens, teasing the dogs as they dragged long pieces of entrails behind them.

'Bradley, what is wrong with you! Don't start the tractor, you'll get killed.'

'Aw, it was only to show him.'

'You're called Bradley?'

'Yup.'

Bradley was the hard case in the gang, by the look of it. He got half undressed just to show her his scars.

'If we put them all together,' he bragged, 'it would make eight inches worth of stitches!'

Camille nodded gravely and drew two Batman pictures: Batman taking off, and Batman versus the giant octopus.

'How do you manage to draw so good?'

'You draw well too. Everyone draws well.'

In the evening, the banquet. Twenty-two people around the table and pork everywhere in sight. The tails and ears were grilling in the fireplace, and straws were drawn to determine whose plates would have the honour. Franck had been working flat out: his first course was a sort of gelatinous and very aromatic soup. Camille dipped her bread in the soup, but didn't go any further; then came the blood pudding, the trotters, the tongue, and that wasn't all. She pushed her chair back a few inches and masked her lack of appetite by holding her glass out to the nearest taker. Afterwards came the desserts – everyone had brought a pie or a cake – and finally, the brandies.

'Ah, my fine young lady, you must taste this. Any fair maid who declines shall remain a virgin.'

'Okay, then, just a drop.'

Camille ensured her deflowering under the wily gaze of her neighbour, an old bloke who had only a tooth and a half, and then she took advantage of the general confusion to go up to bed.

She collapsed on to her bed in a heap and, lulled by the joyful clamour which wafted through the floorboards, nodded off.

She was sound asleep when he came to curl up next to her. She grunted.

'Don't worry. I'm too drunk, I won't do anything,' he murmured.

As she had her back to him, he placed his nose on her neck and slid his arm underneath her to be as close to her as possible. Short strands of her hair tickled his nostrils.

'Camille?'

Was she asleep? Was she pretending? No answer either way.

'I like being with you.'

A little smile.

Was she dreaming? Was she asleep? Who knows . . .

At noon, when they finally awoke, Camille and Franck were on their separate 'beds'. Neither of them mentioned it.

Hangovers, confusion, fatigue; they put back the mattress, folded the sheets, took turns in the bathroom and got dressed in silence.

The stairway seemed unusually treacherous, and Jeannine handed each of them a big mug of black coffee without saying a word. Two other women were already seated at the end of the table, splashing about in the sausage meat. Camille turned her chair to face the fireplace and drank her coffee, her mind empty. Clearly she had had a drop too many, and she closed her eyes between each sip of coffee. Bah: this was the price you paid to lose your virginity.

The kitchen smells made her feel sick. She got up, poured another mug of coffee, reached for her tobacco in her coat pocket and went to sit in the yard on the pig bench.

Franck came to join her after a few minutes.

'May I?'

She moved over.

'Headache?'

She nodded.

'You know, I . . . I have to go and see my grandmother now. So there's three things we can do: either I leave you here and come back for you in the afternoon, or I take you with me and you wait somewhere, long enough for me to chat with her a bit, or I drop you at the station on the way and you go back to Paris on your own.'

She didn't answer right away. Put down her mug, rolled a cigarette, lit it, and exhaled a long, satisfying puff.

'What's your opinion?'

'I don't know,' he lied.

'I don't really feel like staying here without you.'

'Okay, I'll drop you at the station, then. State you're in, the ride will be really unbearable. You'll feel even colder if you're tired.'

'Fine,' she answered.

Oh, shit.

Jeannine insisted. Yes, yes, a piece from the fillet, I'll wrap it up for you. She walked with them down the lane, took Franck in her arms and whispered a few words that Camille could not hear.

And when he put his foot down at the first stop sign before the main road, she lifted their visors:

'I'm coming with you.'

'You sure?'

She nodded with the helmet and was abruptly projected backwards. Ooops. Life was accelerating all of a sudden. Right . . . Never mind.

She squeezed up against him and gritted her teeth.

13

'You want to wait for me in a café?'

'No, no, I'll find a spot downstairs.'

They'd gone only three paces along the hallway when a woman in a sky-blue smock rushed up. She looked hard at Franck and shook her head sadly: 'She's at it again.'

He sighed.

'Is she in her room?'

'Yes but she's bundled everything up again and she refuses to let anyone touch her. She's been lying there with her coat on her lap since yesterday evening.'

'Has she eaten?'

'No.'

'Thanks.'

He turned to Camille. 'Can I leave my stuff with you?'

'What's going on?'

'What's going on is that Paulette is starting to seriously piss me off with her song and dance.'

He was white as a sheet.

'I don't even know if it's a good idea to see her. I'm lost here, you see, completely out of it.'

'Why is she refusing to eat?'

'Because she thinks I'll take her home, the stupid woman. She does this to me every time now. You know, I just feel like taking off, right now.'

'You want me to come with you?'

'That won't change a thing.'

'No, it might not, but it'll distract her.'

'You think?'

'Sure, why not. Come on.'

Franck went in first and announced in a fluty voice:

'Grandma, it's me. I brought you a surpr—'

He didn't have the courage to finish.

The old woman was sitting on her bed, staring at the door. She was wearing her coat, her shoes, her scarf and even her little black pillbox. A poorly closed suitcase was at her feet.

'It breaks my heart . . .' Another impeccably apposite expression, thought Camille, who felt her own heart crumbling suddenly.

Paulette was so sweet with her clear eyes and her pointed face. A little mouse. A little Hunca Munca in desperate straits.

Franck acted as if there were nothing wrong.

'Well, then! You've got too many clothes on again!' he joked, quickly removing her coat. 'But it's not as if they don't heat the place. What's the temperature in here? At least twenty-five. But I told them downstairs, I told them they had the heat way too high, but they never listen. We've just come from slaying the pig over at Jeannine's, and I can tell you that even in the room where they smoke the sausages it's not as hot as in here. How you doing, anyway? Hey, look at that, what a nice bedspread you've got. Does this mean you finally got your catalogue from La Redoute? Took them long enough. And what about the stockings, did I get you the right ones? You know you don't write very clearly. And didn't I look like a plonker when I asked the salesgirl for some Monsieur Michel toilet water. She gave me this sideways look as if I had rocks in my head so I showed her your note. She had to go and get her glasses. You can't imagine the shambles until finally she worked it out, you'd written *Mont-Saint* Michel. How're we supposed to know, huh? Here it is, anyway. Lucky it didn't break.'

He put her slippers on for her and chattered away, punch drunk on his own words so he wouldn't have to look at her.

'Are you young Camille?' Paulette asked, with a lovely smile.

'Uh, yes.'

'Come over here so I can see you.'

Camille sat down next to her.

She took her hands: 'But you're freezing.'

283

'It's the motorbike.'

'Franck?'

'Yes?'

'Well, make us some tea, for heaven's sake! Have to get this little child warm!'

He breathed. Thank you, God. The worst was over. He put her things in the wardrobe and looked around for the kettle.

'Take some little biscuits from my night table.' Then turning back to her: 'So it's you. You're Camille. Oh, I'm so happy to see you.'

'So am I. Thank you for the scarf.'

'Oh that reminds me, just a second.'

She got up and came back with a whole bagful of old knitting catalogues.

'My friend Yvonne brought me these catalogues for you. Tell me what you'd like. But no moss stitch, all right? I don't know how to do that one.'

March, 1984. Oh-kaay . . .

Camille slowly turned the dog-eared pages.

'That's a nice one, no?'

Paulette pointed to an incredibly ugly cardigan with cables and golden buttons.

'Uh . . . I'd prefer a big sweater actually.'

'A big sweater?'

'Yes.'

'But big in what way?'

'Oh, you know, like a turtleneck?'

'Well, keep turning, let's look at the men's designs.'

'That one.'

'Franck, my rabbit: my glasses?'

How happy he was to hear her speak like that. That's good, Grandma, carry on. Give me orders, make me look ridiculous in front of her, and treat me like a baby, but don't cry. I beg you. Please no more crying.

'Well. All right. I'll leave you. Going to take a leak.'

'You do that, leave us.'

He smiled.

What a relief; what a happy relief.

He closed the door behind him and out in the corridor he leapt in the air. He would have kissed the first bedridden invalid he came across. Shit, what joy. 'Leave us,' she had said. Yes, girls, I'll leave you! Fuck, that's all I ask! That is all I ask!

Thank you, Camille, thank you. Even if you never come again, we'll have three months of reprieve with your sweater. The yarn, the colour, trying it on. Conversations guaranteed for a good while yet. Okay, which way were the toilets?

Paulette settled into her armchair and Camille sat with her back to the radiator.

'Are you all right on the floor?'

'Yes.'

'Franck always sits like that too.'

'Did you have a biscuit?'

'Four!'

'That's good.'

They looked at each other and said a host of silent things. They talked about Franck, to be sure, about distance, youth, certain landscapes, death, solitude, the passing of time, the happiness of being together and the relentless struggle of life – without uttering a single word.

Camille really wanted to draw her. Paulette's face evoked little blades of grass from the roadside, wild violets, forget-me-nots, buttercups. A soft face, open, gentle, luminous, fine like Japanese paper. The lines of sorrow disappeared behind the vapour rising from the tea, and gave way to a thousand little kindnesses at the corner of her eyes.

Camille thought she was lovely.

Paulette was thinking exactly the same thing. She was so graceful, this young thing, so calm and elegant in her vagabond's trappings. She wished it were spring so she could show her the garden, the quince branches in bloom and the scent of the seringa. No, this girl was not like other girls.

An angel from heaven, who had to wear huge bricklayer's boots to stay down here among us.

'Has she gone?' asked Franck, looking worried.

'No, no, I'm here,' answered Camille, lifting an arm from behind the bed.

Paulette smiled. No need for glasses to see certain things. A great feeling of peace settled on her chest. She had to resign herself. She was going to resign herself. She had to accept it, finally. For his sake. For herself. For everyone.

No more seasons, okay. Come on . . . That's the way it was. Everyone got their turn. She wouldn't bother him any more. She wouldn't think about her garden every morning. She'd try not to think about anything. His turn to live, now.

His turn to live.

Franck told her about the day at the farm with a fresh new cheerfulness, and Camille showed her the sketches.

'What's this?'

'A pork bladder.'

'And that?'

'Revolutionary slipper-boot-clogs!'

'Who's this little boy?'

'I, uh, can't remember his name now.'

'And this?'

'That is Spiderman. Above all, not to be confused with Batman.'

'It's wonderful to be so gifted.'

'Oh, this is nothing.'

'I wasn't talking about your drawings, young lady, I was referring to the way you see things. Ah! Here's dinner. You'd better think about heading home, you youngsters. It's already dark out.'

Wait . . . She's telling us to leave? Franck was floored. And so flustered that he had to hold on to the curtain to get to his feet, and he pulled the curtain rod off its fitting.

'Shit!'

'Leave it, never mind, and stop talking like a hooligan, won't you?'

'I'll stop.'

He looked down, with a smile. Thatta girl, Paulette. Thatta girl. Don't mind me. Shout. Fuss. Moan. Come back this way.

'Camille?'

'Yes?'

'May I ask you a favour?'

'Of course!'

'Call me when you get home, just to reassure me. He never calls me and I . . . Or if you prefer, just let it ring once and hang up, that way I'll understand and I'll be able to fall asleep.'

'It's a promise.'

They were still in the corridor when Camille realized she'd forgotten her gloves. She hurried back to the room and saw that Paulette was already at the window to watch for them.

'I – my gloves.'

The old lady with the pink hair did not have the cruelty to turn around. She merely raised a hand and nodded her head.

'It's horrible,' she said while he was kneeling by his anti-theft lock.

'No, don't say that, she was really great today! Thanks to you, actually. Thanks.'

'No, it was horrible.'

They waved to the tiny figure on the third floor and rejoined their queue in the ant farm. Franck felt lighter. But Camille, on the other hand, could not find the words to think.

He stopped by their entrance but did not switch off the motor.

'You're not coming up?'

'No,' went the helmet.

'Okay then, ciao.'

14

It must have been a little before nine, and the apartment was plunged in darkness.

'Philou? You there?'

She found him sitting up in his bed. Completely beside himself. A blanket on his shoulders and his hand stuck in a book.

'You okay?'

He didn't answer.

'Are you sick?'

'I've been worried st-stiff, I was expecting you mu-much earlier.'

Camille sighed. Shit. When it's not one, it's the other.

She put her elbows on the mantelpiece, turned her back to him and dropped her forehead into her palms: 'Philibert, please stop. Stop stuttering. Don't do this to me. Don't spoil everything. That is the first time I've been anywhere in years. Pick yourself up, get rid of that moth-eaten poncho, put your book down and ask as casually as you can, "Well, Camille? Did you have a good time on your little trip?"'

'W-well, Ca-Camille? Did you have a good time on your little trip?'

'Great time, thank you! What about you? Which battle today?'

'Pavie.'

'Ah. Great.'

'No, a disaster.'

'Who's this one between?'

'The Valois against the Habsburgs. François I against Charles V.'

'Of course! I know Charles V! He's the one who came after Maximilian I in the German empire!'

'Goodness me, how do you know that?'

'Ah-hah! Got you there, didn't I!'

He took off his glasses to rub his eyelids.

'So you had a good time on your trip.'

'Extremely colourful.'

'Will you show me your sketchbook?'

'If you get up. Is there any soup left?'

'I think so.'

'I'll meet you in the kitchen.'

'And Franck?'

'He took off . . .'

'Did you know he was an orphan? I mean, that his mother abandoned him?'

'That is what I had heard.'

Camille was too tired to fall asleep. She rolled her fireplace into the living room and smoked cigarettes listening to Schubert.

Winterreise.

She started crying and suddenly the nasty taste of stones was there, deep in her throat.

Papa . . .

Camille, stop it. Go to bed. Your soppy romantic dribbling, the cold and fatigue, now the other guy over there getting on your nerves. Stop right now. It's a complete and utter waste of time.

Oh, shit!

What?

I forgot to call Paulette.

Well, then call her.

But it's really late now.

All the more reason! Hurry!

'It's me, it's Camille. Did I wake you up?'

'No, no.'

'I'd forgotten to call.'

Silence.

'Camille?'

'Yes?'

'You take good care of yourself, sweetheart, now, you hear?'

Silence.

'Camille?'

'Okay,' she faltered.

The next day she stayed in bed until it was time to go and do her cleaning. When she got up she saw the plate that Franck had prepared for her on the table with a little note: *'Yesterday's filet mignon with prunes and fresh tagliatelle. Microwave three minutes.'*

And not a single spelling mistake, hey.

She ate standing up and immediately felt better.

She earned her living in silence.

Wrung out the floor mops, emptied the ashtrays and tied the bin bags.

Came home on foot.

Clapped her hands together to warm them up.

Raised her head.

Thought.

And the more she thought, the faster she walked.

Almost running.

It was two o'clock in the morning when she shook Philibert awake: 'I have to talk to you.'

15

'Now?'

'Yes.'

'B-but, what time is it?'

'Who cares, listen to me!'

'Pass me my glasses, please.'

'You don't need your glasses, it's dark in here.'

'Camille, please . . . Ah, thank you. I can hear better with my specs on. Speak, soldier, to what do we owe the honour of this ambush?'

Camille took a deep breath and came out with it. She spoke for a very long time.

'End of report, Colonel, Sir!'

Philibert was speechless.

'Have you nothing to say?'

'Well, if it was a surprise attack you wanted, you've succeeded.'

'You don't want to?'

'Wait, let me think.'

'Coffee?'

'Good idea. Go and make yourself a coffee while I gather my wits about me.'

'What about you?'

He closed his eyes and motioned to her to strike camp.

'Well?'

'I . . . I'll be frank: I don't think it's a good idea.'

'Oh?' said Camille, biting her lip.

'No.'

'Why?'

'Because it involves too much responsibility.'

'That's no excuse. I don't want that kind of answer. That's stupid. People die every day because of people who won't assume their responsibilities . . . people die, Philibert. You didn't ask yourself that sort of question the day you came up to rescue me, when I hadn't eaten for three days.'

'Yes, actually, I did ask myself that question.'

'And? Are you sorry?'

'No. But you can't compare. This is not at all the same sort of situation.'

'Yes it is! It's exactly the same.'

Silence.

'You know full well that this is not my own place. We're living on borrowed time. I can get a registered letter tomorrow morning ordering me to leave the premises in the following week.'

Camille made a dismissive sound. 'You know how all these inheritance stories play out – there's a good chance you'll be here for another ten years.'

'For ten years or one month. Who can tell . . . When there's a lot of money at stake, even the worst sticklers will eventually find common ground, you know.'

'Philou.'

'Don't look at me like that. You're asking too much.'

'No, I'm not asking you a thing. I'm just asking you to trust me.'

'Camille . . .'

'I . . . I've never spoken to you about it but I . . . I had a really shitty life up until the time I met you. Of course, compared to Franck's childhood, it doesn't seem like such a big deal but all the same, I get the impression it's pretty similar. It was more insidious perhaps. Like a slow drip. And then I, I don't know how I managed. I probably handled it badly, but I . . .'

'But you what?'

'I lost all the people I loved in the process and –'

'And?'

'And when I told you the other day that I had no one but you in the world, it was not . . . Oh fuck it, anyway! Look, yesterday was my birthday. I turned twenty-seven and the only person who took

292

any notice was, I'm afraid, my mother. And you know what she gave me? A diet book. Funny, isn't it. How witty can you get, I wonder. I'm really sorry to bug you with all this, but you have to help me one more time, Philibert. Just this once, and after that I'll never ask anything of you again, I promise.'

'It was your birthday yesterday?' he said, his voice full of regret. 'Why didn't you tell us?'

'Who cares about my birthday! If I told you this story it was just to crank up your tear ducts but it really isn't important.'

'But it is! I would have liked to give you a present!'

'Well then go ahead: give it to me now.'

'And if I accept, will you let me go back to sleep?'

'Yes.'

'All right then, it's yes.'

Of course he didn't get back to sleep.

16

At seven o'clock the next morning, Camille was ready for action. She had been to the bakery and brought back a baguette for her favourite officer.

When he came into the kitchen, he found her crouched down under the sink.

'Uh-uh, major manoeuvres already?' he moaned.

'I wanted to bring you breakfast in bed but I didn't dare.'

'You were right. I'm the only one who knows the precise quantity of chocolate to put in.'

'Oh, Camille. Sit down. You're making me dizzy.'

'If I sit down, I'll have to tell you something serious.'

'Oh, Lordy. Then stay on your feet.'

She sat down opposite him, put her hands on the table, and looked him straight in the eye: 'I'm going to start work again.'

'Sorry?'

'I posted my letter of resignation just now, when I went down.'

Silence.

'Philibert?'

'Yes.'

'Speak. Say something.'

He lowered his bowl and licked his whiskers: 'No. What can I say? You're on your own in this, my love.'

'I'd like to set up in the room at the back.'

'But Camille, it's a regular shambles back there!'

'With a billion dead flies, I know. But it's the room with the most light, since it's on the corner with one window to the east and the other to the south.'

'And what about all the stuff?'

'I'll take care of it.'

He sighed: 'What woman wants . . .'

'You'll see. You'll be proud of me.'

'I should hope so. And what about me?'

'What?'

'Do I have the right to ask you for something, too?'

'Well, sure.'

He began to go pink: 'I-imagine that you w-want to g-give a p-present to a young girl that you d-don't know, what d-do you d-do?'

Camille looked at him from under her eyebrows: 'I'm sorry?'

'D-don't p-play dumb, you heard m-me.'

'Well I don't know, depends on the occasion.'

'No p-p-particular occasion.'

'For when?'

'Saturday.'

'Give her some Guerlain.'

'I beg your p-pardon?'

'Perfume.'

'I . . . I would never know what to choo-choose.'

'Do you want me to come with you?'

'Please.'

'No problem. We'll go during your lunch break.'

'Th-thanks.'

'Ca-Camille?'

'Yes?'

'She – she's just a friend, okay?'

She stood up with a laugh.

'Naturally.'

Then, looking at the kittens on the Post Office calendar she added: 'Well, I never! It's Valentine's day on Saturday. Did you know that?'

He dipped his head back into his bowl.

'Okay, I have to leave now, I have work to do. I'll come by for you at the museum at noon.'

*

295

He had not yet made his way back to the surface and was still slurping his way through his Nesquik potion when Camille left the kitchen with her Ajax and her artillery of sponges.

When Franck came back for his nap in the early afternoon, he found the flat deserted and upside down:

'What the fuck is all this bloody mess?'

He emerged from his room at about five o'clock. Camille was struggling with the base of a lamp.

'What the hell is going on?'

'I'm moving.'

'Where are you going?' He turned pale.

'There,' she said, pointing to the mountain of broken furniture and the carpet of dead flies. Then, spreading her arms, 'May I present my new studio . . .'

'Noooh.'

'Yes!'

'And your job?'

'We'll see.'

'And Philou?'

'Oh . . . Philou . . .'

'What?'

'He's making scents.'

'Huh?'

'No, nothing.'

'You want a hand?'

'And how!'

With a man it was a lot easier. In one hour Franck had moved all the stuff into the next room. A room whose windows had been condemned because of 'faulty jambs'.

She took advantage of a quiet moment – he was drinking a cold beer and surveying the extent of the work he had accomplished – to fire off her last salvo: 'Next Monday, at lunchtime, I'd like to celebrate my birthday with Philibert and you.'

'Uh, wouldn't you rather do it in the evening?'

'Why?'

'Well, you know, Monday I'm on granny duty.'

'Oh yes, sorry, I didn't make myself clear: next Monday, at lunchtime, I would like to celebrate my birthday with Philibert and you and Paulette.'

'There? At the hospice?'

'Of course not! You'll have to find us some sort of nice little country inn.'

'And how will we get there?'

'I thought we could rent a car.'

He was quiet and thoughtful until his last swallow of beer.

'Fine,' he said, crumpling the beer can, 'the thing is that she'll be disappointed from now on when I show up on my own.'

'I know . . . there's a good chance she will.'

'Don't feel obliged to do it for her sake, you know.'

'No, no, it's for me.'

'Good. I'll figure something out for the car. I have a friend who'd be only to happy to swap me his car for my bike . . . These flies are really gross.'

'I was waiting for you to wake up before I hoover.'

'And are you okay?'

'I'm fine. Did you see your Ralph Lauren?'

'No.'

'It is-a sublime-a, ze little dogga, is-a very happy.'

'How old will you be?'

'Twenty-seven.'

'Where were you before?'

'Sorry?'

'Before you were here, where were you?'

'Up there, of course!'

'And before that?'

'I don't have time to tell you, just now. Some night when you're around, I'll tell you the story.'

'You always say that, and then –'

'Yes, yes, I feel better now. I'll tell you the story of the edifying life of Camille Fauque.'

'What does that mean, edifying?'

'Good question.'

'Does it mean, "like an edifice"?'

'No, it means "exemplary", but it's ironic.'

'Ah-hah?'

'Like an edifice which is falling down, more like.'

'Like the Tower of Pisa?'

'Exactly!'

'Shit, it's rough living with an intellectual!'

'What d'you mean! On the contrary, it's very pleasant!'

'No, it's rough. I'm always afraid of making spelling mistakes. What did you eat at lunch?'

'A sandwich, with Philou. But I saw you put something for me in the oven, I'll get it later. Thanks, by the way. It's really kind.'

'Don't mention it. Okay, I'm out of here.'

'And you, everything okay?'

'I'm tired.'

'Well, you should sleep!'

'I do sleep actually, but I don't know. I just don't have the energy. Right. Back to the grindstone.'

17

'Well, I never. We don't see you for fifteen years and suddenly you're here nearly every day!'

'Hello, Odette.'

Loud kisses.

'Is she here?'

'No, not yet.'

'Well, we'll get settled while we're waiting for her. I'd like to introduce my friends: Camille . . .'

'Hello.'

' . . . and Philibert.'

'How do you do. Charmed, I'm –'

'Enough, enough! You can do your bowing and scraping later on.'

'Take it easy!'

'I can't take it easy, I'm hungry. Oh, there they are, hello Grandma. Hello Yvonne – will you stay and have a drink with us?'

'No, thanks all the same, but I've got people waiting at home. What time shall I come back for her?'

'We'll take her back.'

'Not too late, all right? Because last time I got told off. She has to be back before five thirty –'

'All right, all right, it's okay, Yvonne. Say hello to everyone at your place.'

Franck let out a sigh.

'Well, Grandma, let me introduce Philibert.'

'My humble respects.'

He leaned over to kiss her hand.

'Come on, let's sit down. No, Odette! No menu! Let the chef decide!'

'A little drink to start with?'

'Champagne!' said Philibert, then turning to his neighbour, 'Madame, do you like champagne?'

'Yes, yes,' said Paulette, intimidated by his grand manners.

'Here you go, here are some pork belly *rillons* while you're waiting.'

Everyone was a bit tense. Fortunately the good little wines from the Loire, the *brochet au beurre blanc*, and the goat cheeses quickly loosened their tongues. Philibert attended to his neighbour's every need, and Camille laughed as she listened to Franck's silly stories: 'I was . . . jeez . . . how old was I, Grandma?'

'Goodness, that was such a long time ago. Thirteen, fourteen?'

'It was the first year of my apprenticeship. I remember I was afraid of René at the time. I used to shake in my shoes. But anyway . . . I learned a mass of things from him. He could drive me up the wall, too. I forget what it was he was showing me . . . spatulas, I think, and he said, "This one we call the big pussy and the other one is the little pussy. You remember that, okay, for when the teacher asks you. 'Cause there may be books and stuff, but this is the real culinary terminology. The real jargon. That's how you can tell a good apprentice. Okay? You got that?"

'"Yes, boss."

'"And what is this one called?"

'"The big pussy, boss."

'"And the other one?"

'"Well, the little . . ."

'"The little what, Lestafier?"

'"The little pussy, boss."

'"Very good, lad, very good. You'll go far." God, I was clueless! The way they used to take the piss out of me! But it wasn't all a laugh, was it Odette? There were some kicks in the butt as well, weren't there?'

Odette, who had sat down with them, was nodding her head.

'Oh, he's a lot calmer now, you know.'

'He'd have to be! Kids nowadays won't put up with that sort of thing.'

'Don't talk to me about kids nowadays . . . You can't say a thing to them any more. They sulk. That's all they know how to do: sulk. I'm bloody fed up. It wears me out, I tell you. It wears me out even more than you lot did, setting fire to the garbage and things.'

'That's right! I'd completely forgotten about that.'

'Well I remember, believe me!'

The lights were dimmed. Camille blew out her candles and the entire room applauded.

Philibert disappeared for a moment and came back with a big package: 'It's from both of us.'

'Yeah, but it was his idea,' said Franck. 'If you don't like it, I'm not responsible. I wanted to rent you a stripper, but he didn't buy it . . .'

'Oh, thank you! This is wonderful!'

It was an artist's easel, especially for watercolours, known as a 'field easel'.

Philibert read the instructions with a quaver in his throat: 'Can be folded and inclined, double-sided, stable, large working area and two storage drawers. This easel has been designed for use when seated. It consists of four folding beechwood feet – that's what we like to hear – which have been assembled in pairs with a crossbar to ensure stability when used open. Closed, they ensure the drawers remained blocked. The work surface can be inclined thanks to a double hinge. It is possible to store a pad of paper maximum format of 68 by 52 centimetres. (A few sheets are included for your use.) An integrated handle allows the entire folded easel to be carried. (And that's not all, Camille . . .) Underneath the handle there is a storage rack for a small water bottle.'

'Only water?' said Franck anxiously.

'But it's not for drinking, you dunce,' said Paulette mockingly, 'it's for mixing colours!'

'Ah yeah, of course, you're right, what a dunce.'

'Do you – do you like it?' said Philibert anxiously.

'It's fabulous!'

'Would – would you have p-preferred a n-naked man?'

'Do I have time to try it right away?'

'Go ahead, go ahead, we're waiting for René in any case.'

Camille hunted for the tiny box of watercolours in her bag, unscrewed the screws and settled by the bay window.

She drew the Loire. Slow, wide, calm, imperturbable. The lazy sand banks, the pilings, the mildewed boats. Over there, a cormorant. Pale rushes and the blue of the sky. A winter blue – metallic, brilliant, bold, showing off its colours between two big weary clouds.

Odette was hypnotized. 'But how does she do it? She has only eight colours in her little box!'

'I'm cheating but hush . . . There. This is for you.'

'Oh, thank you! Thank you! René, come over here and take a look!'

'Dinner's on me!'

'Oh, no, we can't –'

'Yes, yes! I insist.'

When Camille sat back down with them, Paulette slipped her a package under the table: it was a knitted hat to match the scarf. The same holes and the same colours. Classy.

Hunters arrived, Franck followed them into the kitchen with their host, and hard liquor was poured as they commented on their gamebags. Camille fiddled delightedly with her present, and Paulette talked about her wartime experiences to Philibert, who had stretched out his long legs and was listening enraptured.

Then the time came, dusk fell, and Paulette sat down in the death seat in front.

No one said anything.

The landscape became increasingly drab.

They drove around the town and went through the drearily predictable commercial zones: supermarkets, hotels for 29 euros a night with cable, warehouses and storage depots. Finally Franck stopped the car.

Right at the far end of the zone.

Philibert got up to open the door and Camille pulled off her hat.

Paulette caressed her cheek.

'Let's go, let's go,' grumbled Franck, 'let's make it quick. I don't feel like getting told off by the mother superior, okay?'

When he came back, there was already a figure in the window, pulling aside the net curtains.

He got in, made a face, and let out a long sigh before putting the car in gear.

They had not yet left the car park when Camille tapped him on the shoulder: 'Stop.'

'Now what did you forget?'

'Stop, I said.'

18

Franck turned around.

'Now what?'

'How much does it cost?'

'What?'

'This place, here. This hospice.'

'Why do you ask?'

'How much?'

'Roughly ten thousand.'

'Who pays?'

'My granddad's pension, seven thousand one hundred and twelve francs, and the social services something or other.'

'I'll ask for two thousand francs from you, as pocket money, and the rest, you keep, and you stop working on Sundays so that I can have some time off.'

'Hey, what are you talking about, now?'

'Philou?'

'Oh no, this was your idea, my dear,' he simpered.

'Yes, but it's your house, my friend.'

'Hey! What's going on here? What's this about?'

Philibert lit the overhead light: 'If you don't mind . . .'

'And if *she* doesn't mind,' insisted Camille.

'. . . we're taking her with us,' smiled Philibert.

'With you? Where?' said Franck.

'Our place. Home.'

'When?'

'Now.'

'N-now?'

'Tell me, Camille, do I look like such a nitwit when I stutter?'

'Not at all,' she reassured him, 'you *never* have such an idiotic expression on your face.'

'And who is going to look after her?'

'I am. But I just told you my conditions.'

'And your job?'

'No more job! Finito!'

'But, uh –'

'What?'

'Her medication and all that stuff –'

'Well, I'll give it to her! Not so hard to count tablets, is it?'

'And if she falls down?'

'Well, she won't fall down, because I'll be there.'

'But, uh, where will she sleep?'

'I'm giving her my room. Everything has been taken care of.'

Franck leaned his forehead on the steering wheel.

'And you, Philou, what do you think about all this?'

'In the beginning I didn't like the idea, but now I do. I think your life will be a lot simpler if we take her away from here.'

'But that is one bloody heavy responsibility – an old person?'

'You think so? How much does your little granny weigh? Fifty kilos? Not even . . .'

'We can't just take her away like that.'

'No?'

'Well, no.'

'If we have to pay damages, we'll pay.'

'Can I go for a walk?'

'Go right ahead.'

'Camille, can you roll me a cigarette?'

'Here.'

He slammed the door.

'It's a fucking stupid idea,' he concluded when he climbed back in the car.

'Well, we never said it wasn't, did we Philou?'

'Never. We are very lucid, you know.'

'Are you frightened?'

'No.'

'We've seen worse, haven't we?'

'Hell, yes!'

'You think she'll like it in Paris?'

'We're not taking her to Paris, we're taking her to our place.'

'We'll show her the Eiffel Tower.'

'No. We'll show her plenty of things much nicer than the Eiffel Tower.'

Franck sighed.

'Okay then, what do we do now?'

'I'll take care of it,' said Camille.

When they came back to park under her window, she was still there.

Camille went off at a run. From the car, Franck and Philibert watched a performance of Chinese shadow puppets: a little figure turning around, a larger figure by her side, gestures, nodding heads, shoulder movements, and Franck said over and over: 'It's fucking stupid, it's fucking stupid, I tell you it is, it really is, a humongously fucking stupid idea.'

Philibert was smiling.

The silhouettes changed places.

'Philou?'

'Mmm?'

'Who is this girl?'

'I beg your pardon?'

'This girl you found us. What is she exactly – an extraterrestrial?'

Philibert smiled.

'A fairy.'

'Yeah, that's it. A fairy. You're right.'

And, hmm, they . . . are they sexual, fairies, or, uh, what?

'What the hell they doing, shit?'

At last the light went out.

Camille opened the window of Paulette's room and down came a huge suitcase. Franck, who had been biting his fingernails, started: 'Fuck, what is this mania she has for throwing things out the window?'

He was laughing. He was crying.

'Shit, Philou, my friend . . .' Huge tears were flowing down his cheeks. 'It's been months since I could look at myself in a mirror.

Can you believe this? Fuck, do you believe it?' He was trembling.

Philibert handed him his handkerchief.

'Everything is fine. Everything is fine. We'll pamper her and baby her for you, don't you worry.'

Franck blew his nose and edged the car forward then hurried towards the women while Philibert went to get the suitcase.

'No, no, you stay in front, young man. You have long legs.'

Dead silence for a few miles. Everyone wondering whether they hadn't just done the most enormous, insane thing. Then suddenly, artlessly, Paulette chased away the dark clouds: 'Hey. Will you take me to the theatre? Can we go and see those operettas?'

Philibert turned around and began to sing, *'From far Brazil I've come with gold, By ship I left fair Rio, And shot for Paris like an arrow, Far richer than in days of old!'*

Camille took Paulette's hand and Franck smiled at Camille in the rear view mirror.

The four of us now, in this decrepit Clio: free, together, and may the good ship sail on.

'You'll take from me the lot I took!', they sang in unison.

Part Four

1

It's a hypothesis. History won't take us far enough to bear it out. And our certainties never really hold water. One day you feel like dying and the next you realize all you had to do was go down a few stairs to find the light switch so you could see things a bit more clearly. These four, however, were embarking on what might turn out to be the most beautiful days of their lives.

From the very moment they first showed Paulette her new house, waiting with a mixture of emotion and anxiety for her every reaction, her every comment (she made none) and until the next ta-dum! of destiny's clown, a gentle warm wind would caress their tired faces.

A caress, a truce, a balm.

Sentimental healing as someone we know might say.

The family of lame ducks had now acquired a grandmother, and even if their little tribe was incomplete, and always would be, they had no intention of allowing this to get them down.

So what if in their game of happy families, the deck was stacked against them. They could try poker! They'd been dealt an interesting hand, four of a kind. Okay, four aces, maybe not . . . There'd been too many hard knocks and false starts, too many scars for them to make that sort of claim, but, hey. Still four of a kind!

They weren't terribly good players, alas.

Even when they concentrated. Even when they were determined for once not to show their hand, how can you expect an unarmed *chouan* counter-revolutionary, a fragile fairy, an apologetic young man, and an old lady covered with bruises to know how to bluff?

That's asking the impossible.

Bah. Never mind. A careful raise with the hope of a tiny return was still a better bet than throwing in their hands.

2

Camille didn't work to the end of her notice period: Josy B. just smelled too awful. Camille had to go to the head office to negotiate her departure date and arrange to receive her . . . what did they call it, already? Her final settlement. She'd worked there for over a year and had never taken any holiday time. She weighed the pros and cons and decided to do exactly as she pleased.

Mamadou was cross with her: 'Look at you. Look at you,' she kept saying on the last evening, sweeping the broom at her legs. 'Look at you.'

'Look at me, what?' said Camille, eventually growing annoyed. 'Spit it out, for God's sake! Look at me, what?'

'You . . . nothing.'

Camille went off to another room.

Mamadou lived in the opposite direction, but she got on the same deserted metro as Camille and forced her to move over to share the same seat. They were like Asterix and Obelisk squabbling. Camille nudged her elbow into Mamadou's pudgy flesh and Mamadou almost knocked her on to the floor.

They did this several times.

'Hey, Mamadou, don't be mad at me.'

'I ain't mad at you and I don't let you call me Mamadou ever again! That ain't my name! I hate it! It's the girls at work they call me that but my name ain't Mamadou. And since latest news is you're not a girl at work, I don't let you treat me like one ever again, you got that?'

'Really? Well what's your name, then?'

'I won't tell you.'

'Listen, Mama, uh, dear, I'm going to tell you the truth. I'm not leaving because of Josy. I'm not leaving because of the work. I'm not leaving for the pleasure of leaving. I'm not leaving because of the money. Truth is, I'm leaving because I have another profession. A profession where – at least I think – I . . . I guess I'm not sure, but a profession I'm better at than this job here, and where I think I could be happier.'

Silence.

'And that's not the only reason. I'm taking care of this old lady now, and I don't want to be out in the evening, see? I'm afraid she'll fall.'

Silence.

'Okay, this is my stop. If I don't get out here I'll be paying for a taxi again.'

Mamadou pulled her arm and forced her to sit back down.

'Hold on, I'm telling you. It's half past midnight.'

'What is it?'

'Sorry?'

'Your other profession, what is it?'

Camille handed her the sketchbook.

'Hey,' said Mamadou, handing it back, 'this is good. This is okay by me. You can go now but still . . . I've been real glad to know you, you skinny little grasshopper,' she added, turning away.

'I have one more thing to ask you, Mama –'

'You want my Léopold make success guaranteed and plenty of customers too?'

'No. I'd like you to pose for me.'

'To pose what?'

'You! Yourself. Be a model for me.'

'Me?'

'Yes.'

'Hey, you making fun of me or something?'

'From the day I saw you, back when we were working in Neuilly, I remember . . . I've been wanting to do your portrait.'

'Stop it, Camille. I'm not even nice to look at it.'

'To me you are.'

Silence.

'To you I am?'

'To me, yes.'

'What's nice to look at in all this, huh?' she asked, pointing to her reflection in the black window. 'Where you mean?'

'If I manage to do your portrait, if I do it well, in it you'll see everything you've told me since we met. Everything. We'll see your mother and father. And your children. And the sea. And – you know, what was her name already?'

'Who?'

'Your little goat.'

'Bouli.'

'We'll see Bouli. And your cousin who died and . . . And all the rest.'

'You talking like my brother, now! What sort of weird fantasy you jabbering about?'

Silence.

'But I'm not sure I'll manage,' sighed Camille eventually.

'Oh, no? Mind, if we don't see my Bouli on my head that's fine by me!' she giggled. 'But, what you're asking me now, it takes a long time, no?'

'Yes.'

'Well then I can't . . .'

'You've got my number. Take a few days off from All-Kleen and come to see me. I'll pay you your hours . . . We always pay our models. It's a profession, you know. Okay, I'll leave you here. Kiss goodbye, okay?'

Mamadou crushed Camille against her heart.

'What is your name, then, Mamadou?'

'I'm not saying. I don't like my name.'

Camille ran along the platform, miming the gesture of a phone against her ear. Her former co-worker wearily waved her hand. Forget me, little toubab, forget me. You've already forgotten me, anyway.

Mamadou blew her nose noisily.

She liked talking to Camille.

That was true, really it was.

No one else on earth ever listened to her.

3

In the early days, Paulette did not leave her room. She was afraid of disturbing someone, afraid of getting lost, afraid of falling (they had forgotten her walker) and above all, afraid she might regret her sudden impulse.

She often got things in a muddle, saying that she was having a very nice holiday with them, and asking when they meant to take her home.

'Where's your home, then?' Franck would ask, irritated.

'Well, you know perfectly well. At home, my house.'

He would leave the room with a sigh: 'I told you it was a crazy idea. And on top of everything else now she's going gaga.'

Camille looked at Philibert and Philibert looked away.

'Paulette?'

'Oh, it's you, dear. What's your name again?'

'Camille.'

'That's it. And what is it you want, young lady?'

Camille spoke to her frankly, even rather brutally. She reminded Paulette where she came from, why she was with them, what they had changed and would change in their lifestyles in order to keep her company. She added a multitude of other cutting details which completely knocked the stuffing out of the old woman:

'I'm never going back to my house, then?'

'No.'

'Oh . . .'

'Come with me, Paulette.'

Camille took her by the hand and started the tour of the apartment all over again. More slowly this time. And rammed home a few details along the way:

'Here. These are the toilets. You see, Franck is in the middle of putting hand rails along the wall so you can hold on.'

'Bloody stupid,' he grumbled.

'This is the kitchen. Pretty big, isn't it? And cold. That's why I fixed up the table on wheels yesterday. So you can have your meals in your room.'

'. . . or in the living room,' said Philibert, 'you're not obliged to stay shut up in your room all day, you know.'

'Okay now, this is the corridor. It's very long but you can hold on to the wood panelling, can't you? If you need help, we can go to the pharmacy and rent another one of those roller thingies.'

'Yes, I'd rather.'

'No problem! We already have one wheel addict in the house. Here's the bathroom. And this is where we have to have a serious discussion, Paulette. Here, sit down on that chair. Raise your eyes. Look how lovely it is.'

'It really is. We never had anything like this.'

'Good. So, you know what your grandson is going to do tomorrow with his friends?'

'No?'

'They're going to wreck it. They're going to install a shower cabin for you because the bathtub is too high to step over. So before it's too late you have to decide once and for all. Either you stay and the boys get to work, or you think you don't want to stay, and it's not a problem, you do what you want, Paulette, but you have to tell us now, do you understand?'

'Do you understand?' echoed Philibert.

The old lady sighed, fiddled with the corner of her cardigan for a few seconds which seemed like an eternity to them, then raised her head and asked anxiously: 'Did you remember the stool?'

'Pardon?'

'I'm not completely helpless, you know. I can perfectly well take a shower on my own, but I have to have a stool, otherwise –'

Philibert pretended to write on his hand: 'One stool for the little lady in the back! I've written it down! And was there anything else, may I ask?'

She smiled: 'Nothing else.'

'Nothing else?'

Paulette finally let it out: 'Yes. I would like my *TV Star*, my crosswords, some needles and wool to knit for the young lady, a jar of Nivea because I forgot mine, some sweets, a little radio for my night table, some of that fizzy stuff for my dentures, some suspenders, some slippers and a warmer bathrobe because it's so draughty here, some sanitary items, some powder, a bottle of my eau de Cologne that Franck forgot the other day, an extra pillow, a magnifying glass and also I'd like you to move the armchair over by the window, and –'

'And?' Philibert was beginning to get worried.

'And that's all, I suppose.'

Franck, who had come to join them with his tool box, tapped his friend on the shoulder: 'Shit, mate, we've got two princesses here now.'

'Hey, be careful!' shouted Camille, 'You're getting dust all over the place.'

'And stop swearing like that, please!' added his grandmother.

Franck walked off, dragging his heels: 'Oh. My. Lord. This is not going to be easy. We're in a bad way, mate, a bad way . . . I'm going back to work, it's quieter there. If one of you goes shopping, bring back some spuds so I can make a shepherd's pie. And good ones, all right? Have a look at them . . . Potatoes for mashing. It's not complicated, it says on the package.'

'We're in a bad way, a bad way,' was what he had thought, but he was wrong. Never in their lives had they been in such a good way.

When you put it like that, it sounds a bit daft, obviously, but, hey – it was the truth and it had been a long while since any of them had been bothered by ridicule: for the first time, each and every one of them felt like they belonged to a real family.

Better than a real family, even, because this was something they had chosen, desired, and fought for, and this family asked nothing of them in return other than to be happy together. Not even happy, actually, they weren't that demanding. Just to be together, that was everything. And even that they couldn't have imagined.

4

After the bathroom episode, Paulette was a changed woman. She found her bearings and blended into the ambient amiable chaos with astonishing ease. Perhaps it was precisely what she needed, some kind of proof? Proof that they had been waiting for her and that she was welcome in this immense empty apartment where the shutters closed from inside and where no one had disturbed the dust since the Restoration. If they were putting in a shower just for her, well then . . . She had almost lost her bearings because there were a few things she missed, and Camille often thought back on that scene. How people could come undone, often just because of some trivial thing, and how everything could have gone downhill at full speed had there not been a tall patient fellow who asked, 'Was there anything else?' while holding an imaginary notepad. What, in the end, did it hinge on? A wrong magazine, a magnifying glass, two or three bottles of this and that. It was mind-boggling. A little flea-market philosophy which enchanted her, and which turned out to be all the more complex when they found themselves in the toothpaste department of Franprix, reading the descriptions of the various Steradents, Polidents, Fixadents and other miracle glues.

'Paulette, what exactly do you mean by . . . sanitary items?'

'You're not going to make me wear a nappy like the ones they gave us out there on the pretext that it's cheaper!' she said huffily.

'Oh! That kind of sanitary item!' said Camille again, relieved. 'Okay . . . I didn't follow you at all, back there.'

As for Franprix, they knew the place inside out, and it didn't really seem up to scratch any more. So now it was at Monoprix that they minced around with their grocery trolley and the list Franck had drawn up the evening before.

Oh, that Monoprix.

Their whole lives . . .

Paulette was always first to wake up, and she would wait for one of the boys to bring her breakfast in bed. When Philibert was in charge, he brought it to her on a tray with sugar tongs, an embroidered napkin, and a little cream jug. He would help her to sit up, plump up her pillows and pull back the curtains while delivering a little commentary on the weather. No man had ever been so considerate, and what was bound to happen did happen: she began to adore him too. When it was Franck's turn it was, well, more rustic. He placed her bowl of chicory coffee on the night table, and brushed his lips against her cheek while complaining that he was already late.

'Don't you want to have a piss, now?'

'I'm waiting for Camille.'

'Hey, Grandma, that's enough! Leave her alone for a while! You don't know, maybe she wants to sleep for another hour. You can't hold it in all that time.'

Imperturbable, she said again: 'I'll wait for Camille.'

Franck went off, muttering grumpily.

Well then wait for her, go ahead, wait. It's bloody sickening, no one pays attention to anyone but you now. Shit, I'm waiting for her, too! What do I have to do? Break both legs so she'll give me a little smile too? Makes you want to puke, her Mary Poppins act; makes you want to puke.

Camille came out of her room at that very moment, stretching: 'What are you grumbling about this time?'

'Nothing. I live with Prince Charles and Mother Teresa and I'm just having one hell of a time. Out the way, I'm late. Oh, just one thing.'

'What?'

'Give me your arm a second . . . hey, this is great!' he said, more cheerfully now, as he squeezed her flesh. 'Better watch out, fat lady. You might end up in the cauldron one of these days.'

'In your dreams, kitchen boy, in your dreams.'

'Okay then, my little chick, whatever you say.'

One thing was sure. They were much more cheerful.

Franck came back with his jacket under his arm: 'Next Wednesday –'

'What about next Wednesday?'

'It's the day after Mardi Gras but I have too much work that day so Wednesday, wait for me to have dinner.'

'At midnight?'

'I'll try to get back earlier and I'll make you some crêpes, the likes of which you've never had in your entire life.'

'Oh, you scared me! I thought that was the day you'd chosen to screw me.'

'I'll make the crêpes and then I'll screw you.'

'Perfect.'

Perfect? He was deluded, what a jerk . . . What was he going to do until Wednesday? Bump into every lamppost, botch all his sauces and buy new underwear? Fuck, he couldn't bloody believe it! One way or the other she would eventually have his hide, that bitch. Bloody agony. Provided this was for real . . . To be on the safe side he decided to buy new underwear anyway.

Yeah. Well, there'll be plenty of Grand Marnier, I'm telling you, plenty of the stuff. And what I don't use to flambé, I'll drink.

Camille went to join Paulette with her mug of tea. She sat on the bed, pulled over the quilt and they waited until the lads had gone out before switching on the shopping channel. They went into raptures; they giggled and scoffed at the outfits of the airhead models, and Paulette, who still hadn't grasped the transition from francs to euros, was astonished that life was so cheap in Paris. Time had ceased to exist, stretching lazily from the kettle to Monoprix and from Monoprix to the newsstand.

It was like being on holiday. The first one in years for Camille, and the first ever for the old lady. They got along well, finished each other's sentences, and both were growing younger as the days grew longer.

Camille had become what the social services called a 'life carer'. The two words suited her and she made up for her geriatric ignorance by adopting a direct tone and very basic words which stripped them both of any inhibitions.

'Go on, Paulette love, go on. I'll wash your bum with the spray.'

'Are you sure?'

'Of course!'

'You're not disgusted?'

'No.'

It had turned out to be too complicated to install a shower, so Franck had devised a non-skid step to enable his grandmother to climb into the bathtub. Then he had sawn the feet off of an old chair, on which Camille placed a towel before helping her protégée to sit down.

'Oh,' moaned Paulette, 'this bothers me. You have no idea how uncomfortable it makes me to impose this on you.'

'Come on . . .'

'You're not disgusted by my old body? Are you sure?'

'You know, I – I think I don't have the same approach as you. I – I took classes in anatomy, I've drawn nudes who were at least as old as you and I don't have a problem with modesty. Well, I do, but not that one. I don't quite know how to explain. But when I look at old people I don't think, Yuck, wrinkles, droopy breasts, soft belly, those white hairs, flaccid willy or knobbly knees . . . No, not at all. Maybe you won't like this but your body interests me independently of you. I think work, I think technique, light, contour, flesh to be dealt with. I think of certain paintings – Goya's old madwomen, the allegories of Death, Rembrandt's mother or his prophetess Anne. Sorry, Paulette, that sounds terrible but, honestly, I look at you very clinically!'

'As if I were some strange beast?'

'There's a bit of that . . . More like a curiosity.'

'And then?'

'Then nothing.'

'Are you going to draw me, too?'

'Yes.'

Silence.

'Yes, if you let me. I'd like to draw you until I know you by heart. Until you can't take it any more, having me around all the time.'

'I'll let you, but now, really I . . . you're not even my daughter or anything and I . . . Oh, I'm so confused.'

Camille finally got undressed and knelt down beside her on the grey enamel: 'Wash me.'

'What?'

'Take the soap and the flannel and wash me, Paulette.'

She did as she was told and, beginning to shiver on her aquatic prayer stool, she stretched her arm out to the young girl's back.

'Come on! Harder than that!'

'My God, you're so young. When I think I was like you once upon a time. Of course I was not as slim, but still . . .'

'You mean skinny?' Camille interrupted, holding on to the tap.

'No, no, I really meant "slim". When Franck told me about you for the first time, I remember, that was all he said, "Oh, Grandma, she's so skinny. If you could see how skinny she is," but now that I see you how you really are, I don't agree with him. You're not skinny, you're slender. You remind me of that young woman in the book *Le Grand Meaulnes*. You know the one? Oh, what was her name? Help me . . .'

'I haven't read it.'

'She had an aristocratic name, too, she did . . . Oh, isn't this silly.'

'We'll go and check it out at the library. Come on! Lower down, too. There's no reason why not! There. You see? We're in the same boat, old girl! Why are you looking at me like that?'

'I – it's your scar, there.'

'That? It's nothing.'

'No, it's not nothing. When did this happen?'

'It's nothing, I said.'

And after that day there was no more talk of skin between them.

Camille helped her to sit on the toilet seat, then under the shower spray, soaping her, talking about other things. Hair-washing turned out to be the trickiest thing. Every time the old lady closed her eyes she would lose her balance and slip backwards. After a few catastrophic attempts, they decided to buy a series of sessions at a hairdresser's. Not in their neighbourhood, where they were all way over-priced ('Who the hell is Myriam, anyway?' asked that cretin Franck, 'I don't know any Myriams'), but right at the end of one of the bus lines. Camille studied her map, traced the itinerary of the various metropolitan buses with her finger, aimed for exoticism, leafed through the Yellow Pages, asked how much it would cost for a weekly shampoo and set and they decided on a little salon on the rue des Pyrénées, the farthest fare zone of the number 69 bus.

In actual fact, the difference in price didn't really warrant such a long expedition, but it was so nice a ride . . .

So every Friday, at dawn, as soon as it began to get light, Camille would settle a rumpled little Paulette next to the window and do her

323

own running commentary on *Paris by Day*: with sketchbook in hand, and at the whim of traffic jams, she would catch a couple of poodles in Burberry coats on the Pont Royal, and the sort of sausage-shaped carvings which decorated the walls of the Louvre; the cages and boxwoods of the quai de la Mégisserie; the pedestal of the genius on the Bastille or the upper vaults of the Père Lachaise cemetery. Then she would read the stories of pregnant princesses or abandoned singers while her friend beamed with satisfaction underneath the hairdryer. They had lunch in a café on the Place Gambetta. Not at the Le Gambetta café; it was too trendy for their taste, but at the Bar du Métro, which smelled of stale tobacco, of failed millionaires, and of its irritable waiter.

Paulette, who still remembered her catechism, invariably chose trout with almonds and Camille, who had no such qualms, sank her teeth into a croque-monsieur with ham, her eyes closed. They shared a carafe of wine, of course they did, and raised their glasses heartily. To us! On the way back, Camille sat across from Paulette and drew exactly the same things but through the eyes of a trim little old lady brittle with hair spray, who did not dare lean against the window for fear of crumpling her superb mauve curls. (Johanna, the hairdresser, had persuaded her to change her hair colour: 'So, you want to try? I'll give you ash Opaline, okay? Look, it's number 34, see, there?' Paulette wanted to look at Camille for approval, but Camille was immersed in the story of a botched liposuction. 'Won't it look too sad?' she worried; 'Sad? Of course not! Just the opposite, it's really cheerful!')

Indeed, that was the word. It was really cheerful, and that day they got off on the corner of the quai Voltaire to buy, among other things, a half-pot of watercolour paint from Sennelier's.

Paulette's hair had changed from a very diluted Golden Rose to Windsor Violet.

Ah! The effect was immediate. It looked much more chic.

The other days were for Monoprix. They would spend over an hour covering a mere two hundred metres, tasting the latest packaged dessert, answering idiotic surveys, trying on lipsticks or awful chiffon scarves. They took their time, babbled, stopped on the way, commented on the style of the posh ladies from the 7th arrondissement, or the ebullience of adolescent girls: their irrepressible giggling, their unbelievable stories, the constant jangle of their mobile phones, and their backpacks clinking and clanking with trinkets. Camille and Paulette were having a grand adventure, sighing and teasing each other, and feeling their way. They had time, they had their lives ahead of them . . .

5

When Franck was not available to take care of feeding his grand-mother, Camille took over. After a few dishes of soggy pasta, half-cooked frozen dinners and burned omelettes, Paulette decided to inculcate her with a few simple principles of cooking. She sat by the kitchen stove and taught her phrases as basic as bouquet garni, cast iron pot, hot frying pan and stock. She couldn't see well, but guided by her sense of smell she instructed Camille how to proceed: The onions, tiny pieces of bacon, slices of meat and all that, you're fine, all set. Now pour in your stock . . . Go ahead, I'll tell you . . . Fine!

'That's good. I'm not saying I'll make a cordon-bleu cook of you, but anyway . . .'

'And Franck?'

'What about Franck?'

'Are you the one who taught him everything?'

'No, not at all. I gave him the taste for it, I suppose. But all that fancy stuff, that's not me. I taught him home cooking. Simple, country dishes, cheap to prepare. When my husband was laid off because of his heart, I started working for an upper-class family as a cook.'

'And did he go there with you?'

'He did. What else could I do with him when he was little? And then later on, he didn't come any more. After –'

'After what?'

'Well, you know how things are. Later on, I couldn't keep up with him, where he was hanging out. But, he was talented. He really liked doing it. About the only time he ever calmed down was when he was in the kitchen . . .'

'That's still the case.'

'You've seen him?'

'Yes, he took me along as a catering assistant the other day and – I didn't recognize him!'

'You see? But if you knew what a drama there was when we sent him off to do his apprenticeship. He really held it against us.'

'What did he want to do?'

'Nothing. Silly stuff. Camille, you're drinking too much!'

'You must be joking! I haven't drunk a thing since you've been here! Here, a little shot of fermented grape juice, good for the arteries! I'm not the one who said that, it's the medical profession.'

'Okay then, a little glass.'

'Well? Don't make such a face. Does wine make you sad?'

'No, it's the memories.'

'Was it hard?'

'Sometimes, yes.'

'Was he the one who made it hard?'

'He was, life was.'

'He told me.'

'What?'

'About his mother. The day she came to take him back, all that.'

'You – you see, the worst thing when you get older, is this . . . Hey, give me another glass, go on. It's not so much your body going its own way, no, it's the regret. How everything you regret comes back to haunt you, torment you. Day, and night . . . all the time. There comes a point when you don't know any more whether to keep your eyes open or closed to chase all those moments away. There's a point when you – God knows I tried, I tried to understand why it didn't work out, why it all went wrong, all of it. And –'

'And?'

She was trembling. 'I can't do it. I don't understand. I –'

She was crying. 'Where do I begin?'

'I married late, for a start. And like everyone, I had my love story too, you know. Or did I? Anyway, in the end I married a nice boy so everyone would be happy. My sisters had tied the knot long before and I – well, I finally got married too.

'But there was no child coming. Every month I'd curse my belly

327

and cry while I was boiling my linen. I saw doctors, I even came here to Paris to get examined. I saw bone-setters and witch doctors and horrible old women who asked impossible things of me. Some of the things I did, Camille, without evening batting an eyelid . . . Sacrificing ewe-lambs under the full moon, drinking their blood, swallowing . . . Oh, no. It was really barbarian, believe me. Another century. People said I was "tainted". And then the pilgrimages . . . Every year I went to Le Blanc, put a finger in the hole of the Saint Genitor, and then I went to scratch Saint Girlichon in Gargilesse . . . What are you laughing at?'

'Those names.'

'Hey, and that's not all, just wait! You had to make a votive offering in wax of the child you wanted to Saint Froguefault of Pretilly . . .'

'Froguefault?'

'Froguefault! That's what I said! Ah! They were lovely, my wax babies, believe me. Real dolls. You almost expected them to speak. And then one day, although I'd resigned myself years earlier, I fell pregnant. I was well over thirty. You may not realize it, but I was old already. Pregnant with Nadine, Franck's mother. How we spoiled her, how we pampered her, how we babied that child. A princess. I guess we ruined her character. We loved her too much. Loved her badly. We gave in to her every whim. Every one except the last. I refused to lend her the money she wanted to have an abortion. I just couldn't, you understand? I couldn't. I'd suffered so much. It wasn't religion, it wasn't morality, it wasn't gossip that stopped me. It was rage. Sheer rage. The taint of it. I would have killed her rather than help her to gut her own belly. Was I – was I wrong? You tell me. How many lives were wasted because of me? How much suffering? How much –'

'Shh.'

Camille reached across and rubbed Paulette's thigh.

'Shh.'

'So she – she had the little baby and then she left him to me. "Here," she said, "since you wanted it, it's all yours! Are you happy now?"'

Paulette closed her eyes and repeated in a strangled voice, '"You happy now?" and she said it again, packing her bags, "You happy?" How can anyone say such a thing? And how can you forget when someone has said them? Why should I sleep through the night, now that I'm not breaking my back and working my fingers to the bone, huh? Tell me. Tell me. She left him to me, she came back a few months later, took him away, then brought him back again. We were going crazy. Especially Maurice, my husband. I think she drove him to the limits of his patience, his patience as a man . . . Then she had to push him just a little bit further, took the baby away again one more time, came back for money to feed him, or so she said, and ran away during the night and forgot the child. One day, one day too far, she came back whining and Maurice was waiting for her with the shotgun. "I don't want to see you again," he says, "you're nothing but a slut. You're a disgrace to us and you don't deserve this baby. So you're not going to see him. Not today, not ever. Go on, get out of here now. Leave us alone." Camille . . . She was my child. A child I had waited for, every day for over ten years. A child I adored. Adored. How I spoiled that little kid, spoiled her rotten, tried so hard to please her. We bought her everything she ever wanted. Everything! The prettiest dresses. Holidays at the seaside, in the mountains, the best schools . . . Every ounce of goodness in us was for her. And all this happened in a tiny village. She was gone, but the people who had known her since she was a little toddler and who were hiding behind their closed shutters to watch Maurice throw his fit, they were still there. And I kept on meeting them. The next day, and the day after that and the day after that . . . It was . . . it was inhuman. Hell on earth. There's nothing worse than the compassion of good people, I tell you. Those women who say "I'll pray for you" while they're trying to worm the story out of you, and the con-founded men who teach your husband to drink and keep telling him they would have done exactly the same thing, for God's sake! There were days I felt like murdering someone, honestly. Times I'd wished I too had the atom bomb!'

She was laughing.

'And so? Well, there he was, that little boy. He hadn't asked for anything from anyone. So what did we do? We loved him. We loved him as best we could. And maybe there were times we were too hard on him. We didn't want to make the same mistakes so we made others. And aren't you ashamed of yourself, drawing me like this, in the state I'm in?'

'No.'

329

'You're right. Shame doesn't get you anywhere, believe me. Whatever you're ashamed of, it doesn't do you any good. It's only there to please other people who think they're so fine. So when they close their shutters or head back from the bar, they feel good about themselves. They're all puffed up and they put their slippers on and look at each other and smile. They wouldn't have had such a carry-on in their family, oh no! But . . . Tell me one thing, you're not drawing me with this glass in my hand, are you?'

'No.' Camille smiled.

Silence.

'Then after that? Things were all right after that?'

'With the little one? Yes. He was a good boy, what can I say. Mischievous, but straightforward. When he wasn't in the kitchen with me he was out in the garden with his granddad. Or gone fishing. He had a temper, but he was growing up straight, all the same. Growing straight . . . Even if life couldn't have been that much fun every day with two old folks like us, and it was a long time since we'd felt like being talkative, but anyway. We did what we could. We played with him. We stopped drowning kittens. We took him to town, to the cinema. We paid for his football stickers and new bicycles. He worked hard at school, you know. He wasn't top of the class, but he took pride in his work. And then she came back again and that time we thought it was a good idea if he left with her. That a strange sort of mother is still better than no mother. That he'd have a father and a little brother, that it was no life for him, growing up in a half-dead village and that for his studies it would be a real opportunity to be in town. And once again we fell right in the trap. As if we didn't know better. Brainless idiots . . . Well, you know the rest: she broke him in two and put him back on the 4.12 afternoon train . . .'

'And you never heard from her again?'

'No. Except in dreams. In dreams, I see her a lot. She's laughing. She's beautiful . . . Show me what you've drawn.'

'Nothing. Your hand on the table.'

'Why did you let me go on like that? Why are you interested in all this?'

'I like it when people open up.'

'Why?'

'I don't know. It's like a self-portrait, don't you think? A self-portrait with words . . .'

'And you?'

'Oh, I don't know how to tell stories.'

'But for you it's not normal either, to spend all your time with an old woman like me.'

'No? And do you have any idea what *is* normal?'

'You should get out, see people. Young people your age! Come on, lift that lid for me, there. Did you wash the mushrooms?'

6

'Is she asleep?' asked Franck.

'I think so.'

'Hey, I just got stopped by the concierge, you have to go and talk to her.'

'Did we screw up again with the rubbish bins?'

'No, something to do with the guy you're lodging up there.'

'Oh, shit. Has he done something stupid?'

Franck spread his arms and shook his head.

7

Pikou coughed up something and Madame Perreira opened her little French window and put her hand on her chest.

'Come in, come in, sitta down.'

'What's going on?'

'Sitta down, I said.'

Camille pushed aside some cushions and placed half a buttock on a small bench with a leafy design.

'I don't see him any more.'

'Who? Vincent? But, I saw him the other day, he was taking the metro.'

'Whena the other day?'

'I don't know . . . beginning of the week.'

'Wella me, I tella you I don't see him any more. He disappear. With Pikou who wake me up every nighta, I can'ta miss him, you know. And now, nothing. I'm afraida something happened. Go up there, dearie, go up and take a looka.'

'Right.'

'Sweeta Jesus. You think he isa dead?'

Camille opened the door.

'Hey, if he isa dead, you come see me right away, all right? Just that . . .' she added, fiddling with her medallion, 'I don' wanna scandala in the building, you understanda?'

8

'It's Camille, open up.'

Barking, a confusion of sound.

'Are you going to open or should I have someone break down the door?'

'Nah, I can't just now,' said a hoarse voice. 'I'm in bad shape, come back later.'

'When, later?'

'Tonight.'

'You don't need anything?'

'Nah. Leave me alone.'

Camille walked away, then came back: 'Want me to walk the dog?'

No answer.

She went slowly down the stairs.

She was in deep shit.

She should never have brought him here. It's easy to be generous with other people's property. Well, one thing was for sure, she'd earned her halo by now! A junkie on the seventh floor, a granny in her bed, an entire world for which she was responsible, and here she was still having to hold on to the banister not to break her own neck. What a great scene. Clap clap. Really glorious. You must be pleased with yourself; don't your wings bother you when you walk?

Oh shut up, all of you. Sure, when you do nothing –

Nah, but we're just saying . . . don't take it badly, but there are plenty of other tramps in the street. There's one right outside the bakery, as a matter of fact. Why don't you pick him up, too? 'Cause he hasn't got a dog? Shit, if only he'd known . . .

You're turning into a real bore, said Camille to Camille. A major, big-time bore.

C'mon, let's try it. But not a big one, okay? Just a little one. A little bichon frisé trembling from the cold. Yeah, that would be cool. Or a puppy, perhaps? A small puppy all curled up inside his jacket? Bound to give in right away. Besides, there are plenty of rooms left, chez Philibert . . .

Overwhelmed, Camille sat down on a step and put her head on her knees.

Let's go back over this.

She hadn't seen her mother for almost a month. She's better do something about that soon because otherwise her old lady might have another chemical liver attack with emergency medical services and gastric probe to boot. Camille had got used to it over time but, hey, it was never a picnic. It always took her a while to get over it. Tut tut. Still too sensitive, this young lady.

Paulette had a complete grasp of 1930 to 1999 but lost her way between yesterday and today, and things weren't getting any better. Too much happiness, maybe? It was as if she were letting herself float slowly to the bottom. And besides, she really couldn't see a thing. Right. So far, so good. At the moment she was taking her nap, and later on Philou would come and watch *Millionaire* with her and give all the answers without making a mistake. They loved it, the two of them. Perfect.

And while we're on the subject, Philibert was Humphrey Bogart and Oscar Wilde all rolled into one. He was writing now. He locked himself in his room to write, and rehearsed two nights a week. No news from the love front? Right. No news is good news.

As for Franck . . . nothing special. Nothing new. Everything was fine. His grandma was safe and warm and his motorbike too. He only came back in the afternoon to sleep, and he carried on working on Sundays. 'Just a while longer, you know? I can't just dump them like that, I have to find a replacement.'

Well, now. A replacement or an even bigger motorbike? Very clever, this boy. Very clever. And why shouldn't he do as he pleased? What was the problem? He hadn't asked for anything. And once the early days of euphoria had passed, there he was back with his nose in the stewpot. At night he probably leant on his girlfriend and made her get up and switch off the old lady's television. But . . . not a problem. Not a problem. She would still rather put up with all this, documentaries on the swim bladder of gurnards or the old lady's tea-induced nocturnal trips to the toilet, than return to her job at All-Kleen. Of course she could have not worked at all, but she wasn't strong enough to make that leap. Society had trained her well. Was it because she lacked faith in herself, or just the opposite? The fear of finding herself in a situation where she could actually earn her living, but she'd be trampling on her life? She had a few remaining contacts . . . But then what? Spit on herself yet again? Close her sketchbooks and pick up a magnifying glass again? She no longer had the stomach for it. She hadn't become a better person – she had grown older. Sigh.

No, the problem was three flights up. Why had he refused to open up in the first place? Was it because he was high, or in withdrawal? Was it true, his story about the detox? He might fool others . . . Bullshit to charm little bourgeois sorts and their concierges, definitely! Why did he only go out at night? Was it to turn a trick before he could jab himself below the tourniquet? They were all the same . . . Liars who threw dust in your eyes and partied till they dropped, the bastards, while you stood there biting your knuckles until they bled . . .

With Pierre on the phone two weeks earlier, she had gone back to her own brand of bullshit: lying again.

'Camille, this is Kessler. What the devil is going on? Who's this fellow living in my room? Call me back right away.'

Thank you, fat Madame Perreira, thank you.

Our Lady of Fatima, pray for us.

She had to make a pre-emptive attack: 'He's a model,' she announced to Pierre, before even greeting him, 'we're working together.'

That would take the wind out of his sails.

'He's a model?'

'Yes.'

'Are you living with him?'

'No. I just told you: I'm working with him.'

'Camille. I – I want so much to trust you nowadays: can I?'

Silence.

'Who's it for?'

'For you.'

'Oh?'

Silence.

'You – you –'

'I don't know yet. Red chalk, I suppose.'

'Right.'

'Okay, take care.'

'Wait!'

'What?'

'What sort of paper do you have?'

'Good stuff.'

'Are you sure?'

'Daniel's the one who served me.'

'Fine. You okay, otherwise?'

'Actually, I'm talking to the salesman right now. I'll call you back on the other line for a chat.'

Click.

She shook her box of matches with a sigh. She couldn't avoid it any longer.

That evening, as soon as she had tucked in a little old lady who wasn't the least bit sleepy, she would go back up the stairs to talk to him.

The last time she had tried to keep a junkie from going out as night was falling, she'd gotten a stab in the shoulder for her trouble. Okay. That was different. It had been her man, and she had loved him and all, but still . . . A painful sort of present.

Shit. No more matches. Oh, woe. Our Lady of Fatima *and* Hans Christian Andersen, stay where you are, bloody hell. Stay just a bit longer.

And, like someone in the story, she got to her feet, gave a tug to her trouser legs and went to join her grandmother in heaven . . .

9

'What is it?'

'Oh,' said Philibert, shaking his head, 'nothing really, honestly.'

'An ancient tragedy?'

'Noooo.'

'Vaudeville?'

He reached for his dictionary: '. . . *Vatican . . . vaticinate . . . vaudeville. Light comedy, based on sudden reversals of plot, misunderstandings and witticisms.* Yes, that's exactly what it is,' he said, closing the dictionary with a snap. 'A light comedy with witticisms.'

'What's it about?'

'Me.'

'You?' exclaimed Camille. 'But I thought it was taboo in your family to talk about yourself.'

'Well, I'm taking some distance,' he added, striking a pose.

'And, uh, and the little beard you're growing, is that for your part?'

'Don't you like it?'

'Yes, yes, it's very dandyish . . . a bit like the detectives in *The Tiger Brigades,* isn't it?'

'The who?'

'Of course, you're only just discovering television with *Who Wants to Be a Millionaire?* . . . Look, I need to go upstairs, I'm going to see my tenant on the seventh floor. Can I leave Paulette with you?'

He nodded his head, smoothing his thin moustache.

'Go, run, fly and climb up to your destiny, my child.'

'Philou?'

'Yes?'

'If I'm not back down within the hour, can you come up and check?'

10

The room was impeccably tidy. The bed had been made, and he had left two cups and a packet of sugar on the camping table. He was sitting on a chair with his back to the wall, and he closed his book when Camille knocked lightly on the door.

He got up. They were both equally embarrassed. It was the first time they had actually been able to see each other. You could hear a pin drop.

'Would you, would you like something to drink?'

'Please.'

'Tea, coffee, Coke?'

'Coffee would be perfect.'

Camille sat down on the stool and wondered how she had managed to live there for so long. It was so damp, and dark; so inexorable. The ceiling was low and the walls were filthy. No, how had it been possible? It must have been someone else, surely?

He busied himself by the hotplate and pointed to the jar of Nescafé.

Barbès was asleep on the bed and opened an eye from time to time.

He eventually pulled the chair up and sat down across from her. 'I'm glad to see you. You could have come sooner.'

'I didn't dare.'

'Oh?' He paused, then said, 'You're sorry you brought me here.'

'No.'

'Yes, you're sorry. But don't worry about it. I'm waiting for a green light, and then I'll leave. Just a matter of days, now.'

'Where are you going?'

'Brittany.'

'You have family there?'

'No. It's a centre for . . . human detritus. Nah, I'm being stupid. A rehabilitation centre is what you're supposed to call it.'

Camille was silent.

'My doctor found it for me. A deal to make fertilizer with seaweed. Seaweed, shit, and mental retards . . . Fantastic, isn't it? I'll be the only normal worker. Well, "normal" – it's all relative.'

He smiled.

'Here, have a look at the brochure. Classy, isn't it.'

Two idiots with pitchforks stood in front of a sort of cesspool.

'I'm going to be doing Algo-Foresto, a job with compost, seaweed, and horse manure. I can already tell I'm going to love it. That is, apparently it's hard at the start because of the smell but eventually you don't even notice it any more.'

He put down the photo and lit a cigarette.

'Summer holiday, right?'

'How long will you stay there?'

'However long it takes.'

'Have you been taking methadone?'

'Yes.'

'For how long?'

A vague gesture.

'Is it okay?'

'No.'

'Hey, look, you're going to see the sea!'

'Great. And you? Why'd you come up here?'

'The concierge. She thought you were dead.'

'She'll be disappointed.'

'Obviously.'

They laughed.

'You – are you HIV positive too?'

'Nah. That was just to keep her happy. So she'd be good to my dog. Nah, nah. I did it right. I shot up clean.'

'Is this your first detox?'

'Yes.'

'You think you'll make it?'

'Yes. I've been lucky. I guess you have to run into the right people, and I think I have, now.'

'Your doctor?'

'Great woman! Yes, but not only that. A shrink, too. An old geezer who cleaned my head out. D'you know V33?'

'What is it? Medicine?'

'No, it's a wood stripper.'

'Yeah! A green and red bottle, isn't it?'

'If you say so. Well this guy is my V33. He coats me with the stuff, it burns, makes blisters, then next time round he takes his spatula and scrapes off all the shit. Look at me. Under my skull I'm naked as a worm.'

He could no longer smile, his hands were trembling. 'Fuck, it's hard. It's too hard. I didn't think –'

He looked up.

'And then, that's not all. There's someone else, too. A little woman with thighs no thicker than a fly's legs who went and pulled up her trousers before I got a chance to see any more than that, damn.'

'What's your name?' he asked.

'Camille.'

He repeated it and turned to the wall.

'Camille . . . Camille . . . The day you showed up, Camille, I'd had a run-in with a dealer. It was so bloody cold, and I didn't feel like fighting it any more, I think. But anyway. You were there. So I followed you. I'm quite a gallant sort of guy.'

Silence.

'Can I talk some more or are you fed up?'

'Give me another cup of coffee.'

'Oh, sorry. It's because of the old guy, my shrink. I've turned into a real blabbermouth.'

'It's not a problem, really.'

'Nah, but it *is* important. I mean, even for you, I think it's important.'

She frowned.

'Your help, your room, your food, that's one thing, but I tell you, I was really having a bad trip when you found me. I was dizzy, know what I mean? I wanted to go back and see them, I – And then there was this guy who saved me. This guy, and your sheets.'

He reached over for something and put it down between them.

Camille recognized her book. The letters from Van Gogh to his brother.

She'd forgotten she had left it there.

And yet it was not as if she hadn't carried it everywhere with her.

'I opened it to hold myself back, to stop me going out of that door, because there was nothing else here and you know what this book did for me?'

She shook her head.

'It did this, and this, and this.'

He took the book and struck himself on his skull and on each cheek.

'I'm reading it for the third time. It . . . it's everything for me. There's everything in here. I know this guy inside out. He is me. He's my brother. I understand everything he says. How he loses it. How he suffers. How he's always repeating himself and saying sorry and trying to figure other people out, or searching his own soul, how his family rejected him, his parents completely clueless, then he'd stay in the hospital and all of that. I – I'm not going to tell you my life story, don't worry, but it disturbs me on some level. The way he is with girls, how he falls in love with this snooty woman, how everyone treats him with scorn, and the day he decides to set up house with that whore, the one who got pregnant. Nah, I won't tell you my life story but there are coincidences that make me bloody hallucinate. No one believed in him, except his brother. No one. But even though he was fragile and crazy, he believed in what he was doing. At least he says so, that he has faith, that he's strong and, uh . . . The first time I read it, practically straight through, I didn't get the bit in italics at the end.'

He opened the book: '*Letter that Vincent van Gogh had on his person July 29, 1890*. It was only when I read the preface the next day or the day after that I understood he'd committed suicide, the jerk. That he never sent that letter and I – Fuck, that really threw me, you've no idea. Everything he says about his body, I feel it. All his suffering, it's not just words, know what I mean? It's – Well, I . . . I don't care about his work. No, wait, it's not that I don't care but that's not what I was reading about. What I was reading about is that if you're not in your place, if you don't do what other people expect you to do, you suffer. You suffer like an animal and in the end you die. Well hey, no. I'm not going to die. He feels like a friend, a brother – I can't do that to him. I don't want to.'

Camille was glued. Jeez. Her cigarette ash had just fallen into her coffee.

'Is that just a load of bullshit what I just told you?'

'No, no, quite the opposite.'

'You read this?'

'Of course.'

'And you – it didn't make you feel really down?'

'I was mainly interested in his work. He started late. He taught himself. A – you, you know his paintings?'

'Sunflowers, right? Nah. I thought about it for a while, to go and look through a book or something, but I don't feel like it, I like my own images better.'

'Keep it. It's a present.'

'Some day, you know, if I make it through this, I'll thank you. But I can't just yet. Like I told you, I've been gnawed to the bone . . . I've got nothing left, except this old fleabag here.'

'When are you leaving?'

'Next week – supposed to anyway.'

'You want to thank me?'

'If there's a way I can.'

'Let me draw you.'

'Is that all?'

'Yes.'

'Naked?'

'Preferably.'

'Holy shit. You haven't seen my body.'

'I can imagine it.'

He tied the laces on his trainers and his dog began to jump in all directions.

'Are you going out?'

'All night long. Every night. I walk until I'm exhausted, I go for my daily fix as soon as the service opens, and I come back to lie down so I can make it through to the next day. I haven't found a better way up to now.'

Noise out in the hallway. The pile of fur froze.

'There's someone out there,' he panicked.

'Camille? Everything all right? It's – it's your valiant knight, my darling.'

There stood Philibert, in the doorway, with a sabre in his hand.

'Barbès! Down!'

'I am . . . I am r-ridiculous, aren't I.'

She introduced them, laughing, 'Vincent, this is Philibert Marquet de La Durbellière, Commander in Chief of an army in retreat and –' turning the other way, 'Vincent, as in, uh, as in Van Gogh . . .'

'*Enchanté*,' said Philibert, shoving his sabre back into its sheath. 'Ridiculous and delighted to meet you. I will, uh, I will withdraw now, you see.'

'I'm coming down with you,' answered Camille.

'Me too.'

'Will you – will you come and see me?' Camille asked him.

'Tomorrow.'

'When?'

'In the afternoon. Okay? With my dog?'

'With Barbès, of course.'

'Ah! Barbès,' said Philibert regretfully. 'Another madman of the Republic, that fellow. I would have preferred the Abbess of Rochechouart, indeed I would!'

Vincent looked at him quizzically.

She shrugged her shoulders, puzzled.

Philibert, who had turned back, was offended: 'Exactly! The Barbès-Rochechouart metro station! And for the name of poor Marguerite de Rochechouart de Montpipeau to be associated with that good-for-nothing is an absolute aberration!'

'De Montpipeau?' echoed Camille. 'Bloody hell, where do you dig up these names? By the way, why don't you sign up for *Who Wants to be a Millionaire?* yourself?'

'Oh no, don't you start! You know perfectly well why not.'

'No, why?'

'By the time I got the answer out it would be time for the news.'

11

Camille didn't sleep a wink all night. She wandered aimlessly around the flat, wiped at the dust, bumped into ghosts, took a bath, got up late, bathed Paulette and brushed her hair any old how, strolled a while along the rue de Grenelle with her, and couldn't eat a thing.

'You're awfully nervous today.'

'I have an important appointment.'

'Who with?'

'With myself.'

'Are you going to the doctor's?' asked the old lady worriedly.

As was her wont, Paulette dozed off after lunch. Camille set her ball of wool to one side, pulled up the covers and left on tiptoe.

She locked herself in her room, moved the stool a dozen times and inspected her supplies cautiously. She felt sick.

Franck had just come in. He was emptying a washing machine. Since the episode with his Jivaro sweater, he would take out his laundry himself, and held forth like a distraught housewife on the perfidy of dryers which wore out the fibres and chewed up collars.

Heart-stopping.

It was Franck who opened the door.

'I'm here for Camille.'

'Down the end of the hall.'

Then he went off to his room and for once she was grateful for his discretion.

They were both very ill at ease but for different reasons.

No, that's not it.

They were both very ill at ease for the same reason: their guts.

He was the one who broke the ice: 'Okay, then. Shall we get started? You got a changing room? A screen? Something?'

God bless him.

'You see? I turned the heat up to max. You won't be cold.'

'Oh! That's great, that fireplace. Shit, I feel like I'm back with the medics. It makes me nervous. Do I, do I take off my underwear too?'

'If you want to keep it on, then do.'

'But it's better if I take it off.'

'Yes. In any case, I always start from the back.'

'Shit. I'm sure I'm covered in spots.'

'Don't worry, once you're bare-chested in the ocean spray, they'll all vanish before you've even finished loading your first pile of manure.'

'You know you'd make a great beauty consultant?'

'Yeah, really. Go on, get out of there now and go sit down.'

'You could at least have put me by the window . . . So I'd have some distraction.'

'I'm not the one who decides.'

'No? Who does then?'

'The light. And don't complain, you'll be standing up next.'

'For how long?'

'Until you drop.'

'You'll drop before me.'

'Mmm.'

Mmm, meaning: I'd be surprised.

She began with a series of sketches, moving around him. Her belly and her hand began to relax.

But Vincent grew even more tense.

When she came too near he closed his eyes.

Did he have pimples? She couldn't see any. She saw his tensed muscles, his tired shoulders, the cervical bones sticking out at the nape of his neck when he lowered his head, his spinal cord like a long eroded ridge, his nervousness, his febrile quality, his jaw and his prominent cheekbones. The sunken shadows around his eyes, the shape of his skull, his sternum, his hollow chest, his scrawny arms dotted with dark spots. The touching labyrinth of veins beneath his pale skin and the passage of life over his body. Yes. That, above all: the imprint of the abyss, like the caterpillar tread of a huge invisible tank; his extreme modesty, too.

After roughly an hour he asked her if he could read.

'Yes. The time it'll take me to capture you . . .'

'You haven't started, yet?'

'No.'

'Well! Should I read out loud?'

'If you want.'

He kneaded the book for a moment before breaking its spine.

'*I sense what Father and Mother instinctively (I do not say intelligently) think about me. They shrink from taking me into the house as they might from taking a big shaggy dog who is sure to come into the room with wet paws – and is so very shaggy.*

'*He will get in everyone's way. And his bark is so loud.*

'*In short, he is a filthy beast.*

'*Very well, but the beast has a human history, and although he is a dog he has a human soul, and what is more one so sensitive that he can feel what people think about him, which an ordinary dog cannot do.*

'*In fact this dog used to be Father's son once upon a time, and it was Father who left him out in the streets a little too long, so he was bound to become rougher, but seeing that Father forgot this many years ago and has never thought deeply about what the bond between father and son means, we had best say nothing about it.*'

He cleared his throat.

'*The only* – oh, sorry – *the only thing the dog regrets is that he came back, because it wasn't as lonely on the heath as it is in this house – despite all that kindness. The poor beast's visit was a weakness, which I hope will be forgotten, and which he will avoid –*'

'Stop,' she interrupted. 'Stop, please. Just stop.'

'Is it bothering you?'

'Yes.'

'Sorry.'

'Right. I'm there. I've got you now.'

She closed her sketchpad and once again felt her stomach heave. She raised her chin and threw her head back.

'You okay?'

He didn't answer.

'Okay. Now you're going to turn towards me and sit with your legs spread and your hands like this.'

'I have to spread them, you sure?'

'Yes. And your hand, look, you . . . You bend your wrist and spread your fingers. Wait. Don't move.'

She rummaged in her things and handed him the reproduction of a painting by Ingres.

'Exactly like this.'

'Who's this fat guy?'

'Louis-François Bertin.'

'Who's he?'

'The buddha of the bourgeoisie: well-fed, well-off and trium-phant. I didn't say that, Manet did. Sublime, no?'

'And you want me to pose like him?'

'Yes.'

'Uh. My legs, my legs spread. That it?'

'Hey. Stop it with your dick. That's enough. I don't give a damn about it, you know,' she reassured him, leafing through her sketches. 'Here, look. I already drew it.'

'Oh!'

A disappointed, tender little syllable.

Camille sat down and placed her board on her lap, then stood up, tried to use an easel, but that didn't work either. She grew annoyed, cursed, and knew perfectly well that all this fidgeting was merely a pretext to keep the void at bay.

Finally she pinned her paper vertically and decided to sit at exactly the same height as her model.

She took in a long gulp of courage and blew out a little faltering breath of air. She'd been wrong, she shouldn't use red chalk. Graphite, pen-and-ink, and a sepia wash.

The model had spoken.

She raised her elbow. Her hand stayed in the air. She was trembling.

'Whatever you do, don't move. I'll be right back.'

She ran into the kitchen, knocked things over, grabbed the bottle of gin and drowned her fear. She closed her eyes and held on to the edge of the sink. Go on. One more, for the road.

When she came back to sit down, he looked at her with a smile.

He knew.

However compliant they might seem, people like them recognize each other. All of them.

It was like a probe. A radar.

An uneasy complicity and a shared sense of weakness.

'Feeling better?'

'Yes.'

'Okay, get on with it. We've got other things to do, for Christ's sake!'

He held himself very straight. At a slight angle, like the painting. He breathed evenly and stood up to the gaze of the girl who was humiliating him without knowing it.

Dark and luminous.

Ravaged.

Trusting.

'How much do you weigh, Vincent?'

'Around sixty . . .'

Sixty kilos of provocation.

(Even if it wasn't a polite question, it was interesting all the same: had Camille Fauque reached out to this boy to help him, as he truly believed, or to dissect him, naked and defenceless on a red formica kitchen chair?

Compassion? Love for mankind? Really?

Had it not all been premeditated? Moving him in up there, the dog food, the trust, Pierre Kessler's anger – like that kick in the arse, when her back was to the wall?

Artists are monsters.

No, please. That would be just too perverse. Let's give her the benefit of the doubt and keep quiet. There might be something not quite right about our girl Camille, but when she could dig her claws into the heart of her subject, the results were dazzling. And perhaps it was simply that her generosity was only now apparent? When her pupils contracted and she became pitiless . . .)

It was almost dark. She had put on the light without realizing, and was sweating as much as he was.

'Let's stop. I've got cramps. I'm aching all over.'

'No!' she exclaimed.

Her harsh tone of voice surprised them both.

'Forgive me. Don't, don't move, please don't.'

'In my trousers . . . front pocket . . . Valium.'

She went to fetch him a glass of water.

'Please, I beg you, just a little bit longer, you can lean against the chair if you want. I – I can't work from memory. If you leave now my drawing will die. Forgive me, I – I've almost finished.'

'That's it. You can get dressed.'

'Is it serious, doctor?'

'I hope so,' she murmured.

He came back, stretching, patted his dog and whispered a few tender words into its ear. He lit a cigarette.

'Want to see?'

'No.'

'Yes.'

He was stupefied.

'Shit . . . it's – it's raw.'

'No. It's tender.'

'Why did you stop at the ankles?'

'Do you want the real reason or the one I'm going to make up?'

'The real one.'

'Because I'm bad at feet!'

'And the other one?'

'Because . . . There's not much keeping you here, or is there?'

'And what about my dog?'

'There's your dog. I drew him over your shoulder earlier.'

'Oh! This is great! He's gorgeous, gorgeous, gorgeous.'

She tore out the sheet.

You make this huge effort, she thought, mock-grumbling, you break your back, you bring them back to life, offer them immortality and everything that might move them, and it's a scribbled sketch of their mutt . . .

I swear to God . . .

'Are you pleased with yourself?'

'Yes.'

'Will I have to come back?'

'Yes . . . To say goodbye and give me your address. You want something to drink?'

'No. I have to go and lie down, I don't feel so great now.'

As she led him down the hall Camille suddenly struck her forehead with her fist:

'Paulette! I forgot her!'

Her room was empty.

Shiiit.

'Problem?'

'I've lost my flatmate's grandma.'

'Look. There's a note on the table.'

We didn't want to disterb you. She's with me. Come as soon as you can. P.S. Your friend's dog crapped in the entranse.

12

Camille spread her arms and flew above the Champ-de-Mars. She grazed the Eiffel Tower, tickled the stars and came to earth outside the service entrance of the restaurant.

Paulette was sitting in the boss's office.

Swollen with happiness.

'I forgot you.'

'No you didn't, silly child, you were working. Is it done?'

'Yes.'

'Everything okay?'

'I'm hungry.'

'Lestafier!'

'Yes, boss.'

'Do me a nice big steak, plenty rare, for the office.'

Franck turned round. A steak? But Paulette didn't have any teeth.

When he understood that it was for Camille, he was even more astonished.

They communicated through sign language:

'For you?'

'Yes,' she answered, nodding her head.

'A big steak?'

'Yeeees.'

'Did you get a knock on the head?'

'Yeeeees.'

'Hey, you're really cute when you're happy, d'you know that?'

But she didn't really understand the sign language for that, and so she just waved a random acknowledgement.

'Uh, oh,' went the boss, handing Camille the plate, 'it's none of my business, but some people have all the luck.'

The slab of meat was in the shape of a heart.

'Ah, he's really something, that Lestafier,' he sighed, 'really something.'

'And he's so handsome,' added his grandmother, who had been feasting her eyes upon him for the last two hours.

'Yeah, I wouldn't go that far. What would you like with that steak? Go on . . . A little Côtes-du-Rhône, and I'll join you for a glass. And you, Granny? Hasn't your dessert come yet?'

No sooner had he raised his voice than Paulette was tucking into her fondant.

'Well, now,' he added, clicking his tongue, 'he's really shaped up, your grandson. I hardly recognize him.'

Turning to Camille: 'What have you done to him?'

'Nothing.'

'Well, it's perfect! Carry on like that! It really suits him. Nah, seriously. He's a good kid. He really is.'

Paulette was crying.

'Now what? What did I say? Drink something, for Christ's sake! Drink! Maxime!'

'Yes, boss?'

'Go and get me a glass of champagne, would you please.'

'That better?'

Paulette blew her nose and apologized: 'If only you knew what a long, hard road it has been. He was expelled from his first secondary school, then the second, then from his training certificate, his work placements, his apprenticeship, his –'

'But that's not the point!' boomed the chef. 'Look at him now! Look at what a master he is! Everyone's trying to pinch him from me! He'll end up with one or two medals on his arse, your little bichon frisé.'

'Beg pardon?' Paulette asked nervously.

'Stars.'

'Ah . . . not three?' she asked, disappointed.

'No. He's too bad-tempered for that. And too . . . sentimental.'

He winked at Camille.

'By the way, is the meat any good?'

'Delicious.'

'Bound to be. Okay, I'm off. If you need anything, knock on the window.'

When he got back to the apartment, Franck went and stood at the foot of Philibert's bed; his flatmate was chewing on a pencil in the light of his bedside lamp.

'Am I disturbing you?'

'Not at all!'

'We don't see much of each other any more . . .'

'Not a great deal, you're right. And actually are you still working on Sunday?'

'Yes.'

'Well come and see us on Monday if you get bored.'

'What are you reading?'

'I'm writing.'

'Who to?'

'I'm writing a script for my theatre. I'm afraid we're all obliged to go on stage at the end of the year.'

'Will you invite us?'

'I don't know if I dare.'

'Hey tell me, huh . . . How are things going?'

'I beg your pardon?'

'Between Camille and my old lady?'

'Entente cordiale.'

'You don't think Camille is fed up?'

'You want my honest opinion?'

'What?' urged Franck, anxious.

'She's not fed up, but she will be. Remember what you said: you promised to give her time off, two days a week. You promised to slow down at work.'

'Yeah, I know but I –'

'Stop right there. Spare me your excuses. I'm not interested. You know, you've got to grow up a bit, dear boy. It's like this thing –' He pointed to his notebook full of crossed-out lines. 'Whether we want to or not, we all have to take our turn some day.'

Franck got up, thoughtful.

'She'd say if she was fed up, no?'

'You think so?' Philibert held up his glasses to clean them. 'I don't know. Camille is so mysterious. Her past. Her family. Her friends. We don't know anything about this young lady. As far as I'm concerned, apart from her sketchbooks I haven't got a single thing which might conceivably enable me to formulate the slightest hypothesis as to her biography . . . No post, no phone calls, no visitors . . . Imagine if we lost her one day, we would not even know whom to turn to.'

'Don't say that.'

'Yes, I will say it. Think about it, Franck: she convinced me about Paulette, she went to get her, she gave up her bedroom for her, now she's taking care of her with an extraordinary sweetness, more than that, it's more than just taking care – she cares for her. They care for each other. I hear them laughing and babbling all day long when I'm here. Moreover, Camille is trying to get some work done in the afternoon, and you can't even honour your commitments.'

Philibert put his glasses back on his nose and kept Franck in his sights for a few seconds:

'No, I'm not very proud of you, corporal.'

With leaden feet, Franck went to tuck in his grandmother and switch off her television.

'Come over here,' she whispered.

Shit. Not asleep.

'I'm proud of you, my little boy.'

Well, they'd better make up their minds, he mused, putting the remote control down on her bedside table.

'Okay, Grandma, go to sleep now.'

'Very proud.'

Yeah sure, right.

Camille's door was ajar. He pushed it gently and started.

The pale light from the corridor illuminated her easel.

He stood there motionless for a moment.

Stupefaction, fright, and bedazzlement.

Was she right then, yet again?

You could understand things without learning about them first?

So he wasn't so stupid after all? Since, instinctively, he felt like reaching out to that sprawled, loose body on the canvas to help him back to his feet, it must mean he wasn't so thick after all, no?

Evening spider, melancholy. He squashed it and took out a beer.

It sat there and got warm.

He shouldn't have lingered in the hallway.

All this stuff was messing with his basic navigational equipment. Shit.

Though, actually, things were okay, now. For once life was behaving itself.

He quickly moved his hand away from his mouth. He hadn't bitten his nails for eleven days. Except the little finger.

But that didn't count.

Grow up, grow up. That's all he'd ever done.

What would become of them all if she disappeared?

He belched. Well now, this is all very well, but I've got a crêpe batter to prepare.

The picture of ultimate devotion, Franck beat the batter with a hand whisk so as not to disturb the others, then murmured a few secret incantations and let it rest in peace.

He covered the bowl with a clean dishcloth and left the kitchen, rubbing his hands together.

Tomorrow he would make her crêpes Suzette, to keep her there for ever.

Nyak, nyak, nyak . . . Alone in front of the bathroom mirror he imitated the demonic laugh of Dick Dastardly in *The Wacky Races*.

Hoo, hoo, hoo – that was Muttley's.

Wowee . . . Aren't we having fun?

13

Franck hadn't spent the night there for a long time. His dreams were sweet.

He went to get croissants the next morning and they all had breakfast together in Paulette's room. The sky was deep blue. Philibert and Paulette tossed a thousand charming civilities back and forth while Franck and Camille clung to their mugs in silence.

Franck wondered whether he should change his sheets and Camille wondered whether she should change certain details. He tried to catch her eye but she was somewhere else. She was already on the rue Séguier, in Pierre and Mathilde's living room, about to lose heart and run away.

If I change them now, I won't want to lie down this afternoon, and if I change them after my nap, that would be kind of obvious, no? I can already hear her snickering.

Or maybe I should go by the gallery? Drop my portfolio off with Sophie and get straight out of there?

And you know what'll probably happen, anyway, we won't even get anywhere near the bed, we'll just stand there, like in a film, we'll be so, uh –

No, that's not a good idea. If Pierre is there, he won't let me go, he'll make me sit down and talk about it. I don't want to talk. I don't give a damn about all his yadda yadda yadda. He either takes it or he doesn't. Period. And he can keep his yadda yadda for his clients.

I'll take a shower in the locker room before I leave work –

I'll take a taxi and I'll have him double park outside the entrance.

Some worried, others were carefree: but they all shook out their crumbs with a sigh, and quietly went their separate ways.

Philibert was already at the entrance. He opened the door for Franck with one hand and in the other he held a suitcase.

'Are you going on holiday?'

'No, these are props.'

'Props for what?'

'For my part.'

'Holy Moses! What is it? Like an Errol Flynn movie? Will you be swashbuckling all over the place?'

'Yes, of course! I'm going to hang by the curtain and throw myself into the crowd. Come on. Get going or I'll run you through.'

The sky was beautiful, so Camille and Paulette went down into the 'garden'.

The old lady was having more and more trouble walking and it took them nearly an hour to go down the Allée Adrienne-Lecouvreur. Camille had pins and needles in her legs; she gave Paulette her arm and tried to pace herself to her tiny steps, so she could not help but smile when she saw the sign *Reserved for riding, moderate gait*. When they stopped, it was to take tourists' pictures for them, let joggers go by or exchange a few frivolous words with assorted marathon runners in their Birkenstocks.

'Paulette?'

'Yes, dear?'

'Would you be shocked if I talked wheelchairs with you?'

Silence.

'Okay, then. You are shocked.'

'Am I so old?' she whispered.

'No, not at all! On the contrary! But I just thought that . . . Since we get bogged down with the Zimmer, you could push the chair for a while and then when you got tired you could have a rest and I could take you with me to the ends of the earth!'

Silence.

'Paulette, I am tired of this park. I can't stand it any more. I think I have counted every pebble, every bench and every little fence. There are eleven in all. I'm sick of these horrible tourist buses, I'm sick of all these hordes of people with no imagination, I'm sick of constantly running into the same faces. Those park wardens with their smug expression, and that other fellow, too . . . who smells of piss under his medal . . . There are so many other things to see in Paris – boutiques, little cul-de-sacs, courtyards, covered walkways, the Luxembourg, the booksellers along the Seine, the garden outside Notre-Dame, the flower market, the riverbanks, the . . . No, really, this city is magnificent. We could go to the cinema, to concerts, listen to opera, *o mio bambino caro* and all that . . . And here we are stuck in this neighbourhood for old people where the kids all dress the same and all their nannies have the same sour look on their face, and everything is so predictable. It's pointless.'

Silence.

Paulette was leaning more and more heavily on Camille's forearm.

'Okay. I'm going to be up front with you. I'm really trying to win you over but all that's not the real reason. The truth is, I'm asking you as a favour. If we have a wheelchair with us, and you agree to sit in it from time to time, we could go to the head of the queue at the museums and always go first. And you see that would be really convenient for me. There are a whole lot of exhibitions that I dream about going to, but I just don't have what it takes to queue.'

'You should have said so from the start, you little twit! If I can do it as a favour to you, then it's not a problem! That's all I ask, to keep you happy.'

Camille bit the inside of her cheek to keep from smiling. She lowered her head and managed to come out with a little thank you, a bit too solemn to be entirely sincere.

Quick, quick! Strike while the iron's hot! So they hurried to the nearest pharmacy.

'We work a lot with this Sunrise model, Classic 160. It's a folding model and has given complete satisfaction. Very light, easy to manoeuvre, weighing fourteen kilos. Only nine without the wheels. There's a footrest that can be folded away so the patient can push with her feet. Adjustable armrests and backrest . . . Reclining seat . . . Ah, no. That's extra. The wheels are easy to remove. It all fits easily into the boot of a car. You can also adjust the height of, uh –'

Paulette, who had been parked between the dry shampoos and the Scholl display, was making such a dour face that the saleswoman did not dare continue her spiel.

'Okay, I'll let you think about it. I have customers. Here you go, some brochures about it.'

Camille knelt down behind Paulette.

'It's not bad, is it?'

Silence.

'To be honest I expected something worse. It's a sporty model, and the black is quite chic . . .'

'Oh, come on. Tell me it's attractive why don't you.'

'Sunrise Medical . . . Where do they dream up these names . . . 37, isn't that the number of the *département* where you're from?'

Paulette put on her glasses: 'Where?'

'Uh . . . Chanceaux-sur-Choisille.'

'Ah! Of course! Chanceaux! I know exactly where that is!'

It was in the bag.

Thank you, God. Had it been any other *département*, they would have gone out of there with a pedicure kit and a pair of slippers with orthopaedic inner soles . . .

'How much is it?'

'Five hundred and fifty-eight euros, excluding VAT.'

'No, but really . . . Can't we – can't we rent one?'

'Not this model. The rental model is different. Sturdier, and heavier. But, you must be covered one hundred per cent, no? Madame has health insurance, doesn't she?'

The saleswoman had the impression she was talking to two half-witted old maids.

'You shouldn't have to pay for the chair! Go to your doctor and ask him for a prescription! Given your condition, Madame, it won't be a problem. Here, I'll give you this little booklet. All the references are in here. Do you have a GP?'

'Uh . . .'

'If he's not used to this, show him this code: 401 A02.1. And the rest you can arrange with your medical insurance, can't you?'

'Oh, okay, and . . . how do I do that?'

Once they were out on the pavement, Paulette faltered.

'If you make me see a doctor, they'll send me back to the hospice.'

361

'Hey, Paulette dear, calm down. We won't ever go, I hate them as much as you do, we'll figure something out. Don't you worry.'

'They're going to find me. They're going to find me,' she sobbed.

She had no appetite and lay flat out on her bed all day.

'What's wrong with her?' Franck asked, worried.

'Nothing. We went to a pharmacy for a chair and as soon as the woman mentioned seeing a doctor, she went into shock.'

'What sort of chair?'

'A wheelchair!'

'What for?'

'To have wheels, stupid! So we can see the scenery!'

'Shit, what the hell are you doing? She's fine as she is! Why do you want to shake her up like a bottle of Orangina!'

'Oh, hey, you're starting to piss me off, you know that? Why don't you look after her for a change? Why don't you wipe her bum from time to time, you might get some perspective! I have no trouble putting up with her, she's adorable, your grandma, but shit, I need to move, to go for walks, get my head together! Everything's fine and dandy for you, am I right? Tell me there's nothing bothering you? You're all the same, Philou and Paulette and you, it doesn't seem to matter to you guys: these four walls, some grub, your job, then beddy-byes – that seems to be plenty for you. Well it ain't for me! I'm beginning to suffocate, so there! And anyway I adore going for walks and it'll be fine weather soon . . . So I'll say it one more time: I don't mind being the nursemaid, but I need the tourist option too, otherwise you can just figure it out for yourselves –'

'What?'

'Nothing!'

'Don't get in such a state.'

'But I have to! You're so selfish that if I don't yell and scream, you'll never do a thing to help me!'

Franck went out, slamming the door, and Camille shut herself in her room.

When she came back out, there they were, both of them, in the entrance. Paulette was in seventh heaven: her little boy was looking after her.

'Hey, fat lady, have a seat. It's like a motorbike: you need to tune it, if you're going far.'

He was crouched down fiddling with the knobs.

'Your feet feel okay like that?'

'Yes.'

'And your arms?'

'A bit too high.'

'Okay, Camille, over here. Since you're the one who'll be pushing, come here so I can adjust the handles. Perfect. Okay, I've got to get going. Come with me to work, we'll try it out.'

'Does it fit in the lift?'

'No. You have to fold it,' he said irritably. 'But isn't it better that way, she's not completely helpless as far as I know?'

'Vroom, vroom. Fasten your belt, Fangio, I'm running late.'

They went through the park full speed. By the time they reached the red light, Paulette's hair was dishevelled and her cheeks were pink.

'Right, I'm on my way, girls. Send me a postcard when you get to Kathmandu . . .'

Franck had already gone a few yards when he turned around:

'Yo, Camille? Don't forget this evening?'

'What?'

'The crêpes.'

'Shit!'

She put her hand to her mouth.

'I'd forgotten . . . I'm not in.'

He was suddenly a few inches shorter.

'And it's important, I can't cancel. It's for work.'

'And Paulette?'

'I asked Philou to take over.'

'Okay, well, never mind. We'll just eat them without you.'

He was stoical in his despair, the only sign of his discomfort a slight twist as he walked away.

The label on his new underpants was itchy.

14

Mathilde Daens-Kessler was the prettiest woman Camille had ever known. Tall, much taller than her husband, very slender, very lively, and very cultured. She flitted across our little planet as if she scarcely realized where she was; she was interested in everything, could be amazed by the smallest things, knew how to have fun, grew gently indignant, sometimes laid her palm over your hand, always spoke in a soft voice, spoke four or five languages fluently, and hid her intentions behind a discouraging smile.

She was so lovely that it had never even occurred to Camille to sketch her.

It was too risky. She was too full of life.

A little sketch, once. Her profile. The bottom of her chignon and her earrings. Pierre had stolen it from Camille, but it wasn't Mathilde. Her husky voice was missing, and her brilliance, and the deep dimples when she laughed.

Mathilde had the kindness, arrogance and offhand manner of those who are born in finely woven sheets. Her father had been an important art collector, she had always been surrounded by beautiful things, and had never had to count anything in her life – neither possessions, nor friends, still less her enemies.

She was rich, and Pierre was enterprising.

When he spoke, she was silent and covered up his indiscretions when his back was turned. He was always on the lookout for fresh talent. He was unerring in his judgment: he was the one who had launched Voulys and Barcarès, for example, and she did her utmost to keep them.

She kept the ones she wanted.

Camille remembered well the first time they met. It had been at the École des Beaux-Arts during an exhibition of year-end projects. A sort of aura preceded them: the formidable dealer and Witold-Daens's daughter . . . Their visit was much-awaited, they were feared, and their slightest reaction was anxiously anticipated. When they came to greet her and her crowd of grungy fellow artists, Camille felt miserable. She lowered her head when she shook Mathilde's hand, and awkwardly evaded a few compliments, looking for a mousehole to escape into.

That was in June nearly ten years ago. There were swallows giving a concert in the courtyard of the school; and they drank a watery punch while listening devoutly to Kessler's remarks. Camille didn't hear a thing. She was staring at his wife. That day Mathilde wore a blue tunic and a wide silver belt with tiny little bells which tinkled furiously whenever she moved.

It was love at first sight.

Afterwards they were invited to a restaurant on the rue Dauphine and, at the end of a dinner with plenty of wine, Camille's boyfriend had urged her to open her portfolio. She refused.

A few months later, she went to see them. Alone.

Pierre and Mathilde owned drawings by Tiepolo, Degas and Kandinsky, but they had no children. Camille never dared to bring up the subject, nor did she resist when they cast their net round her and reeled her in. Later she turned out to be such a disappointment that the holes in the net were stretched wide . . .

'It's utterly insane! What you're doing is utterly insane!' Pierre shouted.

'Why can you not love yourself? Why?' added Mathilde, more gently.

Camille did not go to the opening nights.

When the two of them were alone, Pierre continued to voice his regret:

'Why?'

'She never had enough love,' answered his wife.

'From us?'

'From anyone.'

He collapsed against her shoulder and moaned, 'Oh, Mathilde, my lovely woman . . . Why did you let this one get away?'

'She'll be back.'

'No. She's going to ruin everything.'

'She'll be back.'

She had come back.

'Is Pierre not here?'

'No, he's having dinner with his Englishmen, I didn't tell him you were coming, I wanted to see you on my own for a bit.'

Then, glancing down at Camille's portfolio: 'But – did you bring something?'

'Nah, it's nothing. Just a little thing I promised him the other day.'

'Can I see?'

Camille didn't answer. Then, 'Okay, I'll wait for him.'

'Is it something you've done?'

'Uh-huh.'

'My God. When he finds out you didn't come empty-handed, he'll scream with despair. I'm going to call him.'

'No, no!' begged Camille, 'Leave it! It's nothing, really. It's between us. A sort of receipt, for the rent.'

'Okay then. Right. Let's eat.'

Everything in their place was beautiful – the view, the *objets*, the rugs, the paintings, the dishes, the toaster – everything. Even their toilets were beautiful. There was a plaster reproduction of the quatrain Mallarmé had composed for his own toilet:

Oh you who relieve your tripe
In this gloomy hall
You may sing or smoke your pipe
And never touch the wall.

The first time, that thing had just killed her: 'Did you – did you buy a chunk of Mallarmé's shitting room?'

'Of course not,' Pierre laughed. 'It's just that I know the fellow who made the cast . . . Have you been to Mallarmé's house? In Vulaines?'

'No.'

'We'll take you there some day. You would love it there. Absolutely *love* it.'

And everything was as it should be. Even their toilet paper was softer than elsewhere . . .

Now, Mathilde seemed delighted: 'You look lovely! And you look great! This short hair really suits you. You've put on weight, no? I'm so happy to see you looking like this. So happy, really! I've missed you so much, Camille. If you only knew how they wear me out sometimes, all those geniuses. The less talent they have the more noise they make. Pierre doesn't care, he's in his element, but as for me, Camille, I . . . It gets so boring. Come and sit here next to me, tell me what's going on . . .'

'I'm not good at that. I'll show you my sketchbooks.'

Mathilde turned the pages and Camille commented on them.

And as she introduced her little universe like this, she really understood how much it meant to her.

Philibert, Franck and Paulette had become the most important people in her life, and she was only just realizing it now, at that very moment, sitting there between two 18th-century Persian cushions. And she felt deeply disturbed.

From the first notebook to the last drawing she had made just a few hours earlier, of Paulette radiant in her chair in front of the Eiffel Tower, only a few months had elapsed, and yet she was not the same person . . . Not the same one holding the pencil. She had given herself a good shake, she had evolved, and she had blasted away the granite blocks which for so many years had kept her from moving forward.

That evening there would be people waiting for her to come home. People who didn't care about her so-called worth. Who loved her for other reasons. For herself, perhaps.

For myself?

For yourself.

'And this?' said Mathilde impatiently, 'You've stopped talking. Who's this?'

'Johanna, Paulette's hairdresser.'

'And this?'

367

'Johanna's boots. Rock 'n' roll, aren't they? How can a girl who works on her feet all day long possibly stand them? Fashion victimhood in the extreme, I suppose.'

Mathilde laughed. The shoes really were monstrous.

'And this one here, I've seen quite a few of him.'

'That's Franck, the chef I was telling you about.'

'He's handsome, isn't he.'

'You think so?'

'Yes. He looks like Titian's young Farnese, ten years older.'

Camille rolled her eyes. 'Whatever.'

'No, really! I promise you!'

Mathilde got up and came back with a book: 'Here. Look. The same dark gaze, the same dilated nostrils, the same jutting chin, the same slightly protruding ears. The same fire burning within . . .'

'That's rubbish,' said Camille, staring cross-eyed at the portrait. 'Mine's all pimply.'

'Oh, you spoil everything!'

'Is that it?' said Mathilde regretfully.

''Fraid so.'

'These are good. Really good. Marvellous.'

'Oh, stop it.'

'Don't contradict me, young lady, I may not know how to do this myself, but I do know how to look at things. At an age when most children are going to puppet shows, my father was already dragging me to the four corners of the earth and lifting me on to his shoulders so I'd be at the right height, so please don't contradict me. Can you leave them with me?'

Camille didn't know what to say.

'For Pierre.'

'All right. But look after them, okay? They're my temperature charts, these things.'

'I'd gathered as much.'

'Don't you want to wait for Pierre?'

'No, I have to get going.'

'He'll be disappointed.'

'It won't be the first time,' answered Camille, resigned.

'You haven't mentioned your mother.'

'Really?' she said, surprised. 'That's a good sign, isn't it?'

Mathilde saw her to the door and kissed her: 'The best. Off you go, and don't forget to come back and see me. Bring your bathchair with the roof down . . . It's only a matter of a few streets . . .'

'I promise.'

'And carry on like this. Keep it light. Have fun with what you're doing. Pierre would surely tell you something completely different, but you mustn't listen to him. Don't listen to others, not to him, not to anyone. Oh, and, by the way?'

'Yes?'

'Do you need money?'

Camille should have said no. For twenty-seven years she had been saying no. No, I'm fine. No, but thanks all the same. No, I really don't need a thing. No, I don't want to have to owe you. No, no, leave me alone.

'Yes.'

Yes. Yes I think I might. Yes, I won't be going back to play chambermaid either for the Italians or for Bredart or any of those bastards. Yes I would like to work in peace for the first time in my life. Yes, I don't want to have to cringe every time Franck hands me the money for Paulette. Yes, I've changed. Yes, I need you. Yes.

'Fine. And use some of it to get yourself some clothes. Honestly, that denim jacket – you were wearing it ten years ago.'

That was true.

15

Camille walked home, looking in the windows of the antique shops. She was right outside the Beaux-Arts (fate, what a clever sod) when her mobile phone rang. She closed it again when she saw it was Pierre calling.

She walked faster. Her heart was racing to keep up.

Second ring. Mathilde this time. She didn't answer that one either.

She went back the way she'd come and crossed the Seine. Our little heroine had a romantic streak, and whether it was to jump for joy or to jump in the water, the Pont des Arts was still the best there was in Paris. She leaned against the parapet and dialled the three digits of her voicemail.

You have two new messages. Today, at twenty-three – She could always drop the phone, not exactly on purpose . . . Splash! Oh, what a pity . . .

'Camille, call me immediately or I'll come and drag you by the scruff of the neck!' he bellowed. 'Right away! You hear me?'

Today, at twenty-three thirty-eight: 'It's Mathilde. Don't call him back. Don't come. I don't want you to see this. He's crying like an overweight cow, your art dealer. Not a very pretty sight, I assure you. No – it *is* a pretty sight, beautiful even. Thank you Camille, thank you. You hear what he's saying? Wait, I'm going to give him the phone, otherwise he's going to yank my ear off.' 'I'll be showing you in September, Fauque, and don't say no because the invitations have already been sent –' The message cut off.

She switched off her mobile phone, rolled a cigarette and smoked it, standing there between the Louvre, the Académie Française, Notre-Dame and the Place de la Concorde.

A perfect place for the curtain to come down . . .

Then she shortened the strap on her shoulder bag and ran as fast as she could, so as not to miss dessert.

16

There was a lingering smell of burnt fat in the kitchen, but all the dishes had been cleared away.

Not a sound, all the lights off, not even a glimmer of light from under the doors of their rooms. Shoot. And here for once she was ready to eat the entire frying pan.

Camille knocked on Franck's door.

He was listening to music.

She planted herself at the end of his bed and put her fists on her hips: 'Well, what the hell?'

'We saved a few for you. I'll flambé them for you tomorrow.'

'Well, what the hell!' she said again. 'You're not going to screw me?'

'Ha, ha. Very funny.'

She began to get undressed. 'Hey, old man, you're not going to get out of it that easily! Promises are made, orgasms are kept!'

He sat up to switch on his lamp, while she was tossing her shoes into the void. 'What the hell are you doing? Where do you think you're going?'

'Well, I'm taking my clothes off!'

'Oh, no.'

'What?'

'Not like that, wait . . . I've been dreaming of this moment for ages.'

'Switch off the light.'

'Why?'

'I'm afraid you won't want me if you see me.'

'But Camille, shit! Stop, stop!' he shouted.

A little pout, disappointed: 'You don't want to?'

Silence.

'Switch off the light.'

'No.'

'Yes!'

'I don't want it to happen like this.'

'And how do you want it to happen? You want to take me rowing in the Bois de Boulogne?'

'Sorry?'

'Take me for a boat ride and recite poetry while I trail my hand in the water?'

'Come and sit beside me.'

'Switch off the light.'

'Okay.'

'Switch off the music.'

'Is that it?'

'Yes.'

'Is that you?' he asked, intimidated.

'Yes.'

'You're really here?'

'No.'

'Here, take one of my pillows. How was your appointment?'

'Fine.'

'You want to tell me?'

'What?'

'Everything. I want to know everything, tonight. Every single thing.'

'You know, if I start . . . You might feel you have to take me in your arms afterwards, too.'

'Oh, shit. Did you get raped?'

'Not that either.'

'Okay then, I can fix that for you if you like.'

'Oh thank you, that's kind of you. Uh, where shall I begin?'

Franck imitated the condescending voice of a TV presenter who has no clue how to behave with children:

'And where are you from, little girl?'

'From Meudon.'

'From Meudon?' he exclaimed, 'That's just great. And where is your mummy?'

'She's at home eating pills and tablets and things.'

'Oh, really? And your daddy, where's your daddy?'

'He died.'

Silence.

'Ah, I warned you, mate! Have you got some condoms at least?'

'Don't jerk me around like this, Camille, I'm pretty bloody stupid sometimes, you know that. Your dad died?'

'Yes.'

'How?'

'He fell into the void.'

Franck was silent.

'Okay, I'll give it to you in order. Come closer because I don't want the others to hear.'

He pulled the duvet up over their heads: 'Go ahead. There, no one can see us now.'

17

Camille crossed her ankles, put her hands on her stomach, and set off on a long journey.

'I was a good little girl, very obedient . . .' she began, in a childish voice, 'I didn't eat much but I worked hard at school and I drew all the time. I didn't have any brothers or sisters. My father was called Jean-Louis and my mother Catherine. I think they were in love when they met. I don't know, I never dared ask them. But by the time I began drawing horses or Johnny Depp's gorgeous face in *21 Jump Street*, by then they didn't love each other any more. I'm sure of that because my dad didn't live with us any more. He only came back at weekends to see me. It was understandable that he went away and I would have done the same in his place. And I would have liked to leave with him on those Sunday evenings but I never could have because my mother would have killed herself *again*. She killed herself plenty of times when I was little. Fortunately it was usually when I wasn't there but then later on, because I'd grown up, she didn't seem to care as much, so, uh . . . Once I was invited to a girlfriend's house for her birthday. In the evening my mum didn't come to get me, so another mum dropped me off outside my house and when I got to the living room, I saw my mother dead on the carpet. The firemen came and I went to live with the neighbour for ten days. After that my dad told me that if she killed herself again he was going to get custody, so she stopped. She just went on taking a ton of medication. My dad told me he had to leave because of his work but my mum said I mustn't believe him. Every evening she repeated that he was a liar and a bastard, that he had another wife and a little girl that he was cuddling every night . . .'

Camille began to speak in a normal tone of voice: 'This is the first time I've ever talked about it. It's like – your mother finished with you before sticking you back in the train, but mine still messes with my head every day. Every single day. There were times she was nice, though. She'd buy me felt tip pens and tell me I was her only happiness on earth.

'When my father came over, he shut himself in the garage in his Jaguar and listened to opera. It was an old Jaguar that didn't have any wheels but that didn't matter, we used to go for a drive all the same. He would say, "Shall I take you to the Riviera, Mademoiselle?" and I would sit there next to him. I adored that car.'

'Which make was it?'

'An MK or something like that.'

'MKI or MKII?'

'Shit, you really are a bloke. I'm trying to tell you a tear-jerker of a story and the only thing you're interested in is the make of the effing car!'

'Sorry.'

'No harm done.'

'Go on, then.'

She gave a sigh of resignation.

'"Well then, Mademoiselle, shall I take you to the Riviera?"

'"Yes," smiled Camille, "I'd like that." "Have you brought your bathing suit?" he'd ask. "Perfect. And an evening gown as well! We must go to the casino. Don't forget your silver fox, it can be cool in Monte Carlo in the evening." There was a nice smell inside the car. The smell of well-worn leather . . . It was all so lovely, I remember. The crystal ashtray, the vanity mirror, the tiny little handle to roll the window down, the inside of the glove compartment, the wood. It was like a flying carpet. "With a bit of luck we'll get there before nightfall," he promised. Yes, he was that kind of man, my dad, a big dreamer who could shift gears on a car up on blocks for hours on end and take me to the far corners of the earth in a suburban garage. He was really into opera, too, so we listened to *Don Carlos, La Traviata* or *The Marriage of Figaro* during the trip. He would tell me the stories: Madama Butterfly's sorrow, the impossible love of Pelléas and Mélisande – when he confesses, "I have something to tell you" and then he can't; the stories with the countess and her Cherub who hides all the time, or Alcina, the beautiful witch who turned her suitors into wild animals. I always had the right to speak except when he raised his hand and in *Alcina*, he raised it a lot. *Tornami a vagheggiar* – I can't listen to that aria any more. It's too happy. But most of the time I didn't say anything. I felt good. I thought about the other little girl. She didn't have all this. It was complicated for me. Now, obviously, I can see things more clearly: a man like him couldn't live with a woman like my mother. A woman who'd turn off the music just like that when it was time for dinner, who'd burst all our dreams like soap bubbles. I never saw her happy, I never saw her smile, I . . . But my father was the very image of kindness and goodness. A bit like Philibert . . . Too nice, in any case, to have to deal with all that. The idea that he might be a bastard in his little princess's eyes . . . So one day he came back to live with us. He slept in his study and left every weekend . . . No more escapades to Salzburg or Rome in the old grey Jaguar, no more casinos or picnics by the seaside. And then one morning – he must have been tired, very, very tired, he fell from the top of a building.'

'Did he fall or did he jump?'

'He was an elegant man; he fell. He was an insurance broker and he was walking on the roof of a tower, something to do with some ventilation conduits, he opened up his file and he wasn't watching where he put his feet.'

'God, that's unbelievable . . . What do you think?'

'I don't. There was the funeral after that and my mother kept turning around to see if the other woman hadn't shown up in the back of the church. Then she sold the Jaguar and I stopped talking.'

'For how long?'

'Months.'

'And then? Can I push the sheet down, I'm suffocating like this.'

'Me too. I became a lonely, ungrateful teenager. I put the number of the hospital into the phone memory but I didn't need it. She calmed down. Not suicidal any more, depressive. That was progress. It was quieter. One death was enough for her, I suppose. After that I had only one thing on my mind: to get the hell out. I left the first time to live with a girlfriend when I was seventeen. One evening, boom, my mother and the cops outside the door. Although the bitch knew perfectly well where I was. It was what we used to call a heavy scene, man. We were having supper with my friend's parents and talking about the war in Algeria, I remember . . . And then knock knock, the cops. I felt really uncomfortable for those people but hey, I didn't want any fuss so I left with my mother. I was going to turn eighteen on 11 February 1995, and on the 10th at one minute past midnight I left, closing the door behind me really quietly. I got my baccalaureate and went to study at the Beaux-Arts. Fourth out of seventy admitted. I'd made a really beautiful dossier based on the operas from my childhood. I worked like a dog and got a commendation from the jury. At that point I had no contact at all with my mother and it was a struggle, life was so bloody expensive in Paris. I lived here and there, no fixed abode. Cut a lot of classes. Cut theory and went to the studio workshops, until I began to piss around. To begin with, I was sort of bored. I guess I really wasn't playing by the rules: I didn't take myself seriously so as a result I wasn't taken seriously. I wasn't an Artist with a capital A, I was a good workman. The kind to whom they'd recommend the Place du Tertre, rather, to daub some Monet and little dancers . . . And then uh . . . I didn't get it. I liked to draw, so instead of listening to the professors' bla-bla, I'd do their portraits, and the whole notion of "visual art" and happenings and installations – it all bored me stiff. I realized that I had got the wrong century. I wish I'd lived in the 16th or 17th century so I could have been apprenticed to a great master. Preparing his backgrounds, cleaning his brushes, grinding his colours. Maybe I wasn't mature enough? I don't know. Second thing was, I fell in with the wrong sort of guy. It was the classic, obvious thing: silly young woman with her box of pastels and her neatly folded rags falls in love with unknown genius. The accursed prince of clouds, the widower, dark and brooding and inconsolable. A real storybook character: long hair, tormented, incredibly brilliant, suffering, passionate . . . Argentinian father and Hungarian mother, what an explosive combination, incredibly cultured, living in a squat and just waiting for it: a dewy-eyed little dodo-brain to fix his meals while he created, in the midst of terrible suffering . . . I fitted the part. I went and bought yards of cloth at the Marché Saint Pierre, and stapled them to the wall to make our little "love nest" look "stylish and charming", and I looked for work to keep the stewpot bubbling. Stewpot, well, camping stove more like. I dropped out of school and sat cross-legged on the floor to think about what sort of job I could do. And the worst of it is that I was proud! I watched him painting and I felt important. I was the sister, the muse, the great woman behind the great man, the one who dragged the wine crates up the stairs, fed the disciples and emptied the ashtrays.'

She laughed.

'I was so proud I became a guard at a museum, really clever that, no? Well, if I'm telling you about my colleagues it's because I really discovered the grandeur of public service. To be honest, I didn't care. I was fine. Because I was in my great master's studio at last. The canvases had been dry for a long time but I was definitely learning more there than in any school in the world. And since I wasn't getting much sleep in those days, I could snooze all I wanted. I was keeping warm. The problem was that I wasn't allowed to do any drawing. Even on a tiny nothing little notebook, even if there was no one around and God knows there were enough days when there was hardly anyone, but it was out of the question that I do anything besides ruminate on my fate, ready to jump whenever I heard the slap slap of the soles of some visitor gone astray or to put my stuff away quick as I could when I heard the jangle of a key-ring. In the end it became the favourite pastime of a certain Séraphin Tico – Séraphin Tico, I love that name . . . he'd creep up on me to catch me red-handed. God, he was pleased, that moron, whenever he could force me to put my pencil away! Then I'd watch as he walked away, spreading his legs so his balls could inflate with delight . . . But every time he startled me it made me move, and that drove me nuts. The number of sketches that were ruined because of him. God! I couldn't take it any more. So I learned how to play the game. My education in life was beginning to bear fruit: I bribed him.'

'Sorry?'

'I paid him. I asked him how much he wanted to let me work. Thirty francs a day? Done deal. The price of an hour's catnap somewhere warm? Done deal. And I gave him the money.'

'Shit.'

'Yup. The great Séraphin Tico,' she added, dreamily, 'now that we have the wheelchair, I'll go and say hello to him some day with Paulette.'

'Why?'

'Because I liked him. At least he was an honest scoundrel. Not like the other prick who was pissed off with me the minute I walked in after a full day's work simply because I'd forgotten to buy him his cigarettes. So what did I do, stupid bitch? I'd go back out to get them.'

'Why did you stay with him?'

'Because I loved him. I admired his work, too. He was free, no hang-ups, sure of himself, demanding . . . Exactly the opposite from me. He would have preferred to die penniless and friendless than accept the slightest compromise. I was barely twenty years old and I was the one supporting him and I admired him.'

'You were a fool.'

'Yes. No. After the adolescence I'd just been through, he was the best thing that could have happened to me. We had all the time in the world, all we talked about was art, painting. We were ridiculous, okay, but we had our integrity. Six of us could eat on two benefit cheques, we were freezing cold and we queued at the public baths, but we had the feeling we were living better than others were. And grotesque as it may seem today, I think we were right. We had passion. The luxury of it . . . I was way naive and I was happy. When I was fed up with one room, I moved into another one, and when I didn't forget the cigarettes, it was party time! We drank a lot, too. I acquired some bad habits. And then I met the Kesslers – I was telling you about them the other day.'

'I'm sure he was a good lay,' scowled Franck.

She cooed: 'Oh yes, best in the world. Oh . . . just thinking about it gives me shivers all over, it still does.'

'Okay-Okay. You made your point.'

'Nah,' she sighed, 'it wasn't really so great. Once the first post-virginal emotion was over with, I – I, well, let's just say he was a selfish man.'

'Ah.'

'Yes. You might know something about that, too.'

'Yeh, but I don't smoke!'

They smiled at each other in the dark.

'After that, things began to go downhill. Lover boy was cheating on me. While I was putting up with Séraphin Tico's corny humour, he was screwing the first-year students, and when eventually we made peace, he confessed that he'd been doing drugs, oh, not a whole lot, just to try, for the beauty of the act . . . And that's something I really don't feel like talking about.'

'Why?'

'Because it was just so sad. It's unbelievable how fast that shit can bring you to your knees. Beauty of the act, my arse, I held out a few more months and then I went back to my mother's to live. She hadn't seen me in nearly three years, she opens the door and says, "I warn you, there's nothing to eat." I burst into tears and I didn't get out of bed for two months. For once she was decent, she had what it took to take care of me, so to speak. And when I was back on my feet, I went back to work. In those days all I ate was pablum and baby food. Hello? Dr Freud? After all the Dolby-surround cinemascope, all the sound and light and blockbuster emotions, I went back to a small-scale life in black and white. I watched TV and my head would go all funny whenever I walked along the river . . .'

'Did you think about it?'

'I did. I pictured my ghost rising up to the heavens to the aria of *Tornami a vagheggiar*, *Te solo vuol amar*, and my papa would be there to open his arms and laugh, "Ah, here you are at last, Mademoiselle! You'll see, it's even nicer than the Riviera up here!"'

She was crying.

'Hey, don't cry . . .'

'I feel like it.'

'Okay then, cry.'

'That's nice. You're not the complicated type.'

'True. I have plenty of faults but I'm not complicated. D'you want to stop there?'

'No.'

'D'you want something to drink? A little hot milk with orange flower water like Paulette used to make me?'

'No, thanks. Where was I?'

'Funny head.'

'Yes, funny head. Honestly, it wouldn't have taken much more than a nudge in the back to tip me over, but instead, fate was wearing fine black kid gloves, and tapped me on the shoulder one morning. That day I was playing with figures from a Watteau painting, I was bent over on my chair when this man went by, behind me. I'd seen him around a lot. He was always wandering in among the students and peering at their work when they weren't looking. I thought he was trying to pick up some girl. I sort of wondered about his sexuality, I watched him chatting up these kids who acted flattered, and I admired the way he went about it. He always wore these superb coats, very long, and classy suits, and scarves. It was like taking a break, to watch him . . . So I was leaning over my sketchpad and all I could see were his magnificent shoes, very fine quality, with an impeccable shine. "May I aska you an indiscreeta question,

Mademoiselle? Can your morality resist all temptation?" I wondered where he was headed with a remark like that. To the hotel? Well, okay . . . could my morality resist all temptation? Here I was corrupting Séraphin Tico and I dreamt of going against the Good Lord's work. "No," I replied, and because of my gallant little reply, off I went down another shit hole. Immeasurably deep, this time.'

'A what?'

'An unspeakable shit hole.'

'What did you do?'

'The same thing as before. But instead of sleeping in a squat and playing housemaid for a lunatic, I lived in one of the grandest hotels in Europe to play parlourmaid for a crook.'

'You didn't –'

'Become a prostitute? No. Although . . .'

'What did you do? '

'Forgery.'

'Forged banknotes?'

'No, art forgery. And the worst of it is, I really enjoyed it. At least in the beginning. Later on it became borderline slavery, the joke was on me, but in the beginning it was a gas. For once I was being useful! And I tell you, I was living in incredible luxury. Nothing was too fine for me. Was I cold? He gave me the best cashmere sweaters. You know that big blue sweater with a hood that I wear all the time?'

'Yeah?'

'Ten thousand francs.'

'No way.'

'Ye-e-s. And I had a dozen more where that one came from. Was I hungry? Ba-boom, room service and all the lobster I could eat. Was I thirsty? *Ma che*, champagne! And if I was bored? Shows, shopping, music! "Enythinga you wanta, you tella Vittorio." The only thing I was not allowed to say was, "I'm quitting." Oh, then he'd get really nasty, *il bello* Vittorio. "If you leava, you go straighta downa." But why would I leave? I was pampered, having fun, doing what I liked, I went to all the museums I had ever dreamt of, met people, at night I wandered into the wrong hotel rooms . . . I'll never be sure but I think I may even have slept with Jeremy Irons . . .'

'Who's that?'

'God, you're hopeless. Anyway, hardly matters. I read, listened to music, earned money. With hindsight I tell myself it was another form of suicide. Just more comfortable. I cut myself off from real life and from the few people who loved me. From Pierre and Mathilde Kessler, who were really angry with me because of it; from my former school friends; from reality, morality, the straight and narrow, my own self.'

'Were you working all the time?'

'All the time. I didn't produce a whole lot but I had to do the same things over and over again because of technical problems. The patina, the type of support and all that. The drawing itself was peanuts, it was the ageing process that was tricky. I worked with Jan, a Dutch guy who supplied us with old paper. That was his metier: going around the world and coming back with rolls of paper. He had a mad chemist side to him and he was tireless, trying to create old from new. I never heard him say a single thing, a fascinating guy. And eventually I lost all notion of time. In a way, I let myself be sucked into this non-life. You couldn't tell, just looking with the naked eye, but I was a wreck. An elegant wreck. Always in need of a drink, shirts made to measure and completely disgusted with my little self. I don't know where it all would have led to if Leonardo hadn't saved me.'

'Leonardo who?'

'Leonardo da Vinci. When he came along I rebelled right away. As long as we were just doing the minor masters, sketches of sketches, prints of prints or touch-ups of touch-ups, we could fob off our illusions on to the less scrupulous dealers; but this was going too far. I said as much but no one listened. Vittorio was getting too greedy. I don't know exactly what he was doing with his money but the more he made, the more he was short of it. He must have had his weaknesses, too. So I kept my mouth shut. It wasn't my problem, after all. I went back to the Louvre, to the graphic arts departments, and I got access to certain documents and learned them by heart. Vittorio, he-a wanted one-a little thing-a. "You see thata study? You getta inspired, but thata character, you keepa her for me." In those days we had already left the hotel and were living in a big furnished apartment. I did as he asked and I waited. He was more and more nervous. He spent hours on the phone, wore out the carpet, cursed the Madonna. One morning he burst into my room like a madman: "I have to go, but you don'a move from here, all right? You don'a go out-a, longa as I don'a tell you. You understan'? You don'a move-a!" That evening I got a call from this other guy I didn't know: "Burn everything," and he hangs up. Right. I gathered up a packet of lies and destroyed them in the kitchen sink. And I went on waiting. Several days. I didn't dare go out. I didn't dare look out the window. I went completely paranoid. But at the end of a week I left. I was hungry, I wanted to smoke, I had nothing left to lose. I went back to Meudon on foot and I found the house all closed up with a For Sale sign on the gate. Had she died? I climbed over the wall and slept in the garage. I came back to Paris. As long as I kept walking, I could stay on my feet. I hung around the building in case Vittorio had come back. I had no money, no compass, no way to get my bearings, nothing. I spent two more nights outside in my ten-thousand-franc cashmere and I bummed cigarettes and got my coat stolen. The third night I rang the bell at Pierre and Mathilde's and collapsed outside their door. They fixed me up and got me this place to live here, on the seventh floor. A week later I was still sitting on the floor wondering what sort of job I could do. All I knew was that I never wanted to do art again in my life. But I wasn't ready to go back out into the world yet either. People frightened me. So I became a night-time cleaning operative. I lived like that for a little over a year. In the meantime I found my mother. She didn't ask any questions. I never knew if it was indifference or just discretion. I didn't scratch the surface, I didn't dare: she was all I had left.

'It was so ironic . . . I had done everything I could to get away from her and there I was, back to square one, minus a few dreams. I pretended to live, rule number one no drinking alone, and I looked for the emergency exit in my ten square metres. And then I got ill at the beginning of the winter and that's when Philibert carried me down the stairs to the room next door. The rest you know.'

Long silence.

'Well,' said Franck, several times. 'Well, well.'

He sat up and folded his arms over his chest.

'Well. Talk about a life. That's crazy. And now? What are you going to do now?'

Camille didn't answer.

She was asleep.

He pulled the duvet up to just below her nose, took his things, and went out on tiptoe. Now that he knew her, he didn't dare lie down beside her. Anyway, she was taking up all the space.

All the space.

18

He was lost.

He wandered through the flat for a while, went to the kitchen, opened the cupboards and closed them again, shaking his head.

On the windowsill the lettuce heart was all wilted. He threw it into the bin then went and sat back down to finish his drawing. He hesitated over the eyes. Should he draw two black dots at the end of the horns, or one single one underneath?

Shit. Even in the snail department he was a loser.

Okay, just one then. It was cuter.

He got dressed. Pushed his motorbike past the concierge's *loge*, tight with apprehension. Pikou watched him go by without making a sound. That's it, good boy, that's the way. This summer you'll have a little Lacoste to seduce the Pekinese bitches. He went another few yards before he dared kick-start then set off into the night.

He took the first street to the left and rode straight on. When he reached the sea, he put his helmet on his lap and watched the fishermen manoeuvring offshore. He used the moment to say a few words to his motorbike. So that it would have some understanding of the situation . . .

And he felt a bit like breaking down.

It was the wind, perhaps.

He gave himself a good shake.

Ah-hah! That's what he'd been looking for earlier on: something like a coffee filter for his thoughts! They were certainly clearing. He walked along the port until he came to the first bar that was open and he drank some coffee amidst the gleaming oilskins. Raising his eyes, he discovered an old acquaintance in the reflection in the mirror:

'Hey, what's up? Look at you!'

'Yeah, hey.'

'What you doing here?'

'I came here for a coffee.'

'You don't look too good.'

'Tired.'

'Still playing around?'

'No.'

'C'mon . . . weren't you with a girl tonight?'

'She wasn't really a girl.'

'What was she then?'

'Don't really know.'

'Easy, mate. Hey, *patronne!* Add a drop of something to his cup, my pal is fading away here.'

'No, no, it's okay.'

'What's okay?'

'Well, everything.'

'What's the matter, Lestaf?'

'Feel sick.'

'Ooh, you wouldn't be in love, maybe?'

'Could be.'

'Well, well. That's good news! Be happy, man! Be happy! Climb up on the bar! Sing!'

'Stop it.'

'What's wrong with you?'

'Nothing. She – she's good, this one. Too good for me, at any rate.'

'Not at all. That's just bullshit. Nobody's ever too good for any-one. Particularly women!'

'She's not a woman, I said.'

'She's a guy?'

'No!'

'She's an android? Lara Croft?'

'Better than that.'

'Better than Lara Croft? Bloody hell. Has she got anything uptop at least?'

'A 34A, I'd say.'

386

He smiled. 'Ah, right. If you fall for a breadboard, you're in deep shit, I get the picture.'

'No, you don't, you don't get a thing!' he said irritably. 'Anyway, you never get it. You're always shooting your big bloody mouth off so no one will notice that you don't get a thing! Ever since you were a kid you've been pissing everyone off. I feel sorry for you, you know that? That girl, when she talks to me, half the words she uses I don't understand at all, you get it? I feel like a piece of shit next to her. If you knew all the stuff she's been through in her life. Shit, I'm really not up to this. I think I'll have to drop the whole idea.'

His reflection pouted.

'What?' grumbled Franck.

'You're a bastard.'

'I've changed.'

'Naw . . . just tired.'

'I've been tired for twenty years.

'What's she been through?'

'Nothing but shit.'

'Well hey! That's good, no? You have something else to give her!'

'What?'

'Yo! You doing this on purpose or what?'

'No.'

'You are. You're doing this on purpose so I'll feel sorry for you. Think about it. I'm sure you'll come up with something.'

'I'm frightened.'

'That's a good sign.'

'Yes, but if I –'

The *patronne* stretched.

'Gentlemen, the bread's here. Who'd like a sandwich? Young man?'

'Thanks, I'll be okay.'

Yeah, I'll be okay.

As I head straight for disaster, or wherever . . .

We'll see.

They were setting up the market. Franck bought some flowers off the back of a truck – got change, young man? – and flattened them beneath his jacket.

Flowers, that was a good beginning, no?

Got change, young man? And how, old girl! And how!

And for the first time in his life, he found himself heading for Paris as the sun rose.

Philibert was taking a shower. Franck took Paulette her breakfast and kissed her, rubbing her jowls. 'So, Grandma, isn't this nice?'

'Hey, you're frozen. Where on earth have you been this time?'

'Doesn't matter,' he said, getting up.

His sweater reeked of mimosas. For lack of a vase he cut a plastic bottle in half with the bread knife.

'Hey, Philou?'

'Hold on, I'm spooning out my Nesquik. Have you made up the shopping list?'

'Yeah. How do you spell Riviera?'

'With a capital R and no accents.'

'Thanks.'

Some mimosas like they have on the ~~rivié~~ Riviera. He folded the note and placed it with the vase by the drawing of the little snail.

He shaved.

'Where did we get to?' asked the other guy, back there in the mirror.

'Nah, it's okay now. I'll manage.'

'Okay, then. Well, good luck.'

Franck made a face.

It was the aftershave.

He was ten minutes late and the meeting had already started.

'Here's lover boy,' announced the boss.

He sat down with a smile.

19

As he did whenever he was exhausted, Franck burned himself badly. His commis insisted on having a look at it and in the end he held out his arm in silence. He didn't have the energy to complain, or to feel the pain. He was a burnt-out machine. Out of order, out of juice, out of trouble, out of everything.

He came home, unsteady on his feet, and set his alarm to be sure he wouldn't sleep through until the next morning; yanked his shoes off without undoing the laces, and fell into bed with his arms across his chest. Now, yes, his hand was throbbing and he stifled a *lllsssh* of pain before dropping off.

He had been sleeping for over an hour when Camille – so light it could be no one else – came to see him in a dream.

Alas, he could not see whether she was naked. She was stretched out on top of him. Thigh against thigh, belly against belly and shoulder against shoulder.

She had her lips by his ear and she was saying, 'Lestafier, I'm going to rape you.'

He smiled in his sleep. First of all because this was one fine hallucination and second of all because her breath was tickling him so badly he wanted to climb the walls.

'Yes. Let's get it over with. I'm going to rape you so I'll have a good reason to take you in my arms. But whatever you do, you mustn't move. If you fight back, I'll smother you, my little one.'

He wanted to pull everything together, his body, his hands, his sheets, to be sure not to wake up, but someone had him pinned down by the wrists.

The pain made him realize he wasn't dreaming and because he was in pain, he understood his happiness.

When she put her palm on his, Camille felt the gauze:

'Does it hurt?'

'Yes.'

'Good.'

And she began to move.

So did he.

'No, no,' she scolded, 'let me.'

She spat out a piece of plastic, slipped on the condom, settled against his neck, a bit lower down too, and passed her hands under the small of his back.

After a short, silent to and fro, she grasped his shoulders, arched her back and came in less time than it takes to write it.

'Already?' he asked, a bit disappointed.

'Yes . . .'

'Oh.'

'I was just too hungry.'

Franck closed his arms around her back.

'Sorry,' she added.

'Not a valid excuse, Mademoiselle. I am going to file a complaint.'

'With pleasure.'

'No, not right away. I'm too comfortable for the moment. Stay like that, I beg of you. Oh, shit.'

'What?'

'I just got burn ointment all over you.'

'So much the better,' she smiled, 'it could always come in handy.'

Franck closed his eyes. He'd hit the jackpot. A sweet, intelligent, bad girl. Oh, thank you God, thank you. It was too good to be true.

Slightly sticky, slightly greasy, they fell asleep together, beneath a sheet that smelled of debauchery and healing skin.

20

When she woke up to go and check on Paulette, Camille stepped on the alarm clock and unplugged it. Nobody dared wake him up. Neither the distracted household, nor his boss, who took over for him without batting an eyelid.

He must be in such pain, poor boy.

He left his room at about two in the morning and knocked on the door at the end of the corridor.

He knelt down at the foot of her mattress.

She was reading.

'Hum . . . hum.'

She lowered her newspaper, raised her head and acted surprised: 'Problem?'

'Uh, Officer Sir, I'm here to file a complaint.'

'Have you had something stolen?'

Okay, easy now! Calm down! He wasn't about to say 'my heart' or any rubbish like that.

'Well, that is, uh, there was a break-in yesterday,' he continued.

'Really?'

'Yes.'

'And were you there?'

'I was asleep.'

'Did you see anything?'

'No.'

'That's very unfortunate. Are you properly insured, at least?'

'No,' he replied sheepishly.

She sighed. 'Your testimony is rather vague. I know such things are never pleasant, but . . . You know . . . It might be best to proceed with a re-enactment of the incident.'

'Ah?'

'Well, yes.'

In one bound he was on top of her. She shrieked.

'Hey, I'm starving too! I haven't had a thing since last night and you're the one who's going to suffer, Mary Poppins. Shit, how long has it been rumbling away in there? I'm going to go mad here . . .'

He devoured her from head to foot.

He began by pecking at her freckles then he nibbled, kissed, crunched, licked, gobbled, chewed, picked, bit and gnawed her to the bone. While he was at it she took her pleasure and gave as good as she got.

They hardly dared speak or even look at each other.

Camille seemed upset.

'What is it?' he asked worriedly.

'Ah, sir, I know, this is really stupid, but I needed a second copy for our archives and I forgot to insert the carbon paper. We're going to have to start again, from the beginning.'

'Now?'

'No. Not now. But we mustn't leave it too long, all the same. Just in case you forget any important details.'

'All right. And you – d'you think I'll be reimbursed?'

'I'd be surprised.'

'The thief took everything, you know.'

'Everything?'

'Almost everything.'

'That's tough.'

Camille lay on her stomach and put her chin on her hands.

'You're beautiful.'

'Oh, stop it,' she said, snuggling into his arms.

'Nah, you're right, you're not beautiful, you're . . . I don't know how to say it. You're alive. Everything about you is alive: your hair, your eyes, your ears, your little nose, your big mouth, your hands, your adorable arse, your long legs, the faces you make, your voice, your softness, your silences, your . . .'

'My organism?'

'Yeah.'

'I'm not beautiful but my organism is alive. Great declaration. I'd never heard that one before.'

'Don't play with words,' he said, clouding over, 'it's too easy for you. Uh –'

'What?'

'I'm even hungrier than before. I really do have to get something to eat now.'

'Okay then, so long. Till we next have the pleasure, as they say.'

He panicked: 'Do, do you want me to bring you something?'

'What do you suggest?' she said, stretching.

'Whatever you like.'

Then, after a moment's thought: 'Nothing. Everything.'

'Okay. I'll get it.'

He was leaning against the wall, his tray on his lap. He uncorked a bottle and handed her a glass. She put down her sketchbook.

They raised their glasses.

'To the future.'

'No. Please, anything but. To now,' she corrected.

Ouch.

'The future. You – uh –'

She looked him straight in the eyes: 'Franck, please tell me: we're not going to fall in love, are we?'

He pretended to choke.

'Am, orrgl, argh . . . You crazy or what? Of course not!'

'Ah! You scared me for a minute. We've already done so many stupid things, the two of us.'

'Yeah, that's for sure. Though we're not really counting, are we?'

'I am. Yes, I am.'

'Ah?'

'Yes. Let's fuck, drink, go for walks, and hold hands; you can grab me by the neck and let me chase after you if you want but . . . Let's not fall in love. Please.'

'Okay. I'll write it down.'

'Are you drawing me?'

'Yes.'

393

'How are you drawing me?'

'The way I see you.'

'Do I look good?'

'I like the way you look.'

He licked the sauce off his plate, put down his glass, and resigned himself to dealing with a few administrative hassles.

This time they did not hurry, and when they rolled apart, sated, at the edge of the abyss, Franck spoke to the ceiling:

'Agreed, Camille, I'll never love you.'

'Thank you, Franck. Me neither.'

Part Five

1

Nothing changed, everything changed. Franck lost his appetite and Camille regained her colour. Paris became more beautiful, more luminous, a happier place. People smiled more and the asphalt seemed more elastic. As if everything was within reach; the contours of the world were more precise and the world itself was lighter.

Microclimate on the Champ-de-Mars? Global warming on their planet? A temporary end to gravity? Nothing made sense any more; nothing mattered.

They navigated from his bed to her mattress, lay down as if on a carpet of eggs, and said tender things while they caressed each other's back. Neither one wanted to be naked in the other's presence; they were a bit gauche and a bit silly, and they felt obliged to pull the sheets up over their modest moments, before lapsing into debauchery.

A new apprenticeship or an initial rough sketch? They were attentive, and applied themselves in silence.

Pikou doffed his dog jacket and Madame Perreira brought her flower pots back out. It was still a bit early for the budgerigars.

'Hup, hup, hup,' she said one morning, 'I've got something for you.'

The letter had been posted from the Côtes-d'Armor in Brittany.

September 10, 1889. Open quotes. *Whatever was in my throat seems to be disappearing, I'm still eating with some difficulty, but at least am able to once again.* Close quotes. *Thank you.*

When she turned the card over, Camille beheld the febrile face of Vincent Van Gogh.

She slipped it into her notebook.

Monoprix had taken a hit. Thanks to the three books which Philibert had given them – *Hidden, Surprising Paris; Paris: 300 Façades for the Curious;* and *Guide to Paris Tea Rooms,* off you go, kids – Camille raised her eyes and no longer said anything bad about her neighbourhood, where Art Nouveau was on display beneath an open sky.

From that time on she and Paulette would ramble from the Russian *isbas* on the boulevard Beau-Séjour to the *mouzaïa* of the Buttes-Chaumont, by way of the Hôtel du Nord and the Saint-Vincent cemetery, where one day they had a picnic with Maurice Utrillo and Eugène Boudin on Marcel Aymé's tomb.

'*As for Théophile Alexandre Steinlen, a marvellous painter of cats and human misery, he has been laid to rest beneath a tree, in the southeastern corner of the cemetery.* That's a nice entry, isn't it?'

'Why are you always taking me to see dead people?' asked Paulette.

'Sorry?'

She didn't answer.

'Where would you like to go, Paulette dear? To a nightclub?'

No answer.

'Yoohoo! Paulette!'

'Let's go home. I'm tired.'

And once again they found themselves in a taxi whose driver groused because of the wheelchair.

It was the perfect moron-detector, that buggy.

Camille was tired.

More and more tired, heavier and heavier.

She didn't like to admit it but she was constantly having to keep Paulette from the edge, to struggle with her to get her dressed, feed her, and oblige her to carry on a conversation. It wasn't even a conversation; more just a response. The stubborn old woman did not want to see a doctor and the tolerant young woman did not try to go against her will, first of all because it was not something she typically did, and secondly because it was up to Franck to convince her. But whenever they went to the library, Camille immersed herself in medical magazines or books to read depressing things about the degeneration of the cerebellum and other Alzheimeresque delights of old age. She then put away these Pandora's boxes with a sigh, and took bad good resolutions: if Paulette didn't want to get care, if she didn't want to show any interest in the modern world, if she didn't want to finish her plate and would rather wear her coat over her bathrobe to go for her walk, that was, after all, her right. Her most legitimate right. Camille didn't want to pressure her, and if there were people who had a problem with that then let them get her to talk about her past – about her mother, about the evenings during the grape-picking, about the day the abbot nearly drowned in the Louère because he had thrown the casting net a bit too quickly and the thingammy got caught on one of the buttons on his cassock, or about her garden – let them try to put the spark back in her eyes, – eyes which had become almost opaque. In any case, as far as Camille was concerned, there was nothing else to be done.

'Which sort of lettuces did you grow?'

'May Queen or Fat Lazy Blonde.'

'And the carrots?'

'La Palaiseau, of course.'

'And the spinach?'

'Ooh . . . spinach. Monstrueux de Viroflay. That was a good variety, grew well.'

'But how can you manage to remember all those names?'

'And I remember a whole lot more. I'd leaf through the seed catalogue every night, the way others would get their prayer books all sticky. I loved it. My husband dreamt about cartridge pouches when he read his hunting and fishing catalogue, and I loved my plants. People came from all over to admire my garden, do you know that?'

She would put her in the light and draw her while she listened.

And the more she drew her, the more she loved her.

Would Paulette have struggled harder to stay on her feet if it hadn't been for the wheelchair? Had Camille infantilized her by begging her to sit the whole way so that they could go faster? Probably . . .

Never mind. What they were experiencing together – the looks they exchanged, hand in hand, while life was crumbling away with every passing memory – was something no one could ever take away from them. Neither Franck nor Philibert, both of whom were leagues away from even conceiving the wild, improvised nature of Camille and Paulette's friendship, nor the doctors, who would never prevent an old woman from returning to the riverbank, eight years old again and shouting, *'Monsieur l'abbé! Monsieur l'abbé!'* through her tears, because if the abbot went under, it would be straight to hell for all his choir children . . .

'I tossed my rosary out to him – what on earth good do you think that could have done the poor man? I think I began to lose my faith that day, because instead of begging God to save him, he was calling for his mother. Now that seemed fishy to me.'

2

'Franck?'
  'Mmm?'
  'I'm worried about Paulette.'
  'I know.'
  'What should I do? Force her to have some tests?'
  'I think I'm going to sell my motorbike.'
  'Right. I can see you care diddly-squat about what I'm saying.'

3

He didn't sell it. He swapped it with the grill man at work for his pretentious Golf. He had reached the bottom of the abyss that week but he was careful not to show it and, the following Sunday, he gathered all of them around Paulette's bed.

Stroke of luck, the weather was fine.

'Aren't you going to work?' she asked.

'Oh, I don't know. Don't much feel like it today. Say, uh, wasn't it the first day of spring yesterday?'

The others were confused, between Philibert who lived in his fog of unintelligible scribbles, and Paulette and Camille who'd lost all notion of time for weeks now; so he was deluding himself if he hoped to get any sort of response.

But he didn't give up: 'It is, you Parisians! It's spring, I swear!'

'Oh?'

Not very enthusiastic, this audience.

'You don't care?'

'Yes, yes . . .'

'No, you don't, I can see you don't.'

He went over to the window: 'Nah, I was just saying that. Just saying that because it's a pity to stay here watching the Chinese tourists sprouting on the Champ-de-Mars when we have a nice country house like all the rich people in the building, and if you got a move on we could stop at the market in Azay and buy what we need to make a good lunch. At least I – well, that's what I think, okay? If you're not interested, I'll go back to bed.'

Like a tortoise, Paulette stretched out her old wrinkly neck from her carapace:

'Pardon?'

'Oh, just something simple. I thought maybe veal chops with assorted vegetables. And strawberries for dessert. If they're good ones, right? Otherwise I'll make an apple pie. We'll have to see. A little Bourgueil from my friend Christophe to wash it all down and a nice nap in the sun, what do you say?'

'And your work?' asked Philibert.

'Bah. I do enough as it is, don't I?'

'And how will we get there?' said Camille with a touch of irony. 'In your top case?'

He took a sip of coffee and announced calmly: 'I have a beautiful car, waiting outside the door: that scum Pikou has already baptized it twice this morning, the wheelchair is folded up in the back and I filled her up a little while ago.'

He put his cup down and reached for the breakfast tray: 'C'mon. Get a move on, guys. I've got peas to shell, you know.'

Paulette fell out of bed. It wasn't her cerebellum, it was the hurry.

No sooner said than done, and what was done was repeated every week.

Like all their wealthy neighbours – but without them, since they were one day out of synch – they would get up very early on a Sunday morning and come back on Monday night, their arms filled with victuals, flowers, sketches and a sweet fatigue.

Paulette revived.

There were times when Camille suffered from spells of lucidity and she would look things squarely in the face. This thing with Franck was truly pleasant. Let's be happy, let's be crazy, let's nail the doors shut, carve the bark, exchange our blood samples, not think about it any more, let's discover each other and pluck daisy petals and suffer a bit and gather our rosebuds and yadda yadda yadda – but it could never work. She didn't feel like going into it at length but whatever, their affair was bound to be a washout. There were too many differences, too much – anyway. Let's move on. She just couldn't put the wanton Camille side by side with the watchful Camille. One was always looking at the other, wrinkling her nose.

It was sad, but that was the way it was.

403

But sometimes it wasn't that way. Sometimes she managed to hold it all together and the two bickering bitches would melt into one single Camille, a silly and helpless Camille. Sometimes, he really won her over.

On that first day, for example. The business with the car, the nap, the sweet little market and all that, that wasn't bad, but it got even better.

It was when he stopped on the way into the village and turned around: 'Grandma, you should walk a little and do this last bit on foot with Camille. We'll go on ahead and open up the house in the meantime.'

That was a stroke of genius.

Because you should have seen her, the little dame in her quilted slippers, grasping the arm of her youthful cane, the same lady who for months had been withdrawing from the edge while sinking into the mud, how slowly she moved forward to start with, slowly slowly so as not to slip, then she raised her head, lifted her knees and loosened her grip . . .

You should have seen her so you could appreciate words as corny as *happiness* or *bliss*. Paulette's suddenly radiant face, her queenly bearing, those little nudges with her chin towards the furtive net curtains, and her implacable commentary on the state of people's windowboxes or porches.

How quickly she was walking all of a sudden, her blood flowing with memories and the smell of warm tar . . .

'Look, Camille, there's my house. There it is.'

4

Camille just stood there.

'Well, what is it? What's wrong?' asked Paulette.

'This – this is your house?'

'Well, I should think so! Oh, just look at this jungle. Nothing's been cut back. What a sad state of affairs.'

'The house looks like mine . . .'

'Pardon?'

Her house: not the one in Meudon where her parents scratched each other's eyes out, but the one she used to draw for herself from the time she was old enough to hold a felt tip pen. Her little imaginary house, the place where she sought refuge with her dreams of hens and metal biscuit tins. Her Polly Pocket, her Barbie camper van, her nest for the Marsupilamis, her blue house clinging to the hill, her Tara, her African farm, her promontory in the mountains.

Paulette's house was like a square and solid little woman, showing off and greeting you with one hand firmly planted on her hip and the knowing look of someone who gives herself airs. The kind who lowers her eyes and acts modestly when really, everything in her oozes happiness and serene satisfaction.

Paulette's house was a frog that wanted to become as big as an ox. A little railway guard's bungalow that was not afraid of competing with Chambord and Chenonceaux.

Dreams of grandeur, like a pushy little peasant woman proclaiming: 'Take a good look, sister dear. It this enough, tell me? My slate roof with that white limestone which nicely sets off the door-and window-frames – I've made it, don't you think?'

'I fear not.'

'Ah, you don't think? And my two dormer windows, there? Aren't they pretty, my cut-stone dormer windows?'

'Not in the least.'

'Not in the least? And the cornice? The cornice was carved by a journeyman!'

'You don't even come close, my dear.'

The timid country bumpkin became so upset that she covered herself in a trellis, dolled herself up with unmatching flower pots and pushed her contempt to the limits – body piercing with a horseshoe above the door. Ha! They had nothing like it, those Agnès Sorels and other royal mistresses of Poitiers!

Paulette's house *existed*.

Paulette didn't feel like going inside, she wanted to see her garden. Oh, woe . . . Everything's ruined . . . Weeds everywhere . . . And this is when we should be sowing . . . Cabbages, carrots, strawberries, leeks . . . All this fine soil gone to the dandelions. Oh, woe. Fortunately I have my flowers. Well, it's still a bit early, yet. Where are the narcissi? Oh, there they are. And the daffodils? And here, Camille, bend down so you can see how pretty they are. I can't see them but they must be around here somewhere . . .

'Little blue ones?'

'Yes.'

'What are they called?'

'Grape hyacinths . . . Oh,' she moaned.

'What?'

'Well, they have to be divided.'

'No problem. We'll take care of it tomorrow. You'll tell me what to do.'

'You would do that?'

'Of course. And you'll see, I'll be a better student than I was in the kitchen.'

'And sweet peas, too. They need planting. They were my mother's favourite flower.'

'Whatever you like.'

Camille felt her bag. Good, she hadn't forgotten her watercolours.

They rolled the wheelchair out into the sun and Philibert helped her sit down. Too much emotion.

'Look, Grandma, look who's here!'

Franck stood on the porch, a huge knife in one hand and a cat in the other.

'Actually, I think I'd rather make you some rabbit!'

They brought out some chairs and picnicked in their coats. By dessert, they had undone their buttons and, eyes closed, head back, legs outstretched, they breathed in the good country sunshine.

The birds were singing, Franck and Philibert were squabbling:

'I say it's a blackbird.'

'No, a nightingale.'

'A blackbird!'

'A nightingale! Shit, this is where I live! I should know!'

'Stop,' sighed Philibert, 'you spent all your time fiddling with mopeds, how could you possibly hear the birds? Whereas I was reading in silence, and had all the time in the world to become familiar with their dialects. The blackbird trills, whereas the robin's song is like little drops of water falling. I promise you, that is a blackbird. Can you hear how it's trilling? Pavarotti practising his singing exercises.'

'Grandma. What is it?'

She was asleep.

'Camille. What is it?'

'Two penguins spoiling the silence.'

'Fine. If that's the way things are. Come, Philou dear, I'll take you fishing.'

'Ah? Uh . . . It's just that I . . . I'm not very good at it, and I al-always tangle up . . .'

Franck laughed.

'Come on, Philou dear, come on. Come and tell me about your lover so I can explain to you where the reel is.'

Philibert rolled his eyes in Camille's direction.

'Hey! I didn't say a thing!' she protested.

'No, it's not her. It's my little finger . . .'

The tall Mutt with his bow tie and monocle and the little Jeff with his pirate's headband walked off into the distance, arm in arm.

'Tell me, lad, tell Uncle Franck what sort of bait you've got. Very important, bait is, you know that? Because those beasts are not stupid, ooh, noo, not stupid at all.'

When Paulette woke up, the two women walked around the hamlet with the wheelchair, then Camille forced her to take a bath to warm up.

She was biting the inside of her cheek.

All this was not very sensible.

Never mind.

Philibert lit a fire and Franck prepared dinner.

Paulette went to bed early and Camille sketched the boys playing chess.

'Camille?'

'Mmm?'

'Why do you draw all the time?'

'Because that's all I know how to do.'

'And what are you drawing right now?'

'The Bishop and the Knight.'

They decided that the boys would sleep on the sofa bed and Camille would take Franck's old bed.

'Uh,' protested Philibert, 'wouldn't it be better if Camille, hmm, took the big bed, hmm.'

They looked at him with a smile.

'I may be short-sighted, to be sure, but not that short-sighted, you know.'

'No, no,' Franck countered, 'she goes in my room. We're like your cousins: never before the wedding.'

Because he wanted to sleep with her in his childhood bed. Beneath his football posters and his moto-cross trophies. It would be neither very comfortable nor very romantic but it was the proof that life was a good lay in spite of everything.

He'd been so bored in that room. So, so bored.

If someone had told him that one day he would bring home a princess and that he would lie down there, next to her, in this little brass bed where there was a deep hole, once upon a time, in which he used to get lost as a child, and where in later years he would rub himself as he dreamt about creatures who were not nearly as pretty as she was . . . he would never have believed it. That pimply boy with his big feet and his bronze trophy above his head . . . No, it wasn't a foregone conclusion, not by a long shot.

Yes, life was a strange chef: years in the cold store and then boom! From one day to the next, you're on the grill, mate!

'What are you thinking about?' asked Camille.

'Nothing . . . bullshit. You okay?'

'I can't believe you grew up here.'

'Why not?'

She sighed. 'It's so far from everything. It's not even a village. There's . . . there's nothing here. Just little houses with little old people in the window. And this house, where nothing has changed since the fifties. I'd never seen a kitchen stove like that one. And the other stove takes up half the room! And the toilets out in the garden! How can a child grow and flourish here? How did you manage? What did you do to survive?'

'I went looking for you.'

'Stop . . . None of that, we said.'

'*You* said.'

'Come on.'

'You know how I managed, you went through the same thing. Except that I had nature. That was lucky for me. I was outside all the time. And Philou can say what he likes, it was a nightingale. I know so because my granddad told me and my granddad was like a singing magpie. He didn't need any bird whistles.'

'So how do you manage to live in Paris?'

'I don't live.'

'Isn't there any work down this way?'

'No. Nothing interesting. But if I have kids some day, I swear I won't let them grow up in the middle of traffic, that's for sure. A kid who doesn't have a pair of boots, a fishing rod, and a catapult isn't a real kid. Why are you smiling?'

'Nothing. You're cute.'

'I'd rather you said something else about me.'

'You're never satisfied.'

'How many do you want?'

'Pardon?'

'Kids?'

'Hey,' she whined. 'Are you doing this on purpose or what?'

'Hold on, I didn't say it had to be with me!'

'I don't want any.'

'Really?' He sounded disappointed.

'No.'

'Why?'

'Because.'

He caught her by the neck and held her by force close to his ear.

'Tell me.'

'No.'

'Yes. Tell me. I won't tell anyone.'

'Because if I die, I don't want the child to be all alone.'

'You're right. That's why you have to have lots of kids. And besides, you know . . .'

He squeezed her even tighter.

'You're not going to die, not you. You're an angel . . . and angels don't ever die.'

She was crying.

'Hey, what's up?'

'Nah, it's nothing. It's because I'm about to get my period. It's always the same. It gets me down and the littlest thing makes me cry.'

She smiled through her runny nose:

'You see I'm no angel.'

5

They'd been in the dark for a long time, uncomfortable and entwined, when Franck suddenly came out with, 'There's something been bugging me.'

'What?'

'You have a sister, right?'

'Yes . . .'

'Why don't you see her?'

'I don't know.'

'That's lame. You have to see her.'

'Why?'

'Because! It's great to have a sister. I would have given anything to have a brother. Anything! Even my bike. Even my most secret fishing holes. Even my extra balls at pinball. Like that song by Maxime Le Forestier, you know. The one about the brother he never had . . .'

'I know. I thought about trying to see her at one point but then I didn't dare.'

'Why?'

'Because of my mother, maybe.'

'Stop going on about your mother. She's done nothing but hurt you. Don't be masochistic. You don't owe her a thing, you know.'

'But I do.'

'No you don't. You're not obliged to love your parents when they behave badly.'

'Yes you are.'

'Why?'

'Precisely because they're your parents.'

He gave a sigh of disgust. 'It's not hard to become a parent, all you have to do is fuck. It's afterwards that it gets complicated. In my case, for example, I'm not about to love a woman just because she got laid in a car park. I can't do anything about that.'

'But it's not the same for me.'

'No, it's worse. I can see the state you're in every time you come back from a meeting with your mother. It's horrible. Your face is all –'

'Stop. I don't feel like talking about it.'

'Okay, okay. Just one last thing. You're not obliged to love her. That's all I have to say. And you'll say that I'm like this because of all the bad stuff I'm carting around and yeah, you're right. But it's precisely because I've been down this road myself that I'm showing you where to go: you're not obliged to love your parents when they behave like big shits, that's all.'

Camille didn't respond.

'Are you mad at me?'

'No.'

'Forgive me.'

She was silent.

'You're right. It's not the same for you. She always took care of you, after all. But she mustn't stop you from seeing your sister if you have one. Frankly, she's not worth that sacrifice.'

'No . . .'

'No.'

6

The next day, Camille set to work in the garden, following Paulette's instructions. Philibert settled at the bottom of the garden to write, and Franck prepared a delicious salad.

After coffee, it was Franck who fell asleep on the chaise longue. God, what a backache he had . . .

He was going to order a mattress for next time. He couldn't spend another two nights like that. No way. Life was a good lay but there was no point in taking stupid risks. No way.

They came back every weekend. With or without Philibert. Usually with.

Camille – and she had always known she would – was becoming a regular pro at gardening.

Paulette tried to calm her enthusiasm: 'No. We can't plant that! Bear in mind that we're only coming once a week. We need sturdy, hardy plants. Lupin if you like, phlox, cosmos . . . Cosmos is really pretty. So light. You'd like it, I think.'

And Franck, through the brother-in-law of Fat Titi's sister's co-worker, dug up an ageing motorbike he could use to go to the market or to drop in on René.

He'd lasted thirty-two days without a bike and he was still wondering how he'd managed.

It was an old, ugly bike, but the noise it made when it revved was magnificent.

'Listen to that,' he shouted to them from the lean-to where he hung out when he was not in the kitchen, 'listen to this baby!'

They all raised their heads half-heartedly from their seeds or their book.

'Ptttttt . . . put put put put.'

'Well? Amazing, no? It sounds like a Harley!'

Yeah, whatever . . . They went back to their individual occupations without a word of encouragement.

Franck breathed a sigh of disappointment. 'You just don't get it.'

'Who is Arlette, anyway?' Paulette asked Camille.

'Arlette Davidson . . . A fantastic singer.'

'Don't know her.'

Philibert invented a game for the trip. Each of them had to teach something to the three others in order to pass on some form of knowledge.

Philibert would have been a great teacher.

One day, Paulette told them how to catch cockchafers:

'In the morning, when they're still numb from the nighttime chill and they're not moving on their leaf, you shake the trees where they're hiding, stir the branches with a pole and then gather them on to a canvas sheet. You pound them, cover them with lime and put them in a ditch, it makes very good nitrogen compost. And don't forget to cover your head!'

Another day, Franck carved up a calf for them:

'Prime cuts to start with: eye, leg, rump, loin, filet mignon, ribrack – that's the first five ribs and the three secondary ribs – and the shoulder. Second category: breast, tendrons, and flank. Finally the third category: knuckle, shank, and . . . Shit, I'm missing one.'

As for Philibert, he tutored these miscreants who knew nothing about Henri IV – apart from the story of the chicken in the pot, his assassin Ravaillac, and his famous prick, about which *he did not know it was not a bone* . . .

'Henri IV was born in Pau in 1553 and died in Paris in 1610. He was the son of Antoine de Bourbon and Jeanne d'Albret. One of my distant cousins, let it be said in passing. In 1572 he married the daughter of Henri II, Marguerite de Valois, one of my mother's cousins, actually. Head of the Calvinist party, he abjured Protestantism to escape the Saint-Bartholomew's Day massacre. In 1594 he was consecrated in Chartres and entered Paris. With the Edict of Nantes in 1598 he re-established religious peace. He was very popular. I won't go into all

414

his battles, I expect you're not really interested. But it is important to remember that his entourage included, among others, two great individuals: Maximilien de Béthune, the Duke of Sully, who cleaned up the country's finances, and Olivier de Serres, who was a blessing for the agriculture of the era.'

Camille didn't feel like telling any stories.

'I don't know anything,' she said, 'and I'm not sure what I believe.'

'Talk to us about art!' the others urged. 'Movements, periods, famous paintings, or even your painting supplies if you want!'

'No, I wouldn't know how to talk about all that. I'm afraid I'd give you the wrong information.'

'What's your favourite period?'

'The Renaissance.'

'Why?'

'Because. I don't know . . . Everything is beautiful. Everywhere. Everything.'

'Every what?'

'Everything.'

'Come on,' joked Philibert, 'can't get much more precise than that! For those who would like to know more, I refer them to Élie Faure's *History of Art*, which is located in our bathroom behind the special issue of Enduro 2003.'

'And tell us who you like,' added Paulette.

'Painters?'

'Yes.'

'Well, in any old order, then . . . Rembrandt, Dürer, Leonardo, Mantegna, Tintoretto, La Tour, Turner, Bonington, Delacroix, Gauguin, Vallotton, Corot, Bonnard, Cézanne, Chardin, Degas, Bosch, Velasquez, Goya, Lotto, Hiroshige, Piero della Francesca, Van Eyck, the two Holbeins, Bellini, Tiepolo, Poussin, Monet, Zhu Da, Manet, Constable, Ziem, Vuillard and . . . it's awful, I must be forgetting loads.'

'And can't you tell us something about one of them?'

'No.'

'At random – Bellini. Why do you like him?'

'Because of his portrait of the Doge Leonardo Loredan.'

'Why?'

'I don't know . . . you have to go to London, to the National

Gallery if I remember right, and look at the painting and you know for sure that it is – It is . . . it is . . . No. I'm no good at this.'

'Okay,' they said, resigned, 'it's just a game, after all. We can't force you.'

'Ah! I know what I forgot!' said Franck, exultantly, 'the neck, of course! That goes in the blanquette . . .'

Camille felt her two selves at odds with each other again there, no doubt about it.

One Monday evening, however, in the traffic jam after the motorway toll at Saint-Arnoult, when they were all tired and a bit grumpy, she suddenly declared, 'I've got it!'

'Sorry?'

'My knowledge! The only knowledge I have! Something I've known by heart for years!'

'Go on, we're listening.'

'It's Hokusai, an artist I adore . . . You know? The wave? And the views of Mount Fiji? Come ooonn, you know. The turquoise wave edged with foam? Well, he's just marvellous. If you knew all he's done – you just can't imagine.'

'Is that it? Other than "Just marvellous", do you have anything else to add?'

'Yes, wait, I'm concentrating.'

So there in the twilight of that predictable suburb, between a factory outlet to the left and a huge home decoration store to the right, amidst urban gloom and the animosity of the flock returning to the fold, Camille slowly uttered these words:

'*At the age of six, I was seized by the mania of drawing the shape of objects.*

'*By the age of fifty, I had published an infinite number of drawings, but everything produced before the age of seventy is not worthy of consideration.*

'*It was at the age of sixty-three that I gradually began to understand the structure of true nature, of animals, trees, birds, and insects.*

'*As a result, by the age of eighty, I will have made still greater progress; at ninety I will penetrate into the mystery of things; at one hundred I will have attained a degree of wonder and by the time I am one hundred and ten, whether I create a point or a line, everything will be alive.*

'*I ask those who live as long as I do to see if I keep my word.*

416

'Written at the age of seventy-five by me, Hokusai, the old man mad about painting.'

'Whether I create a point or a line, everything will be alive,' she repeated.

As each of them had probably found grist for their own poor mill, the rest of the journey continued in silence.

7

They were invited to the château for Easter.

Philibert was nervous.

He was afraid of losing some of his prestige.

He said '*vous*' to his parents, his parents said '*vous*' to him and to each other.

'Hello, Father.'

'Ah, there you are, my son. Isabelle, kindly go and inform your mother. Marie-Laurence, do you know where the bottle of whisky is kept? I cannot seem to find it.'

'Pray to Saint Anthony, my friend!'

At the beginning, such formality seemed strange to them but then they ceased to notice.

The dinner was laborious. The Marquis and Marquise asked them a host of questions but did not wait for their replies to judge them. Moreover, some of the questions were rather awkward, such as:

'And what does your father do?'

'He's dead.'

'Ah, forgive me.'

'Don't worry about it.'

'Oh . . . and yours?'

'I didn't know him.'

'Ah, I see. You – would you like a bit more fruit salad, perhaps?'

'No, thank you.'

A convoy of angels passed over the panelled dining room.

*

'And so you – are a chef, isn't that right?'

'Uh, yes.'

'And you?'

Camille turned to Philibert.

'She's an artist,' he answered for her.

'An artist? How quaint! And are you able to live from your art?'

'Yes. Well, I think so.'

'So very quaint. And you live in the same building, is that correct?'

'Yes. Just above.'

'Just above, just above.'

He made a mental search on the hard drive of his society directory.

'. . . so you must be a little Roulier de Mortemart!'

Camille panicked.

'Uh, my name is Camille Fauque.'

And she brought out the full artillery:

'Camille Marie Elisabeth Fauque.'

'Fauque? How quaint. I used to know a chap named Fauque. A fine man, I do recall. Charles, believe it was. A relation of yours, perhaps?'

'Uh, no.'

Paulette did not open her mouth all evening. For over forty years she had been in service to people of this mould and she was too ill at ease to put her two cents' worth on their embroidered tablecloth.

Even the coffee was laborious.

This time, it was Philou who was in their sights:

'Well, son? Still in postcards?'

'Yes, father.'

'Fascinating, isn't it?'

'You said it!'

'Don't be ironic, I beg you. Irony is the defence of dunces, and it's not for lack of having repeated this to you, I believe.'

'Yes, father. *Citadel,* by Saint-Ex . . .'

'I beg your pardon?'

'Saint-Exupéry.'

His father winced.

When at last they were able to leave the gloomy room where all the local animals had been stuffed and stuck above their heads – even a pheasant for fuck's sake, even Bambi – Franck carried Paulette up to her room. 'Like a young bride,' he whispered in her ear, and he shook his head sadly when he realized that he would be sleeping light years away from his princesses, two floors higher up.

He turned round and played with a lattice-work boar's foot while Camille was undressing Paulette.

'Can you believe it? Did you see how badly we ate? What sort of crap was that? It was disgusting! I would never dare serve anything like that to my guests. You'd be better off making an omelette or boiling up some pasta!'

'Perhaps they can't afford it?'

'Fuck, everyone can afford to make a good runny omelette, can't they? I just don't get it. I really don't. Eating shit with sterling silver cutlery and serving a revolting cheap wine in a crystal carafe: maybe I'm thick but there's something here I just don't get. If they sold even one of their umpteen chandeliers they'd have enough to eat properly for a year.'

'They don't see things that way, I suppose. The idea of selling one single family toothpick must seem as strange to them as the idea of serving your guests Russian salad from a tin is to you.'

'Fuck, it wasn't even the good stuff! I saw the empty tin in the garbage, it was from Leader Price! Can you believe it? Live in a château like this with a moat and chandeliers and thousands of acres and all that and eat Leader Price! I really don't get it, it's beyond me. You've got the guard calling you *Monsieur le Marquis* and then you fucking put mayo from a tube on your poor man's vegetable salad, I swear, it doesn't add up.'

'Come on, calm down. It's no big deal.'

'Yes it is a big deal, fuck! Yes it is! What does it mean to hand on your legacy to your kids if you can't even speak kindly to them? Nah, did you see how he spoke to old Philou there? Did you see how his upper lip curled when he said, "Still in postcards, my son?", meaning, "my stupid dork of a son?" Swear to God, I wanted to headbutt him one. Philou's like a god to me, he's the most wonderful human being I've ever met in my life and then you get that other cretin dumping on him like that.'

'Shit, Franck, stop swearing, damnit,' lamented Paulette.

Gotcha there, you pleb.

'Puh. And on top of that I'm sleeping up in Boonieville. Hey, I warn you, I'm not going to mass tomorrow! To give thanks for what, anyway? Whether it's you or Philou or me, we'd have been better off meeting in an orphanage.'

'Yeah, really! In My Little Pony house for example?'

'What?'

'Nothing.'

'You going to mass?'

'Yes, I like it.'

'And you, Grandma?'

Paulette didn't answer.

'You stay here with me. We'll show these hicks what a good meal is. Since they can't afford better, well, we'll feed them.'

'I'm not much good at anything any more, you know.'

'Do you remember the recipe for your Easter pâté?'

'Of course.'

'Well, let's not waste any time, okay? String up the aristocracy! Okay, I better get going, otherwise I'll find myself in the dungeon.'

And the next day, imagine Marie-Laurence's astonishment when she went down into her kitchen at eight o'clock and found that Franck had already come back from the market and was rallying his invisible flunkeys.

She was flabbergasted:

'My God, but –'

'Everything's fine, Madaaame la Marquise. Everything is hunky-dory, tip-top, right as rain!' he sang, opening all the cupboards. 'Don't worry about a thing, I'll be taking care of the luncheon.'

'And . . . and my leg of lamb?'

'I put it in the freezer. Tell me, I don't suppose you have a conical strainer by any chance?'

'I beg your pardon?'

'No, never mind. A sieve, then?'

'Uh, yes, in this cupboard.'

'Oh, this is fantastic!' he said ecstatically, picking up a device which was missing a foot. 'What era does this date from? Late 12th century, looks like, no?'

They arrived famished and cheerful. Jesus was back among them, and they all clustered around the table with their mouths watering. Oops, Franck and Camille sprang back to their feet. They had, once again, forgotten they must say grace.

The pater familias cleared his throat:

'Bless us, Lord, bless this meal and those who have prepared it – a wink from Philou to his kitchen boy – and bla-bla-bla give bread to those who do not have it.'

'Amen,' replied the chorus-line of adolescents, quivering.

'Since we're doing things this way,' he added, 'let us do honour to this marvellous meal. Louis, go and fetch two of Uncle Hubert's bottles, please.'

'Oh, dear heart, are you sure?' said his lady wife tremulously.

'Absolutely. And you, Blanche, refrain from combing your brother's hair, we are not, as far as I know, at a hairdresser's salon.'

They were served asparagus in a mousseline sauce so delicious you could faint, then the Easter pâté AOC Paulette Lestafier, then a roasted *carré d'agneau* accompanied by tians of tomatoes, and courgettes with thyme flowers, then a tart of strawberries and wild strawberries with home-made whipped cream.

'Whipped with pure elbow grease, I'll have you know.'

Rarely had they been happier around that table with its twelve extension leaves, and never had they laughed so heartily. After a few glasses, the Marquis removed his cravat and told preposterous hunting tales which did not always show him in the best light. Franck was in and out of the kitchen and Philibert took care of the service: they were perfect.

'They should work together,' murmured Paulette to Camille, 'my little grandson cooking away at his stove, and that tall courteous fellow waiting tables in the restaurant – that would be amazing.'

They had coffee on the porch; Blanche brought out fresh petits-fours then settled again on Philibert's lap.

Phew. Franck was done at last. After a service like this, he would have loved to roll a little – but, maybe better not . . . So he pinched a cigarette from Camille instead.

'What's that?' she asked, indicating the basket everyone was eagerly dipping their hands into.

'Nun's farts,' he laughed, 'it was too much, I couldn't resist.'

He went down a step and sat with his back against his sweetheart's legs.

She put her notebook on his head.

'Doesn't this feel good?' he asked.

'Very good.'

'Well, you should think about it, my chubby princess.'

'About what?'

'About this. How we feel here, now.'

'I'm not sure what you mean. You want me to look for lice?'

'Yeah. De-louse me and I'll es-pouse you.'

'Franck,' she sighed.

'Naw, c'mon, it's a symbolic thing! I'm resting against you, and you can work on me. Something like that, don't you see?'

'You're just too much.'

'Yeah. Well, I'd better go and sharpen my knives, while I have time. They're bound to have what I need here.'

They toured the property with the wheelchair, and parted without any inappropriate displays of emotion. Camille offered Philou's family a watercolour of the château and to Philibert she gave Blanche's profile.

'You're for ever giving your work away. You'll never get rich.'

'Doesn't matter.'

At the end of the drive lined with poplars, Philibert struck his forehead: 'Holy Moses! I forgot to tell them . . .'

No reaction among the passengers.

'Holy Moses! I forgot to tell them,' he said again, more loudly.

'Huh?'

'What?'

'Oh, nothing. Minor detail.'

Right.

Silence, again.

'Franck, Camille?'

'Yes, we know, you're going to thank us because you saw your father laugh for the first time since the fall of the vase of Soissons.'

'No, no not at all.'

'What is it?'

'Would you be w-w-wi-, w-w-willing to b-be my w-w-wi . . .'

'Your what? Your witches?'

'No, my wi-wi—'

'Your wimps?'

'N-no, my wi-wi –'

'What? Out with it, shit!'

'W-w-wi-tnesses, at my w-w-wedding?'

Franck slammed on the brakes and Paulette bashed into the headrest.

8

He wouldn't tell them any more than that.

'I'll let you know when I know more myself.'

'Huh? But wait, put our minds at rest, at least . . . You do have a girlfriend, right?'

'A girlfriend,' he sniffed, 'not on your life! A girlfriend . . . that's vulgar. A fiancée, my dear.'

'But, uh, is she aware of this?'

'I beg your pardon?'

'That you're engaged?'

'Not yet,' he confessed, looking down.

Franck sighed: 'Uh-oh, I sense work ahead. Pure unadulterated Philou, this one. Okay, then. Don't wait till the day before to invite us, right? So I'll have time to buy myself a nice suit?'

'And a dress for me!' added Camille.

'And a hat . . .' said Paulette.

9

The Kesslers came to dinner one evening. They walked around the flat in silence. Two old bourgeois Bohemians; they couldn't get over it. It was a very gratifying spectacle indeed.

Franck wasn't there and Philibert was exquisite.

Camille showed them her studio. Paulette was present in every pose, every technique and every format. It was a temple to her joyfulness and sweetness, to the memories and regrets which sometimes furrowed her face.

Mathilde was moved, and Pierre was confident: 'This is all wonderful! Really good! With last summer's heat wave, the elderly have become very trendy, did you know that? It will take off, I'm sure it will.'

Camille was devastated.

De-va-stated.

'Don't mind him,' said Mathilde, 'he's just provoking you. The old man finds it all rather moving . . .'

'Oh, and this, isn't this sublime?'

'It's not finished.'

'You'll keep it for me, won't you? You'll put it aside for me?'

Camille agreed.

No. She would never give it to him because it would never be finished, and it would never be finished because her model would never come back. She knew it.

Never mind.

So much the better.

This sketch would stay with her then. It wasn't finished. It would be on hold for ever. Like their impossible friendship. Like everything which separated them here on earth.

One Saturday morning, a few weeks back, Camille was working. She hadn't even heard the chime of the doorbell when Philibert knocked on her door:

'Camille?'

'Yes?'

'The . . . the Queen of Sheba is here. In my sitting room.'

Mamadou was magnificent. She was wearing her finest African cloth and all her jewels. Her hair had been shaved from over two-thirds of her skull and she was wearing a little scarf that matched her tribal garment.

'I told you I would drop by but you better be quick because I'm going to a wedding in my family at four o'clock. So this is where you live, huh? This is where you working?'

'I'm so happy to see you again!'

'Come on . . . Don't waste time, I said!'

Camille settled her comfortably.

'There. Sit up straight.'

'But I always sit up straight, anyway!'

After she had done a few quick sketches, Camille put her pencil down on her pad: 'I can't draw you if I don't know your name.'

Mamadou raised her head and stared at her with magnificent disdain: 'My name is Marie-Anastasie Bamundela M'Bayé.'

Marie-Anastasie Bamundela M'Bayé would never come back to this neighbourhood dressed like a queen from Diouloulou, her child-hood village, Camille was sure of that. Her portrait would never be finished, and it would never be for Pierre Kessler either, and he would never have the eyes to see Bouli the little goat in the arms of this 'beautiful Negress'.

Other than these two visits, and a party where all three of them went to celebrate the thirtieth birthday of one of Franck's co-workers and where Camille went wild and shouted, I have more appetite than a barra-cuda, bar-ra-cu-da, nothing worthy of notice occurred.

The days were getting longer, the Sunrise wheelchair had been broken in, Philibert went to his rehearsals, Camille worked and

Franck lost a bit more self-confidence with each passing day. Camille liked him but she didn't love him; she offered herself to him but did not give herself; though she tried, she just didn't believe in it.

One night he didn't come home. Just to see.

She made no comment.

Then a second night, and a third. To get drunk.

He slept at Kermadec's place. Alone most of the time; with a girl one night on a binge of Sudden Death beer.

He made her come, then turned his back.

'Well?'

'Leave me alone.'

10

Paulette could hardly walk any more and Camille avoided asking her about it. She found other ways to keep her back from the edge. In the daylight, or beneath the halo of the lamps. There were days when she was absent, and other days when she was full of beans. It was exhausting.

Where did respect for others end and the notion of not assisting a person in danger begin? This question tormented Camille, and every time she got up during the night, determined to make an appointment at the doctor's, the old lady would show up the next morning bright and fresh as a rose.

And Franck could no longer persuade one of his former conquests, a lab worker, to provide them with medication without a prescription.

Paulette hadn't been taking anything for weeks.

The evening of Philibert's performance, for example, she wasn't up to it and they had to ask Madame Perreira to keep her company.

'No problema! I hadda my mother-in-law at home for twelva yearsa, so, what d'you expect . . . I know all abouta old people!'

The performance was held in a youth hall at the very end of the A line on the suburban rail network.

They took the 'Zeus' at 7.34, sat across from each other and worked out their differences in silence.

Camille looked at Franck with a smile.

Keep your shitty little smile, I don't want it. That's all you know how to give. Little smiles to lead people astray. Keep it, why don't you. You'll end up all alone in your ivory tower with your coloured pencils, and it will serve you bloody right. I can tell I'm running out of steam, now. The earthworm in love with a star – that's gone on long enough.

Franck looked at Camille with his teeth clenched.

You're so cute when you're angry, you really are. You're so handsome when you start to lose it. Why can't I let myself go with you? Why do I make you suffer? Why do I wear a corset beneath my suit of armour and two cartridge belts across my chest? Why do I get hung up on the most trivial details? Get a tin-opener, for Christ's sake! Look in your little knife case, I'm sure you have what it takes to help me breathe . . .

'What are you thinking about?' he asked her.

'Your name. The other day I read in an old dictionary that an *estafier* was a tall footman who followed a man on horseback and held the stirrup for him.'

'Oh?'

'Yes.'

'A doormat in other words.'

'Franck Lestafier?'

'Present.'

'When you're not sleeping with me, who are you sleeping with?'

No answer.

'Do you do the same things to them as you do to me?' she added, biting her lip.

'No.'

They held hands as they rose to the surface.

Hands are good.

Not too much is required of the one giving, and the one on the receiving end feels a great sense of calm.

The venue was pretty gloomy.

There was an air of outmoded beards, warm Fanta and fading dreams of glory. Day-Glo yellow posters announced the triumphant concert tour of one Ramon Riobambo and his llama-skin orchestra. Camille and Franck took their tickets and had a super-abundance of seats to choose from.

Gradually the hall filled with people. It felt like a cross between a country fair and a youth club. Mothers were all dressed up and fathers double-checked their camcorder batteries.

As was his tendency whenever he was agitated, Franck began jiggling his foot. Camille put her hand on his knee to calm him.

'To think our Philou is going to have to get up in front of all these people – it kills me. I don't think I can take it. What if he blanks out, forgets something? What if he starts stuttering? Jeez. We'll have to pick up the pieces.'

'Ssh. It will be fine.'

'If one single person giggles, I swear, they'll be toast.'

'Calm down, now.'

'Calm down, calm down! I'd like to see how you'd be in his shoes! Would you get up and prance around like a clown there in front of all these strangers?'

The children came out first. If you were in the mood for Scapin, Queneau, the Little Prince and the Wizard of Oz, you could have it all.

Camille didn't manage to draw anything, she was having too much fun.

Then a cluster of gangling teenagers who were in the middle of an experimental rehabilitation programme rapped out their existentialism, shaking heavy gold-plated chains.

'Yo, man, what have they got on their heads,' said Franck, 'tights or what?'

Intermission.

Shit. Warm Fanta and still no sign of Philibert on the horizon.

When darkness fell again, an unbelievable creature of a girl made her appearance.

A pint-sized young woman, wearing pink custom new-look Converse trainers, multicoloured striped tights, a green tulle mini-skirt and a little bomber jacket covered in pearls; her hair colour matched her shoes.

An elf. A handful of confetti. The sort of touching, extravagant little child you love the moment you clap eyes on her – or that you'll never understand.

Camille leaned over and saw that Franck had a silly smile on his face.

'Good evening. So, uh. Anyway. I – I have given a lot of thought to the way I might introduce the . . . the next act and in the end I – I thought that . . . the best would be to – to tell you how we met . . .'

'Uh-oh. Stuttering. Here comes our bit,' he murmured.

'So, uh . . . It was last year, roughly . . .'

The girl was waving her arms all over the place.

'You know I've been organizing workshops for children at the Pompidou Centre and uh . . . I noticed him because he was always going round his stands to count his postcards over and over. Every time I went by, I found a way to surprise him and it never failed: he'd be counting his postcards again and moaning. That . . . Like Charlie Chaplin, d'you know what I mean? With that sort of grace that grabs you by the throat . . . When you don't know whether you should laugh or cry . . . When suddenly you're clueless. When you stand there like a fool and your heart goes hot and cold. One day I gave him a hand and . . . I really liked him, simple as that. You will too, you'll see. You can't help but like him. This boy is – he is – He's the city lights, all by himself.'

Camille was kneading Franck's hand.

'Oh! And one more thing. When he introduced himself for the first time, he said, "Philibert de La Durbellière", so since I'm sort of normal and polite I answered same thing, "Suzy, uh, *de*, you know, from Belleville." "Ah!" he exclaimed, "you must be a descendant of Geoffroy de Lajemme de Belleville who fought the Habsburgs in 1672?" Oh, my gosh! "Nah," I garbled, "from Belleville in Paris." And you know the most amazing thing of all? He wasn't even disappointed.'

She gave a little hop.

'So there we are, that's it, I've said it all. And please applaud very loudly.'

Franck whistled through his fingers.

Philibert came out, heavily. In a suit of armour. With his coat of mail, a plume in the breeze, a long sword, a shield and all the clanking hardware.

Tremors in the audience.

He began to speak but you couldn't understand a thing.

After a few minutes a little boy went up to him and, standing on a stool, raised his visor.

Philibert, imperturbable, was finally audible.

Faint smiles.

Hard to tell yet, where all this was heading.

Philibert began a brilliant striptease. Every time he would remove a piece of metal, his little page shouted out the designation of the object, good and loud:

'Helmet . . . basinet . . . gorgerin . . . breastplate . . . brassards . . . cubitieres . . . gauntlet . . . corselet . . . cuisses . . . kneecaps . . . greaves . . .'

Completely de-boned, our knight eventually collapsed and the little boy removed his 'shoes'.

'Sollerets,' he announced at last, raising them above his head and holding his nose.

Genuine laughter this time around.

There's nothing like some good slapstick to warm up an audience.

Meanwhile, Philibert Jehan Louis-Marie Georges Marquet de La Durbellière, in a flat and blasé voice, detailed the branches of his family tree, enumerating the armed exploits of his illustrious lineage.

Granddaddy Charles against the Turks with Saint Louis in 1271; Grandpa Bertrand gone to glory at Agincourt in 1415, Uncle Thingamijig at the battle of Fontenoy, Granddad Louis on the banks of the Moine at Cholet, Great-Uncle Maximilien at Napoleon's side, Great-Grandfather on the Chemin des Dames and his maternal grandfather imprisoned by the Krauts in Pomerania.

With a wealth of detail. The children were silent as lambs. The History of France in 3D. Sublime art.

'And the last leaf on the tree,' concluded Philibert, ' – here it is.'

He stood up straight. All white, skinny as could be, clothed in nothing but a pair of white boxer shorts with a fleur de lys print.

'Here I am, do you see? The fellow who counts his postcards.'

His page brought him a military greatcoat.

'Why?' he asked. 'Why, you might ask, does the scion of such a great convoy stand there counting and re-counting bits of paper in a place he abhors? Well, I shall tell you why . . .'

And then, the wind shifted. Philibert told the story of his birth – chaotic because he was presenting in the wrong position, 'already,' he sighed, and his mother refused to go to a hospital where they practised abortions. He told the story of his childhood – isolated from the world, he was taught to keep his distance from the common people. He told the story of his years in boarding school with Liddell and Scott as spearhead, and the innumerable mischievous and malicious pranks to which he fell victim, this boy who knew nothing of power struggles beyond the ponderous movements of his tin soldiers.

And the audience laughed.

They laughed because it was funny. The one about the pee glass, the taunting, the spectacles thrown into the toilet, how he was goaded into wanking, the cruelty of the Vendée peasant children and the dubious consolation offered by the supervisor. His mother's directives about the white dove, the long evening prayers to forgive those who trespass against us and lead us not into temptation and his father asking every Saturday if he had maintained his rank and been worthy of his ancestors while he wriggled and writhed because, yet again, they were washing his willy with soft soap.

Yes, people were laughing. Because he was laughing, and they were with him on this one now.

All of them princes . . .

All behind his white plume . . .

All of them touched.

He talked about his obsessive-compulsive disorder. His tranquilizers, the papers from the social security where his name never fitted on the forms, his stuttering, the muddles he would get in whenever his tongue got bogged down in his distress, the panic attacks in public places, his root canals, his balding scalp, his back beginning to hunch over and all the things he'd already lost along the way by virtue of being born in the wrong century. He'd been raised without television or newspapers, without experience of the outside world, without humour and above all, without ever witnessing an act of kindness towards the world around him.

Philibert gave lessons in deportment and the rules of etiquette, to remind people about good manners and other ways of being in the world, and he could recite his grandmother's manual by heart:

'Generous, delicate persons never, when in the presence of a servant, use a comparison which might be injurious. For example: "Whatsisname behaves like a lackey." Great ladies in times gone by were scarcely so considerate, you might say, and I do know that there was indeed a duchess

in the 18th century who was in the habit of sending her people to the Place de Grève at every execution, and she would say, roughly, "Go to school!"

'Nowadays we show greater care for human dignity and the righteous vulnerability of the small and humble; it is the honour of our era.

'But nevertheless,' he insisted, 'the politeness of masters towards their servants must not degenerate into a base familiarity. For example, there is nothing quite so vulgar as listening to the gossip of one's servants.'

And the smiles continued. Even if it was not really a laughing matter.

Finally, he spoke some Ancient Greek, recited prayers in Latin like there was no tomorrow, and confessed he had never seen *La Grande Vadrouille,* because they made fun of nuns in the film . . .

'I think I must be the only Frenchman alive who has never seen *La Grande Vadrouille,* don't you think?'

And kind voices reassured him: No, no, you're not the only one.

'Fortunately I . . . I'm better now. I think I've lowered the drawbridge. And I . . . I have left my lands behind to embrace life. I have met people who are far more noble than I am and I . . . Well . . . Some of them are here in the room and I would not like to make them feel uncomfortable but . . .'

Because he was looking at them, everyone turned to Franck and Camille, who were desperately trying to – rrr . . . umm – to swallow the lump in their throats.

Because this fellow who was talking now, this beanpole who made everyone laugh when he told them about his misfortunes, was none other than their own Philou, their guardian angel, their SuperNesquik from out of the blue. The one who had saved them, closing his long skinny arms around their dejected shoulders . . .

While people were applauding, Philibert finished getting dressed. He was now wearing a top hat and tails.

'And there we are. I think I've told you everything. I hope I haven't troubled you unduly with these dusty old trinkets of mine. If such were, alas, the case, I beg you to forgive me and to present your grievances to this loyal damsel with the pink hair, for she is the one who compelled me to appear before you this evening. I promise you I will not begin again, but uh . . .'

He waved his walking stick towards backstage and his page reappeared with a pair of gloves and a bouquet of flowers.

435

'Have you noticed the colour?' he asked, slipping on his gloves. 'Fresh butter. Dear Lord, I am hopelessly traditional. Now where was I? Oh, yes! Pink hair. I . . . I . . . know that Monsieur et Madame Martin, the parents of the young maiden from Belleville, are in the theatre and I – I – I – I . . .'

He went down on one knee: 'I – I do stutter a b-b-bit, d-don't I?'

Laughter.

'I stutter and it's perfectly normal for once because I am here to ask for the hand of your dau—'

At that moment a cannonball flew across the stage and knocked him over. His face disappeared behind a corolla of tulle and all you could hear was:

'Heeeeeeeeeeeeeeeeeee, I'm going to be a marquiiiiiiiiiiiiiiiiiiiise!'

His glasses all askew, Philibert stood up and lifted Suzy in his arms:

'A marvellous conquest, don't you agree?'

He smiled.

'My ancestors can be proud of me.'

11

Camille and Franck did not attend the troupe's year-end party because they couldn't afford to miss the last train at two minutes to midnight.

They sat next to each other this time, and were no more talkative than on the way out.

Too many images, too much excitement.

'Do you think he'll come back tonight?' asked Franck.

'Mmm. She doesn't seem to be particularly burdened with a sense of propriety, that girl.'

'It's crazy, isn't it?'

'Completely crazy.'

'Can you imagine the look on Marie-Laurence's face when she sees her future daughter-in-law?'

'If you ask me, it won't be any time soon.'

'Why do you say that?'

'I don't know . . . Female intuition . . . The other day, at the château, when we went for a walk with Paulette after lunch, he said – and he was trembling with rage: "Can you imagine? It's Easter and they didn't even hide any eggs for Blanche . . ." Maybe I'm wrong but I got the impression that that was the straw that cut the apron strings. They made him go through all sorts of stuff and he never took offence, or hardly at all, but this time . . . Not hiding any eggs for the little girl, that was just disgraceful. Pathetic. I got the feeling he was venting his anger and making some dark decisions at the same time. So much the better, you might say. You were right: they don't deserve him.'

Franck nodded and they spoke no more of it. Had they pursued the issue, they would have been obliged to speak of the future in the conditional (and what if Philibert and Suzy get married, where will they live? And where will we live?) and they weren't ready for that discussion. Too treacherous to head down that path.

Franck paid Madame Perreira, while Camille broke the news to Paulette, then they had a bite to eat in the sitting room, listening to just bearable techno.

'It's not techno, it's electro.'

'Ah, excuse me.'

Philibert did indeed not come back that night, and the flat seemed horribly empty. They were happy for him, and unhappy for themselves. The familiar aftertaste of abandonment welling up in their throats.

Philou . . .

They didn't need to pour their hearts out to communicate their distress. They really could read each other loud and clear.

Their friend's marriage became a pretext for opening the strong liquor, and they drank to the health of all the orphans on the planet. There were so many of them that Camille and Franck had to bring the evening to a close by getting utterly and superbly wasted.

Superbly, and bitterly.

12

Philibert Jehan Louis-Marie Georges Marquet de La Durbellière, born 27 September 1967 at La Roche-sur-Yon (Vendée), married Suzy Martin, born 5 February 1980 at Montreuil (Seine–Saint-Denis) at the town hall of the 20th arrondissement in Paris on the first Monday of the month of June, 2004, beneath the emotional gazes of his witnesses, Franck Germain Maurice Lestafier, born 8 August 1970 in Tours (Indre-et-Loire), and Camille Marie Elisabeth Fauque, born 17 February 1977 in Meudon (Hauts-de-Seine), and in the presence of Paulette Lestafier, who refuses to give her age.

Also present were the bride's parents and her best friend, a tall boy with yellow hair, scarcely more restrained than Suzy herself.

Philibert was wearing a suit of magnificent white linen, a pink handkerchief with green polka dots tucked in his pocket.

Suzy was wearing a magnificent pink miniskirt with green polka dots, with a bustle and a train of over two metres long. 'My dream!' she said over and over, laughing.

She laughed all the time.

Franck wore the same suit as Philibert, of a more caramel hue. Paulette was wearing a hat which Camille had made, a sort of little pillbox nest with birds and feathers going in every direction, and Camille wore a white tuxedo shirt that had belonged to Philibert's grandfather and which went down to her knees. She had knotted a tie around her waist, and inaugurated a pair of adorable red sandals. It was the first time she'd put on a skirt since . . . Gosh, longer than that even.

After the ceremony all these lovely people went to have a picnic in the gardens of Buttes-Chaumont. They had the huge La Durbellière wicker basket as their caterer, and they were especially crafty so that the park wardens wouldn't see them picknicking.

Philibert moved 1/100,000th of his books into his spouse's tiny two-bedroom flat; Suzy could not dream even for a second of leaving her beloved neighbourhood for a first-class burial on the other side of the Seine.

That just goes to show how disinterested she was, and how truly in love he was.

But he kept his room in the old flat all the same, and they slept there whenever they came for dinner. Philibert used the opportunity to bring some books back and take others home with him, and Camille used the opportunity to continue Suzy's portrait.

She couldn't quite get her: yet another subject who evaded capture. Whatever – the risks of the trade.

Philibert no longer stuttered, but he stopped breathing the moment Suzy was out of eyeshot.

And whenever Camille seemed surprised by how quickly they had got engaged and married, they gave her a funny look. Why should they wait? Why waste time, where happiness was at stake? What an idiotic thing to say, Camille.

She shook her head, doubting and suddenly moved, while Franck gave her a furtive glance.

Just drop it, it's not something you could ever understand. You just don't get it. You're all in a knot. Only your drawings are beautiful. You're all shrivelled up inside. When I think that I believed that you were alive . . . Shit, I must really have been hooked on you that night to have been able to kid myself to that degree. I thought you'd come to make love to me, but in fact you were just starving. What a cretin I was, I swear.

Y'know what you need? You need to have your head cleaned out the way you clean out a chicken, pull out all the crap that's inside you once and for all. He'll have to be a bloody saint, the guy who's gonna manage to sort you out. Not sure such a guy exists, anyway. Philou says that it's because you're like this that you draw so well, well shit, at what a cost . . .

*

'Hey Franck, old boy?' Philibert was shaking him, 'you seem all out of sorts just now.'

'Tired.'

'Come on. Holiday time soon.'

'Yeah, really. The whole month of July to get through still. Anyway, I'm going to bed because I have to get up early: I'm taking the ladies out into the countryside for a break.'

To spend the summer in the country. It was Camille's idea and Paulette didn't see anything wrong with it. She wasn't any more enthusiastic than that, though, his old grandma. But game. Game for anything as long as she was never forced into it.

When Camille announced her plan, Franck finally began to accept the idea.

She could live apart from him. She wasn't in love and never would be. And hadn't she warned him, anyway: 'Thanks, Franck. Me neither.' After that it was his problem if he thought he was stronger than her, stronger than the whole world. Well, mate, guess what, you're not the strongest one. 'Fraid not. And it's not as if people hadn't tried to make you understand, is it. But you're so stubborn, so full of yourself . . .

You weren't even born yet and already your life was halfway up shit creek so why should it change now? What were you thinking? That because you were fucking her with your whole heart in it, and you were nice to her, that happiness would land fully baked on to your plate . . . Puh! What a shame. Just take a look, have you seen the hand you've been dealt? Where did you think you were going with it, tell me? Where were you headed? Honestly?

Camille left her bag and Paulette's suitcase by the entrance and went back to join Franck in the kitchen.

'I'm thirsty.'

He didn't respond.

'You pissed off? Does it bother you that we're leaving?'

'Not at all! I'll be able to have some fun!'

She got up and took him by the hand: 'Come on.'

'Where?'

'Come to bed.'

'With you?'

'Who else?'

'No.'

'Why?'

'Don't feel like it. You turn soft when you've had one drink too many. All you ever do is cheat with me, I'm sick of it.'

'Right.'

'You blow hot and cold. That's a piss awful way to behave.'

Silence.

'Disgusting.'

'But I like being with you.'

'"But I like being with you,"' he echoed in a whiny voice. 'I don't give a fuck if you like being with me. I wanted you to be with me, period. All the rest, who cares. Your little ways, your artsy fartsy attitude, the little deals you cut with your cunt and your conscience: keep them for some other sucker. This one is emptied out. You'll get nothing more from me for the time being and you can drop the whole business, princess.'

'You've fallen in love, is that it?'

'God you piss me off, Camille! Go on, then. Speak to me as if I were some terminal patient now! Fuck, d'you have no modesty or what! A bit of human decency! I don't deserve this, do I? Go on. You're going to split and it'll be good for me. What the fuck am I doing, anyway, getting myself tangled up with some girl who gets off on the idea of spending two months in the middle of nowhere all alone with an old woman? You're not normal, and if you had one ounce of honesty, you'd get yourself looked at before grabbing on to the first motherfucker who comes your way.'

'Paulette was right. It's incredible how vulgar you can be.'

The trip, the following morning, seemed, shall we say, rather long.

He left them the car and headed off again on his old motorbike.

'Will you come again next Saturday?'

'To do what?'

'Uh . . . to have a break.'

'We'll see.'

'I was just wondering . . .'

'We'll see.'

'Not going to kiss me?'

'Nah. I'll come and fuck you next Saturday if I have nothing better to do, but I'm not kissing you.'

442

'Right.'

Franck went to say goodbye to his grandmother then disappeared down the end of the lane.

Camille went back to her big cans of paint. She was having a go at interior decoration for the moment.

She started thinking, then went: no. Took her brushes out of the white spirit and wiped them for a long time. He was right. They would see.

And their little life resumed its course. Like in Paris, yet even slower. And in the sun.

Camille met an English couple who were doing up the house next door. They swapped things, clever ideas, tools, and glasses of gin and tonic just as the swifts began to make their swooping passes.

They went to the Fine Arts museum in Tours. Paulette waited under an immense cedar tree (too many stairs) while Camille discovered the garden, the lovely wife, and the grandson of the painter Edouard Debat-Ponsan. He wasn't in the encyclopedia, that one. Like Emmanuel Lansyer too, whose museum they had visited in Loches a few days earlier. Camille really loved these painters who were not in the encyclopedia. These minor masters, as they were known. Regional painters of stopping-off points, whose only glory was to be found in the town which they had made their home. Debat-Ponsan would for ever be the grandfather of Olivier Debré, and Lansyer had been Corot's student. What the hell. Unburdened by genius or posterity, their paintings lend themselves more easily to a quiet love. And, perhaps, more sincerely.

Camille was constantly asking Paulette whether she didn't need to go to the toilet. It was idiotic, this incontinence thing, but she clung to her idée fixe just to keep her from slipping away. The old lady had let herself go once or twice, and Camille had scolded her profusely: 'Oh, no, my dear Paulette, whatever you want, but not this! I'm here just for you, so ask me, all right? Stay with me, for Christ's sake! What the hell do you mean, shitting yourself like that? You're not locked up in a cage that I can see?'

Paulette didn't reply.

'Hey! Yoohoo, Paulette! Answer me! You going deaf as well?'

'I didn't want to disturb you.'

'Liar! You didn't want to disturb *yourself!*'

The rest of the time she gardened, pottered around fixing things, worked, thought about Franck, and read, at last, *The Alexandria Quartet*. Out loud sometimes. To put Paulette in the mood. And then it was her turn to tell the stories of operas.

'Listen here, it's really beautiful. Don Rodrigo suggests to his friend that he go and die in the war so that he'll forget he's in love with Elisabeth.

'Wait, I'll turn up the volume. Listen to this duet, Paulette. "God, you sowed in our souls . . ."' she hummed, wiggling her wrists, 'na ninana ninana . . .

'Beautiful, isn't it?'

Paulette had nodded off.

Franck did not come the following weekend but they had a visit from the inseparable Monsieur and Madame Marquet.

Suzy had placed her yoga cushion in the wild grass, and Philibert sat reading in a deck chair – guides to Spain where they would be heading the following week for their honeymoon.

'To Juan Carlos's domain: my cousin by marriage.'

'I might have guessed.' Camille smiled.

'Wait a minute, where's Franck? He's not here?'

'No.'

'Off on the motorbike?'

'I don't know.'

'You mean he stayed in Paris?'

'I suppose so.'

'Oh, Camille,' he said sorrowfully.

'What, Camille?' she replied, annoyed. 'What? You're the one who told me when you first talked about him that he was impossible. That he never read a thing except *Motorjerk Magazine*, that . . . that . . .'

'Shh. Calm down. I'm not criticizing you.'

'No, what you're doing is worse.'

'You seemed so happy.'

'Yes. Precisely. Enough, let's stop right there. Let's not spoil everything.'

'You think they're like your pencil leads? That they get worn down when you use them?'

444

'What?'
'Feelings.'

'When did you last do your self-portrait?'
'Why do you ask?'
'When?'
'A long time ago.'
'That's what I thought.'
'It's got nothing to do with it.'
'No, of course not.'
'Camille?'
'Hmm?'
'1st October 2004, at eight in the morning . . .'
'Yes?'
He handed her the letter from Maître Buzot, notary in Paris.
Camille read it, handed it back, and stretched out in the grass by his feet.
'I beg your pardon?'
'It was too good to last.'
'I'm so sorry.'
'Stop.'
'Suzy is looking at ads for places in our neighbourhood. It's a good one too, you know. It's . . . quaint, as my father would say.'
'Stop it. And does Franck know?'
'Not yet.'

He informed them he'd be coming the following weekend.
'Are you missing me too much?' purred Camille on the phone.
'Nah. I've got stuff to do on my motorbike. Did Philibert show you the letter?'
'Yes.'
He was silent.
'You thinking about Paulette?'
'Yes.'
'Me, too.'
'We've been playing yo-yo with her. We would've done better to leave her where she was.'
'Do you really believe that?' added Camille.
'No.'

13

The week went by.

Camille washed her hands and went back out into the garden to join Paulette, who was enjoying the sun in her chair.

She'd made a quiche. Well, a sort of pie with bits of bacon in it. Well, something to eat, let's say.

A genuine submissive little woman, waiting for her man.

She was already on her knees scratching the soil when her elderly companion murmured to her back: 'I killed him.'

'Pardon?'

Heaven help us.

She had been talking nonsense more and more lately.

'Maurice . . . my husband . . . I killed him.'

Camille sat up straight without turning round.

'I was in the kitchen looking for my wallet to go down to the bakery and I . . . I saw him fall. He had a bad heart, you know. He was groaning and sighing and his face was . . . I – I put on my cardigan and went out.

'I took my time. I stopped outside every house. "And your little boy, how's he doing? And your rheumatism, has it got any better? And have you seen the storm that's brewing?" I'm not a very chatty person but that morning I was particularly friendly. And the worst of it is that I bought a lottery ticket. Can you imagine? As if it were my lucky day. Anyway. And then I went on home and he was dead.'

Silence.

'I threw out my lottery ticket because I never would've had the

446

nerve to check all the winning numbers, and I called the ambulance. Or the emergency rescue people . . . I don't remember exactly. But it was too late. And I knew it.'

Silence.

'You have nothing to say?'

'No.'

'Why aren't you saying anything?'

'Because I think his time had come.'

'You think so?' Paulette implored.

'I'm sure of it. A heart attack is a heart attack. You told me once that he'd had fifteen years of borrowed time. Well there you go, he'd used them up.'

And to prove her good faith, Camille went on digging as if nothing had happened.

'Camille?'

'Yes?'

'Thank you.'

When Camille stood up a good half-hour later, Paulette was sleeping, a smile on her face.

Camille went to fetch her a blanket.

Then she rolled a cigarette.

Then she cleaned her nails with a matchstick.

Then she went to check on her 'quiche'.

Then she chopped three little heads of lettuce and some chives.

Then she washed them.

Then she poured herself a glass of white wine.

Then she took a shower.

Then she went back out into the garden and pulled on a sweater.

She put her hand on her shoulder: 'Hey, you'll catch cold, Paulette, love.'

She shook her gently: 'Paulette?'

Never had a drawing taken so much out of her.

She made only one.

And perhaps it was the finest.

14

It was after one o'clock when Franck woke the entire village.

Camille was in the kitchen.

'Still getting sozzled?'

He put his jacket down on a chair and reached for a glass in the cupboard above her head. 'Don't move, I'll get it.'

He sat down facing her.

'My grandma already in bed?'

'She's in the garden.'

'In the gar—'

And when Camille looked up, he began to moan.

'Oh no, fuck. Oh no.'

15

'What sort of music? Any preference?'

Franck turned to Camille.

She was crying.

'You can think of something nice, can't you?'

She shook her head.

'And what about the urn? Have you – have you had a chance to look at their rates?'

16

Camille didn't have the strength to go back to town to look for a decent CD. Moreover, she was not sure she'd find one. And, well, she just didn't have the strength.

She took the cassette from the car stereo and handed it to the gentleman from the crematorium.

'Nothing to do, then?'

'No.'

Because this really was Paulette's favourite music. The proof was that he'd even sung a song just for her, so what more . . .

Camille had compiled the tape for Paulette to thank her for the horrible sweater she'd knitted that winter, and they'd listened to it again religiously just the other day on their way back from the gardens at Villandry.

She'd watched her smiling in the rear view mirror.

When that tall young man began to sing, Paulette was twenty years old again, too.

She'd seen him in 1952, back in the days when there was a music hall next to the cinema.

Ah, he was so handsome, she sighed, so handsome.

So it was to Yves Montand that they entrusted the task of delivering the funeral oration.

And the requiem . . .

Quand on partait de bon matin
Quand on partait sur les chemins
À bicyclette
Nous étions quelques bons copains

Y avait Fernand y avait Firmin
Y avait Francis et Sebastien
Et puis Paulette

On était tous amoureux d'elle
On se sentait pousser des ailes
À bicyclette

And what about Philou, who wasn't even here.
Off somewhere in his castles in Spain.
Franck stood very straight, hands behind his back.
Camille wept.

La, la, la . . . Mine de rien,
La voilà qui revient,
La chansonnette
Elle avait disparu,
Le pavé de ma rue,
Etait tout bête

Les titis, les marquis
C'est parti mon kiki

Camille smiled. *Les titis, les marquis* . . . Street urchins and
marquises – that's us, Monsieur Montand is singing about us . . .

La, la, la, haut les coeurs
Avec moi tous en choeur
La chansonnette

Madame Carminot was fumbling with her rosary and sniffling.
How many of them were there in this fake chapel made of fake
marble?
Perhaps a dozen?
With the exception of the English couple, only old people.
Mostly old ladies.
Mostly old ladies nodding their heads sadly.
Camille collapsed on Franck's shoulder and he went on kneading
his knuckles.

Trois petites notes de musique,
Ont plié boutique
Au creux du souvenir . . .

C'en est fini d'leur tapage
Elles tournent la page,
Et vont s'endormir

The man with the moustache gestured to Franck.

He nodded.

The door to the oven opened, the coffin rolled, the door closed again and . . . Ffffffoooooooff . . . .

Listening to her beloved crooner, Paulette burned for him one last time.

Et s'en alla . . . clopin . . . clopant . . . dans le soleil . . .
Et dans . . . le vent*

And hobbling along, left us behind, in the sun, and in the wind . . .

People kissed and hugged. The old women reminded Franck that they had loved his grandmother very much. And he smiled at them. Grinding his molars, to keep from crying.

People went their way. The undertaker had Franck sign some papers and another man handed him a little black box.

Very nice. Very chic.

Shining in the variable intensity light of the fake chandelier.

Enough to make you puke.

Yvonne invited them for a little pick-me-up.

'No, thanks.'

'Sure?'

'Sure,' answered Franck, clutching her arm.

And they found themselves out in the street.

All alone.

The two of them.

A fifty-something woman came up to them.

She asked them to come to her home.

They followed her by car.

They would have followed anyone.

---

* For a translation, see page 474.

17

She made them some tea and took a sponge cake out of the oven.

She introduced herself as the daughter of Jeanne Louvel.

Franck didn't get it.

'That's not surprising. When I came to live in my mother's house, you'd been gone a long time already.'

She let them take their time to eat and drink.

Camille went out into the garden for a smoke. Her hands were trembling.

When she came back to sit with them, their hostess went to fetch a large box.

'Now let's see, hold on. It must be here somewhere. Ah! Here it is.'

A tiny little cream-coloured photo with a notched border and a fussy signature in the bottom right-hand corner.

Two young women. The one on the right was laughing and staring at the camera, and the one on the left stared at the ground, beneath a black hat.

Both of them were bald.

'Do you recognize her?'

'Pardon?'

'There . . . that's your grandmother.'

'This one?'

'Yes. And that's my aunt Lucienne next to her. My mother's older sister.'

Franck handed the photo to Camille.

'My aunt was a teacher. They said she was the prettiest girl for miles around. They also said she was really stuck-up . . . She was educated and she'd turned away more than one suitor – so yes, a strange stuck-up little woman. On 3rd July 1945, Rolande F., a seamstress by profession, declared – and my mother knew the accusation by heart: *I saw her having fun, laughing, joking with them –* the German officers – *and one day even in the schoolyard splashing herself in a bathing suit, in their presence.'*

Silence.

'They shaved her head?' Camille eventually asked.

'Yes. My mother told me she couldn't get up on her feet for days and days, until one morning her good friend Paulette Mauguin came for her. She'd shaved her head with her father's cut-throat razor and she stood laughing outside their door. She took Aunt Lucienne by the hand and forced her to go with her to town to a photographer's. "Come on," she said, "it will be a souvenir for us. Go on, hold your head up, little Lulu. You're so much better than they are, go on." My aunt didn't dare go out without her hat and she refused to take it off at the photographer's, but your grandmother . . . Look at her. That mischievous air. How old would she have been at the time? Twenty?'

'She was born in November 1921.'

'Twenty-three years old. A courageous little woman, don't you think? Here. It's for you.'

'Thank you,' said Franck, his mouth all twisted to one side.

Once they were out in the street, Franck turned to Camille and said bravely: 'She was something else, my grandma, wasn't she?'

And began to cry.

At last.

'My little old girl,' he sobbed. 'My very own little old girl, the only one I had in the whole world.'

Camille suddenly froze, then ran back to fetch the black box.

He slept on the sofa and got up very early the next day.

From the window of her room, Camille watched him scattering a fine powder over the poppies and the sweet peas.

She didn't dare go out right away and when she finally made up her mind to take him a mug of steaming coffee, she heard the roar of his motorbike in the distance.

The mug broke and she collapsed against the kitchen table.

18

Camille got up several hours later, blew her nose, took a cold shower and went back to her cans of paint.

She had begun painting this bloody house and she would finish the job.

She tuned in to FM and spent the following days at the top of a ladder.

She sent a text message to Franck every two hours or so to tell him how far she'd got:

09.13 Indochine, top of the sideboard
11.37 *Aïsha, Aïsha, écoute-moi*, windowframes
13.44 Souchon, cigarette in the garden
16.22 Nougaro, ceiling
19.00 News, ham and butter sandwich
10.15 Beach Boys, bathroom
11.15 Bénabar, *C'est moi, c'est Nathalie*, haven't moved
15.30 Sardou, washing out the brushes
21.23 Daho, dreamland

He only answered once:

1.16 Silence

Did he mean: my work's over for the night, peace and calm; or did he mean, shut up?

Uncertain, she switched off her mobile.

19

Camille closed the shutters, went to say goodbye to . . . the flowers, and stroked the cat with her eyes closed.

End of July.

Paris was stifling.

The flat was silent. It was as if the place had already chased them out.

Hold your horses, she replied, I still have something to finish.

She bought a very fine notebook, glued the idiotic charter they had written that night at La Coupole to the first page, then gathered all her drawings, maps, sketches and so on, to create a record of everything they would be leaving behind, everything that would disappear with their departure.

There was room enough to build ten luxury rabbit warrens in this huge ship.

Only later would she start to empty out the adjacent room.

Only later . . .

When the hairpins and the tube of Polident had died, too.

While sorting her drawings Camille put the portraits of her friend Paulette to one side.

Up to now she had not been very enthusiastic about the idea of an exhibition, but suddenly she was. It became an obsession: to keep Paulette alive a while longer. To think about her, talk about her, show her face, her back, her neck and hands. Camille was sorry she had not recorded her while she was talking about her childhood memories, for example. Or about the great love of her life.

'This is between you and me, okay?'

'Yes, yes.'

'His name was Jean-Baptiste. It's a nice name, don't you think? If I'd had a son, I would have called him Jean-Baptiste . . .'

At the moment, Camille could still hear the sound of Paulette's voice but . . . for how long?

Since she had grown accustomed to listening to music while doing the painting, she went into Franck's room to borrow his stereo.

She couldn't find it.

And for good reason.

Everything was gone.

Except three boxes stacked along the wall.

She rested her forehead against the door frame and the parquet floor was transformed into shifting sands.

Oh, no. Not him. Not him *too*.

She bit her wrists.

Oh, no. It was starting, again. She was losing everyone again.

Oh no, fuck.

Oh, no.

She slammed the door and ran to the restaurant.

'Is Franck here?' she asked, breathless.

'Franck? Nah, don't think so,' replied a tall limp boy, limply.

She was squeezing the end of her nose not to cry.

'He . . . he doesn't work here any more?'

'Nah.'

She let go of her nose and . . .

'After tonight that is . . . Hang on . . . There he is, actually.'

Franck was on his way up from the locker room with all his linen rolled into a ball.

'Well, well,' he went when he saw her, 'here's our lovely gardener.'

Camille was crying.

'What's wrong?'

'I thought you'd gone . . .'

'Tomorrow.'

'What?'

'I'm leaving tomorrow.'

'Where?'

'England.'

'Wh – why?'

'First to have some holiday, and then to work. My boss found me a great job.'

'You going to feed the Queen?' She tried to smile.

'Nah, better than that. *Chef de partie* at the Westminster.'

'Ah?'

'Top of the line.'

'Ah?'

'You okay?'

Silence.

'C'mon, come and have a drink. We're not going to leave each other just like that, surely.'

20

'Inside or on the terrace?'

'Inside.'

Franck looked at Camille, peeved: 'You've already lost all the kilos I gave you.'

She didn't reply; then, after a pause, 'Why are you leaving?'

'Because, I told you. It's a great promotion and then, uh . . . Well, that's it. I can't afford to live in Paris. You might tell me I can always sell Paulette's house, but in fact I can't.'

'I understand . . .'

'Nah, nah, it's not that. As far as the memories I have left there, uh . . . Nah, it's just that . . . The house doesn't belong to me.'

'Does it belong to your mother?'

'No. To you.'

Stunned silence.

'Paulette's last wish,' he added, pulling a letter from his wallet. 'Here. Read it.'

My dear little Franck,

Please ignore my slatternly handwriting, I can't see a thing nowadays.

But I do see that our little Camille loves the garden, and that is why I'd like to leave it to her if you don't mind.

Take care of yourself and of her if you can.

With all my love,

Grandma.

'When did you get this?'

'A few days before . . . before she left us. I got it the day Philou told me about the sale of the flat. She . . . she understood that . . . that it was a shit situation, whatever.'

Jeez. The sensation of a leash pulling like mad on a choke collar . . .

Fortunately the waiter arrived.

'Sir?'

'A Perrier with lemon, please.'

'And the young lady?'

'Brandy. Double.'

'She's talking about the garden, not the house.'

'Yeah, well, we're not going to quibble, okay?'

'You're going away?'

'I just told you. I already have my ticket.'

'When?'

'Tomorrow evening.'

'What?'

'I thought you were sick of working for other people.'

'Sure I'm sick of it, but what else do you want me to do?'

Camille rummaged in her bag and brought out her sketchbook.

'Nah, nah, that's all over with,' he protested, crossing his hands in front of his face. 'I'm not here any more, I told you.'

She turned the pages.

'Look,' she said, showing him the sketchbook.

'What's this list?'

'It's all the places Paulette and I found when we were out on our walks.'

'What places?'

'All the empty places where you could start your business. We thought it through, you know. Before we wrote down the address, we would talk about it a lot, the two of us. The ones that are underlined are the best ones. This one especially, it would be fantastic. A little square behind the Panthéon. An old café still in its lovely original state, I'm sure you'd like it.'

She gulped down the last of her brandy.

'You're completely out of your mind. Do you know how much it costs to open a restaurant?'

'No.'

460

'Off your fucking head. Okay, well. I have to finish sorting through my stuff. I'm having dinner at Philou and Suzy's tonight, you coming?'

She grasped his arm so he wouldn't get up.

'I have money.'

'You? You live like a little beggar girl!'

'Yes, because I don't want to touch it. I don't like it, but I'd be willing to give it to you.'

He said nothing.

'You remember when I told you my father was an insurer and that he died in an – in an accident at work, remember?'

'Yes.'

'Well, anyway, he did the right thing. Since he knew he was going to abandon me, at least he thought of protecting me.'

'I don't follow.'

'Life insurance. In my name.'

'And why do you – why have you never even bought yourself a decent pair of shoes, then?'

'Because, like I said . . . I don't want that money. It stinks of, of death. I wanted a father who was alive, that's what I wanted. Not money.'

'How much?'

'Enough for a banker to smile sweetly and offer you a good loan, I think.'

She picked up her sketchbook.

'Hold on a sec, I think I drew it here somewhere.'

He grabbed the notebook from her hands.

'Stop it, Camille. Stop it right there. Stop hiding behind this fucking notebook. Stop. For once, I'm begging you.'

She looked over at the bar.

'Hey! I'm talking to you!'

She looked at his T-shirt.

'Nah, me. Look at *me*.'

She looked at him.

'Why don't you just say, "I don't want you to go?" That's how I am. I don't give a fuck about the money if it means spending it all on my own. I – I – shit, I don't know. "I don't want you to go," is that such a hard thing to say?'

'Awreadysaidit.'

'What?'

'I already said it.'

'When?'

'On New Year's Eve.'

'Yeah but that . . . that doesn't count. That was to do with Philou.'

Silence.

'Camille?'

He articulated each syllable, distinctly: 'I . . . don't . . . want . . . you . . . to . . . go.'

'I –'

'That's it. Go on. "Don't –" '

'I'm afraid.'

'Afraid of what?'

'Afraid of you, of myself, of everything.'

He sighed.

And sighed again.

'Look. Do what I do.'

He struck the pose of a body-builder strutting his stuff for a beauty contest.

'Clench your fists, round your back, bend your arms, cross them and bring them right under your chin . . . Like this.'

'Why?' she asked.

'Because . . . You have to snap out of it, this skin of yours that's too tight for you. See? You're suffocating inside. You have to get out of it now. Go ahead. I want to hear the seam ripping down your back.'

She smiled.

'Fuck, no! Keep your pathetic little smile. I don't want it. That's not what I'm asking you! I'm asking you to live, for fuck's sake! Keep your smile! There are plenty of women on the evening weather forecast for that. Okay, well I'm out of here 'cause otherwise I'll just lose it again. See you tonight.'

21

Camille burrowed deep into Suzy's myriad multicoloured cushions, didn't touch her plate, but drank sufficient amounts so that she could laugh in the right places.

Even though there was no slide show, they were treated to a strange session of *The World Around Us*.

'Aragon or Castile . . .' Philou pointed out,

'. . . are the lifeblood of destiny!' trumpeted Suzy after every photo.

She was in high spirits.

Sad, with her high spirits.

Franck left early because he was on his way to bury his life as a Frenchman with some co-workers.

When Camille finally managed to get up, Philibert walked with her to the street.

'Are you going to be okay?'

'Yes.'

'Would you like me to call a taxi?'

'No thanks. I feel like walking.'

'Okay. Have a nice walk, then.'

'Camille?'

'Yes.' She turned round.

'Tomorrow afternoon. Five fifteen, Gare du Nord.'

'You'll be there?'

He shook his head.

'I'm afraid not. I'm working.'

'Camille?'

She turned round again.

'You. Go there for me. Please.'

22

'Come to wave your handkerchief?'

'Yes.'

'That's nice of you.'

'How many of us here?'

'Of what?'

'Girls who've come to wave our hankies and smear lipstick all over you?'

'Just look around.'

'Only me!'

'Yeah, looks that way . . .' He made a face. 'Times are hard. Fortunately, English girls are hot. Well, that's what I've heard, anyway.'

'You going to teach them to French kiss?'

'Among other things. Coming with me to the platform?'

'Yes.'

Franck looked at the clock.

'Right. You've only got five minutes to get it together and say one six-word sentence, that's doable, no? Go on,' he teased, with false joviality, 'if six is too much, I'd settle for three. But the right ones, okay? Shit! I didn't get my ticket punched. Well?'

Silence.

'Never mind. I guess I'll stay a frog.'

He put his big bag on his shoulder and turned his back on her.

He ran to catch up with the ticket collector.

She saw him take his ticket and wave to her.

And the Eurostar slipped between her fingers.

And she began to cry, silly goose that she was.

And all you could see was a little grey dot in the distance.

Her mobile rang.

'It's me.'

'I know. It tells me on the screen.'

'I'm sure you're in the middle of a hyper romantic film, there. I'm sure you're all alone on the platform, like in a film, crying for your lost love in a cloud of white smoke . . .'

Her own smile brought tears to her eyes.

'Not – not at all,' she managed to say, 'I – I was just leaving the station, actually.'

'Liar,' said a voice behind her.

She fell into his arms and held him so so so tight.

Until she felt her skin snap.

She was crying.

Opened all the valves, blew her nose against his shirt, cried some more, letting go of twenty-seven years of solitude, of sorrow, of nasty blows to the head, crying for the cuddles she never had, her mother's madness, the paramedics on their knees on the fitted carpet, her father's absent gazes, the shit she went through, all those years without any respite, ever, the cold, the pleasure of hunger, the wrong paths taken, the self-imposed betrayals, and always that vertigo, the vertigo at the edge of the abyss and of the bottle. And the doubt, her body always in hiding, and the taste of ether and the fear of never being good enough. And Paulette, too. The sweet reality of Paulette, pulverized in five and a half seconds.

Franck closed his jacket round Camille and put his chin on her head.

'There . . . there,' he murmured softly, not knowing if he wanted to say, There, cry some more, or There, dry your tears.

It was up to her.

Her hair was tickling him, he was covered in snot and he was insanely happy.

Insanely happy.

He smiled. For the first time in his life, he was in the right place at the right time.

He rubbed his chin across her scalp.

'C'mon, sweetheart. Don't worry, we'll make it. We won't do any better than anyone else but we won't do any worse, either. We'll make it, you hear? We'll make it. We've got nothing to lose, since we have nothing to begin with. C'mon. Let's go.'

Epilogue

'Fuck, I don't believe it! I don't believe it,' he moaned, to hide his happiness. 'All he talks about is Philou, the bloody idiot! And the service this, and the service that . . . Yeah, sure! It's not hard for Philou, he's got good manners tattooed in his blood! And the welcome, and the décor and Fauque's drawings and bla-bla . . . And what about the cuisine, huh? Nobody gives a stuff about my cuisine?'

Suzy snatched the paper from his hands.

'*A genuinely heart-warming bistrot bla-bla-bla, where young chef Franck Lestafier arouses our taste buds and indulges us with a host of delights by reinventing a livelier, lighter, brighter style of home cooking, bla-bla-bla . . . In a word, it's the joy of Sunday lunch every day of the week without one's old aunts and no Monday on the horizon* . . . What the – what are they talking about? Stock prices or roast chicken?'

'No, it's closed,' Franck shouted to the people who were looking round the curtain. 'Oh well then, yes, come on . . . Come in, there should be enough for everyone. Vincent, can you call off your fucking dog or I'll stick him in the freezer!'

'Rochechouart, heel!' ordered Philibert.

'Barbès, not Rochechouart.'

'I prefer Rochechouart. Don't I, Rochechouart? Come and see your old uncle Philou, you'll have a big lovely bo-bone.'

Suzy laughed.

Suzy still laughed all the time, even now.

'Ah, there you are! Terrific, you took off your sunglasses for once.'

She simpered.

Even if he hadn't managed to subdue the young one yet, as far as Fauque Senior was concerned, it was in the bag. Camille's mother was always impeccably behaved around Franck, and looked at him with the damp eyes of someone purring on Prozac.

'Mum, I'd like to introduce Agnes, a friend . . . Peter, her husband, and their little boy Valentin.'

She preferred to say 'a friend' rather than 'my sister'.

No point risking a psychodrama when no one could care less. And besides she really had become her friend, so . . .

'Ah! Finally! Here come Mamadou and Co!' shouted Franck. 'Did you bring me what I asked, Mamadou?'

'Oh I did, and I beg you please be special careful, this is no spice for chickens, you know. No way!'

'Thanks, this is great, why don't you come and give me a hand back here.'

'I'm coming. Sissi, watch out for that dog!'

'It's okay, he's friendly,' said Franck.

'You mind your own. Don't mess with my childrearing. So? Where you make up the grub? It's so small in here!'

'Well, duh, you're taking up all the room!'

'Oh . . . that's the old lady I met at your place, no?' she asked, pointing to the print on the wall.

'Hey, hands off. That's my own private black magic.'

Mathilde Kessler was vamping Vincent and his friend while Pierre stole a menu on the sly. Camille was deep in the *Chronicle of the Victual*, a journal from 1767 where she was finding inspiration for some extraordinary dishes to draw . . . It was magnificent. And, uh, where could she find the originals?

Franck was firing on all cylinders, he'd been in the kitchen since dawn. For once everyone was here.

'C'mon, quick, take your seats, it'll get cold! Hot! Mind your backs, it's hot!'

He put a big stewpot down in the middle of the table and went back for a ladle.

Philou filled the glasses. Perfect, as always.

Without him, success would not have come so quickly. He had a marvellous gift for making people feel at ease: he could always come up with a compliment, a topic of conversation, a droll expression, a touch of oh-so-French *coquetterie*. And he greeted all the locals with a hug. All distant cousins.

When it was up to him to be maître d', he could *see* himself in the role, could speak clearly, and could always find the right words.

And as the food critic had stated so baldly in his article, he was the 'soul' of this chic little eatery.

'Come on, come on,' grumbled Franck, 'pass me your plates.'

Just then Camille, who had spent the last hour going gaga over Valentin, playing peekaboo with her napkin, suddenly blurted, 'Oh Franck, I want one just like this . . .'

Franck finished serving Mathilde, and sighed . . . shit, I really have to do everything around here, I do . . . He put the ladle back in the dish, untied his apron, placed it over the back of his chair, took the baby, put it back in its mother's arms, lifted up the woman he loved, held her over his shoulder like a sack of potatoes or a half-carcass of beef, groaned, she's put on weight this little thing . . . opened the door, walked across the square, went into the hotel across the street, shook hands with Vishayan, his concierge friend whom he fed between faxes, thanked him and marched on up the stairs with a smile.

We'd head off in the early hours
We'd head off down the lane
On our bicycles
A handful of the finest friends
Fernand, Firmin, Francis and Sebastien
And then Paulette . . .

We were all in love with her, could feel our hearts take flight
On our bicycles . . .

La, la, la . . . May not seem like much
But here it comes again
That little tune
It had disappeared
And the pavement of my street
Felt hard beneath my feet . . .

Street urchins and marquises
Off we go, my lovely

La, la, la . . . Take heart and
Sing along
This little tune . . .

Three little notes of music
Have closed up shop
Lost in memories . . .
Had enough of their rampage
And now they've turned the page
And off they go to sleep . . .